STREER PATRA

AND OTHER STORIES

SELECTIONS FROM GALPAGUCHCHHA 3

STREER PATRA
AND OTHER STORIES

Rabindranath Tagore

Translated by

Ratan K. Chattopadhyay

Orient BlackSwan

In loving memory of my parents

The Translator

ORIENT BLACKSWAN PRIVATE LIMITED

Registered Office
3-6-752 Himayatnagar, Hyderabad 500 029 (A.P.), India
e-mail: centraloffice@orientblackswan.com

Other Offices
Bangalore, Bhopal, Bhubaneshwar, Chandigarh, Chennai, Ernakulam, Guwahati, Hyderabad, Jaipur, Kolkata, Lucknow, Mumbai, New Delhi, Noida, Patna

First published 2010

ISBN: 978-81-250-4098-9

Typeset in Adobe Garamond 11/14.2 by
InoSoft Systems, Noida

Printed in India at
Aegean Offset Printers, Greater Noida

Published by
Orient Blackswan Private Limited
1/24 Asaf Ali Road, New Delhi 110 002
e-mail: delhi@orientblackswan.com

Contents

Translator's Preface

Galpaguchchha (Bengali for 'bunch of stories') is held among the finest of Tagore's literary creations; in fact, next only to his songs and poems. Besides the domain of poetry, over which he reigns, in the entire range of his prose writings, short stories offered him a medium for his genius to flourish. There his two distinct identities—that of a poet and that of a narrator—have met in perfect harmony. Tagore's communion with Nature, his identification with man, his general preference for real-life tales to romanticised history or myth, his emphasis on theme rather than plot, and on the intricacies of character rather than intrigues set the stories apart. To a reader, these are no mere narration of events by a story-teller: rather they are works of art that retain strong contemporary appeal and can be enjoyed at various levels.

It is always difficult to translate any great author. It is even more difficult in the case of a multi-faceted writer like Rabindranath, if only because his prose is often infused with his instinctive rhythm and rhetoric with varied overtones of words: words he often improvises by compounding effortlessly, which in fact enhance the beauty and lyricism of his long sentences with their resonance.

A master of his own language, he adapts it as necessary to suit the topic. In his earlier days, when he used to stay in his houseboat on the river Padma, he wrote simple stories based on the joys and sorrows of riparian rural life that he had observed: the language of those idyllic tales is limpid and lilting like a flowing river. Again, in the stories of his later life, when the theme extends from simple narrative to the complex working of human psychology, when he writes a social or political satire, or when inspired by a profound realisation of life, he wants to show us the way in the garb of a story, he adopts a different style of language—sharp, shining, subtle—that appeals more to the intellect of the modern-day individual. Whether it is the lyrical prose steeped in the colours of Nature, as in *Cloud and Sunshine* and *The Visitor,* or the majestic diction of *Hungry Stones*, or humour, wit and stark, unblinking reality as in *House Number One*, the charm of his language is hard to resist.

It is a challenging task to render the stories in a generally acceptable register appropriate to this language. My aim has been to acquaint the reader with the flavour of the original as far as possible within the natural constraints of translation. I have tried to be faithful to the text, for I feel any addition or deletion would lessen its appeal.

Again, the target language, English, may not always be adequate for getting across to the reader the connotations of the idioms and references in the Bengali context that appear abundantly in the stories. These have mostly been retained as such in italics and either annotated at the end of the story or explained in the glossary. This will I hope enable readers to better appreciate the nuances of Tagore's unique style.

This collection of sixty-one stories had to be divided into three volumes to avoid an unwieldy size. That no definite order in chronology or strict thematic unity was maintained—the latter I feel is neither feasible nor desirable—is because each volume was intended to be self-contained in giving the flavour of *Galpaguchchha* as a whole.

If, in spite of my shortcomings as a translator, the reader emerges enriched, the credit is all Tagore's.

I must mention the invaluable role of my sons Rajib and Somnath in the project. Were it not for their suggestions, of considerable literary and critical value, the work would not have been whatever it is worth.

Kolkata, 15 August 2010 RATAN KUMAR CHATTOPADHYAY

Hungry Stones (*Kshudhita Pashaan*)

My relative and I, having completed a tour of the country during the *puja* holidays, had been returning to Calcutta, when on the train we encountered the Bengali gentleman. Observing his dress and demeanour, at first we had mistaken him for a north Indian Muslim; hearing him speak was even more puzzling. He kept talking on every conceivable topic with such aplomb as if only after consulting him did the Lord of the universe get down to any work. That so many unheard-of momentous events were happening behind the curtain all over the world—that the Russians had advanced so far; that the British had such clandestine designs; that a grave discontent was simmering among the native kings[1]—knowing absolutely nothing, we had remained so blissfully unconcerned. Our new acquaintance said with a patronising smile in chaste English: *There happen more things in heaven and earth, Horatio, than are reported in your newspapers*[2]. This was the first time we had ever stepped out of our homes; naturally, we were amazed at his ways. On the slightest pretext, he would now talk science, now expound the Vedas, and then suddenly recite Persian couplets. As we were completely innocent of science, the Vedas, and Persian, we found ourselves admiring him with increasing awe. My relative, who was a theosophist, was even convinced that there was some supernatural association with the man—a sort of strange magnetism, some occult power, or an astral body, or something of the kind. He was listening with awe-struck wonder even to the most ordinary talk of this extraordinary man and taking notes secretly. By all appearances, the extraordinary man also could discern it and felt rather flattered.

When the train stopped at a junction station, we moved into the waiting room for the connecting train. It was half past ten at night. We heard that our train was running very late for some kind of disruption on the way. I had meanwhile decided to roll out my bed on the table and get some sleep when that no-nonsense gentleman launched into a story. There was no getting any sleep that night.

Because of some differences over administrative matters, when after quitting my job under the state of Junagadh, I entered the services of the Nizam[3] of Hyderabad, finding me young and sturdy, they first engaged me in the collection of cotton revenues at Barich.

Barich is a most fascinating place. Through extensive forests beneath the range of desolate hills, bickers down the river Shusta (a corruption of the Sanskrit *svachchhatoya* [river with transparent water]) along its pebbly course, meandering at every step like the nimble footwork of a skilled danseuse. Right upon that riverbank, at the head of a flight of one hundred and fifty steps in stone, stands a white marble palace in grand isolation set off by the hilly background: there is no human habitation around. The cotton market and the village of Barich are far away from here.

Some two hundred and fifty years ago, Shah Mahmud II had built the palace at this isolated spot as a luxurious resort of revelry. Ever since, fountains in bathing cubicles had been spurting rose-scented water. Ensconced in the cool mist of droplets in those secluded chambers, young Persian damsels sitting on soothingly cold marble platforms used to sing vineyard ghazals[4] strumming sitars on their laps, their soft bare petal-like feet dipping in the pool of crystal water, their hair untied before the bath.

No longer now do those fountains play or those songs are sung; those fair feet no longer register their graceful stamp on the white marble. Now the palace is a terribly big, horribly empty residence for the likes of us tax collectors languishing in banishment without female company. An old-timer in my office, the clerk Karim Khan, however, had warned me repeatedly against living in the palace. 'Stay there during the day, if you like,' he had said, 'but don't ever spend the night.' I laughed him off. The servants said they would work until dusk, but would not spend the night there. 'So be it,' I said. The palace had earned such notoriety that not even robbers would have ventured into it at night.

Immediately after I had come here, the stony desolation of the deserted mansion kept bearing down on my heart like a crushing weight. I used to stay away as much as possible working ceaselessly by day, only to return at night and retire, exhausted.

Nevertheless, barely a week had passed before I felt a strange sense of obsession with the mansion gradually enfold me. That state of mine is difficult to describe, and it is as much difficult to make others believe the story as well. I felt as if the whole building, like a living entity, kept macerating me insidiously in its gastric juices of enchantment.

Perhaps the process had started the moment I had stepped into the house, but the day I came to sense its onset is vivid in my memory.

At the beginning of the summer then, business was sluggish; I had no work to do. A little before sundown, I was sitting in an armchair on the bottom rung of the flight of steps leading to the river. The Shusta had then become a depleted stream: on the other side, stretches of sandy shores were coloured with the afternoon tint; here at the foot of the steps, pebbles were shimmering under the shallow transparent water. There was not a whiff of wind anywhere that day. A thick scent of basil, spearmint and aniseed rising from the undergrowth of the hill not far away permeated the still afternoon sky.

When the sun dipped below the hilltop, an extensive curtain of shadow descended on the stage of day all at once: because of the mountain barrier, crepuscular light did not last long here. Thinking of enjoying a ride, I was on the point of getting up when I heard footsteps on the stairway. Looking back, I found there was nobody there.

Dismissing it as a false perception and turning back, as soon as I sat down, the simultaneous tread of a number of feet was heard, as if several people were trooping down animatedly. An exquisite delight laced with a creeping fear filled every pore of my body. Although there was no image in front of me, yet I had a distinct, visually perceptible sensation that on this summer evening a bevy of pleasure-seeking women had descended to bathe in the waters of the Shusta. Although at that hour of the evening, in the still mountain valley, on the riverbank, in the lonely palace, nowhere was there any sound, yet it seemed I could distinctly hear the bathers brushing past me in a rapid file with gurgling laughter like the myriad streams of a waterfall. They did not seem to notice me: as they were invisible to me, so perhaps was I to them. The river lay calm as before. But I had a distinct impression that the shallow stream of the river water was being stirred up by a number of arms thrashing about with tinkling bracelets; the laughing damsels were teasingly sprinkling one another with water, their kicking feet sending droplets of water like fistfuls of pearls in arcs into the sky.

I began to feel a sort of tremor in my heart. Whether that tumult was excited by fear, joy, or curiosity I cannot tell. I was very eager to have a good look, but ahead, there was nothing to see. It occurred to me that once I strained my ears, all their talk could be distinctly heard, but straining intently, all I could hear was the grating of crickets from the forest. I thought the dark curtain of two hundred and fifty years hung right in front of me: let me lift a corner timidly and peer behind it; I might see a royal court in session, but in the deep darkness, nothing could be seen.

Suddenly a wind rose sweeping away the suffocating sultriness. Soon the placid surface of the Shusta was crimped like the crinkled tresses of a nymph, and the entire woodland steeped in the evening darkness instantly murmured in one breath, as if waking from a nightmare. Whether you call it a dream or reality, the invisible mirage reflecting from the mist of two hundred and fifty years that had descended before me vanished in the twinkling of an eye. The illusory nymphets, running over me with brisk disembodied footsteps and silent shrieks of laughter, who had hurriedly jumped into the Shusta, did not retrace their steps wringing out water from their wet clothes. Like a breeze wafting away a whiff of scent, one single breath of springtime had whisked them away.

Then I had a gut feeling: I began to suspect that perhaps, finding me alone, the muse of poetry had descended on my shoulders. A poor tax collector sweating it out for a living, now perhaps I was going to be befuddled by the ominous deity. I decided I must eat properly: the underfed are the easiest prey to all kinds of serious diseases. I called my cook and ordered a regular Moghlai dinner rich in ghee and aromatic spices.

Next morning, the whole thing seemed utterly ridiculous. Cheerfully, wearing a sola topi like a sahib, driving the carriage myself, I rattled down on my way to inspection. That day I was to write my quarterly report and expected to be late returning home. Nevertheless, hardly had the evening descended when I began to feel being drawn to the house. Who kept pulling I cannot tell, but I felt I could not afford to dawdle any longer: everyone was waiting for me. Leaving the report unfinished, I put back the topi on my head and startling the deserted, twilit-grey, densely wooded path with the clattering of carriage wheels, arrived at that dark silent massive mansion sequestered beneath the hills.

The stairs led to an enormous hall. Three rows of colossal columns supported the extensive ceiling on arches carved with intricate patterns. This gigantic hall reverberated day and night with its immense emptiness. It was early evening then, and so no lamps had been lit yet. Pushing open the door, as soon as I entered the room, I sensed a great pandemonium set in, as if abruptly dismissing a court in session, the participants, running pell-mell through the doors, windows, balconies and corridors, fled wherever they could. Finding nothing anywhere, I stood transfixed; a strange sense of rapture thrilled my body. I felt as if a faint scent of shampoo and attar lingering down the ages tickled my nostrils. Standing between rows of ancient marble columns in that giant unlit uninhabited hall, I had an astounding aural sensation: spray from the fountains falling with a gentle clatter on white marble, sitar playing some unknown tune, tinkle of gold ornaments coming from somewhere, jingle of anklets from somewhere else, the sound of a giant copper gong striking the hour, an *alap*[5] from some distant concert, clinking of crystal chandeliers swinging in the breeze, song of bulbuls in cages from the balcony, call of trained herons from the garden: they kept orchestrating a symphony of Hades around me.

Such a hallucination was induced in me that this impalpable, inaccessible, unreal world seemed to be the only truth in the world, everything else false, an illusion. That I was myself—that is, Mr So-and-so, eldest son of the late So-and-so who earned a salary of four hundred and fifty rupees collecting cotton-revenues, that I went to my office sporting a sola topi and kurta in a carriage—seemed so laughably absurd, baseless and fictitious that I burst into a guffaw, standing in the middle of that big dark silent room.

Just then, my Muslim servant entered with a lighted kerosene lamp in his hand. Whether he thought me mad, I do not know; but I at once recollected that I was really Mr So-and-so, eldest son of the late So-and-so. I also contemplated that whether or not anywhere within or outside this world any formless fountain had been spurting perpetually, or any place was resounding with endless ragas on an illusory sitar plucked by invisible fingers was stuff for our great poets and mystics to conjecture, but it was certainly true that collecting taxes at the cotton markets of Barich I received four hundred and fifty rupees a month as remuneration. Then again, when I remembered my strange attachment of the previous moment, I kept laughing in jest, taking the newspaper near my kerosene-lit camp-table.

After reading the newspaper and eating a Moghlai dinner, I went to bed in a small corner room after putting out the lamp. Through the open window in front of me, a brilliant star billions of miles above the dark forested Arali[6] Mountains was intently watching Mr Tax-collector lying on a miserable camp-cot. As I kept thinking this with wonder and amusement, I do not know when I drifted into sleep. Neither do I know how long I had slept. Suddenly I woke up with a shiver, not because there had been any sound in the room, nor apparently, anyone had entered. The unblinking star had then dipped below the dark mountain, and faint moonlight of the dark fortnight had entered through my window, pale as if shy of intrusion.

I could not see anybody in the room. Yet I seemed to have a clear feeling that someone was nudging me gently. As soon as I woke up, the apparition, without speaking a word, with only the motion of all five ring-studded fingers bade me follow her very cautiously.

I crept out of bed and walked gingerly. In that enormous palace with a hundred rooms and cubicles, filled with immense emptiness, with sleeping sounds and wakeful echoes, I was apprehensive at every step, in case anyone might wake up, though there was not a single soul except me. Most of the rooms used to be kept closed, and into those rooms, I had never gone before.

On that night, following that invisible beckoning figure with subdued breath and muffled footsteps where and by which alleys I was going is something I cannot clearly recollect today. Dark narrow passages, long corridors, large sombre durbar-halls, small asphyxiating secret chambers, how many we went through one after another I have no count.

Though I had not seen her with my eyes, the image of my invisible guide was not beyond the vision of my mind. She was an Arab woman: her firm perfectly shaped arms, as if carved out of white marble, showing beneath her loose sleeves; a fine veil hanging down her face from the rim of her fez, a curved knife tied to her waistband. It seemed to me that one night from *A Thousand and One Nights* of the Arabian fiction had descended from the realm of fiction today: as if, in the dead of night on the unlit alleys of slumbering Baghdad I had ventured out for some dangerous assignation.

Finally, my guide stopped dead before a deep blue curtain and seemed to point to something on the floor. There was nothing there, but the blood in my chest froze in fright. I sensed that on the floor in front of the curtain, a fearsome Kaffir eunuch in a brocade robe sat dozing, with a drawn sword in his lap, his legs sprawled out. The guide stepped nimbly across his legs and lifted a corner of the curtain.

A part of the room was visible behind, its floor covered with a Persian carpet. Someone was sitting on a throne, partially obscured by the curtain. All I could see was the ankle lengths of her saffron-coloured baggy pyjamas projecting two elegant feet shod in gold-threaded sandals resting lazily on a pink velvet fabric. On one side of a table was a bluish crystal saucer with apples, pears, oranges and bunches of grapes neatly laid out; next to it were two small goblets and a decanter of golden wine waiting for the guest. A strange intoxicating scent of some exquisite variety of incense wafting from inside the room overwhelmed me.

My heart beating fast, I was just about to cross the eunuch's out-stretched legs when he gave a start, and his sword dropped on the marble floor with a horrendous clang.

Startled out of sleep by a horrible scream, I found myself sitting on my camp-cot, soaked all over in sweat: in the first light of dawn the crescent moon of the waning phase looked pale like a patient of insomnia; and our insane Meher Ali was making his customary morning round of the empty roads, shouting, 'Keep away! Keep away!'

This is how the first night of my Arabian fiction came to an abrupt end; a thousand others were still to go, nevertheless.

A serious conflict now arose between my day and my night. By day, I used to go out to work weary and exhausted, and kept cursing the delusive night full of empty dreams; then again, at the approach of the evening, my work-bound existence seemed utterly trivial, false and laughable.

In the evening, I would be entangled in a bewildering web of intoxication. I would become a mysterious doppelganger, a strange character from some unrecorded centuries-old history; no longer then would my anachronistic short English jacket, tight pantaloons, and cigarette do justice to my noble mien. I would then dress up fastidiously—baggy pyjamas, embroidered kurta, long silk overcoat, red velvet fez complete with a coloured attar-scented handkerchief. Then, discarding the cigarette, I would pick up the biggest hubble-bubble with its many-coiled pipe and bowl of rose water, and finally sink into a multi-layered cushioned chair, as if waiting avidly for an extraordinary tryst of love at night.

Thereafter, as darkness thickened, strange, uncanny events would begin to happen: just what they were is beyond my ability to recount. I can imagine them as several pages from a grand fiction borne by a sudden spring breeze, skimming through the strange rooms of this imposing palace; to some distance, they could be followed, after which no end would be in sight. I too spent my nights wandering from room to room pursuing the flitting fragments.

In the swirl of these fragmentary dreams, amidst these whiffs of henna here, snatches of the sitar there, or wafts of air sprinkled with scented water elsewhere, I caught every now and then glimpses of a prima donna like the flashes of lightning. Hers were the saffron pyjamas, her two soft pink feet shod in gold-threaded curve-nosed sandals, her breasts bound in a gold-embroidered tight-fitting bodice, her head wearing a red fez, hanging from whose rim a ruche of gold threads framed her fair forehead and cheeks.

She had driven me crazy with infatuation. Hers was the assignation for which I roamed every night in the tortuous alleys and rooms of a dream palace in the nethermost land of sleep.

On some evenings, standing in front of a large mirror flanked by two lighted candles I would be dressing up thoroughly like a prince when suddenly, I could see a momentary reflection of the same Persian woman alongside my image in the mirror. In the twinkling of an eye, tilting her neck, darting an anguished look with intense yearning in her large dark eyes, forming inarticulate phrases with her moist ruddy lips, twirling her slender vine of blooming youth in a graceful pirouette, and showering sparks of pain, desire and illusion, of smiles, frowns and glinting jewellery all at once, she melted into the mirror again.

Thereupon, a wild gust of wind plundering all the fragrance of the hilly woodland would strike, blowing out the candles; then, after discarding my princely attire, I would sprawl out on the bed in the antechamber of the dressing room, my eyes closed in rapturous delight. In that wind over and around me, in that admixture of scents from the Aravalli forests, I could sense many kisses, many caresses, and many tender strokes of a soft hand swimming about in the secluded darkness. I could hear murmurs of delight next to my ears; I could feel warm perfumed breath upon my forehead and the flowing end of a faintly scented delicate veil brushing my cheeks. An enchanting serpent seemed to be gradually enfolding me in her intoxicating coils, and then heaving a deep sigh, I would sink into deep slumber, my body limp and flaccid.

One afternoon, I decided to go out for a ride. Someone, I do not know who, repeatedly told me not to, but that day, I paid no heed. My English hat and short jacket were hanging from a wooden peg; picking them up, I was about to put them on when suddenly a mighty whirlwind fluttering the ensign of the Shusta's sands and the Aravalli's dry leaves carried away my hat and jacket circling in its vortex. An extremely sweet gurgle of laughter spiralling in the wind and striking every note of amusement rising to higher and higher octaves finally dissolved into the realm of sunset.

There was no going out riding that day, and from the next day on, I had given up wearing that funny kurta and hat altogether.

The same day again, waking up at midnight on my bed I could hear someone weeping her heart out with a low wrenching moan; under my bed, beneath the floor, from within a dark mouldy grave below the stone foundations of this massive mansion, someone seemed to be wailing, 'Take me out of this dungeon! Break down the barriers of this cruel illusion, this deep slumber, this frustrated dream. Lift me on your horse, and pressing me close to your heart, carry me away through the forest, across the mountain, across the river into the sunlit room of yours. Deliver me!'

Who was I anyway? How could I rescue her? And what drowning seductress of desire should I drag ashore from this swirling, shifting flow of dreams? When did you exist, and where did you live, you divine beauty? By which cool spring in the shade of a palm grove, and to which desert nomad were you born? What Bedouin brigand plucked you from your mother's arms like a sprouting bud from a wild creeper? Then mounting his galloping horse across blistering sands, to the slave market of which palace did he carry you? There, which emperor's vassal, after watching your newly sprouted youthful beauty drooping in abashment, counted out the price in gold, and then fording the sea and carrying you in a gold palanquin gifted you to his master's harem? And what is your history there? The known tale of the tunes of the sarangi[7], tinkling of anklets and the golden wine of Persia—interspersed with flashes of dagger, stings of poison, lash of oblique glances! What immeasurable wealth, what interminable incarceration: two bondswomen on either side waving fans, their bracelets coruscating with diamonds; the Shah-en-shah[8] Badshah abasing himself near the bejewelled slippers under your fair feet; outside, a frightful Abyssinian, veritable messenger of death dressed as messenger of God, standing at the door, drawn sword in hand! Thereafter, drifting along in that appallingly resplendent opulence tainted with blood, frothing with envy, fraught with intrigue, O desert shoot, into what cruel life of damnation did you sink, or into what crueller life of dignity were you catapulted!

Just then, the lunatic Meher Ali suddenly yelled out, 'Keep away, keep away! It's all a lie, it's all a lie!' I opened my eyes; it was morning. My peon handed me the mail, and the cook asked with a salaam what kind of dish he should make that day.

I told him, 'No, there is no staying here any longer.' That very day, I packed up and moved into my office. The old clerk Karim Khan gave a wry smile, which annoyed me; making no comment, I settled down to work.

The further the day advanced to dusk, the more I became distracted: I thought, 'Was I not to go out somewhere?' My cotton-tax accounting seemed very trivial; even the Nizamate of Hyderabad held no lure for me: whatever was the living present, whatever was happening around me with people coming and going, working and eating seemed abjectly petty, senseless and inconsequential.

Throwing away my pen, slamming shut the enormous ledger, at once I jumped onto the carriage. Precisely at dusk, involuntarily it stopped at the portals of that stone palace. Rushing up the stairs, I entered the hall.

Today everything stood still. The dark rooms seemed to be sulking from offence taken. My heart swelled with remorse; but I did not find anyone around whom to tell or to ask for forgiveness. With a blank mind, I kept wandering from room to room. I wished to sing my heart out to someone, strumming an instrument, 'O flame of fire, here is the moth that tried to flee you; it has come back to die. Have mercy on it this once; singe its wings, burn it to ashes.'

Suddenly from above, two drops of tears fell on my forehead. Thick clouds had gathered over the Aravalli hills. The dark forest and the inky waters of the Shusta were lying still in some grim expectation. Water, land and sky suddenly quaked, and all at once, a howling storm baring its fangs of lightning came raging like an unfettered lunatic through the distant impenetrable forest. The vast vacant rooms of the palace banging their doors began to wail convulsively in intense anguish.

All my servants were at the office then; there was no one here to light a lamp. On that clouded moonless night, in the pitch-black darkness inside, I distinctly felt the presence of a woman lying face down on the carpet under the bedstead—tearing her dishevelled locks of hair with clenched fists, her fair forehead dripping blood; sometimes bursting into gales of mirthless laughter, sometimes into spasms of sobs; tearing apart her bodice and beating her bare chest wildly; through the window, winds came roaring, bringing in sheets of rain which drenched her thoroughly.

All night long, neither did the storm subside nor her sobs abate. I kept wandering from one dark room to another in futile remorse. There was no one anywhere: whom could I comfort? Whose was this devastating resentment? Where did this inconsolable lament originate ?

'Keep away, keep away!' cried out the lunatic. 'It's all a lie, it's all a lie!'

I looked out: it was dawn, and even in this terrible weather, Meher Ali was as usual circumambulating the palace shouting away as was his wont. Suddenly it occurred to me that perhaps Meher Ali too had once lived in this palace; now, even after coming out of it, if only as a maniac, he was still under the spell of the stone ogress, so went round revisiting it every morning.

At once, in that rain I ran out to the lunatic and asked, 'What's a lie, Meher Ali?'

Without giving any reply, he pushed me aside and, crying like a hypnotised bird hovering within the gaze of a python, continued to run around the house. Just to warn himself desperately, he kept saying, 'Keep away, keep away. It's all a lie, it's all a lie.'

In that squally weather, insanely going to my office I called up Karim Khan and said, 'Tell me frankly what all this means.'

This is essentially, what the old man said:

Once in this palace there raged the flames of many an unfulfilled desire, many a wild lust. In the blaze of all that agony, by the curse of all those frustrated desires, every single stone of this palace is simmering with hunger and thirst, baying like a demon with a lolling tongue to devour any living person ever entrapped. Of those who had spent three nights in that palace, only Meher Ali survived, though completely mad; no one else so far could escape its clutches.

I asked, 'Is there no way for my escape?'

'There is only one way, which is extremely difficult,' said the old man. 'Let me tell you that, but first, it is necessary to recount the story of a Persian slave girl who lived in that rose-garden. So strange and heart-rending an event had never happened in the world.'

At that point of time, the coolies came in to announce that the train was arriving. So soon? By the time we rolled up our bed, the train had pulled in. From the first-class compartment of that train, an Englishman, jerked off his snooze, stuck his head out of the window trying to read the name of the station. Recognising our fellow traveller, he shouted out, 'Hallo!' and called him over to his compartment. We got into a second-class carriage. The identity of our gentleman remained unknown. Neither was the end of the story heard.

I said, 'The man found us fools and had a good laugh at our expense; the story was false from beginning to end.'

On the pretext of the arguments that followed, my theosophist relative and I agreed to part company for ever.

NOTES

1 Rajas and Maharajas who were titular heads of their states under the British Raj.

2 *Reported in your newspapers:* Tagore's own insertion in a lighter vein for the original 'dreamt of in your philosophy' occurring in Shakespeare's Hamlet.

3 The title of the ruler of Hyderabad, from 1724 to 1948.

4 A class of Indian love songs; lyrical ballad; especially the Moghul court singers' forte.

5 A form of Indian classical music that demonstrates the correct notes of a particular raga sung not necessarily to beats but always without any specific composition.

6 Corruption of the name of Aravalli mountains in Rajasthan.

7 A stringed instrument played with a bow, rarely solo, in accompaniment to Indian classical music.

8 King of kings, supreme emperor.

Hidden Treasure
(*Guptadhan*)

1

It was dead of night on the new moon day. Mrityunjay sat down to worship their ancestral deity *Jaykali* according to the *tantric* rites[1]. By the time he finished his *puja*, the first crow had announced the dawn from the nearby mango grove. Mrityunjay turned back to check that the door was closed. Then bowing down at the deity's feet, he removed her throne. Out came a box made of jackfruit timber. The key was tied to the holy thread round his neck; with it he opened the box. The moment it opened, he started back and struck his head in despair.

The garden in Mrityunjay's inner courtyard was enclosed by a wall. In a corner of that garden, at a dark spot shaded by trees there stood this small temple. Inside, there was nothing else apart from the deity; the temple had a single entrance. Mrityunjay examined the box thoroughly. The box was locked all right when he had gone to open it; there had been no tampering. Mrityunjay fumbled around the deity for the umpteenth time, but found nothing. Driven to distraction, he swung open the door; the day was then breaking. Mrityunjay kept searching around the temple interminably hoping against hope.

When the morning became brighter, he came to the *chandimandap* in the outer house and sat down brooding, holding his head. Weary after a sleepless night, he had just dozed off when he was startled to hear, 'May victory be yours, son.' A *sannyasi* with matted hair stood in front of him. Mrityunjay bowed at his feet reverently. The sannyasi blessed him by touching his head, and said, 'Son, you're nursing senseless grief in your mind.'

Mrityunjay was stunned. 'You must be all-knowing,' he said. 'How else could you have known my grief? To no one have I uttered a word.'

The sannyasi said, 'I tell you, son, whatever you've lost, rejoice that you've lost it; don't lament.'

Mrityunjay clutched his feet and said, 'So you must know everything. If you don't tell me how it was lost and where I can get it back, I won't let go of your feet.'

'If I had wished you ill,' said the sannyasi, 'I would have answered your queries. But don't be sad for what the goddess has graciously removed.'

To gratify the sannyasi, Mrityunjay served him with various offerings all day. Next morning, when he came to treat him to a bowl of frothy milk from his own cattleshed, the sannyasi was gone.

2

When Mrityunjay was a child, one day when his grandfather Harihar had been sitting at this chandimandap smoking his hookah, a sannyasi had similarly come and stood in the courtyard, uttering, 'May victory be yours.' Harihar put him up in his house for several days and duly served him to his satisfaction. Before leaving, the sannyasi asked Harihar, 'Son, what do you want from me?' Harihar said, 'Baba, if you are pleased with me, kindly listen to my story. We had once been the most affluent of all in this village. My great-grandfather had married off one of his daughters to a *kulin* boy from a faraway place. His grandson's clan by that daughter, having cheated us, has since become rich under our noses. Now, we are not well-off, and hence, put up with their vanity. But we can bear it no more. Tell me how our family can regain its glory. Please give me your blessings.'

The sannyasi said with a gentle smile, 'Son, be happy to remain poor. There is ultimately no good in trying to be rich.' But Harihar was adamant; he was ready to do his utmost to uplift his family.

The sannyasi then took out from his shoulder bag a parchment manuscript wrapped in a rag. The paper was long, rolled up like a horoscope. He smoothed it out on the floor. Harihar found inscribed in it various cryptic signs in wheels of different kinds, and at its foot a long doggerel which began thus:

Paye dhare sadha / Ra nahi dei Radha / Sheshe dilo Ra / Pagol chharo Pa
Tentul bater kole / Dakshine jao chole / Ishankone Ishani / Kahe dilam Nishani.

(Supplicating at Radha's feet / Yet Radha doesn't speak / Finally she speaks up / *Madman, let go of the feet*

From tamarind and banyan / Go southward / The goddess in the north-east / Knowest as the limit.)

'But I can't make out anything at all, Baba,' said Harihar.

'Keep it with you,' said the sannyasi. 'Worship the goddess. By her grace, someone or another of your descendants will be able to decode this writing. He will then acquire wealth unparalleled in all the world.'

'Won't you explain it, Baba?'

'No. You have to understand it through perseverance.'

Just then, Harihar's younger brother Shankar appeared. Harihar tried to hide the paper hastily. The sannyasi said with a smile, 'Right here begins the misery on the path to riches. But you need not hide it, because its mystery can be solved by one particular person; no one else can, howsoever he may try. Nobody knows who amongst you is that person. So you can leave it open to everybody without fear.'

The sannyasi departed, but Harihar had no peace until he had put it away in a secret place. Lest someone else should benefit from it, and what's more, lest his brother Shankar should come to reap its fruits, Harihar locked it up in a chest made of jackfruit wood, and hid it under the throne of their family deity Jaykali. Every new moon night after finishing the goddess's worship, he would take a look at that paper, in case the goddess graciously empowered him to decipher it.

For some days thereafter, Shankar had been pleading with Harihar, 'Dada, can't I have a good look at the paper for once?'

'Silly boy,' said Harihar, 'do you think it's still with me? That scoundrel, hypocrite of a sannyasi, has deceived me with just some meaningless scribble. I've burnt it.'

Shankar kept silent. Suddenly one day he could not be found in his house. Since then he was missing.

Harihar lost all interest in his work; he could not keep off his thought of the hidden treasure for a moment. Before his death, he passed on the paper to his eldest son Shyamapada. Armed with the paper, Shyamapada gave up his job. He never knew how his entire life was spent worshipping Jaykali and learning how to decipher the script.

The Mrityunjay of our story was Shyamapada's eldest son who inherited this cryptic writing after his father's death. The more his condition worsened, the more avidly he became obsessed with the writing. At this point of time, after the last new moon night worship, he could find it no more; the sannyasi had disappeared as well.

Mrityunjay promised to himself: this sannyasi mustn't go untraced. He alone can give the clue.

With this, he left home to track down the sannyasi. A year passed by.

3

The name of the village was Dharagol. There in a grocer's shop Mrityunjay sat smoking tobacco and thinking on various things casually. Some distance away along the edge of the field, a sannyasi passed by. At first Mrityunjay had not taken notice of it. A little later, it suddenly occurred to him that the man who had just passed was *that* sannyasi. Quickly putting aside the hookah, he leapt out of the shop startling the grocer. But the sannyasi could not be seen.

The evening had become dark. He could not decide where to look for the sannyasi in an unknown place. He came back to the shop and asked the grocer, 'What's there in the big forest over there?'

'Once it was a town,' said the grocer. 'By sage Agastya's curse, the king and the subjects all perished in an epidemic. If searches are made, they say, huge wealth can be found even today. But nobody has the courage to venture into that forest even by day. Whoever went never returned.'

Mrityunjay's heart grew restless. He lay all night on a mat in the grocer's shop smarting all over from mosquito bites and thinking—about the forest, about the sannyasi, about the missing scroll. He had read the script repeatedly and knew it almost entirely by heart. So it kept rolling in his head as he lay awake:

Paye dhare sadha / Ra nahi dei Radha / Sheshe dilo Ra / Pagol chharo Pa

His head became hot; he could not obliterate these few lines from his mind. Finally, when he dozed off towards dawn, he had a dream which revealed their meaning. *Ra nahi dei Radha*: if Radha doesn't give *Ra*, what remains is *Dha*; *Sheshe dilo Ra*: finally she gives *Ra*, hence *Dhara*; then *Pagol chharo Pa*: if *Pa* is discarded from *Pagol*, what remains is *gol*. Hence the whole jumble works out to Dharagol, and lo, that's the name of this place.

The dream snapped, and Mrityunjay jumped up.

4

After roaming the forest all day, and finally finding the way out of it with great effort, Mrityunjay returned to the village in the evening, completely worn out from fasting.

The next day, tying up some *chinra*[2] in his chuddar, he set out for the forest once again. In the afternoon, he arrived near a large pond, which had clear water in the middle and a dense growth of water lilies along its edges. The *ghat* paved with marble was broken-down. He soaked his chinra in water there, ate it, and then went around the pond inspecting. At the western end of the pond, Mrityunjay stopped dead. He saw a large banyan tree circumscribing a tamarind tree. At once, the lines came to his mind: *Tentul bater kole / Dakshine jao chole.* So he walked some distance to the south and soon found himself in a thick jungle, where it was impossible to penetrate the thickets of cane. However, Mrityunjay decided that he could ill afford to miss this one tree. While retracing his path to this tree, he caught sight of the spire of a temple through the gaps between trees. Walking in that direction, he arrived at a dilapidated temple. Near it lay an oven, some cinder and ash. Nervously he peeped into the temple through its broken door. He found no man or deity there; only a rug, a *kamandalu*[3], and a saffron scarf lay strewn.

The evening had been drawing near by then. The village was far away; he had doubts whether he could negotiate his way out of the dark forest, so he brightened up when he found signs of human presence in the temple. A huge chunk of stone chipped off the temple lay at its door. Mrityunjay sat down on it thinking, with his head bent low. Suddenly, he noticed something etched out on the stone. Stooping over it, he noticed a wheel; it was divided by two rectangular strips and two diameters into several sections and sectors, each containing a symbolic letter or number, some distinct, others nearly faded out.

This wheel was quite familiar to Mrityunjay. On several new-moon nights in his own temple, poring over the parchment scroll amid fumes of scented incense under a ghee-fuelled lamp, he had prayed for the goddess's blessings to break the mystery. Now that he had come within an ace of fulfilment, he seemed to tremble all over. Lest there was a slip betwixt the cup and the lip, lest everything should be spoilt by a hasty step, and worst, in case the sannyasi had already gathered everything, he felt a great turmoil in his heart. He was at a loss to decide what to do. It occurred to him maybe he was sitting right on top of his treasure-trove, yet unable to know anything.

He sat there telling the name of goddess Kali, even as the evening grew darker and the woodland resounded with the call of crickets.

5

It was then that, some distance into the dense woods, the glow of a flame was visible. Mrityunjay rose from his stone seat and proceeded in the direction of that flame. After proceeding a few steps with difficulty, he saw clearly from behind a peepul tree that the sannyasi he had known was absorbed in some calculations on a square of ash with the help of a stick, the scroll spread out beside him under the flame. The same parchment Mrityunjay had inherited from his forefathers! 'Hypocrite, thief! So that's why he had advised him not to grieve!'

The sannyasi, once he had finished a round of calculation, went on to measure the land with a yardstick. After measuring up to a point, he shook his head despairingly, then returning to his seat started calculating all over again. This went on until the night was nearly over, and the leaves on the top branches of the banyan tree murmured in the cool breeze at daybreak, when the sannyasi rolled up the scroll and went away.

Mrityunjay did not know what he should do. But what he certainly knew was that it was well-nigh impossible for him without the sannyasi's help to decipher the writing. That the sannyasi, himself covetous, would never help him was certain as well. Naturally, there was nothing he could do except keep watch on him secretly. But he had to procure his food, and unless he went to the village by day, he would get none. Obviously, he needed to go to the village in the morning at the earliest.

Towards dawn when darkness had somewhat faded, he got down from the tree and carefully examined the site where the sannyasi had been working with numbers on ash; he could make out nothing. Going around in the forest he could discern no difference whatever with any other tract. When it was slightly brighter, Mrityunjay made for the village very circumspectly, afraid that the sannyasi might notice him.

Near the shop where Mrityunjay had taken shelter, a *kayastha* housewife was feeding Brahmins after keeping a ritual vow. Mrityunjay had his meal there. Having eaten scantily for the last couple of days, he ended up eating rather too much today. After the overeating, once he had taken a few puffs at his hookah and lain on the mat inside the shop for a short nap, he fell fast asleep, exhausted from the previous night's vigil.

Mrityunjay had decided that he would set out rather early today after his meals. His plan was upset: when he woke, the sun had set. That could not daunt him, though; he entered the forest in spite of the darkness. Soon the night advanced; his vision was obstructed by shadows of trees, his passage blocked by the jungle. He had no idea where and in which direction he was heading. When the night ended, he found he had ambled over the same tract all night.

A flock of crows flew out in the direction of the village cawing raucously, which sounded in Mrityunjay's ears like taunts of reproach.

6

After several attempts of miscalculation and recalculation, the sannyasi had finally discovered the way into the tunnel. He entered it with a torch. The stone walls had gathered moss, and water was leaking at places. Here and there frogs were sleeping in a cluster. After he had gone some distance down this slippery path, he encountered a wall blocking further progress. Bewildered, he struck vigorously with an iron rod all over the wall: no hollow sound came from anywhere, nor was there any hole in it; that this path ended here was certain, he concluded. Once again he took out the paper and sat down to calculate, racking his brains all through the night.

The next day, he entered the tunnel after a fresh round of calculation. Following a secret code, he arrived at a particular spot, from where he removed the stones and found a byway. Advancing some distance, he found this one too was blocked at some point. At last on the fifth night, upon entering the tunnel, the sannyasi cried out: today I've found out the path; today I'm not going to make any blunder.

It was a most tortuous path; there was no end to its branches and lanes which were at places so narrow that one had to crawl to make any progress. Holding the torch very carefully, he walked on until he arrived at what looked like a room circular in shape. At its centre, there was a large masonry well, whose bottom was not discernible in torchlight. A thick iron chain hung from the ceiling down into the well. When the sannyasi pushed it with utmost strength shaking it only slightly, a clang rose from within the well reverberating all through the room. 'I've found it!' he cried out. Hardly had he uttered this before a slab of stone tumbled out of the worn-out wall. The same moment, another object—something animate—fell with a thud letting out a yell. The sannyasi, startled by this sudden sound, dropped the torch, and it went out.

7

'Who're you?' asked the sannyasi. When there was no reply, he groped about and touched a human body. 'Who're you?' he asked again, but got no reply. The man had fainted. The sannyasi then lighted a torch with great effort by striking flints. By now the man had recovered too; he tried to rise giving out a yell of pain.

'My goodness, it's Mrityunjay!' said the sannyasi. 'What made you do this?'

'Baba, forgive me. God has punished me. I wanted to hit you by throwing a stone, but was off balance. I lost my footing and fell together with it. I must have fractured my leg.'

'What would you have gained by striking me?'

'Gain! You're talking of gain?' said Mrityunjay. 'What are *you* after,' he taunted, 'when having stolen the scroll from my prayer room you're scouring the tunnel? You are a cheat, hypocrite. The sannyasi who had given this scroll to my grandfather had said that someone from our family alone could decipher it. It is we who deserve this hidden treasure. That's why I've shadowed you without food or sleep for the last few days. Today when you cried out that you had found it, I could contain myself no more. I followed you up to that pit where I hid myself. From there I loosened a chunk and aimed at you, but my body being weak and the place slippery, I fell. Now I'm at your mercy. You can kill me if you wish, and I'll guard this wealth as *Yaksh*, but you can't take it for yourself. No, never! And if you try to take it, mind you, I'm a Brahmin; I'll curse you and kill myself by jumping into this well. The wealth that you will then acquire shall be tantamount to Brahmin's blood, cow's blood. You can never happily enjoy it. Our father and grandfather had their minds on this treasure when they died. This treasure has been our sole target, and we've become poor meditating on it. To find this treasure, I've left my wife and children uncared-for at home and have been roaming about like a wretched lunatic without food or rest. You can never take this away in front of my eyes.'

8

'Listen then, Mrityunjay,' said the sannyasi. 'Let me tell you everything. You know that your grandfather had a younger brother named Shankar.'

'Yes, I do, but he left his home and went missing.'

'I'm that Shankar.'

Mrityunjay gave out a deep sigh of despair: the sole claim to this hidden treasure that he had so long decided was his, now a relation from his own clan had come to lay waste to.

Said Shankar, 'Right from the moment Dada got the scroll, he had been trying desperately to hide it from me. But the more he tried, the more I became curious. He had kept it under the throne of the deity; I found it out. I then acquired a duplicate key and copied out the entire scroll little by little each day. The very day I had finished copying, I set out to trace the wealth, leaving my home. I too had my helpless wife and a small child at my home. They are no more today.

'Needless to narrate how I went travelling from one land to another. Deciding that only a sannyasi could explain a script from another sannyasi, I served quite a few of them. Some fake ones even tried to steal it when they had got scent of it. Years passed by in this way, and I did not have a moment's peace, a moment's happiness.

'Finally, by sheer virtue acquired from my previous birth, I was blessed with the company of Swami Swarupananda in the Kumayun mountains. He said, "Son, give up your greed. Only then will the eternal wealth in the universe come to you on its own."

'He assuaged the affliction of my heart. By his grace, the light of the sky and the green of the earth became a royal treasure for me. Sitting on a rock at the foot of the mountain one winter evening, when the Baba had kindled a fire in his incense-holder, I consigned my paper into the flame. Baba had a faint smile. I had not realised then what that smile meant. Today I do. He must have said to himself: it is easy to burn the paper to ashes, but not so easy to burn your desires to ashes.

'When there was no sign left of the paper, I felt as if a serpent's snare that had enfolded me until now released its hold. My heart filled with an ecstasy of freedom. I thought that from this moment I had nothing to fear, nothing to want from this world. Not long after this, I got separated from the Baba. I searched for him extensively, but found no trace of him anywhere.

'Eventually I became a sannyasi and wandered about with a detached heart. Many years passed by, and I had almost forgotten about the writing when one day I happened to be in this forest of Dharagol; I took shelter in a deserted temple. In two or three days I noticed that various symbols were inscribed here and there on its walls. These symbols were well known to me. So what I had once pursued for a long time was no doubt within my reach. I said to myself: no more staying here. I'm off this moment leaving this forest behind.

'But it just did not happen. I thought: why don't I see what's here? Better to satisfy my curiosity once and for all. I racked my brains long over the symbols, with no result. It kept coming back again and again to my mind: why did I burn the paper after all? What harm would there have been even if I had preserved it?

'I then went to my native village. When I saw the abject condition of our ancestral home, I thought: I'm a sannyasi; what do I care for gems and jewels? But these poor people? They are only family men; if I recover that hidden treasure for them, there indeed can be no fault in it. I knew where that paper was; to obtain it was not at all difficult for me.

'For a whole year after that I have been in this lonely forest working with figures and searching for the wealth; I had no other thought in my mind. Every time I encountered an impediment, I grew more eager. Like one possessed, I was absorbed day and night in this one pursuit.

'I did not know when in the meanwhile you had been following me. If I had been my usual self, you could never have hid yourself from me. But I was engrossed single-mindedly; no external event attracted my notice.

'Thereafter today, just now, I have discovered what I had been looking for. No king or emperor of the world possesses as much wealth in his store as is embedded here. There's only one more symbol to decode, and the wealth will be found. This is the hardest code, but I've decoded this one as well in my mind. That's why I had cried out in joy, "I've found it!" If I wish, I can arrive in a moment right in the middle of that storehouse of jewels.'

Clutching Shankar's feet, Mrityunjay said, 'You're a sannyasi; you've no need for wealth. Take me into that store. Do not deprive me.'

'Today my last tie has been severed,' said Shankar. 'The stone you had hurled with intent to hit me missed my body, but its impact has broken through my shell of delusion. Today I have seen the appalling image of craving. My guru *Paramahansa Dev's* benign, mystical smile has at last kindled an inextinguishable flame in the hallowed lamp of my heart.'

Falling at his feet, Mrityunjay pleaded once again piteously, 'You are an emancipated soul; I am not, and I don't want to be one, either. You must not deprive me of this wealth.'

'Son, here then is your writing,' said the sannyasi. 'If you can find out the wealth, well, take it away.' Leaving his staff and the scroll with Mrityunjay, the sannyasi departed. 'Have pity on me,' wailed Mrityunjay. 'Do not leave me behind; take me there.' He got no reply.

Mrityunjay then tried to get out of the tunnel fumbling about with the staff. But in the intricate, labyrinthine path he met too often with obstacles to make any progress. At last, tired out from endless wandering, he lay down at a place and soon fell asleep. When he woke up, there was no way he could ascertain whether it was night or day, or what hour it was. When he felt very hungry, he took out some chinra from his chuddar-end and ate it. He then made another attempt to grope his way out of the tunnel. Encountering obstruction at several places, he sat down in desperation. 'Do you hear, O Sannyasi? Where are you?' he screamed; the voice reverberated through every duct and channel. A reply came from not far away, 'I am close by; tell me what you want.'

'Show me for heaven's sake where the treasure is,' Mrityunjay pleaded woefully. But this time round, there came no reply. Mrityunjay called repeatedly, but got no reply. In the eternal underground night not marked by minutes and hours, Mrityunjay dozed off for another spell. When he woke, he woke back to that darkness again and yelled out, 'Do you hear? Where are you?' Reply came from somewhere nearby, 'Here I am. What do you want?'

'I want nothing else; take me out of this hell.'

'Don't you want wealth?'

'No. I don't.'

Flints were then struck, and a while later the torch was alight. The sannyasi said, 'All right, Mrityunjay. Let's go out of this tunnel.'

'Baba, must everything come to naught?' Mrityunjay urged miserably. 'Even after so much suffering, don't I get any wealth in the end?'

Instantly the light went out. 'Oh, how cruel!' Mrityunjay cried and flopped on to the ground. He began to contemplate. Time had no measure; darkness no end. Mrityunjay wished he could, with the last ounce of strength in his body and mind, crush this darkness into smithereens. His heart began to pine for the light, sky, and variety in the picturesque earth. 'O sannyasi!' he beseeched, 'Listen, you cruel sannyasi! I don't want wealth. Only take me out.'

'Don't want wealth?' said the sannyasi. 'Hold my hand then. Come along.' No light was lit this time, however. Clutching the staff in one hand and the sannyasi's chuddar in the other, Mrityunjay walked slowly on. After traversing a network of alleys and rounding many corners, the sannyasi came to a certain spot and said, 'Stop here.'

Mrityunjay stopped. A rusted iron door creaked open. Holding his hand, the sannyasi said, 'Come in.' Mrityunjay walked into what looked like a room. Once again flints were struck. When the torch was alight, what an amazing sight it revealed! Stacked against the walls glinted piles of thick gold bars resembling frozen sunbeams incarcerated underground. Mrityunjay's eyes began to glow. Like a madman he cried out, 'This gold is mine; I shan't go leaving this behind.'

'All right, you needn't go,' said the Sannyasi. 'Here is the torch. And here is some *chhatu*[4], some chinra, and a big jar of water.' Out came the sannyasi, and the iron doors of this goldmine slammed shut.

Mrityunjay ambled around the room stroking the heaps of gold again and again. He pulled down the smaller bars on the floor, lifted them on to his lap, struck them together to hear their clang, brushed them all over his body to get their feel. Finally he made a bed of them, lay on it and fell asleep, exhausted.

He woke up only to find gold sparkling all around him, nothing else besides gold. He began to reflect: on the earth, perhaps by now, the day has dawned; men and animals have woken up delightedly; the soothing smell rising every morning from their pondside garden illusively entered his nose; ducks waddling and quacking their way to the pond, their maidservant Bama, her sari-end tucked to her waist, carrying a heap of utensils to the ghat on her uplifted right arm distinctly appeared in his mind.

Mrityunjay banged on the door shouting, 'Do you hear, Sannyasi-*thakur*?' The door opened. 'What do you want?'

'I want to go out. But can't I take just one or two bars with me?'

Without giving any reply, the sannyasi lit the torch afresh, put down a water-filled kamandalu, then taking out a few morsels of chinra from his chuddar put it on the floor and went out, shutting the door behind.

Mrityunjay pulled out a thin bar and bent it double until it broke into pieces. When he had made a lot, he strewed the pieces around like clods of earth. Now he grabbed a bar and bit dents on it, now he threw another and stamped away on it. He kept saying to himself: how many kings are there in the world who can trifle with gold like this? Mrityunjay seemed to have been seized with a destructive spree. He wished he could grind all the gold to dust and sweep it up with a broom, thereby deriding all the kings and emperors of the world hankering after gold.

Rampaging with the gold in all manner of disdain as long as he could, he felt tired and dropped off to sleep. When he woke, all he could see was the same heap of gold. Thumping on the door, he shouted out, 'Hear me, sannyasi? I don't want this gold; I don't want any gold.'

But the door did not open. He shouted himself hoarse, still the door did not open. He went on picking lumps and hurling at the door, with no result. His heart sank: won't the sannyasi come again then? Have I to die little by little, minute by minute, withering in this dungeon of gold? The very sight of gold now struck terror in his heart: that golden mound standing still loomed with a silent frigid grin of horror—no pulsation, no change—the heart now beating away in Mrityunjay had no relation to them, its pangs nothing to do with them! The lumps of gold wanted no light, no sky, no air, no life and no freedom. In this perpetual darkness, they remained forever bright, rigid, and immobile.

Was it now dusk on earth? O for that crepuscular gold: the gold that soothes the eye for a moment, only to fade away dolefully into darkness; thereafter the evening star gazes upon the courtyard; the housewife lights a lamp in the cattle-shed and another in a corner of her room; the prayer bell rings in the temple.

The smallest and the pettiest things of village life now stood out in Mrityunjay's imagination: even the thought of their pet dog Bhola dozing off, coiled up in a corner of their courtyard after the evening seemed to torment him. The grocer at Dharagol in whose shop he had taken shelter for a few days must by now have put out the lamp, downed the shutter and proceeded homewards for his meal. How happy the grocer is, he sighed. Who knows what day of the week it is? If it is Sunday, people must now be returning from market to their homes, shouting at their straying companions, crossing the river by ferry boats; farmers making their way to different villages along mud-paths, along dykes in cornfields, by courtyards littered with dry bamboo leaves, one or two fish in their hands and baskets on their heads in the faint light of stars.

To mingle as the meanest and most insignificant creature with this vast, varied, bustling life on the firm ground overhead, he heard calls of habitation from above a hundred layers of earth. That life, that sky, and that light seemed priceless compared to all the gems and jewellery of the world put together. Even if for once, lying on the dusty lap of that verdant Mother Earth under the bright bare sky, I could take in a lungful of that grass-scented air in one last breath, my life would have been fulfilled, he thought.

Just then, the door opened. Entered the sannyasi. 'Mrityunjay, what do you want?'

'I want nothing else,' he burst forth. 'I want to go out of this tunnel, of this darkness, of this labyrinth, of this prison of gold once and for all. I want light; I want the sky; I want freedom.'

'There is a more precious store of gems here than this stock of gold. Won't you go there once?'

'No, I shan't.'

'Don't you feel curious just to have a look?'

'No, I don't want even to look at it. If I have to go begging with a loincloth on, still I don't want to stay here a moment longer.'

'All right. Come along.'

The sannyasi led Mrityunjay by the hand to that deep well. Placing the scroll in his hand, he asked, 'What will you do with this?'

Mrityunjay tore it into pieces and cast them away into the well.

Kartik 1311 (1904)

NOTES

1 A special ritual of worshipping Kali, which combines magical and mystical elements.
2 Beaten rice.
3 A priest's copper water-pot.
4 Barley or gram ground into powder.

The Editor
(*Sampadak*)

As long as my wife was living, I never really had to worry about Prabha. I had been a bit too much preoccupied then with Prabha's mother rather than Prabha. That was a time when merely watching her play and laugh, hearing her half-formed words, and getting her gentle caresses I remained quite contented. I would dandle her as long as I liked; the moment she started crying, I would deposit her in her mother's lap, finding immediate relief. That she had to be brought up with a great deal of care and effort had not occurred to me.

Eventually, my wife having prematurely died, one day the little girl rolling off her mother's lap dropped near mine. I hugged her close to me.

I contemplated that it was my duty now to nurture the motherless daughter with twice as much care, but I cannot exactly tell whether she had more strongly felt that it was her duty now to tend to her wifeless father with utmost diligence. But right from when she was six, she had begun to act as a regular matron. It was evident that the wisp of a girl was growing to be the sole guardian of her father.

With an inward smile, I surrendered myself to her hands. Then I noticed that the more I proved incompetent and helpless, the more she was pleased: if I picked up my dhoti or umbrella for myself, she would assume such a posture as if I had infringed her right. She had never before found such a big doll as her father; so feeding him, dressing him, sending him to bed, she was very happy all day. Only while teaching the Multiplication Tables or the Book of Poems–Part I, did I have to activate my fatherhood somewhat.

But sometimes I was worried to think that getting her married with a respectable groom would require a lot of money: where was I to get it? I was giving her the best possible education within my capacity all right, but what would happen to her if she ended up in the hands of a complete dunce?

I was persuaded, finally, to get down to earning money. I had already become age-barred for government service, and was not competent for any other service, either. After much deliberation, I started writing books.

A perforated bamboo reed cannot hold any oil or water: the essential property itself is lost; the reed as such serves no practical purpose whatever, but when blown into it, makes a flute free of cost. I definitely knew that an unfortunate good-for-nothing person, who had no brains for any other work in the world, would certainly make a good writer. With the courage of my conviction, I wrote a satirical skit, which found popular appreciation and was played at the theatre.

I was so fascinated by the sudden taste of fame that I could not stop writing satires. Throughout the day, in an anxious and reflective mood I kept writing only satires.

Prabha came, and giving me a cuddle, asked with an affectionate smile, 'Won't you go to bathe, Baba?'

'Go away, go away. Don't disturb me now,' I snapped.

Perhaps, her face had darkened like a lamp blown out with a single puff: I did not even notice when she had slipped out of the room quietly with a tear-laden heart.

I would shoo away the maid, lunge at the servant, and chase the whining beggar, raising a stick. My reading room being right on the road, when an innocent pedestrian from outside the window enquired about the direction to his destination, I would politely tell him to go to some undesirable place called hell. Alas, nobody tried to understand that I was writing an uproarious burlesque.

But the money I had made was nothing in comparison to the extent of fun and fame I was getting. Neither was money on my mind at that time. Meanwhile, Prabha's prospective matches had been growing up blithely for delivering other people from the burden of their daughters, to which I had been blissfully oblivious.

Unless pinched by hunger, I would never have woken from my slumber. But at that time there was a favourable turn. The zamindar of Jahirgram having launched a journal offered to appoint me its salaried editor. I accepted the assignment. For a few days, I kept writing so brilliantly that whenever I came out in public, people would point me out to each other, and I would consider myself as blindingly luminous as the midday sun.

Next to Jahirgram, was Ahirgram. The zamindars of the two villages were sworn enemies. Previously, they had been at loggerheads. Later, giving an undertaking to the magistrate they stopped violence. Now I, a docile fellow, had been appointed to replace Jahirgram's murderous stick-fighting squad. Everyone said I had proved equal to my status.

My acerbic columns completely shattered Ahirgram. I had managed to tarnish the history of their caste, clan, and ancestry thoroughly.

This was a time when I normally felt euphoric. My health picked up, adding some extra flab; my face always wore a contented smile. Targeting the ancestors of Ahirgram, I used to hurl heart-rending verbal spears, and entire Jahirgram burst into laughter like ripe muskmelons. I really had a jolly nice time then.

Eventually, Ahirgram too, brought out a journal of its own. It never minced its words. So enthusiastically did it curse in the common dialect that even the words in print virtually screamed the curse standing in front of the reader's eyes. Naturally, people of either village could very clearly understand what it said.

On the other hand, as was my wont, I used to assail my opponents so wittily with such subtle irony that whether friend or foe, nobody could make out what I meant.

Consequently, even though I triumphed, everyone thought I had been vanquished. I was obliged to write up a homily on the importance of refined tastes. Later I found that this had been a grave mistake, because it is not so easy to ridicule the ridiculous as to ridicule the sublime. Anthropoid apes[1] can easily hold humans to ridicule; but humans[2] are never quite successful at mocking the Anthropoids. Therefore, the latter banished civility from the land straightaway by baring their teeth.

My master no longer treated me warmly. No more was I treated with respect in public gatherings either. When I went out, no one came forward to strike up a conversation. Some of them had even begun to laugh at me.

Meanwhile, my satires had been altogether forgotten. Suddenly I felt as if I was a safety match: after blazing for a minute or so, I had burnt myself out.

I felt so demoralised that howsoever I banged my head, not a single line of writing would come. I began to feel there was no happiness in remaining alive.

Prabha was now scared of me. She did not dare to approach me at any time, uninvited. She must have realised that a clay doll was a far better companion than a humorist father.

Eventually, the Ahirgram-Prakash, sparing our zamindar, instead made me the butt of their ridicule. Several ugly insinuations had been made. All my acquaintances, one after another picking up the journal, read it out to me with evident relish. One or two even remarked that whatever the subject matter, the language was indeed admirable. In other words, the vituperation was obvious from the language itself. Throughout the day, I heard the same thing from a score of people.

There was a sort of garden in front of my house. One evening I was strolling there alone, utterly dejected. When the birds, after returning to their nests and stopping their chatter, retired comfortably into the evening calm, I realised that among birds there was no such tribe as witty writers and no such thing as debate over refined tastes.

I was preoccupied with drafting a suitable rejoinder. One great disadvantage of politeness is that not everyone everywhere can appreciate it. The language of incivility is comparatively familiar, so I was contemplating a riposte of that kind: there was no question of accepting defeat. It was then in that darkness of the evening that I heard a familiar tender voice, and next felt a soft warm touch in my palm. I was so tense and distracted that I could not recognise the voice or the touch even though I had known them too well.

But the very next moment, the trail of that voice became prominent in my ears and that gentle touch soothed my palm. The little girl coming quietly had once called in her mild voice, 'Baba.' After getting no reply, picking up my right hand, and with it stroking her tender cheek once, she was going back quietly.

For a long time now, Prabha had not called me so piteously or coming willingly given me a fond caress. That is why today this loving touch suddenly made my heart extremely anxious.

After a while, going back into the room I saw Prabha was lying in her bed. She looked distressed, her eyes half-closed; she was sprawled like a drooping flower shed at the end of the day: her head felt very hot; her breath was warm; veins of her forehead were throbbing.

I realised that afflicted by the oncoming illness, she had gone with her thirsty heart to obtain her father's love and tender care; her father was then formulating a tough reply on behalf of Jahir-Prakash.

I sat beside her. Without saying a word, she took my hand between her febrile palms, and resting her cheek on it, lay quietly.

I made a bonfire of all the copies of the Jahirgram and Ahirgram journals. No rejoinder was written. I had never been so happy acknowledging defeat.

When her mother had died, I had picked up the girl into my lap. Today, having finished the funeral rites of her stepmother, I gathered her once again into my arms and went indoors.

Baishakh 1300 (1893)

NOTES

1 In Bengali, *Hanu* for Hanuman, the monkey chief of Hindu mythology and devoted to Rama. Rabindranath has wittily made this homonymous adaptation to compare 'sons of *Hanu*' with 'sons of *Manu*': Manu's sons are supposedly law-abiding compared to Hanu's sons who have inherited the monkey-chief's knack of incendiarism and vandalism.

2 In Bengali, Manu, the Hindu lawgiver (see Glossary).

The Gift of Sight
(*Drishtidan*)

I have heard that daughters of many Bengalis nowadays have to find their husbands through their own endeavour. So did I, albeit with god's help: I had kept many vows, and performed many Shiva[1] *pujas* from my childhood.

I had hardly completed eight years of age when I was married. But because of sins of an earlier life, even though I had such a cherished husband, I succeeded in possessing him but not fully. The three-eyed goddess (*Durga)* claimed my two eyes, and I was denied the pleasure of continuing to see my husband up to the last moment of my life.

My ordeal had begun right in my childhood. I was just past fourteen when I gave birth to a stillborn baby and was myself at death's door. But how could one destined to suffer afford to die prematurely? A lamp meant to burn has enough oil in it to burn all night before it extinguishes. I did survive, but whether from debility, depression, or whatever, my eyes were affected.

My husband was then studying medicine. In the excitement of acquiring new learning, he exulted at the least chance of trying it out. He started treating my eyes himself.

My elder brother was at college studying for his BL examination that year. He came one day to my husband and said, 'What are you doing? I'm afraid you're going to damage Kusum's eyes. Get her treated by a good doctor.'

'What new treatment is a good doctor supposed to do?' said my husband. 'As for medicines, what else is there I don't know?'

'So am I to suppose,' said my brother with some irritation, 'there's no difference between you and the head of your college?'

'You're studying law,' countered my husband, 'What would you know about medicine? When you get married, suppose there is litigation over your wife's property; will you then go by my advice?'

I thought to myself: when giants fight, it is the midgets who get trampled over.[2] My brother has locked horns with my husband, but I have to suffer and nobody else. But then, once my parents have given me away, why this squabble over fixing responsibilities about me, I wondered. My sorrow or happiness, my sickness or health, was entirely my husband's concern.

That day, over this petty issue, my brother and my husband apparently fell out a bit. My eyes had already been watering; now the tears became even more copious with neither my husband nor my brother realising the true reason.

When my husband was at college, in the afternoon my brother arrived with a doctor. After examining me, the doctor said unless proper care was taken, the condition might worsen. He wrote out some medicines, which my brother sent someone to fetch. When the doctor had gone, I said, 'Dada, I beg you, please do not interfere with the treatment I am receiving at the moment.'

I had held my brother in great awe since childhood; I was amazed that I had managed to speak so bluntly to him. But I had realised that the treatment my brother was arranging behind my husband's back could ultimately do no good, if not worse.

Perhaps my brother too was surprised at my brusqueness. He thought for a while and said, 'All right, I'll never bring the doctor again. But at least try the medicine as advised.' When the medicine arrived, he explained to me how to take it, and left. Before my husband could return from college, I disposed of the phials, prescription and all the rest of it into the well in our courtyard.

Patently, out of grudge against my brother, my husband now took over my treatment with a vengeance. Medicines were replaced mornings and evenings; I put on blinkers and spectacles, applied drops and ointments, gulped horrible-smelling cod-liver oil swallowing the gut-churning nausea. When he asked me how I was feeling, I would say, 'Much better.' I even tried to persuade myself so: when the eyes streamed profusely, I thought it was a good sign; when they stopped streaming, I decided I was on the recovery path.

After some time, however, the pain grew unbearable; my vision became blurred, and I had maddening headaches. My husband too looked somewhat embarrassed; apparently, he could not think of any adequate ground for calling a doctor now so late.

'What's the harm in giving the doctor a call,' I told my husband, 'if only to placate my brother? He's showing his displeasure, if unfairly, over this, and that hurts me. When the treatment will be done by you, isn't it better to have a doctor to take the blame?'

'That's a good idea,' said my husband. That very day he called in an English doctor. I don't know what the sahib actually said, but apparently, he gave my husband a bit of a reprimand; he stood silently, bending his head low. When the doctor had gone, I said to my husband holding his hand, 'Where did you find this bull-headed, white-skinned fool? Wouldn't a native doctor do? How is this man more competent to know my condition than you?'

'It's become necessary to operate on your eyes,' said my husband abashedly.

'Come on,' I said with some pretence of anger, 'you had always known surgery was necessary, but from the very beginning you've kept it from me. Did you think I would panic?'

His shyness gone, he said, 'When it comes to surgery on the eyes, how many among males are bold enough not to recoil?'

'Males are bold to their wives only,' I said jokingly.

'True enough,' he said, at once turning pale and solemn. 'Vanity is all they are capable of.'

I brushed aside his solemnity saying, 'Do you think you can beat us even in being vain? There also we win.'

Meanwhile, when my brother came, I took him aside and said, 'Dada, by following that doctor's advice, my eyes had been doing fairly well; but one day by mistake, smearing the medicine meant for oral use, I've damaged my eyes almost beyond repair. My husband says they'll need an operation.'

'I thought you were having your husband's treatment,' said my brother. 'That's the main reason why in my annoyance I haven't come so long.'

'Far from it,' I said. 'Secretly I'd been going by that doctor's advice. I hadn't told my husband, lest he should get angry.'

What gross lies women have to tell! I could not hurt my brother. Nor could I lower my husband's repute. As mother, to placate her baby; as wife, to keep baby's father in good humour: what deception do women need!

One by-product of this dissimulation was that before I finally became blind, I had found my brother and my husband reconciled. My brother thought secret treatment had brought about this mishap; my husband thought it would have been better to heed my brother's advice at the outset. The two repentant souls inwardly begged each other's forgiveness and thus drew closer together. Henceforth, they began to rely on and consult each other with humility.

In the end, they agreed to call in an English surgeon, who came and operated on my left eye. Already weakened, it failed to withstand the trauma, and the guttering flame went out. Little by little, the other eye too went into complete darkness. A curtain was drawn forever over the sandalwood-bedecked image I had seen for the first time at *shubhadrishti*[3] one childhood day.

One day, my husband came to my bedside and said, 'No more false bragging to you; it was I, I who impaired your eyes.' His voice was choking with tears as he said this. I clasped his right hand with both my hands and said, 'Never mind. You have taken away what was yours. Just think if they had been damaged at a doctor's hand, what consolation would I have had? When fate cannot be averted, could anyone have saved my eyes? That they have been lost to you is the sole comfort in my blindness. When flowers for worship were too few, Rama was about to gouge out his two eyes to offer his god.[4] To my god I have offered my eyes: my moonlight of the full moon, my light of the morning, my blue of the sky, my green of the earth, I offer all I have unto you. Whatever pleases your eyes tell me in your own words, and I will accept it as the gift of your sight.'

I could not say so many words. Neither is it possible to speak actually in this fashion. These are words of long reflection: sometimes when I felt depressed and my devotion lost its ardour, when I deemed myself to be deprived, distressed and wretched by misfortune, I would make my mind utter these words. This solace, this devotion gave me the impetus for trying even to transcend my sorrow. That day, partly by my words, partly by my silence, perhaps I managed to convey my feelings in some sort of way. He said, 'Kumu, what I destroyed through my stupidity, I can never give you back, but I will keep you constant company to make up for your lost eyes to the best of my ability.'

'That's no sensible thing to say,' I said. 'I shall never allow you to make your home a sanatorium for the blind. You must marry again.'

Before I began to explain why marriage was an immediate imperative, my voice cracked slightly. After clearing the throat and recovering a little, I was just about to begin when my husband burst forth with surging emotion, 'I may be stupid, I may be conceited, but that does not mean I am a scoundrel. I have made you blind by my own hand; if in the end I desert you on the pretext of that flaw and take another wife, I swear by our deity[5] that it will be tantamount to committing patricide or some unspeakable crime.'

He could not have uttered so terrible a vow; I would have cut him short. But tears welling up in my breast and choking my voice were on the verge of streaming down my eyes which I found too hard to restrain for speech. His words so overwhelmed me that I cried out in joy sinking my face in the pillow: I am blind, but he will not leave me; he would clasp me to his heart like the sorrow of a sufferer! I did not want such good fortune; but then, the mind is selfish.

At last, when the first shower of my tears had poured down with full force, I drew his face close to my breast and said, 'Why did you make such a dreadful vow? Do you think I wanted you to marry for your own happiness? I would have my co-wife to serve my own interest: the work I could not do for you personally being blind, I would get done by her.'

'Doesn't a maidservant work as well?' protested my husband. 'Can I for that matter marry a servant girl and place her alongside this goddess of mine?' He lifted my face and placed one single kiss on my brow that seemed to open up a third eye; it marked the moment I was raised to the pedestal of a goddess. I said to myself: let it be so. Now that I am blind I can no longer be a mistress in the domestic world; I will rise above it, and as a goddess bring welfare to my husband. No more falsehood, no more deception: I brushed aside whatever was mean and deceitful about being a female homemaker.

The whole day long, I was locked in a conflict with myself. That my husband could never marry a second time, overriding his sacrosanct vow, was an exultation I could no way banish from my mind. The goddess now instituted in me said: a time may come when marriage rather than adherence to the vow will do your husband good. But the erstwhile woman in me countered: true, but once he has taken a vow, he cannot retract from it. The goddess said:

even so, you have no reason to exult over it. The woman insisted: granted, but when he has made a vow—so on and so forth; the same thing repeatedly. The goddess scowled silently; the shadow of a terrible foreboding engulfed my entire self.

My contrite husband, after forbidding my servants, started doing my work himself. Such helpless dependence on the husband even in trivial matters was flattering enough to begin with, because that way I got him always by my side. His invisibility to me intensified my desire to feel his presence. Of my pleasure in a husband, the portion originally allocated to my eyes was now usurped by the other senses to enhance their individual shares. If my husband was long away on work, I felt as if I was hovering in the air, as if there was nothing I could hold, as if I had lost everything. Earlier, when my husband went to college, if he was late, I would wait for his return, slightly opening the window facing the road. The world he roamed I had bound to myself with my eyes. Now destitute of vision, my whole body tried to seek him out. The principal bridge spanning his world and mine had collapsed; now there was an insurmountable gulf of blindness between him and me; all I could do was sit with helpless eagerness waiting for him to come willingly from his shore to mine. That is why now, whenever he withdrew from me, even if briefly, my entire body bereft of sight became keen to catch him, silently calling him in despair.

But such longing, such dependence was not right: a wife herself is burden enough to her husband; surely, I shouldn't weigh him down additionally with the enormous load of blindness. The all-pervasive dark is mine and I will bear it all by myself. I must not tie my husband to me with my perpetual blindness.

Within a short time, I learnt to carry out my accustomed tasks through the senses of sound, smell and touch. I could now even perform much of the household work with greater skill than before. It began to seem vision distracts us far more than it helps in our work. Eyes see much more than is necessary to do a job well. When the eyes keep their vigil, the ears remain idle and hear less than they ought to. Now, in the absence of restless eyes, my other senses accomplished their duties with perfection and poise.

Henceforth, I never allowed my husband do my work and instead got back to doing his work myself as before.

'You're preventing me from making amends,' grumbled my husband.

'I don't know what you're trying to make amends for,' I said, 'but why should I aggravate my sin?'

Whatever he might say, in truth, when I released him, it was only to his great relief. A lifelong vow of service to a blind wife was something beyond the capacity of males to keep.

My husband, after qualifying as a doctor, went to the suburbs taking me with him. Coming to the countryside, I felt as if I had returned to my mother's lap. I was eight years old when I had left my village to come to the city. In the next ten years, my birthplace had become indistinct in my mind like a shadow. As long as I had my eyes, the city of Calcutta had encompassed me shutting out all other memories. Once I lost them, I realised that the city merely fascinated the eyes; it had no appeal for the mind. The moment I lost my vision, my childhood village reappeared in my mind like the world of stars at day's end.

Towards the end of *Agrahayan* we went to the village of Hasimpur. It was a new place; I could not perceive how the landscape looked, but it enfolded me with the scents and sensations I had had in my childhood. That morning breeze wafting in from the freshly tilled dew-sodden field, the soft sweet scent of golden mustard and pea permeating the sky, the pastoral songs of cowherds, and even the clatter of bullock-carts on jagged paths thrilled me to the core. The dormant memory of my early life returned to the living present to enthral me with its ineffable sounds and smells; my blind eyes were no hindrance. I returned to that childhood; only I did not get back my mother. I could see with my mind's eye the day when my grandmother, her tenuous strands of hair let loose, with her back to the sun, laying rows of *boris*[6] in the courtyard; but her old tremulous voice humming the tunes of our village saint Bhajandas was not heard. The *nabanna*[7] festival was resuscitated in the bedewed sky of winter, but where had my playmates among the crowd of threshing girls at the husking-shed gone? In the evening, cows lowing somewhere near reminded me of my mother going to show the evening lamp to the cowshed. I felt at the same time the smell of damp fodder and smoke of burning straw creeping into my heart and heard the clang of cymbals and bells coming from the shrine of the Vidyalankars[8] across the pond. It was as if someone had filtered the gross material out of the first eight years of my life and immersed me in their quintessential extract and flavour.

This also reminded me of the days when I used to keep vows and pluck flowers in the morning for my Shiva-*puja*. But the hurly-burly of Calcutta admittedly has a disorienting effect on the mind. Religious practices lose their innocent simplicity. I remember the day shortly after I had lost my eyes when a friend from my old village came to me in Calcutta and said, 'Aren't you angry, Kumu? If this were to happen to me, I would never see such a husband's face again.' 'Seeing his face has ended, indeed,' I said, 'and for this, I am angry with my cursed eyes, but why should I be angry with my husband?' Since my husband had not called a doctor in time, Labanya was terribly cross with him and tried to make me so as well. I explained to her that as long as you are in the world, you have to have happiness as well as sorrow, no matter whether you like it, whether they come wittingly, or whether they are caused through your follies. But if you are steadfast in devotion, you find some kind of peace even in your distress; otherwise you spend the rest of your life in angry squabbles and conflict. Isn't it sufficient sorrow for me to be blind? Why should I aggravate it with malice towards my husband? Labanya was not pleased to hear such old-fashioned sermon from a girl like me; she went away in a huff perhaps holding me in contempt. But then, words do have poison, and they are not altogether without effect. Labanya's harsh words did create a few sparks in my mind, but I stamped them out; nevertheless, one or two scars remained. That is why I say there is too much talk, too much conflict in Calcutta; one soon becomes shrewd and insensitive.

In the village, the cool scent of *shiuli*-flowers revived all my heart's hopes and faith, just as fresh and radiant as they had been in my childhood. My soul and my home were imbued with god's aura. I bowed my head and said, 'O Lord, if my eyes have gone, well and good; after all, you are with me.'

Alas, I was mistaken. Even to say, 'You are mine' is presumptuous; 'I am with you,' is all we have any right to say; a day was to come when my god would compel me to say this. Nothing may exist for me, but I will have to exist nevertheless. On nobody can one lay any claim; all one's claim lies only on oneself.

Days passed quite happily for some time. My husband continued to thrive in his profession, and we made decent savings as well.

But money is something which is not good; it bottles up the mind. When the mind reigns supreme, it can generate its own happiness; but when wealth assumes the task of obtaining it, the mind has nothing left to do; goods, furniture and ceremony then occupy its domains of happiness, and all we get is commodities instead of happiness.

I cannot cite any particular instance or occasion to corroborate this, but because of the enhanced power of perception of the blind, or I know not what reason, I could well perceive a change in my husband as he continued to prosper. The sensitivity of his youth about justice and morality seemed to grow inert by the day. At one time, he used to say, 'I am studying medicine not merely to earn my living, but to help the poor as well.' He had vehement hatred for those doctors who refused even to take the pulse of their patients without getting their fees in advance. I realise those days are gone. A poor woman begged him clasping his feet to save her only son's life, and he ignored it. Finally, with much swearing and pleading,

I persuaded him to go, but his mind was not in it. I knew what my husband's attitude had been towards improper earnings in the days we were in rather straitened circumstances. Now when we had lots in the bank, a rich man's representative came the other day and had two days of secret conference with him; what the man said I do not know, but when thereafter my husband came back to me talking breezily about other things, I had the extra-sensory perception that he had done something shameful.

Where was my husband, the one I had last seen before my blindness; the man who had once installed me as a goddess by kissing me between my sightless eyes? What could I do about him? Those who succumb to a sudden storm of vices can pick themselves up once again through a different surge of emotion. But I cannot contemplate how to remedy this brutalising callousness being ingrained in the marrow day by day, minute by minute, this stunting of the inner core bit by little bit while growing externally.

My visual separation from my husband was nothing compared to the asphyxiating torment in my heart when I thought that he was not where I was. With my blindness, I dwelt in an inner world devoid of light with the sprouting love, unflagging devotion and unwavering trust of my tender ages. The *shephali* flowers I had once offered with girlish devotion in my shrine on the threshold of my life were still moist with dew. But where in the arid sands of life was my husband vanishing in pursuit of money leaving this cool, shadowy, evergreen land? Whatever I believed in, revered as my religion, and held superior to all material bliss, he glanced at from afar with a contemptuous sneer. But time was when this rift did not exist: we had started out on the same path. Thereafter when our paths had begun to diverge he did not know, nor did I; today I get no response to my call any more.

Sometimes I thought perhaps because of my blindness I made too much of a trifle; with sight, I might have recognised the world in its true colors. My husband also explained the same thing for me one day. That morning an old Muslim had come begging him to treat his granddaughter for cholera. I overheard the man say, 'Baba, I am poor, but Allah will bless you.' My husband said, 'What Allah will do won't be enough for me; tell me what you will do.' The moment I heard it, I asked myself: God has made me blind; why did He not make me deaf? The old man departed with a deep sigh, 'O Allah!' At once I got my maidservant to bring him back at the rear door and said, 'Baba, here is some money for your granddaughter's treatment. Pray for the good of my husband and take along Dr Harish from the neighbourhood.'

I had no appetite for food all day. My husband, waking from his afternoon nap, said, 'Why do you look glum?' A customary reply came to my mouth, 'No, it's nothing.' But those days of deception were gone; I decided to be frank. 'I have often thought of saying this, but every time I attempted, I didn't seem to know exactly what there was to say. I do not know whether I can explain myself, but you must know in your heart that the way we started our lives together has now bifurcated.' My husband smiled and said, 'But isn't change the way of the world?' I said, 'Things like wealth, beauty and youth do change, but is there nothing eternal?' Now somewhat grave, he said, 'Other women rue what they actually lack: someone's husband hasn't any income; someone else's doesn't love her; you simply pluck misery out of the air.' At once I realised that my blindness had smeared an ointment on my eyes dissociating me from this changing world: I was not like other women; my husband will not understand me.

Meanwhile an aunt of my husband's arrived from her village to see how her nephew was doing. The first thing she said after we had made our *pronam*s was, 'Well, *Bouma*, it was only your lot to have lost your eyes, but how's our Abinash supposed to run his house with a blind wife? Get him married again.' If my husband had said in jest, 'All right, *Pishima*. Why don't you start taking the bother of match-making,' he would have been candid enough. But he said with some embarrassment, 'Oh, come on, Pishima.'

'Have I said anything wrong ?' said Pishima. 'Well, let's hear what *Bouma* has to say.'

I spoke with a smile, 'The right person to ask indeed! If you want to pick someone's pocket, do you seek his consent?'

'That's true, of course,' said our aunt. 'Well then, Abinash, we'll confer privately, right? Even so, I tell you, Bouma, the more co-wives a *Kulin* girl has, the prouder she becomes of her husband. If this child went on taking wives instead of practising medicine, would he have to worry about an income? A patient must eventually die in the hand of a doctor, and once dead, he does not pay his fees. But a Kulin's wife is cursed by fate never to die, and the longer she lives, the better it is for her husband.'

Two days after this, my husband asked his aunt in my presence, 'Pishima, can you find me a woman from a good family who could help my wife like a relative? She can't see, and if someone were to keep her company, I would feel reassured.' This would have made sense if said immediately after my blindness; but I can't understand how it particularly affects any personal or domestic task now so long after. However, I kept silent without demur.

'Is there any dearth?' said Pishima. 'Why, there's my elder brother-in-law who has a daughter; she is as good-natured as she is beautiful. The girl is quite grown up; they are only waiting for a suitable match. If they find a Kulin like you, they would at once marry her off.'

Startled, my husband said, 'Who's talking about marriage?'

'Good heavens! Did you think an unmarried girl from a good family would otherwise come to stay at your house?' Pishima enquired.

True enough and my husband found no reasonable answer.

Forlorn in my infinite darkness, I prayed: may God save my husband!

A few days later, as I came out after my morning prayers, my aunt said, 'Bouma, our Hemangini, the niece I mentioned, has just come from her village. And Himu, this is your Didi, touch her feet.'

Just then, my husband appeared, and as if finding an unfamiliar woman was about to leave.

Pishima said, 'Where are you going, Abinash?'

'Who is she?' he asked.

'This is the girl I was speaking about, my niece Hemangini,' she replied. My husband started showing unwarranted curiosity asking when she had come, who had brought her, and such other questions. I said to myself: can't I perceive what is going to happen? Why then this chicanery into the bargain? Evasiveness, secretiveness, falsehood! Commit impiety if you must; that is for the sake of your turbulent passion, but why demean yourself for my sake? Why this falsehood for the sake of deceiving me?

I led Hemangini by the hand into my bedroom. I *saw* her by stroking her face and her body; I sensed she was pretty, and her age not less than fourteen or fifteen.

The girl suddenly broke out into loud sweet laughter. 'What's that you're doing?' she asked. 'Do you want to exorcise the ghost in me?' Her free and frank laughter seemed to sweep away a dark cloud hovering between the two of us. 'I'm *seeing* you, dear,' I said putting my right arm across her neck, and then I caressed her face again.

'Seeing me!' She began to laugh. 'Am I brinjal or beans of your garden that you're trying to guess how big I've grown?'

It then suddenly occurred to me that maybe Hemangini did not know I was blind. 'I'm blind, you know, sister,' I said. Taken aback, she remained grave for a while. I could perceive she was looking intently into my face and my sightless eyes with her wide, luminous, curious eyes. Then she said, 'So, that's why you've brought my auntie over here?'

'No, I did not invite her. Your auntie has come on her own.'

'As an act of kindness?' she said, laughing. 'The kindly soul is not going to leave any time soon, then. But why did my father send me here?'

Pishima entered at that moment. She had been having a talk with my husband. Hemangini said, 'When are we going back, Auntie?'

'Good heavens!' said Auntie, 'Wanting to leave the moment she's come! Whoever has seen such a flighty girl?'

'Auntie,' said Hemangini, 'you seem to be in no hurry to leave, I can see. Well, this is your relative's house, you can stay here as long as you like. But I'm not going to stay any longer, and that's that.' She then addressed me holding my hand, 'What do you say, sister? You aren't really any relative of mine, are you?' Without giving any reply, I drew her close to my heart. I could see that however overbearing Pishima might be, she could not dominate this girl. Without betraying her annoyance, she tried to cajole her; the girl apparently brushed it aside. Pishima laughed off the whole thing as a pampered child's joke and was about to leave, but turned back having other thoughts, saying, 'Himu, come along, it's time for your bath.' Hemangini turned to me and said, 'Both of us will go to the *ghat*; how about it, sister?' Pishima, despite her reluctance, rested her case. She knew that if she tried to apply force, Hemangini would win, and the conflict between them would take a nasty turn in front of me.

As we walked to the ghat in our backyard pond, Hemangini asked me, 'Why haven't you had any children?' I said with a slight smile, 'How can I know why? God hasn't given me any.'

'You must have had some sins in you.'

'That too is known to God.'

As proof, the girl said, 'Don't you see Auntie has so much crookedness in her that her womb wouldn't grow any children.'

Such loaded things as vice and virtue, happiness and misery, punishment and reward I have never understood myself, nor did I try to explain for the girl. I merely sighed, thinking, 'Lord, you only know.' Hemangini at once clasped me in an embrace, and bursting into a laugh, said, 'Dear me, even a girl like me made you sigh! You don't know, but no one cares a fig for what I say.'

I noticed that my husband's medical practice was getting short shrift. He avoided distant calls altogether and made short work of the nearby ones. Earlier, whenever he was off-duty and stayed at home, he used to visit the inner rooms only for his midday meal and siesta. Now Pishima summoned him as often as she liked, and he too came to ask after her unnecessarily. When I heard her calling aloud, 'Himu, would you bring me my *paan*-box?' I knew that my husband was in her room. For the first two or three days, Hemangini did fetch her paan-box, vermilion box, oil pot and so on. Thereafter she would never budge and instead send the maidservant with the things. Pishima called her, "Hemangini, Himu, Himi!' and the girl clung to me, as if with a piteous appeal; some dismay and sadness engulfed her. She never mentioned my husband in my presence.

Meanwhile my elder brother came to see me. I knew how keenly watchful he was. It would have been practically impossible to hide from him what was on the horizon. My brother was too stern a judge to forgive the slightest wrong. That my husband would have to stand trial before such a judge was my worst fear. I wrapped everything up with exaggerated cheerfulness: by talking too much, by fussing unusually, by keeping up a show, I tried to put up a smokescreen all around. But this was so unnatural for me that I would have been detected even because of it. However, my brother did not stay very long—rather he could not: my husband betrayed restlessness that took the form of blunt rudeness. Before he left, he blessed me, placing his trembling hand on my head for quite a while with fatherly affection; I seemed to feel what he blessed solicitously; his tears fell on my moist cheeks.

I remember it was a market day in *Chaitra*. In the evening, people were making their way home. A storm was approaching from afar bringing rain in its wake; the sky was laden with its damp wind and smell of sodden earth. People who had strayed from their companions were loudly calling one another anxiously in the dark fields. In the evening, I never sat alone with a lamp alight in my bedroom, in case my clothes brushed against it or some other accident happened. In the dark solitary room, I sat on the floor with clasped hands praying to the Almighty of my endless blind world. 'O Lord, when I do not feel your mercy, when I do not understand your designs, I press with both hands the rudder of my shattered and abandoned heart desperately hard to my breast, which spurts blood, but the tempest continues to rage. What further ordeals must I suffer? You only know what little strength I have.' Tears were welling up; laying my head on the bed, I wept. Having to do housework all day with Hemangini keeping me company like a shadow, I hardly found any respite to shed the tears that accumulated within me; today at last they burst forth. Then I felt a slight jerk in the bed, a rustle of footsteps, and a moment later Hemangini came, flung her arms round my neck and wiped my tears with her sari-end. I did not know why and since when before evening she had been lying in my bed. She asked no questions of me; neither did I say anything to her. She slowly ran her soothing hand over my forehead. I had not noticed when in the meantime, there had been a storm with accompanying thunder and torrents of rain; after a long time, a refreshing tranquillity came over me soothing my scorched heart.

The following day Hemangini said, 'Auntie, if you decide not to go back now, I tell you I'll be leaving with *Kaibarta* Dada[9].'

'There's no need for that,' said *Pishima*. 'I'm also going tomorrow; we can go together. Look at this, Himu, what a wonderful pearl-studded ring my Abinash has bought for you!' She proudly thrust it into Hemangini's hand.

'And look at this, Auntie,' said Himu, 'how good I am at hitting a target.' She flung the ring through the window into the backyard pond leaving Pishima stunned and bristling. Holding my hand, Pishima told me repeatedly, 'Bouma, do not report this frivolity to

Abinash; be on guard, please; my child will be very much offended then. For heaven's sake, Bouma, please don't.' 'You don't have to say any more, Pishima,' I said. 'I shall not utter a word.'

The day after this, when she was leaving, Hemangini embraced me and said, 'Remember me, Didi.' With both hands, I caressed her face and said, 'The blind never forget a thing, sister. I have no word to speak of; all I have is my mind.' With this, I drew her head close, smelt its scent and kissed it, my tears streaming into her hair.

When Hemangini departed, my world turned arid. When the fragrance, sweetness and music, the radiance and supple youthfulness she had instilled into my heart were gone, I stretched out my arms into my world and around myself trying to locate whatever if any I still possessed. My husband came, and said with unusual exhilaration, 'So they're gone. Thank God, now we'll have some time for work.' Shame on me! Why such play-acting for my sake? Was I afraid to confront the truth? Had I ever feared a blow? And didn't my husband know this? When I gave up my eyes, did I not accept eternal darkness calmly?

So long, blindness had been the only divide between my husband and me; today another rift sprang up. My husband, never even by mistake, uttered the name of Hemangini to me, as if from his contextual world Hemangini had been obliterated, as if she had never left the faintest impression there. Yet, I intuitively knew he had been in regular correspondence with her. Whenever there is an inflow of floodwater into a pond, the lotus stalk feels the pull: whenever my husband had the slightest elation in him, I could similarly sense it from the core of my heart. Which day he got her news and which day he did not was perfectly within my knowledge. Nevertheless, I could not ask him about her. I dearly wished to hear a word about her, to talk about her: the wild lusty bright beautiful star that had briefly appeared in the dark firmament of my heart; but I had no right to mention her even casually to my husband. There steadily existed between us this one silence replete with words and agony.

One day about the middle of *Boishakh,* the maidservant came to say, '*Ma-thakrun* I saw there's a great flurry at the *ghat* doing up the boat; where's the master going?' I knew something was in the offing: in the firmament of my fate, there had been a lull for a few days, and thereafter, tattered clouds of ominous foreboding had been gathering; the full fury of the god of distruction[10] was now looming over my head. I told her, 'Is that so? But they haven't told me anything yet.' The maidservant did not dare to ask any more questions and left with a sigh.

Late at night, my husband came and said, 'I've a call from some distant place. Tomorrow at dawn itself I've to leave. Probably it'll be two or three days before I come back.'

I rose from my bed and said, 'Why are you lying?'

He muttered in a shaky voice, 'What lie did I tell you?'

'You're going to get married,' I said.

He fell silent. I stood still as well. There was no sound in the room for a long time. At last, I said, 'Say something. Say yes, I am going to get married.'

'Yes, I am going to get married,' he echoed me.

'No, you shall not go,' I remonstrated. 'I will save you from this great disaster, this terrible sin. If I cannot do that, what sort of wife am I? Why had I been worshipping Shiva?'

Once again, there was a long silence. I sat down on the floor, and clasping his feet said, 'What was my fault? Where did I go wrong? Why do you need another wife? For heaven's sake, tell me the truth.'

My husband then said gently, 'Frankly speaking, I fear you. Your blindness has enfolded you in an endless veil, which is impossible for me to penetrate. You are my goddess—forbiddingly awesome like a goddess—not just the sort for everyday domestic living. I want an ordinary woman—one I can scold, show my temper to, caress and buy ornaments for.'

'Cut open my breast,' I said. 'You will see an ordinary woman there. In my mind, I am none other than the girl you married. I want to trust you, rely upon you, to worship you; abasing yourself and bringing me insufferable misery, do not elevate me to a higher pedestal than yours; keep me at your feet in every matter.'

I do not remember the exact words I said: can a sea hear its own roaring? All I remember is that I said: 'if I have been true to you, let God be witness, by no means shall you be able to break your pious vows. Before you commit this heinous sin, either I will be widowed or Hemangini shall not live.' With this, I collapsed in a faint.

When I came to, birds had not announced the dawn yet, and my husband had gone.

I went into my prayer room, shut the door and sat down to worship my deity. I stayed there all day long. In the evening, a devastating nor'wester struck. Instead of saying, 'O my god, save my husband who is now on the river,' I prayed fervently, 'O god, whatever is fated to me, let it be, but let my husband desist from this sin.' That night passed; even the next day I did not leave my prayer seat. Who gave me the strength to sit through the ordeal without food or sleep I do not know, but I was sitting like an image in stone before the idol of stone.

In the evening, banging and pushing on the door began. When they broke open the door, I had collapsed. The first word I heard on recovering was, 'Didi!' I found myself lying on Hemangini's lap. As I turned my head, her new Benares sari rustled. O god, you did not heed my prayer! My husband has fallen at last! I moaned.

Hemangini lowered her face to my ears and said, 'I have come to seek your blessing, Didi.'

I felt I was dead like a log, but sat up the next moment and said, 'Of course, I will. What's your fault after all?'

Hemangini laughed aloud in her dulcet tone and said, 'What fault! When you married, if it was not a fault, then how can it be so if I do?'

Hugging her, I laughed too, asking myself: is my prayer expected to decide things in the world? Isn't Lord's wish final? The curse that has befallen me let it strike my head, not the core of my heart, which encases my faith, and my religion. I shall remain as I was. Hemangini bowed down to take the dust of my feet. I blessed her, 'May fortune be forever with you. May you be forever happy.'

'Mere blessing won't do,' said Hemangini. 'You must usher in your brother-in-law and me with your pure hands. You mustn't shy away from him. I can bring him up here if you permit.'

'Bring him,' I said.

A little later, there was a new footfall in my room and an affectionate question, 'Are you well, Kumu?'

I hurriedly got off the bed and bowed at his feet, crying, 'Dada!'

'What do mean "Dada"?' said Hemangini. 'Rather, make some practical joke with him. He is your younger *bhagnipati*!'[11]

It was then that I understood everything. My brother had vowed not to get married. In the absence of my mother, there was practically no one to persuade him. Eventually I had now got him married. Tears poured in torrents from my eyes. My brother stroked my hair fondly, as Hemangini, hugging me, laughed away.

I had no sleep that night, waiting anxiously for my husband to return. I could not ascertain how he would hide his discomfiture and disappointment. Very late at night, the door creaked open. I sat up with a start; it was my husband's footsteps. My heart pounded. He came to my bed, and holding my hand said, 'Your brother has saved me. I was going to my ruination in a moment of infatuation. God alone knew the weight that was bearing down on my heart as I got into the boat that day. When the storm overtook us in the river, I feared for life and yet, I thought that if I drowned, then only would I be saved. Reaching Mathurganj I heard that Hemangini had married your elder brother the previous day. What was my shame as well as my joy when I returned to the boat is beyond words. I have realised in these few days that I will never be happy leaving you. You are my goddess.'

I smiled and said, 'No, I don't want to be a goddess. I am simply your homemaker, just an ordinary woman.'

'I too have a request,' said my husband. 'Never embarrass me by calling me a god.'

The following day the neighbourhood resounded with *ululations*[12] and hoots of conches. Hemangini started teasing[13] my husband in a hundred ways all through the day without any respite. But where he had gone or what had happened no one mentioned the least bit.

Paus 1305 (1898)

NOTES

1 Unmarried Bengali girls cherish the desire to find a husband who would be handsome, self-composed, easily contented, and imperturbable like Shiva. He is worshipped in his shrine through a most austere ritual on the fourteenth lunar day of the dark fortnight of *Phalgun.*

2 The Bengali proverb *Rajay Rajay yuddha hay, ulukhagrar pran jay* means: when kings fight, the grass of the battleground is the first casualty. The message is clear: ordinary folks being most vulnerable ought not to come in the way of two mighty rivals trying to fight it out.

3 When the bride and the groom see each other for the first time ceremonially (see Glossary).

4 The winter solstice from *Shravan* through *Paus* is gods' night when they go into hibernation. According to the shashtras, a hibernating god or goddess cannot be validly and fruitfully worshipped. However, Rama, urged by the immediacy of war against Ravana and the consideration that autumn was scripturally congenial to war, decided to worship goddess *Durga* in *Ashwin*, even though

it would be untimely. This aroused the goddess who put Rama's devotion to test by making two lotuses vanish from the prescribed complement of one hundred and eight. Rama at once aimed his arrow at his lotus-like eyes when the goddess condescended.

5 *Ishtadevata* (see Glossary): Gopinath is the image of Lord Krishna which is worshipped as ishtadevata or household deity installed at the shrine in one's home.

6 A preparation of mashed pulses and spice, in the shape of small cones, dried in the sun, used as such or as an ingredient; making boris is a favourite pastime of elderly women in the winter when an uninterrupted sun is almost guaranteed.

7 A festival to celebrate the first harvested rice (new rice) in *Agrahayan*; rice from parboiled paddy, mixed with jaggery and coconut corn forms *nabanna*.

8 A scholarly decoration for a pundit.

9 A servant of that name; *Kaibarta* is the caste name of fishermen, which in this case, was his name also; children are taught to address servants as Dada or Didi, as the case might be.

10 Lord Shiva (see Glossary).

11 Husband of one's sister or any cousin by extended relation. Since Hemangini is on sisterly terms with Kusum and loves her very dearly, she prefers to call her husband Kusum's brother-in-law rather than her brother (Dada). Ordinarily, Kusum would have called Hemangini sister-in-law or *Baudi* (wife of one's own or extended brother).

12 This is exclusively a women's ritual, in which women join in producing a chorus of *ulus*–begin with '*u*', followed by '*lu*' until they run out of breath, while rapidly swinging the tip of the tongue between the corners of lips all through the exhalation, repeated thrice over. It would sound like: *u–lululu*..... This is a small, innocent, yet indispensable, rite on all auspicious occasions like pujas and weddings.

13 Under the redefined relationship following their marriage, Hemangini was sister-in-law (*Shali*) to Kusum's husband—a loving relationship admitting of light banter and even slightly amorous repartees (see Glossary).

Elder Sister
(*Didi*)

1

Having elaborately narrated the misdeeds of an unjust and tyrannical husband of a certain wretched woman of the village, Shashi's neighbour Tara pronounced her judgement very briefly, 'Let there be fire to the mouth of such husbands.[1]'

Jaygopal-babu's wife Shashi was aghast to hear this: under no circumstances whatever does it behove a woman to wish any kind of fire other than the smouldering cheroot's in her husband's mouth. So when she expressed some reservation about this, the hard-hearted Tara said with twice as much vehemence, 'Better to be widowed in seven lives than have such husbands.' With this, she went away half way through the encounter.

Shashi said to herself: I can't imagine any fault in a husband that can make his wife feel so harshly about him. Even as she pondered thus, her tender heart swelled with affection for her absent husband. She lay with her hands sprawled over the part of the bed her husband used to occupy, kissed the vacant pillow and sniffed the scent of his hair from it. She then closed the door and took out from a wooden box an almost faded photograph of her husband and the letters he had written, spending the still afternoon in her secluded room in solitary thought, old memories and tears of melancholy.

Shashikala and Jaygopal were no newly-wed couple. They had been married in their childhood; meanwhile they had had children too. They had lived together for long years, and it was a relaxed normal life; neither had ever made any extravagant display of passion. After about sixteen years, when suddenly her husband went to work elsewhere, an intense love arose in her. The harder her separation stretched their bond, the firmer her love tightened its knot in her soft heart. The bond of love that she had not felt as long as it was loose, she now felt like an aching pain.

Today, so many years after marriage, despite her age, despite being a mother, she lay on her lonely bed on a spring afternoon daydreaming like a youthful bride. Suddenly today, waking to the murmur of love that had been flowing unbeknown to her, she drifted upstream very far, visualising many golden cities, many bowers of love on the banks, but there was no room now to set foot on that lost chance of pleasure. 'This time when I get back my husband,' she thought, 'I won't allow life to be dull and springtime to be barren.' She remembered remorsefully how often she had exasperated her husband squabbling over silly matters. Today she resolved with all her heart that she would never again be impatient with him, never oppose his wishes; she would obey his commands, take his actions whether good or bad in good grace with all humility: a husband was all a woman could possibly have; he was her dearest; he was her deity.

For many years Shashikala had been her parents' only child, and beloved too. That was why Jaygopal, although living on a petty job, was never worried about the future. His father-in-law Kaliprasanna had enough wealth for him to live a princely life, village-style.

Meanwhile, quite unexpectedly, virtually in old age, Shashikala's parents had a male child. In fact, Shashikala was scandalised by this undesirable, indiscreet act of her parents, and Jaygopal was not too happy either.

Towards the son of their advanced age, parents grew deeply affectionate. So when this tiny newly arrived suckling, sleepy brother-in-law grabbed all Jaygopal's hopes in its tiny clenched fists, he had found himself this job in an Assam tea garden.

All had urged him to look for a job near home. But whether out of resentment for the people or intimation of bright career prospects in a tea garden, he paid no heed to them. Leaving Shashi with her children in her father's house, he went off to Assam. In their married life, this was the first time the couple separated.

This development made Shashi very angry with her little brother: one most resents the disappointment that cannot be spoken out for formality's sake. The little man just sucked away and slept happily, and his good old sister worried herself and harried others on various pretexts like hot milk, cold rice, son's late attendance at school, and so on.

Within a few days, the boy's mother died, leaving his charge to her daughter's care. Now that the boy was motherless, it was not long before he captured his sister's heart very easily. Often he would come running with a whoop and hurl himself upon her, eagerly trying to grab her face, nose and all into his little toothless cavity. Clutching a tuft of her hair in his little fist, he would hold on refusing to let go of it. Waking up even before the sun, he would roll over the bed and nestle up thrilling her with his tender touch and gurgle of delight. Soon he was calling her *Jiji* and *Jijima.* He started up a regular nuisance doing forbidden things, eating forbidden food and trying to explore forbidden places during her work or leisure. Now Shashi could hold herself no longer; she surrendered completely to this self-willed little monster. Since the boy had no mother, he enjoyed far more domination over her than otherwise.

2

The boy's name was Nilmani. When he was two years old, his father fell seriously ill. Jaygopal received an urgent call. When, on a hard-earned leave, he finally arrived, Kaliprasanna was dying.

Before his death, Kaliprasanna entrusted Jaygopal with the guardianship of his minor son and made a will entitling his daughter to a quarter of his estate. To manage the estate therefore Jaygopal had to resign his job.

After a long time, husband and wife were reunited. If a material object breaks apart, it can be reconstructed precisely along the grooves; when two human beings are separated, they never rejoin exactly along the line of fissure. For, the mind is something animate, which matures and changes every moment.

This reunion generated a novel emotion in Shashi, as if she had married her husband all over again. The effeteness from the old habituated conjugal life was removed by the longing born out of separation; she seemed to have her husband in a more complete manner than ever before. She promised to herself: whatever future may come, however long I may live, never shall I allow the lustre of this burning love for my husband to fade.

Jaygopal's feelings were different at this reunion, though. When they had lived together without break, when all his interests and strange habits had been bound identically with his wife, she had been a permanent truth in his life; life without her would have meant an abrupt break in the network of his routine life. That's why when he had been away on work, he had found himself in deep waters to start with. Gradually however, that discontinuity in habits was patched up with new ones.

Not only that. Formerly, his days had passed without the least endeavour or care. Thereafter for the last two years, he had been so keen to improve his lot that there was nothing else before his mind. In contrast with the intensity of this new passion, his earlier life had begun to look like a formless shadow. In women's nature what brings about the greatest change is love; in men's, it is soaring ambition.

When Jaygopal came back after two years, he did not get back his wife exactly as she had left her. His little brother-in-law had added a new dimension to his wife's life. This aspect was completely unknown to him, where he had no connection whatever with his wife. His wife tried hard to share her love of the child with him; whether or not she was exactly successful is hard to tell.

Carrying Nilmani in her arms with a smiling face, Shashi would sometimes hold him in front of her husband; Nilmani would bury his face into her shoulder desperately clutching her neck without acknowledging any courtesy due to kinship. Shashi wished that her little brother should demonstrate before Jaygopal whatever ingratiating tricks he had in his command. But neither did Jaygopal feel too keen about it nor did the child evince much interest. Jaygopal simply could not understand just why so much affection was being wasted on this scrawny, big-headed, dark-skinned, serious-faced boy.

Women are very quick to sense love's ways. Shashi soon realised that Jaygopal did not like Nilmani very much. She then took great care to keep her brother out of sight of her husband, trying to insulate him against his loveless, and rather hateful eyes. In this way, the child grew to be her secret treasure, her sole property of love. As everyone knows, love is stronger the more it is secret, the more it is secluded.

When Nilmani cried, Jaygopal became visibly irritated; Shashi would then quickly pick him up and press him to her breast trying to placate him with all her heart. Particularly, if at night, his cries disturbed her husband's sleep, and he growled with a stricken heart betraying savage hatred for the boy, Shashi would be flustered and embarrassed no end as though a culprit. At once, carrying him away in her arms she would try to put him to sleep with coaxing words like 'My jewel, my treasure, my gem' and so on.

It is quite natural that children would quarrel on various pretexts. Earlier, in such cases Shashi would punish her own sons, taking her brother's side because he had no mother. Now the penal code had changed with the change of judge. Now Nilmani had to suffer severe punishments most unfairly and often without trial. Shashi felt shell-shocked at this injustice. Therefore, taking her ill-treated brother into her room she would ply him with sweets and toys, caresses and kisses trying to repair his injured heart as far as possible.

Eventually, the more Shashi loved Nilmani, the more Jaygopal resented him. Again, the more Jaygopal betrayed his aversion for Nilmani, the more Shashi showered him with her love. After all, Jaygopal never behaved with his wife rudely, and Shashi used to serve him quietly with the devotion and love due to a husband. Only because of Nilmani, they were hurting each other inwardly all day and night.

The covert repercussion of such silent conflict is harder to bear than open strife.

3

In all Nilmani's body, his head was the most conspicuous. If you saw him, you would have thought it was just a thin hollow stick with a large bubble blown at its end by puffing. Even his doctors sometimes expressed apprehension that the boy would be as frail and short-lived as a bubble. For a long time he had not learnt to talk or walk. His sad, unsmiling face would give the impression that his parents had dumped their worries of advanced age upon this little child's head.

His sister's careful nursing saw him through the critical years, and he was now five years of age.

On *Brothers' Day* in the month of *Kartik*, Shashi dressed Nilmani up like a babu in new red-bordered dhoti, chuddar and apparel and then sat performing the *tilak* ritual when the aforementioned outspoken neighbour Tara appeared and picked up a quarrel in course of conversation. 'There's no point of all this fuss of tilak,' she said, 'after bringing about the brother's ruin secretly.' Shashi was almost thunderstruck with surprise, anger and pain to hear this. In the end, she heard that they, husband and wife together, were planning to have minor Nimani's estate auctioned off owing to unpaid revenues and buy back the same in the name of Jaygopal's cousin. Hearing this, Shashi cursed that those who had circulated such monstrous lies might have leprosy in their mouths.

She then went to her husband tearfully and told him about the rumour.

'You can trust no one these days,' said Jaygopal, 'Upen is the son of my father's sister; I left the management of the estate to him never worrying about it. I had no idea when he had secretly defaulted on payment and bought the estate at Hasilpur for himself."

Shashi was stunned. 'Aren't you going to sue him?'

'How can I sue my cousin?' said Jaygopal, 'And even if I sue,' he argued, 'no good will come of it in the end; it's sheer waste of money.'

To believe her husband's words was Shashi's sacred duty, but she could not do so by any means. This happy home, this dearly loved family life then suddenly assumed a hideous and loathsome appearance before her. The home she had known for a secure refuge suddenly seemed to be a cruel trap enfolding the two of them from all sides. A lone woman, how could she protect her helpless Nilmani? She was absolutely at a loss; the more she thought, the more her heart filled with dismay and indignation and boundless affection for her imperilled brother. She thought that if she knew the way, she could have appealed to the Governor-General, or even the Queen of England to retrieve her brother's property. The Queen would never have allowed Nilmani's Hasilpur estate, which fetched seven hundred fifty-eight rupees a year in revenue, to be sold off.

While she was in the process of thinking out how to appeal directly to the Queen to bring her cousin-in-law to his knees, suddenly one day Nilmani came down with fever, frequently passing out with convulsions.

Jaygopal called a local native[2] doctor. When Shashi begged him to call a qualified doctor, he said, 'Why? Is Matilal a bad doctor?'

Shashi then fell at his feet and pleaded desparately. 'All right,' said Jaygopal, 'I'm sending for a doctor from the town.'

Shashi remained with Nilmani in her arms or close to her breast. Nilmani too would not leave her out of sight for a moment; lest she should give him the slip, he would cling to her so hard that not even when asleep would he loosen his grip of her sari-end.

The whole day having passed in this way, Jaygopal returned rather late in the evening and said, 'The doctor is out of town visiting some patient at a distant place.' He also said, 'I've to leave today itself for a court case. I've told Matilal to visit the patient regularly.'

That night Nilmani had delirium in his sleep. In the morning, Shashi, without a thought, took a boat carrying her sick brother and went straight to the doctor's house in the town. The doctor was very much there; he had not gone anywhere out of town. Seeing a married woman from a middle-class family, he promptly rented a house, left Shashi in the care of an elderly widow and started to treat the boy.

Right next morning Jaygopal arrived there. Furious, he ordered his wife to return immediately with him. 'Even if you should kill me,' said his wife, 'I shan't go back now. You want to kill my Nilmani. He has no father, no mother; he has no one but me. I will protect him.'

'Stay here then,' fumed Jaygopal. 'Don't ever return to my house.'

'How do you call it your house?' said Shashi, now enraged. 'Isn't it my brother's house?'

'All right, we'll see.'

People in the neighbourhood made a great furore for a few days over this event. 'If you must quarrel with your husband,' said Tara, 'why don't you do so sitting in your home? Why must you step out? After all he's your husband.'

Spending all the cash she had with her and then selling off her ornaments, she managed to save her brother from the jaws of death. Her father owned a large plot of land at Dwarigram. This land, on which he had his own house, had an annual income of nearly one thousand five hundred rupees. Shashi now heard that Jaygopal with the connivance of the zamindar had appropriated it by effecting mutation. Now the entire property was legally theirs, not her brother's.

After recovering from his illness, Nilmani started whining, 'Didi, let's go home.' He very much missed the company of his nephews back home. So he kept on pleading, 'Please, Didi, let's go home to that old house of ours.' His sister could only weep. 'Where's our house any more?'

But mere weeping was no use: except for his sister, the brother had no one now in the world. Realising this, she wiped her tears and went straight to the deputy magistrate Tarini-babu's house where she appealed to his wife for help.

The deputy magistrate knew Jaygopal. That a woman of a respectable family should have stepped out of home wanting to litigate with her husband over property left him very much annoyed with Shashi. Consoling her with some prevarication, he at once wrote to Jaygopal. Jaygopal came and forcibly lifting his wife along with his brother-in-law in a boat took her back home. After the second separation between husband and wife, this was their second reunion. As decreed by the god of marriage!

Returning home after a long time, Nilmani was very much delighted to get back his companions and play with them all day. As she saw his carefree delight, Shashi's heart broke asunder silently.

4

It was winter. The British district magistrate, out on survey duty, had camped in the village for hunting around. Nilmani came across the magistrate on the village path. All other boys categorising the sahib among those with talons, teeth or horns, discreetly gave him a wide berth. But the solemn-faced Nilmani stood watching him quietly with unending curiosity.

The sahib walked up to him and asked him with some amusement, 'Do you go to school?' The boy silently nodded yes.

'What texts do you read?'

Nilmani kept looking at his face, unable to understand the meaning of the word 'text'. Later, he narrated this meeting with the sahib to his sister with great enthusiasm.

That afternoon, Jaygopal dressed in long robe, trousers and turban went to pay his respects to the magistrate. Many people whoever had any business with him had crowded around besides his staff in attendance. To escape the heat inside the tent, the sahib sat at a camp-table in the shade outside. Offering Jaygopal a stool, he was questioning him about local affairs. Jaygopal was bloated with conceit to have been given this privileged status in front of the villagers and was thinking: it would be great if someone from the Chakrabortis and the Nandis now came to see this.

At that point, a woman, her face veiled, came along with Nilmani and stood right in front of the magistrate. 'Sahib,' she said, 'I entrust this orphan brother of mine to you. Please protect him.'

Seeing the large-headed, unsmiling boy he had previously met and a woman apparently from a respectable family, the sahib at once stood up and said, 'Please come into the tent.'

'All I have to say,' said the woman, 'I'll say right here.'

Jaygopal turned pale and began to fidget in his seat. Curious onlookers tried to come closer out of sheer fun. When the sahib raised his cane, they ran away.

Shashi then holding her brother's hand narrated the whole story of the orphaned boy from beginning to end. Jaygopal tried to interrupt her at times; but the magistrate, red in the face, bellowed, 'Shut up!' and motioned to him with the point of his cane to leave the stool and stand in front of him. Jaygopal stood silently, seething and raging at Shashi in his heart. Nilmani stood near his sister listening with wonder.

When Shashi had finished, the magistrate asked Jaygopal some questions, and after hearing his replies, remained silent for quite a while. 'Dear child,' he then said to Shashi, 'although this case can never come to my court, you can rest assured that I will do whatever needs to be done. You can return home with your brother without fear.'

Shashi said, 'So long as he does not get back his rightful house, I dare not take him there. If you do not keep him with you, he is not safe anywhere else."

'And what about you?' asked the sahib.

'I'll return to my husband's house; I am not worried about myself.'

Finding no alternative, the sahib agreed with a slight smile to take this lean-bodied, dark-skinned, solemn-faced, calm, meek, amulet-wearing Bengali boy with him.

In the end, when Shashi was about to leave, the boy clutched her sari. The sahib said, 'Don't be afraid, son. Come with me.' Tears streaming down behind her veil, Shashi said, 'Dear brother, do go. You will see your Didi again.' She embraced him, stroked his head and his back, and then extricating her sari with difficulty walked away quickly. The sahib held Nilmani with his left arm round him; Nilmani kept crying, 'Didi, O Didi!' Shashi looked back once and waved at him with her right hand, sending him silent consolation from a distance. She finally went on her way, her heart shattered.

Once again, husband and wife were united in their old familiar home. As decreed by the god of marriage!

But this union did not last long. Soon after this, one morning people of the village heard that Shashi had died of cholera overnight and had been cremated that very night.

No one made any comment on this. Only Tara sometimes wanted to burst forth, but others forced her to shut up.

Shashi had promised her brother that she would see him again. I do not know where she may have fulfilled that promise.

Chaitra 1301 (1894)

NOTES

1 According to Hindu custom, fire is ritually brought into contact with the mouth of a dead person before being cremated by the next of kin, especially the son or in the son's absence, the deceased's spouse: *mukhagni.* The implication here is clear: Tara is cursing that man with immediate death.

At Dead of Night
(*Nishithe*)

'Doctor! Doctor!'

What a bother! In the middle of the night–

Looking out, I saw it was our zamindar Dakshinacharan-babu. Scrambling out of bed, I pulled out the backless chair and offered it to him and peered anxiously at his face. It was half past two by the clock.

'That old trouble has come back again tonight; your medicine was no good,' said Dakshinacharan-babu, his face ashen and eyes wide open.

With some diffidence I said, 'Perhaps you have increased your intake of liquor.'

Very much annoyed, Dakshinacharan-babu snapped, 'That's a great misconception of yours. It's not liquor; unless you hear the whole story, you can't guess the true reason.'

In a niche in the wall, in a small tin container a kerosene wick was burning dimly. I stoked it up; the flame rose a little and kept emitting much smoke. Pulling the dhoti end to cover myself, I sat down on a packing case over which an old newspaper was spread. Dakshinacharan-babu began his story.

A homemaker like my first wife was very rare. But I was rather young then, and effortlessly brimming with passion; on top of that, I had learnt poetics quite well, so her unremitting housewifery did not satisfy me. One particular verse from Kalidasa often came to me–

A wife is to husband
Counsel, friend, and associate,
An earnest disciple in fine arts as well.

But to my wife no lecture on the fine arts had any effect, and if I tried to address her lovingly as a friend, she would laugh it off. Just as the mighty *Airavat* of *Indra* had been harassed no end by the flowing Ganges, so the finest gems of poetry and fondest greetings of love were swept away in an instant by the sheer force of her laughter. She had an amazing faculty to laugh.

Thereafter, it has been nearly four years now since I fell terribly ill. I suffered from carbuncle and delirious fever; I was at death's door. Eventually, the doctor gave up. Just then a relative brought in a hermit-like man who gave me a potion of some dry root pounded with ghee. Whether it was because of that medicine or owing to luck, I survived that time.

During my illness, my wife had never rested for a moment. All through those days, a frail woman with the limited powers of a human, with relentless earnestness, had battled continually with Death's envoys at the threshold. With all her love, heart and care, she had preserved my unworthy life as if shielding and covering it with her two hands like a child snuggled to her breast. She had forgotten her meals, forgotten her sleep, and took no notice of anything else whatsoever in the world.

Like a worsted tiger, *Yama* dropped me from his jaws beating a retreat, but not before mauling my wife with his massive paw.

My wife was pregnant then, and sometime later, delivered a stillborn baby. After that she developed various complicated diseases. Now it was my turn to nurse her; but she felt embarrassed. 'Oh, what are you doing?' she would murmur, 'What will people say? Don't keep frequenting my room like this day and night.'

Pretending as if I was fanning myself, at night if I tried to fan her when she ran a temperature, a great tussle for the fan would ensue. If occasionally in connection with her nursing, my usual time of dinner was delayed by ten minutes, it would give her cause for much complaint, pleading, and coaxing. The slightest attempt to care for her would prove counterproductive. 'It's not good for men to go to such lengths,' she would demur.

Perhaps you have seen our house at Baranagar. In front of the house is a garden which looks out on the flowing Ganga. Just below our bedroom, enclosing a small plot of land in the south with henna creepers, my wife had carved out a small garden plot to her liking. In the entire garden, that corner was the most ordinary, and it was purely native. What I mean is that there was no splendour of colours in preference to fragrance, no variety of leaves in preference to flowers, nor was there in the flowerpots, beside nondescript plants, any stick-hoisted paper flags of Latin names. *Bel*, jasmine, rose, gardenia, oleander and tuberose were mostly in evidence. The foot of a huge *bakul* tree was paved with white marble. Before her illness, under her personal supervision she used to get it washed clean mornings and evenings. On summer evenings, after housework, that was where she sat. From there, the Ganga could be seen, but from the Ganga, the babus cruising by in their boats could not see her.

Having been bed-ridden for a long time, one moonlit evening of *Chaitra*, she said, 'Remaining confined in the room, I feel restless; today for once I would like to go and sit in that garden of mine.'

Holding her with great care, slowly walking her to that marble platform, I helped her lie down. I could have rested her head on my knees, but I knew she would have found it odd, so fetching a pillow I placed it under her head.

Fully bloomed bakul flowers kept dropping in ones and twos, and from behind the cover of branches, moonlight patterned with shadows fell on her emaciated face. It was serene and silent all around; in that thickly scented shadowy moonlight, sitting quietly at one side, as I looked at her face, my eyes moistened with tears.

I slowly went near her and gently picked up her hot thin arm; she did not object. For some time, sitting silently in this way, I felt a surge of emotion. 'I'll never forget your love,' I spoke out.

I then realised that there was no need of saying that. My wife laughed. In that laugh, there was shyness, pleasure, and slight disbelief, and besides, there was a strong element of derision as well. Without uttering a single word in protest, only with that laugh she seemed to convey, 'That you'll never forget is impossible, and I don't hope for it, either.'

It was for fear of that sweet mordant laugh that I had never had the courage to indulge in serious amorous talk with my wife. The thoughts that came to my mind in her absence seemed sheer nonsense in her presence. To this day, I have not understood why the same thing, which when read in print makes our eyes stream with tears, sounds laughable, when spoken.

You can argue with someone's words, but not with someone's laughter. Therefore, I stayed silent. Moonlight became brighter; a stray cuckoo cooed continually. I sat wondering: even in this moonlit night, was the bird's consort deaf to the call?

Despite prolonged treatment, my wife showed no sign of improvement. The doctor advised change of air. I took her to Allahabad.

At this point, Dakshinacharan-babu suddenly paused, eyed me suspiciously, and then holding his head with both hands kept thinking. I remained silent as well. In the niche, the kerosene lamp burned dimly, and in the stillness of the room, the buzzing of mosquitoes became prominent. Suddenly breaking his silence, Dakshina-babu resumed his story.

In Allahabad, Doctor Haran took up my wife's treatment. In the end, her condition having remained static for a long time, the doctor as well as I realised, as did my wife too, that hers was no curable disease and she would have to live as a chronic patient.

Then one day, my wife told me, 'When neither my disease will be cured nor is there any hope of my dying soon, how long will you live with one who is as good as dead? Marry again.'

She said this apparently as something logical and well thought-out; there was not the least hint in her expression that there was some greatness, some heroism or something extraordinary about her words.

It should have been my turn to laugh. But did I have the ability to laugh in that manner? Like the protagonist of a novel, I began to say in a solemn and lofty manner, 'As long as there is life in this body –'

'Come, come,' she cut me short, 'You do not need to say any more. Your words are too much for me.'

Without acknowledging defeat, I said, 'In this life, I'll never be able to love anyone else.'

Hearing this, my wife broke into loud laughter. Then I had to stop.

I do not know whether even to myself I had ever confessed, but now I can realise that this nursing without hope had tired me out inwardly. That I would stop this task was beyond my imagination, yet the thought that I would have to drag on with this chronic patient all my life was agonising as well. Alas, when at the advent of youth I had looked forward to the future, in the delusion of love, in the promise of happiness, in the illusion of beauty there had been the vista of a cheerful life. From now until the end, there stretched only a vast desert of hopelessness and unquenchable thirst.

In my nursing, my wife must have noticed that ennui in my heart. I did not know then, but now there is no doubt that she could read me as easily as the first book of a children's primer without double consonants. That is why whenever in the vein of a fictional hero I went to wax poetical before her, she would laugh out with such profound affection, yet unmistakable fun. Even my innermost thoughts beyond my own consciousness she knew fully well like my good old Lord. When I remember this, I wish to die in shame even today.

Doctor Haran was the same caste as we were. He would invite me to dinner at his house quite often. After I had been to his place a couple of times, one day he introduced me to his daughter. The girl was unmarried; she was about fifteen. The doctor used to say that since he had not found a suitable groom he had not given her in marriage yet, but from others I had heard the rumour of a taint in the family.

However, the girl had no other fault. She was as good-looking as well-educated. For this reason, occasionally on some days, I would be talking with her over various subjects, and thereby would be quite late in returning home at night. The prescribed time for giving medicine to my wife would have passed by then. She knew that I had gone to the doctor's house, but never once asked me the reason for the delay.

Once again, I saw a mirage in the midst of the desert. When I was thirsting right down to my heart, a brimming pool of crystal water was splashing and spilling before my eyes. However hard I tried, it was then impossible for me to rein in my mind.

The patient's room turned doubly gloomy for me. Thereafter, breach of regularity in nursing as well as administering medicine kept happening very often.

Doctor Haran would often comment that those who had no chance of recovering from their illness had better welcome death, because they were themselves not happy with their lives, and others were unhappy as well. There is no harm in saying this as a general observation; yet keeping my wife in view, he ought not to have said this. But doctors are so inured to life and death that they do not quite realise our feelings.

Suddenly one day I heard from the next room that my wife was telling Haran-babu, 'Doctor, by making me swallow some useless medicines why are you increasing our debt to your dispensary?

When the problem is with my life itself, why not just give me the medicine so it stops soon?'

'Shame on you, you shouldn't say such things,' said the doctor.

I was deeply hurt to hear this. After the doctor had left, going into her room, I sat by her bedside, and began to caress her forehead gently. She said, 'It is very hot in here. You go outside. It is time for you to go out to stroll. Without going out a bit, you won't have good appetite at night.'

To go out on a walk meant going to the doctor's house. I had myself explained to her the benefit of the outdoors as an appetiser. Now I can certainly say that every time she saw through this deception. I was a fool; I thought she could be fooled.

Having said this, Dakshinacharan-babu sat silently for a long while, his head resting on his hands. At last, he said, 'Bring me a glass of water.' He resumed after drinking water.

One day, the doctor's daughter Manorama expressed her desire to come on a visit to my wife. I do not know why, but I did not like her proposal. Yet I had no reason to refuse either. She arrived one evening at our house.

That day my wife's pain had become severer than usual. On days when her pain was worse, she used to lie still and motionless; only at times, her fists clenched and her face took on a bluish hue, which indicated the intensity of her pain. There was no sound in the room; I was sitting quietly at the end of her bed. That day, she was physically unable even to request me to go out to walk, or maybe, she wished that in times of her great distress I give her company. To avert the glare, the kerosene lamp was kept near the door. The room was half-dark and hushed. Only occasionally on slight relief of pain, her heavy sighs could be heard.

At that time, Manorama appeared at the door. Light from the lamp fell on her face. In the haze of light and darkness, she could not make out anything at first in the room and waited hesitantly.

My wife, giving a start, clutching my hand, asked, 'Who's she?' In that weak state, suddenly seeing a stranger, she was frightened and asked me a couple of times indistinctly, 'Who's she? Who is she, dear?'

Some perverse streak made me blurt out, 'I don't know.' The moment I said this, someone seemed to whip me. The next moment I corrected myself, 'Oh, she's our Doctor-babu's daughter.'

My wife looked once at my face; I could not look at her. The next moment, she told the guest in her feeble voice, 'Please come in.' She asked me to hold the lamp.

Manorama came into the room and took her seat. She kept chatting with the patient casually, when the doctor came on a visit.

He had brought from his dispensary two phials of medicine with him. Holding them before my wife, he said, 'Look, this blue phial contains massage oil, and this one, pills for oral use. Take care you do not mix them up; the oil is deadly poison.' After once cautioning me as well, he put the medicines on the bedside table. When taking leave, he called his daughter.

'Why don't I stay back, father?' Manorama said, 'There's no woman around. Who'll look after her?'

My wife protested anxiously, 'No, no, please, don't take the trouble. I have my old maid; she cares for me like a mother.'

The doctor smiled and said, 'She is the Mother Goddess! She has always nursed others, and can't take nursing from others.'

When the doctor was about to leave along with his daughter, my wife said, 'Doctor-babu, he has been sitting for a long time in this stuffy room. Can you take him out for a walk?'

The doctor told me, 'Why not come along? Let us go for a walk on the riverside.'

After showing a slight reluctance, I agreed almost immediately. Before finally leaving, the doctor warned my wife once again about the two phials of medicine.

That day, I had my meals at the doctor's house. When I came back, it was quite late in the night. On entering the room, I found that my wife was tossing in the bed. Stung by remorse, I asked her, 'Is your pain worse?'

She could not utter a word, only looked at my face. Her voice had choked.

At once at that hour of the night, I called in the doctor.

The doctor at first could not make out anything for quite a while. At last, he asked her, 'Has that pain aggravated? Can't we try the massage oil once?'

Having said this, picking up the phial from the table, he found it empty. 'Have you swallowed this medicine by mistake?' he asked my wife.

She nodded.

Immediately, the doctor rushed home in a tonga to fetch the suction pump. I threw myself on her bed, almost in a faint.

Then, in the manner of a mother comforting her ailing child, drawing my head close to her breast, with the touch of her hands she tried to convey what she wanted to say. Only through that pathetic touch, she kept telling me repeatedly, 'Do not grieve. Whatever has happened is for the best; you will be happy, and keeping that in mind, I die happy."

By the time the doctor came back, all my wife's torments along with her life had ended.

Dakshinacharan, after taking another draught of water said, 'It is too hot here,' and then after pacing up and down the veranda a couple of times, came back to his seat. It was evident, he was reluctant to carry on with his story, but as if by hypnotising him, I had been extracting it. He began from where he had left off.

I married Manorama and returned to my native home.

Manorama had married me with the consent of her father. But when I told her affectionate words and tried to capture her heart with words of love, she would not laugh, and would remain grave. How could I know where and at which nook of her heart what misgiving had formed?

At this time, my addiction to drinks became excessive.

One early autumn evening, along with Manorama I was walking in the garden of our Baranagar house. It was growing eerily dark. There was not even the sound of birds flapping their wings in their nests. Only, the dense shadowy *jhau* trees lining both sides of the avenue were rustling in the breeze.

Feeling tired, Manorama came to that marble platform under the bakul tree, and lay down resting her head on her hands. I too came and sat nearby.

Darkness was even denser there; the small patch of the sky overhead was thickly studded with stars; the chirping of crickets under the tree seemed to be weaving a slender border of sound at the end of the fabric of silence falling from the heart of the endless sky.

That day also, I had taken some drinks; my mind was in a rather buoyant state. When the eyes had got used to the darkness, under the shadow of the wooded surroundings, the indistinct figure of that languid dishevelled woman painted in a pale colour instilled in me an irresistible passion. It seemed she was a shadow, as if I could no way grasp her with two hands.

Just then, the crest of the dark fir trees seemed to catch fire. By and by, the wan yellow moon at the fag end of the dark fortnight rose above the trees; moonlight fell on the face of that woman clad in a white sari, wearily sprawled on the white marble. I could restrain myself no more. I drew up close, picked up her hand lovingly, and said, 'Manorama, you do not trust me, but I do love you. I will never forget you all my life.'

As soon as I said this, I was startled: I remembered that these were the exact words I had spoken some other day to some other person. And the next moment, from over the branches of the bakul tree, above the heads of the jhau trees, under the yellow dark-fortnightly crescent moon, from the eastern to the far western bank of the Ganga there swept a fast rolling laughter, 'ha-ha–ha-ha–ha-ha'. Whether that was a heart-rending laugh, or a sky-piercing wail

I cannot tell. Instantly I fell in a faint from the marble platform down to the ground below.

When I came to, I found myself lying on the bed in my room. My wife asked, 'Why did it happen to you all of a sudden?'

I said with a shiver, "Did you not hear that roll of laughter sweep by filling the entire sky?'

'Did you think it was laughter?' said my wife with a laugh. 'Forming a column, a long flight of birds had swept past; it was the flapping of their wings that we had heard. You get scared so easily?'

At daytime, I could clearly understand that indeed it had been the sound of a flight of birds. During this time of the year, flocks of ducks flew in from the far north to roam the sand-beds of the river. But when evening fell, I could not hold on to that conviction. I would then feel that on all sides, throughout the darkness, dense laughter lay in heaps, waiting to burst forth on a slight pretext piercing the darkness and overflowing the sky. Eventually, I was in such a state that after dusk, I had not the courage to talk to Manorama.

Then leaving our Baranagar house, taking Manorama along, I went out on a boat-trip. In the month of *Agrahayan*, the cool river breeze blew away all my fear. For a few days, we were very happy. Fascinated by the landscape, Manorama too seemed at last to be opening the closed door of her heart to me little by little.

We sailed past the Ganga, past the estuary, and finally into the Padma. The terrible Padma, then at the advent of winter, was lean and lifeless like a serpent in a hole in a state of long hibernation. To the north, a desolate, denuded sand-bed stretched out endlessly to the hazy horizons. On the high banks to the south, mango groves of villages stood trembling with joined palms before the jaws of this monstrous river. From time to time, the Padma turned over in her sleep, and ruptured shores came crashing down with a splash. Finding the spot convenient for walking about, we moored the boat.

One day, strolling on the riverbank, we wandered very far from our boat. Soon after the golden tinge of sunset had disappeared, the moon of the bright fortnight came up. Across that endless silvery sandbank, when copious, boundless, beaming moonlight extended far into the frontiers of the sky, it seemed we were the only two humans wandering in the uninhabited, unbounded dreamland of the moon. A red shawl covered Manorama's head and flanking her face swathed her body. When the stillness grew dense, when there remained nothing but a limitless directionless whiteness and void, Manorama slowly taking out her hand pressed mine; snuggling up to me, she reclined on me as if reposing her body and soul, life and youth upon me. With an ecstatic and throbbing heart, I wondered if it was possible to love passionately enough within the four walls of a room. Could two human beings be accommodated except under this open, free and endless sky? Then it seemed we had no homes, no roots, nowhere to go back to; thus holding each other's hand, along the path with no destination, in aimless wandering we would be gliding without hindrance through the moonlit void.

Walking in this way, coming to a certain place, I noticed that in the middle of that mass of sand, not far away, there was a sort of a pool; after the Padma had receded, water was trapped there.

Upon that ripple-less, motionless, dormant bowl of water in the midst of the desert sand, a long streak of moonlight lay in a faint. Coming to that spot, the two of us stood on its edge. What Manorama was thinking I knew not, but she looked up to my face and the shawl slipped from her head. Lifting her moonlit face, I kissed it.

At that time, in that solitary desert without a single soul, someone called out thrice in a solemn voice, 'Who is she?'

I started; my wife too shuddered. But the next moment we realised that this sound was neither human nor extra-human—just the call of water-birds who were scouring the sandbanks. Suddenly at that hour of night finding human presence near their safe secluded haunt, they were alerted.

In our fright, we hurried back to our boat and after dinner went to bed as usual. A tired Manorama soon fell asleep. Then in the dark, someone standing next to my mosquito net, pointing a single long thin bony finger at the deeply sleeping Manorama, as if into my ears very secretly in an inarticulate voice, kept asking repeatedly, 'Who is she, who is she, who is she, dear?'

Scrambling out of the bed, I lighted the lamp by striking a match. That very moment, the apparition vanished, and shaking my mosquito net, rocking the boat, freezing the blood of my perspiring body, a gale of laughter flowed through the dark night. It crossed the Padma, crossed the sandbanks and then beyond it went away across all the sleeping fields, towns and villages. It seemed as if for ever, crossing land after land, world after world gradually becoming fainter and fainter it was melting away infinitely far; as if gradually it transcended the realm of life and death; as if gradually it became as minute as the point of a needle. So faint a sound I had never heard or imagined: as if in my head there was an endless sky, and no matter howsoever farther and farther that sound receded, it could not overstep the boundaries of my head. At last, when I could endure it no more, I thought unless the lamp was put out, no sleep was possible. As soon as I blew out the lamp and lay down, next to my mosquito-net, next to my ears in the dark, the same hushed voice spoke out, 'Who's she, who's she, who's she, dear?' At the same rate as the blood pulsing through my heart, the words sounded incessantly, 'Who's she, who's she, who's she, dear? Who's she, who's she, who's she, dear?' In the dead of night, in that soundless boat, even my round clock on the shelf coming to life, pointing its hour hand at Manorama and keeping time with its tick-tock, kept asking, 'Who is she, who is she, who's she, dear? Who is she, who's she, who's she, dear?'

As he went on, Dakshina-babu grew pale, his voice nearly choked. Touching him, I said, 'Have some water.'

Then suddenly my kerosene lamp after flickering for some time went out. I saw the night was almost over. Crows cawed. Robins whistled. On the path in front of my house, the creaking of a bullock-cart was heard. Then Dakshina-babu's face wore an altogether different look; there was no trace of fear in it. That under the spell of night and in the frenzy of imaginary fright, he had revealed so much of himself made him feel very ashamed and extremely angry with me. Without even saying a word of courtesy, he got up abruptly and rushed out.

That very day in the middle of the night, he again came to knock on my door, calling, 'Doctor! Doctor!'

Magh 1301 (1894)

A Problem Solved
(*Samasyapuran*)

1

The zamindar of Jhinkrakota, Krishnagopal Sarkar, after entrusting the management of his estate and household to his eldest son, went to spend the rest of his life in Benares. All the poor and destitute people of the land kept crying their hearts out for him: everyone said such generosity and piousness was rarely seen in *Kaliyug*.

His son Bipinbihari was a well-educated BA of the modern day. He grew a beard, wore glasses and did not mix too much with others. He was virtuous to a fault; he never smoked, never even played cards. He had an extremely innocent appearance, but he was a very strict person.

His tenants were soon to get a taste of this. With the old master, remission of rent was possible, but with this person, there was no hope on any pretext of even a paisa worth of exemption from the due rent. Nor in any case was the due date to be relaxed by a day.

Soon after taking over, Bipinbihari found that his father had patronised a great number of Brahmans with lands free of rent and countless other people by reducing their rents. If anyone begged him for anything, he just could not deny it: it was one of his weaknesses.

'This can never go on,' said Bipinbihari. 'Surely I can't allow half the estate to go rent-free.' Two arguments came to his mind:

First, those lazy beneficiaries who sat at home putting on flab by subletting their lands were mostly worthless and undeserving of kindness. Such charity merely gave indulgence to idleness in the country.

Second, means of livelihood had become rarer and costlier now as compared to his father or grandfather's times. Wants had multiplied. To live with self-respect today it cost a man four times as much as it used to previously. Obviously, the way his father had squandered money blithely in indiscriminate charity would no longer do now; on the contrary, what had gone out ought to be retrieved and augmented.

He started doing whatever he ought to do following the dictates of his conscience. He carried on by observing a definite principle.

What had gone out of the coffers began to trickle back into the coffers again. He retained very few of his father's charitable arrangements, and that too, after providing that they were not deemed as good as permanent settlement.

Staying in Benares, Krishnagopal could hear the cries of his tenants through letters; some of them even going all the way to him broke into tears. Krishnagopal wrote to Bipinbihari that what he was doing was most atrocious.

In reply, Bipinbihari wrote: 'Earlier, in the same way that gifts were freely made, there were receipts of various kinds as well. In those days, between the zamindar and the tenant it was customary to exchange gifts. Recently, new laws having been enforced, and except the legitimate rent, all other kinds of receipts have stopped altogether, and other prestigious rights and privileges of the zamindar have been abolished as well. Naturally, in these days if I do not keep a strict watch on my rightful dues, then what else is left? Today, neither will the tenants give me anything extra; nor shall

I give the tenants anything extra: now our relationship is purely commercial. If we keep making gifts and donations, we will end up bankrupt; preserving the property and the family name will be well-nigh impossible.'

Krishnagopal became deeply concerned over such enormous changes over time; he contemplated: 'Boys of modern times are doing what is only appropriate in this age; the traditional rules of our time will not apply. If I try to interfere from this distance, they will say, "Then you take back your own property; we can't take the responsibility." Why take the bother for nothing? Better spend these few days chanting Lord Krishna's name.'

2

Things went on accordingly. After a great deal of litigation and troublesome measures, Bipinbihari managed to settle things more or less, as he had planned.

Most tenants acknowledged submission; only Mirza Bibi's son Achhimaddi Biswas could by no means be brought under control.

Bipinbihari's anger and indignation too was the strongest for him: lands given away to Brahmans were in a way justifiable, but how a Muslim's son could own so much land free of rent or at nominal rents was something he could not understand. Son of a lowly Muslim widow, he had barely learnt to read and write at the village junior scholarship school, but was so vain of his fortune, he just did not respect anyone.

Bipin learnt from his older employees that since his father's time the family had indeed been receiving favours for long, but they could not ascertain any particular reason for this favour. Maybe the hapless widow had aroused the master's pity by narrating her misery.

But to Bipin, this one instance of patronage seemed most unjustified: especially because their previous state of poverty Bipin had not seen for himself; from their present affluence and arrogant pride, he felt that they had cheated his emotionally weak simple-minded father out of a portion of his property.

Achhimaddi, also, was an insolent type of young man. He said, 'I stake my life on it, I will not surrender the least bit of my right.' A fierce battle ensued between the two parties.

Achhimaddi's widowed mother repeatedly advised him: it is better not to quarrel with a zamindar; someone by whose benevolence so many days of our lives have been spent, it is our duty to depend on his consideration alone. Let us agree to cede a part as demanded by the zamindar.

'Ma, these aren't things you can understand,' said Achhimaddi.

Achhimaddi lost the litigations one after another. But the more he lost, the more obstinate he grew: for the sake of all he had, he went as far as to stake all he had.

One afternoon, Mirza Bibi, with a hamper of her own garden's vegetables met Bipin-babu secretly. The old woman, as if affectionately carressing Bipin all over with her doleful motherly eyes, said, 'You are like my son, may Allah bless you. Baba, do not ruin Achhim; by this, you will not be doing justice to your religion. In your hand, I do surrender him; accept him as a worthless younger brother whom you cannot disown. Only because he has got a grain of your immense wealth, do not resent, dear.'

Seeing that out of a natural impertinence of advanced age the old woman was speaking so presumptuously with him, Bipin became very much annoyed. 'You are a mere woman,' he said, 'You don't understand these things. If you have anything to say, send your son.'

Both from her own son and from another woman's son Mirza Bibi heard that she understood nothing in this matter. Remembering Allah's name, wiping her eyes, the widow went back home.

3

The case dragged from the criminal court to civil court to district court up to the High Court; nearly eighteen months passed by in this way. When Achhimaddi had sunk neck-deep in debt, he was awarded partial victory in the appeals court.

But whatever was saved from Scylla fell into the clutches of Charybdis[1]. The money-lenders took the opportunity to obtain a decree. A day was fixed for putting all Achhimaddi's property to auction.

It was Monday, a market-day. The market sat on the bank of a small river. In the monsoon, the river was full; transactions were going on partly on the bank, partly in boats, amidst continuous din. As for the commodities, in the month of Asharh now, supply of jackfruit was most abundant; hilsa-fish was plentiful as well. The sky was overcast; many of the vendors, fearing rain, had put up tents on bamboo poles.

Achhimaddi too had come to the market to buy something, but he did not have a single paisa, and no one these days dealt with him on credit either. He had brought a chopper and a brass plate to raise money by pawning.

Bipin-babu had been out on his afternoon stroll, attended by two or three footmen holding sticks. Attracted by the hubbub, he wanted to make a round of the market. On entering the market out of curiosity, he was asking Dwari the oilman about the state of his business, when Achhimaddi roaring like a tiger, brandishing his chopper came charging at him. The vendors intercepted him and at once disarmed him. He was soon handed over to the police, and it was business as usual again.

No one would say that over this incident Bipin-babu had not been gloating in his mind. For a quarry to turn back charging at the hunter is villainy at its worst; the insolence of it is intolerable. Anyway, the wretch was such a scoundrel he would get condign punishment.

The women of Bipin's house were horrified to hear about the day's incident. Everyone said, 'Goodness, what a wicked dastardly fellow!' At the possibility of his impending punishment, they found some comfort.

Meanwhile, that evening, without food and without her son, the widow's house seemed even darker than death. Everyone forgot the matter, had their dinner, went to bed and slept; only to an old woman, among the happenings in the world, this incident assumed the greatest importance of all. Yet, to fight it, there was no one else in the entire world, except in the corner of a light-less hut, a few decrepit bones and a despairing timorous heart.

4

In the meanwhile, two or three days had passed. The following day had been fixed for a hearing before the deputy magistrate. Bipin too would have to be present as a witness. So far, no zamindar ever had to appear in person at the witness box; but Bipin had no objection to it.

Next day, after putting on his turban and sporting his pendant watch, riding a palanquin Bipin-babu duly arrived at the court with great pomp. The courtroom was packed to capacity; such a sensational event had not happened at the court for long.

When only a short time was left for the hearing to begin, a footman came up to Bipin-babu and whispered something into his ear; extremely perturbed, he excused himself and came out of the courtroom.

Outside, he saw that at some distance away, under a banyan tree his old father was standing. Barefoot, his body wrapped in a *namabali* with a Krishna-rosary in his hand, his slender frame seemed to exude a refreshing glow; from his forehead, a calm compassion was radiating into the world.

With his *chapkan*, *jobba* and tight-fitting pantaloons, Bipin had to make quite an effort to touch his father's feet in obeisance. His turban came down to the tip of his nose, and his watch came out from the inside pocket. Hastily readjusting them, he requested his father to come to his lawyer's house nearby.

Krishnagopal said, 'No, what I have to say, let me say right here.'

Bipin's footmen kept the curious bystanders at bay.

'You must see that Achhim is acquitted,' said Krishnagopal. 'Also his property which you have forcibly acquired should be returned.'

Taken aback, Bipin asked, 'Is that why you have come all the way from Benares? Why do you show them so much favour?'

'What will you gain by hearing that, son?'

Bipin refused to give up. 'On the ground of unfitness, so many grants I have recalled from so many men; among them were several Brahmans as well; you interfered with none of the cases. And for this Muslim fellow so much is your perseverance! Today, after making all this fuss, if I have to secure Achhim's release and return everything, what shall I say to the people?'

Krishnagopal kept silent for a while. Then with trembling fingers going over his rosary, he said in a rather tremulous voice, 'If you think it necessary to tell everything to people frankly, tell them Achhimaddin is your brother, my own son.'

Startled and aghast, Bipin said, 'By a Muslim woman?'

'Yes, my son,' said Krishnagopal.

After remaining silent for quite some time, Bipin said, 'Well, more of it afterwards, now come home.'

Krishnagopal said, 'No, for I'll never enter home again. I'm going back right now from here. Do what your conscience says is proper.' Then after blessing him, resisting his tears, he turned back with a trembling body.

Bipin did not know what to do or say; he kept standing silently. But this little bit of thought appeared in his mind that such indeed had been the devotion to religion in those days. In education and character, he found himself far superior to his father. This was but the consequence of the lack of some principle, he concluded.

Back to the court, he saw Achhim emaciated and distressed, his lips dry and pale, his eyes glowing, held by two guards, standing outside in dirty rags. He was Bipin's brother!

Bipin was on friendly terms with the deputy magistrate. The case was dismissed on some technical ground. Shortly thereafter, too, Achhim got back his previous estate. But, not only was he unable to comprehend the reason of this, but other people were astonished as well.

That Krishnagopal had come during the trial soon became public; salacious gossip kept doing the rounds.

Shrewd lawyers surmised the entire matter. Lawyer Ramtaran whom Krishnagopal had brought up and educated at his own expense had all along suspected, but now at last realised perfectly that every sadhu[2], subjected to close scrutiny, would ultimately be exposed. 'Howsoever devoutly he may count his rosary beads, in the world everyone is a wretched fellow like me.' The difference between a sadhu and non-sadhu is that sadhus are hypocrites, and non-sadhus are candid. Anyway, deciding that Krishnagopal's widely acclaimed generosity, nobility and piety were all sham, Ramtaran seemed to have finally found the solution to an old knotty problem, and by what logic I do not know, at this finding the burden of gratitude felt a great deal lighter as well. He found great comfort.

Agrahayan 1300 (1893)

NOTES

1 English equivalent of the Bengali proverb: *Jale kumir, dangai bagh*: between the crocodile in the water and the tiger on the bank (faced with two equally dangerous options).

2 A Hindu wandering holy man.

Atonement
(*Prayashchitta*)

1

In between heaven and earth, there is an indefinable, anarchic realm where King Trishanku[1] is hovering, where sky-flowers[2] are cultivated in plenty. This continent ringed by forts of air is called 'Might-Have-Been'. Blessed are the souls who have acquired immortality by accomplishing great deeds; blessed too are those who with their meagre power are assisting ordinarily among the masses in the discharge of daily duties of life. But persons who, through the mistake of Providence, have fallen in between, have no means of escape. They *might have been* something whatever, but that is precisely why it is impossible for them to *have been* something whatever.

Our Anathbandhu was a fate-struck young man suspended in that intermediate land. Everyone believes that he could have been successful at everything if he wished. But neither did he wish at any time nor did he succeed in anything, and everyone's confidence in him remained unshaken. They said, 'He'll be first in the exams,' and he took no examinations at all. Everyone believe that if he joined a service, he could easily rise to the highest position in any department; he never took a job. He was particularly contemptuous of ordinary people, because they were insignificantly small. He had scant regard for extraordinary people, because if he had wished, he could have been even more extraordinary than them.

Anathbandhu's entire earning in honour and fame, wealth and fortune had been deposited in the vault of non-impossibility beyond time and space. In the realm of the real, the great Dispenser had gifted him with a wealthy father-in-law and a docile wife. The wife's name was Bindhyabasini.

Anathbandhu did not like the name of his wife; neither did he regard his wife worthy of him in looks or virtues; but in Bindhyabasini's mind, there was no end of pride in being blessed with such a husband. She did not have a shade of doubt in her mind that her husband was superior to any other husband of any other wife in every respect; neither did her husband have any, and public opinion was favourable to this conviction as well.

Bindhyabasini lived in constant apprehension lest this pride in her husband be dented in the least. She would have peacefully devoted her life to his worship if by elevating her husband to the highest peak of the mountain of her unwavering devotion she could shield him from all the cynical glances of foolish mortals. But in the material world, with devotion alone one cannot elevate and keep one's object of devotion hoisted up indefinitely, and people who did not regard Anathbandhu as the paradigm of the male were not rare either. This had brought Bindhyabasini much distress.

When Anathbandhu was in college, he used to stay in his father-in-law's house. The examination came; he did not appear, and the next year he left college. At this, Bindhyabasini, or Bindi, felt small before the public. At night, she murmured to him, 'You had better take the exam.' Laughing sardonically he said, 'Does one get two extra hands[3] by taking the exam? Has our Kedar not passed the exam?' She found consolation: when many stupid fellows of the country were passing such examinations, how could taking those exams have enhanced Anathbandhu's glory any further?

Her neighbour Kamala came jubilantly to her childhood friend Bindi with the news that her brother Ramesh had won a scholarship, passing his exam this year. Quite unreasonably, Bindhyabasini thought that this jubilation of Kamala was not genuine, but laced with some secret insinuation at her husband. So, instead of sharing her friend's joy, rather obtrusively in a contentious vein she remarked that the LA exam was not reckoned as an exam at all; in fact, at colleges in England there was even no examination below the BA. Obviously, all this information and argument she had collected from her husband.

After coming to give a happy news, Kamala was at first somewhat surprised on suddenly receiving such a hurt from her most beloved friend. But she too was a creature of the female race, wasn't she? Therefore, she could immediately perceive Bindhyabasini's feelings, and at the insult of her brother, at once there appeared a drop of lethal poison on the tip of her tongue too: 'Women like us, my dear, have neither gone to England nor married Englishmen. How can we know about such things? We are foolish women; we know more or less this: Bengali boys have to take the LA in colleges. Even so, not everyone can make it.' Saying these words in an extremely innocent, sweet, and friendly manner, she went away. Not given to quarrelling, Bindhyabasini bore it without giving any reply, and then going into her room began to weep silently.

Within a few days, another incident happened. A distant wealthy relation coming to Calcutta on a short trip put up at the house of Bindhyabasini's father. The occasion set off a flurry of activity in her father Rajkumar-babu's household. The son-in-law was requested to vacate for a few days the large drawing room he had been occupying, for special reception of the guests.

Anathbandhu was filled with resentment from injured pride. First, going to Bindhyabasini, by reviling her father and reducing her to tears, he avenged himself on him. Then by boycotting meals and adopting other drastic measures, he tried to exhibit his umbrage. Bindhyabasini was mortified to see this. With her natural sense of dignity, she realised that there was nothing so disgracefully self-demeaning as to make a public display of resentment in such cases. Abasing herself at his feet, weeping a lot, she persuaded him with great effort to desist from this infantile behaviour.

Bindhya was not an insensible woman, and so did not blame her parents; she realised that this was a trifling matter and quite normal. But at the same time, she also felt that her husband, by staying as a resident son-in-law, was being deprived of the proper reception due to a marital relation. From that day on, she kept insisting on her husband, 'Take me back to your house. I don't want to stay here any more.'

Anathbandhu had a great deal of vanity, but no sense of self-respect. He was least inclined to return to the destitution of his own home. Then his wife, showing some firmness, said, 'If you do not go, I'll go alone.'

Keeping his annoyance to himself, Anathbandhu decided to take his wife to their mud-built thatched hut in a remote village outside Calcutta. On the eve of their departure, Rajkumar-babu and his wife requested their daughter repeatedly to stay back a little longer. Without saying a word, sitting gravely with lowered head she indicated silently that that was not to be. Her sudden inflexible stand made her parents suspect that perhaps they had somehow hurt her unwittingly. Rajkumar-babu asked her sadly, 'My child, has anything we did unknowingly offended you?'

'Not at all, even for a moment,' she said looking at her father pitifully. 'I have been very happy all these days with your love and care.' She wept, but remained firm in her resolve. Her parents sighed and said to themselves: 'Howsoever affectionately, howsoever caringly you might bring up your daughter, once you give her in marriage, she no longer remains your own.'

Finally, with moist eyes taking leave of everyone, parting from her family, friends and the loving father's home she had lived in since birth, Bindhyabasini got into the palanquin.

2

There is a gulf of difference between a wealthy home in Calcutta and an ordinary household in a village. But not even for a day did Bindhyabasini betray any discontent by her conduct or demeanour. She continued cheerfully to assist her mother-in-law in domestic chores. Aware of their poor condition, her father had sent a maidservant with his daughter at his own expense. Bindhyabasini, soon after arriving at her husband's house, sent her back home; that the maidservant from a wealthy home should turn up her nose every moment at the poverty of her father-in-law's house seemed an intolerable apprehension to her.

Her mother-in-law, out of affection, tried to keep Bindhya away from work requiring hard labour, but Bindhya, participating in every work tirelessly with a cheerful face, won over the heart of her mother-in-law, and the village women were all praise for her charming behaviour.

But the consequence of this was not perfectly satisfactory, because the laws of the world are not simple sermons written in pristine Bengali like the First Book of Fables. A devil fond of cruel jokes intervening in the middle has scrambled up all the moral edicts into a tangled web. That is why good work does not always produce a perfectly good result possible in a certain situation; all at once, trouble begins.

Anathbandhu had one elder and two younger brothers. The eldest brother working at a distant place earned some fifty rupees, which took care of the family expenses and paid for the younger two brothers' education as well.

It is impossible these days with fifty rupees a month to improve the lot of a family, but for inflating the vanity of his elder brother's wife Shyamashankari, even that sum was enough: husband worked all the year round; hence, wife was entitled to the privilege of rest all the year round. She did absolutely no work, but behaved in such manner as if she had done the whole family proud merely by being the wife of her breadwinner husband.

When Bindhyabasini, after coming over to her father-in-law's house, devoted herself like a devout homemaker to housework day and night, Shyamashankari began to feel as if someone was holding her ungenerous heart in a tight squeeze. The reason is difficult to comprehend: perhaps *Barobau* thought that even though *Mejobou* came of an affluent family, she engaged in the lowly household chores only to show off to people, thereby only embarrassing her in the eye of others. Whatever the reason, the wife of 'fifty-rupees-a-month' could not at all stand the daughter from a rich family. She discovered signs of intolerable arrogance in her humility.

In the meanwhile, Anathbandhu, now coming back to his village, founded a library; after collecting ten to twenty school students and becoming their president, he started telegraphing reports to newspapers. He even amazed the whole village by becoming special correspondent of some English language dailies. Nevertheless, to his poor family he did not fetch a single paisa, but on the contrary, incurred many needless expenses.

Bindhyabasini kept pestering him for taking up some job of any kind whatever. He paid no heed. To his wife he said jobs suitable to him were there, but in those posts, the biased British government employed only influential Englishmen; a Bengali, howsoever eligible, had no hope.

Shyamashankari kept applying verbal stings directly or indirectly to her brother-in-law and his wife. Bragging about their own poverty, she kept saying, 'We are poor people. How can we maintain a rich man's daughter and son-in-law? There they were quite well off, had no cause for sorrow. Here eating our gruel of rice and lentils, can they suffer so much hardship?'

The mother-in-law feared the eldest wife; she did not dare to say anything in favour of the weak. The younger wife too, eating the rice-and-lentil provided by the 'fifty-rupees-a-month' brother-in-law peppered with his wife's acrid words, continued to digest them quietly.

Meanwhile, the eldest brother on coming home for a few days on leave found himself at the receiving end of a series of inspiring and powerful lectures from his wife. At last, when disturbance of sleep started being progressively greater, one day calling Anathbandhu he said calmly with affection, 'You ought to look out for some job. How can I run the family all by myself?'

Reacting like a trampled snake, Anathbandhu burst out with a roar: just two fistfuls of extremely filthy coarse rice twice a day; thereafter, such jibes were unbearable. He at once decided to leave with his wife for his father-in-law's house.

But his wife did not agree at all. She held that in an elder brother's rice and his wife's abuse, the younger brother had a family right, but in his father-in-law's shelter there was utter disgrace. In her father-in-law's house, Bindhyabasini was ready to accept abject humility and meanness, but in her father's house, she wanted to walk with her head held high preserving her own dignity.

At this point, the post of the third pundit fell vacant in the village entrance school. Both Anathbandhu's elder brother and Bindhyabasini requested him importunately to take up this work. But this too brought an adverse effect. That his own brother and his own co-religionist wife should think him worthy of a most trivial job excited unconquerable resentment in his mind and he grew far more indifferent to all worldly occupation than he had been ever before. Then again, it took his brother a lot of coaxing to placate his anger. Everyone decided that it was better not to pester him any more; only if somehow he remained in the house would the family be fortunate enough.

After exhausting his leave, the elder brother went back to his work; Shyamashankari lived with her pent-up anger distending her face into a huge unsightly disc[4]. Anathbandhu came and said to Bindhyabasini, 'Nowadays, unless one goes to England, one never gets a respectable job. I have decided to go to England. You better go to your father and on any pretext collect some money.'

In the first place, hearing of his proposed visit to England Bindhya felt she was struck by a thunderbolt. On top of that, she just could not think how to approach her father begging for money, and trying to find a way she was mortified with shame.

Anathbandhu's vanity prevented his begging from his father-in-law himself, and yet, he could not comprehend why the daughter could not extract money from her father by any means, fair or foul. Anath became hotheaded on the issue and a distressed Bindhyabasini had to shed copious tears.

In this way, days went by amidst household wants and mental distress until it was autumn when the *Durga Puja* approached. Rajkumar-babu sent men and carriages with much ceremonial splendour to invite his daughter and son-in-law cordially. After one year, the daughter along with her husband entered her father's house. This time the son-in-law received much more cordial treatment than what was once given to the rich relative to his great irritation. Bindhyabasini also, after a long time discarding the veil of her head, kept amusing heerself day and night with the ripples of affection and festivity.

That day was *shashthi*[5], the next day the puja would begin. There was no end of hustle and bustle in the house swarming with relations, near and distant. That night, Bindhyabasini went to bed very tired. This was not the same room she used to sleep in earlier; as part of special treatment to her son-in-law, her mother had spared her own bedroom. Bindhyabasini did not know when Anathbandhu had come to sleep; she was fast asleep then.

Very early in the morning the *shehnai* started playing. It did not wake Bindhyabasini who had been so tired out. Her two friends, Kamal and Bhuban, who had been trying in vain to eavesdrop, finally broke out into loud laughter. Startled out of sleep Bindhya found that her husband had already risen. Feeling ashamed, getting out of bed, she noticed that her mother's iron safe was wide open and her father's cash-box was not there either.

It suddenly crossed her mind that last evening there had been a clamour over her mother's bunch of keys that had gone missing. Obviously, someone had deliberately removed the keys to commit the theft. Then suddenly she had the apprehension that maybe the thief had harmed her husband, and she felt a pounding in her heart. Going to search under the bed, she found at its foot a letter under her mother's missing keys.

The letter was written in her husband's hand. From it, she learned that one of his friends had helped him secure a passage by ship to England. Now finding no other means of paying for his maintenance there, he had stolen his father-in-law's money, and then descending the wooden stairs from the veranda into the inside garden, escaped by scaling the wall. The ship had departed this morning.

When she had finished reading the letter, blood froze in her; right there she collapsed on the floor clutching the bedpost. Deep within her body, within the cavity of her ears, a noise like the call of crickets of a still deathly night kept buzzing. It was accentuated by the incongruous medley of shehnais from the courtyard, from the houses of neighbours, from the distant mansions. The whole of Bengal had then become delirious with festive joy.

The autumn sun tinged with festive laughter peeped amusedly into the room. It was so late in the morning, yet the doors were closed: Bhuban and Kamal began to thump it, giggling and joking. With no responses still coming, they panicked and started shouting, 'Bindi, Bindi!' Bindhyabasini said in a cracked, choking voice, 'I'm coming. You go away now.'

Fearing their friend was ill, they called her mother, who came and said, 'Bindu dear, what is the matter? Why is the door still closed?'

Resisting her welling tears, Bindhya said, 'Go and bring back father.'

Greatly alarmed, her mother immediately returned with Rajkumar-babu. Opening the door, Bindhya let them in and at once shut the door. Then falling on the floor, holding her father's feet she burst into a wail that broke her heart asunder. 'Baba, forgive me. I have stolen money from your safe.'

They sat down on the bed, dumbstruck. Bindhya said she had done it to send her husband to England.

'Why did you not ask it from us?' asked her father.

'I was afraid you might not let him go to England.'

Rajkumar-babu became very angry. Mother started weeping; so did the daughter, while the entire city resounded with various strains of joyful music.

Bindhya was a daughter who could never beg money from her father; Bindhya was a wife who could have died trying to conceal the slightest of her husband's dishonour from the closest of her relations. The same Bindhya today saw her wifely pride, her daughterly dignity, her self-respect crumbling down and wallowing in the dust at the feet of everyone, dear or disliked, familiar or stranger, right in the midst of the rejoicing crowd.

A censorious gossip swept through the house teeming with friends and relations: it was all pre-planned; after conspiring with his wife, removing the key, then with her assistance stealing the money overnight, Anathbandhu had fled to England. Standing outside the door, not only Bhuban and Kamal, but also many other relations, servants and neighbours had heard everything. They had come with anticipation and curiosity at the unusual sight of parents barging anxiously into their son-in-law's bedroom.

Bindhyabasini refrained from showing her face to anyone; after closing the door, she lay in her bed unfed. No one shared her sorrow. Everyone was staggered by the sheer wickedness of the conspiring woman. They concluded that Bindhya's character had so far remained dormant only because of lack of opportunity. In the sombre house, the puja festival passed off in some sort of way.

3

Bindhya returned to her husband's home, bowed down by disgrace and ennui. There an even more intimate bond was forged between the widowed mother-in-law and the wife, both languishing from the estrangement of one man. Coming closer to each other under the shadow of silent grief, they continued with profound equanimity to perform their household duties to the smallest detail. The closer her mother-in-law came, the farther her parents receded. Bindhya felt within her heart; 'My mother-in-law is poor, so am I, we two are bound by a tie of suffering. My parents are wealthy; they are far away from us.' In the first place, because of her poverty, Bindhya was far removed from her parents; now by admitting to the theft, she had fallen even lower. Who knew whether the thread of affection could withstand so huge a load of difference?

Anathbandhu, after he reached England, initially used to write to his wife regularly, but gradually the letters became rarer and started betraying a note of indifference unconsciously. Many accomplished English girls, far superior in every respect from intellect to beauty to his illiterate, homespun wife, admired Anathbandhu for his competence, intelligence and appearance. When such was the state, it was nothing strange that he would not regard his single-sari clad, veiled, non-fair skinned wife on par with him in any respect.

Nevertheless, when he fell in straitened circumstances, he felt no hesitation in sending a telegram to this resource-less Bengali girl as the only person to fall back upon. And this very Bengali woman kept sending money by selling her jewellery one after another wearing just two glass bangles on her hands. Since there was no suitable place for keeping gold safely in a village, all her costly ornaments had been put away in her father's house. On the pretext of having to attend invitations from her husband's relatives, she had them all brought back on various occasions. Finally, when she had sold off her bracelets, silver bangles, Benarasi sari, everything down to the shawl, writing a letter pouring profuse humble entreaties and oaths, smudging each word with tears, she requested him to come back.

Anathbandhu returned a barrister, dressed as an Englishman, his hair close-cropped and his beard clean-shaven. He moved into a hotel. Going back to his paternal house was out of the question:

first, there was lack of suitable accommodation. Second, a poor middle-class family in a village, having once lost its caste, was utterly helpless. His in-laws were devout orthodox Hindus; they too could not give shelter to an outcaste[5].

Being cash-strapped, he soon had to scale down his accommodation from hotel to a rented house, where he was not prepared to bring his wife. After returning from England, only on two or three days during the day he had gone visiting his wife and his mother; no further meeting with them had taken place since.

The two grief-stricken women had one consolation that Anathbandhu was in the proximity of relatives in his own country. At the same time, at Anathbandhu's extraordinary barrister-ial feat, there was no end of pride in their minds. Bindhyabasini kept reproaching herself as an unworthy wife of a renowned husband; then again, because she was unworthy, she felt even prouder of her husband. She became shrunken in sadness and puffed up in pride. She hated pagan ways, yet looking at her husband, she said to herself: 'Nowadays, many a man becomes a sahib, but does anyone look it so befittingly? A sahib right from England, every inch of him! Who could tell he was a Bengali?'

When his maintenance expenses began to be increasingly unaffordable, when in exasperation, Anathbandhu concluded that there was no recognition for talent in this accursed land, that out of jealousy his colleagues were secretly planting obstacles on the path to progress, when his lunch and dinner dishes started showing increasingly greater volumes of vegetables than fish and meat, fried shrimps almost completely ousted the prestigious roasted chicken, the polish of his dandyish dress and the arrogant sheen of his clean-shaven visage began to wane, when his life-string attuned to the flamboyant highest note of the octave began to scale down to the doleful lower middle, just then, a serious accident in Rajkumar-babu's family brought about a change in Anathbandhu's critical existence. One day, while returning by boat from his uncle's house across the Ganges, Rajkumar's only son Harakumar drowned with his wife and only son when the boat collided with a steamer. This incident left no one except Bindhyabasini in Rajkumar's line of descent.

His terrible grief somewhat assuaged, Rajkumar-babu approached Anathbandhu and said, 'Baba, you must undergo the atonement rites[7] so you can return to caste. I have no one else except you.'

Anathbandhu enthusiastically agreed to the proposal. He contemplated that in this way he could take revenge upon those bar library-frequenting native barristers who were jealous of him and did not show adequate respect to his extraordinary intellect.

Rajkumar-babu consulted the pundits versed in the scriptures. They said that if Anathbandhu had not eaten beef, there was a way to restore him to his caste.

Even though while abroad, the forbidden quadruped used to constitute his favourite dishes, he had no hesitation at all to deny it altogether. To his close friends he said, 'When society willingly wants to listen to lies, I see no sin in obliging it by just uttering it. To sanctify the tongue that has tasted beef with two abominable things, namely cow dung and lies, is the edict of modern society. I do not wish to transgress it.'

An auspicious day was fixed for his atonement and reinstatement in society. Meanwhile Anathbandhu not only reverted to his former dress code of dhoti and chuddar, but also devoted himself by means of argument and sermon to smearing black tar on the face of the British society and whitewashing the Hindu society. Whoever listened was pleased.

In exhilaration and pride, Bindhyabasini's tender heart suffused with affection began to overflow everywhere. She said to herself: 'Whoever returns from England returns a complete British sahib; there is no way one can tell from his looks he is a Bengali. But my husband has come back absolutely unchanged; rather, his devotion to Hinduism has become even stronger than before.'

On the appointed day, Rajkumar-babu's house swarmed with Brahmins and pundits. No expenses were spared. Arrangements for feast and after-dinner honorarium[8] were adequate.

There was no end of ceremony in the inner quarters either. All the rooms as well as the courtyard buzzed with the din and bustle of reception of the guests. Amidst that tumultuous flurry of activity, Bindhyabasini was floating cheerfully like a feathery sliver of cloud borne by the morning breeze and tinged by the autumn sun. Of all that was happening in the world today, her husband was the central character. Today entire Bengal had, as it were, become one single theatre, which on raising the curtain was presenting Anathbandhu as the only performing artiste before the surprised audience. Not that atonement meant confession of sin, rather display of condescension: by returning from England and re-entering the Hindu society, Anath had covered it with glory. The effulgence of that glory dispersing in a myriad beams from all over the land was radiating a celestial glow on Bindhyabasini's love-lustred face. All the misery and little insults of her petty life of so many years having been dispelled, today in the humming home of her father before the eyes of her friends and relations she ascended the glorious throne holding her head high. The reflected glory of the husband rendered an unworthy wife honourable to the world.

The ritual was over; Anathbandhu had been rehabilitated in his caste. Guests, relations and Brahmins sitting with him in the same row ate contentedly. The relatives in the inner rooms then sent for the son-in-law. The latter, in high spirits chewing *paan*, beaming a smile of delight, his chuddar trailing along the floor, walked leisurely towards the inner rooms.

Their eating over, while their remuneration was being arranged, the Brahmins sitting in a cluster were quibbling over the scriptures with an animated display of pedantry. Rajkumar-babu, by way of a little rest, was sitting in the learned assembly listening to them arguing over *Smriti*[9], when his doorman handed him a visiting card and said, 'Memsahib of an Englishman has come.'

Rajkumar-babu felt amazed; the next moment looking at the card, he saw on it printed in English: *Mrs Anathbandhu Sarkar*—meaning Anathbandhu Sarkar's wife.

Rajkumar-babu, looking at it for quite a while, could not at all comprehend the meaning of this one small word. In the meantime, a rosy-cheeked, auburn-haired, blue-eyed, fair-as-milk froth, nimble-as-doe, just-arrived-from-England, Englishwoman herself walked into the assembly, watching everyone's face intently. But she could not spot her familiar beloved face. The sudden sight of a memsahib stopped all the discourses on *Manusamhita* and the assembly fell profoundly silent like a cremation ground.

Enter Anathbandhu sauntering into the stage with his trailing chuddar once again. Instantly, the memsahib running over to him, holding him in an embrace planted on his *paan*-stained lips a kiss of conjugal reunion.

The *Manusamhita* debate could not be raised any more in the assembly that day.

Agrahayan 1301 (1894)

NOTES

1 See *Patra o Patri.*
2 Literally, 'where *sky-flowers* are cultivated': absurd dream, fool's paradise.
3 Vishnu and many other gods have four hands; hence the suggestion of greatness. This is Bengali idiomatic style of suggesting, with evident scorn, that someone has suddenly assumed a superior posture after achieving something. Another expression uttered in a similar vein: 'he has sighted a five-footed snake!'
4 The text has *kudarshanchakra*, a pejorative adaptation of *Sudarshanchakra*, Lord Vishnu or Krishna's wheel-shaped weapon.
5 The Durga (see Glossary) puja is a five-day ritual; from the *shashthi* (sixth lunar day) through the *dashami* (tenth lunar day) of the bright fortnight of Ashwin. On the sixth, the goddess is ritually invoked, and on the tenth, she is given ritual farewell when the idol is immersed, elaborate rites being performed on the intervening days. The puja being an expensive ritual, it is chiefly a

community festival. However, in many affluent families, the goddess is traditionally worshipped with grandeur.

6 A caste Hindu is held to have fallen from his caste, and by extension, from society, by committing the perceived offence of crossing the black (*kala*) waters (*pani*) of the sea; other arbitrarily decreed social transgressions include not marrying off one's daughter within an upper age limit of, say, eleven, usually the pubertal age. The offending family is handed down the devastating penalty of social ostracism (*ekghare*). Such customs are on the wane.

7 Atonement rite is the farce of purification supposedly achieved by performing some religious mumbo-jumbo including tasting cow dung or cow urine or some such ghoulish stuff.

8 In Bengali *bidai:* money and other gifts offered to Brahmins at the time of departure after being treated to a ritual feast; also called *bhojan-dakshina,* see *Notes* to In Quest of a Bride.

9 A scripture containing the essence of the Vedas, ascribed to Manu the law-giver, compiled from memory (smriti), hence the name; containing Hindu social, religious and domestic teaching.

The Inscrutable Woman (*Aparichita*)

1

I am all of twenty-seven now. This life is neither great in its number of years nor great in its accomplishments. Yet it has some significance of its own. It is like a flower, which was once visited by a honeybee; the history of that visit has germinated in it like a fruit.

That history is small in volume, and I will present it in a rather small way. Those who do not confuse 'small' with 'trivial' will savour its flavour.

I have passed all the university examinations. In my childhood, my handsome features gave my schoolteacher an opportunity to ridicule me by finding a parallel in *shimul*[1] flower and *makal*[2] fruit. This was quite embarrassing then. Later on, I felt that if one could be reborn I would still have wished a recurrence of my good looks and the derision of the teacher.

My father had once been poor. Later he earned lots of money as a lawyer never finding any respite to enjoy it. Leisure came to him for the first time when he breathed his last.

I was then barely past my childhood. I was practically brought up by my mother. As she came of a poor family, never did she forget that we were rich and ensured that I too did not. I was cosseted all through my childhood—that is perhaps why I have never quite matured. Even at twenty-seven, I look an infant spoon-fed by his mother[3].

My true guardian was my maternal uncle. He was hardly six years my senior. Even so, like the sandy bed of the *Phalgu,*[4] he had sucked up our entire family into his heart. Without digging into him, there was no way one could get a trickle of charity from our resources. Naturally, I did not have to bother about anything whatsoever.

Fathers of unmarried girls must find me a most sought-after bachelor. I do not even smoke. As it takes no hassles to be a good man, I am a good man and a perfect one too. I am capable of obeying my mother's commands; in fact, I lack the courage to disobey her. Actually, I have been trained to go by the dictates from women's quarters. A girl, who would choose her own husband, might remember this attribute.

Proposals came from many affluent families. However, my uncle, who was my Destiny's chief agent on earth, had his pet notions about marriage. He disapproved of daughters of rich fathers. The bride he wanted for our family had to come with her head bowed in subservience. Yet the craving for money was ingrained in his marrow. He wanted as my father-in-law someone who would not be moneyed, yet would not flinch from supplying it; someone who could be exploited, yet coming on a visit, if treated to the ordinary hookah[5] instead of the hubble-bubble[5] was not supposed to complain.

My friend Harish worked in Kanpur. He came home to Calcutta on leave and distracted my mind. 'Well,' he said, 'If you're considering girls, I know of an excellent one.'

I had since taken my master's degree. As far as I could see, holidays stretched away endlessly before me: no examinations, no canvassing, and no job. As for supervising my property, not only did I have no worry, I had neither the training nor the inclination for it. All I had was my mother inside the house and my uncle outside.

In this wasteland of idle time, my mind was fantasising over the illusory feminine form pervading the macrocosm: in the sky, there was her gaze; in the breeze, her breath; in the murmur of leaves, her secrets.

It was at this point of time that Harish came and said, 'If you're considering girls –.' My body and mind throbbing in the spring breeze like freshly sprouted leaves of the *bakul* grove, kept weaving a brocade of light and shade. Harish was a connoisseur of things romantic; he had a flair for instilling passion into his descriptions, and my mind was thirsting for it.

I asked him to mention the matter to my uncle.

Harish was unparalleled in captivating his audience, and hence was much sought-after in company. Even my uncle was a fan of his. The matter was broached in one of his sessions. To him the report about the girl's father was more important than that of the girl. Financially, the father's condition was just what he wanted. At one time, in their family Lakshmi's pitcher[6] was full to the brim. Now it was all but empty, yet a fistful was left at the bottom. Since it was not easy to keep up the family status in his native town, he had moved into the anonymity of a north Indian town, living there like any ordinary householder. This daughter was his only child, so for her sake, he would not hesitate to empty out the pitcher.

So far so good. But the girl was already fifteen! This upset my uncle. Could there be some blemish in the line? No, there was not any; the father had not found a suitable match for his daughter. Not only were bridegrooms an expensive commodity, he had made them even dearer by sticking to his uncompromising stand. Therefore, he was only waiting, but the girl's age just would not.

Thanks to Harish's unctuous tongue, my uncle relented. The preparatory part of marriage went off smoothly. In my uncle's perception, the world beyond Calcutta entirely lay in the Andaman Islands. He had undertaken his farthest ever trip on a certain occasion to Konnagar[7]. Had he been Manu[8], he would have specifically prohibited journey across the Howrah Bridge[7] in his code of laws. I fondly wished to go to see the bride for myself, but lacked the courage to propose it.

The person sent to bless[9] the girl was my elder cousin Binu Dada. I had full faith in his taste, wisdom and opinion. He came back to report, 'Not bad, my boy.' Binu Dada was discreetly conservative with his words. Where we would say 'splendid', he would say 'not too bad'. That's why I knew that in my lot there was no conflict between the god of marriage and the god of love.

2

Needless to say[10], the bride's side had to come all the way from Lucknow to Calcutta. The bride's father Shambhunath-babu saw me for the first time only three days before the wedding when he came to bless me; this goes to show how sincerely he trusted Harish. His age was more or less forty. His hair was black and his moustache had just started greying. A handsome man, he could easily stand out in a crowd.

I believe he was happy to see me. One could not tell, of course, because he spoke only sparingly, and the little he spoke apparently lacked the force of expression. My uncle was then talking incessantly: that in wealth and honour we were inferior to none in the city was the recurring theme he brought up. Shambhunath-babu paid no heed to this publicity; he did not even put in a *yes* or *no*. Had it been me, I would have been put out completely, but my uncle was not one to be disheartened so easily. From Shambhunath-babu's reticent manner, he concluded that the man was a lifeless fellow completely devoid of spirit. Whatever else the tribe of fathers-in-law may have, spirit is taboo for them, and so my uncle was pleased inwardly. When Shambhunath-babu got up to leave, my uncle made short work of saying goodbye to him from upstairs, without going to see him off into the carriage.

The dowry had already been finalised between the two sides. My uncle prided himself on being extraordinarily smart. He had left no ambiguity or loophole in the agreement; not only was the exact quantity of cash specified, the weight of gold in *bhari*[11] and its purity in terms of price were laid down as well. As I had kept aloof from these negotiations, I did not know the deal exactly. All I knew was that even this crude deal was a major part of the entire proceedings, and the charge of that part lay on someone who would not be cheated out of a paisa. In fact, as a man of astounding shrewdness, my uncle was the principal object of pride in our family. Wherever our interests were involved, that he would win the battle of wits was a foregone conclusion. That is why even though we had no want and the other party was in dire straits, we must win; that was the inviolable stand of our family, no matter who lives or dies by it.

The gifts of the turmeric ritual[12] were sent with extraordinary pomp. You would have to employ an enumerator to keep a tally of the footmen bearing the gift trays. Imagining how the bride's people would be harassed giving them baksheesh my mother and uncle laughed together heartily.

Mixing every conceivable high-pitched noise like bands, flutes, amateur concert and so on, and generally creating a rampaging barbaric cacophony, finally I arrived at the wedding venue. Festooned all over with rings, necklaces and ornaments, I looked like a jewellery shop put to auction, as though I was going to encounter my would-be father-in-law with a part of their would-be son-in-law's price clearly advertised all over.

Inside the wedding house, my uncle found little to his liking. The courtyard was too small to accommodate the groom's party, and the arrangements were absolutely dull and commonplace. Moreover, Shambhunath-babu himself was very cold in his reception: he did not demonstrate sufficient humility, apart from the fact that he spoke few words. There would have been an immediate showdown were it not for a lawyer friend of his—an obese, dark, hoarse, bald man with a shawl tied round his waist—who plied everyone from the groom's guardian down to the cymbalist of the concert party with effusive courtesies and gentle smiles of politeness, his hands joined and head nodding.

Immediately after I had been taken into the wedding assembly, Shambhunath-babu took my uncle aside into the next room. I did not know what they talked over, but Shambhunath-babu came back in a while and asked me to follow him.

This is what happened. Some people, though not all, have a certain objective in life. My uncle's was that by no means would he be cheated by anyone. He had suspected that the girl's father might dupe him over gold and once the marriage had been solemnised there would be no way of rectifying it. He had already had evidence of the man's niggardliness from such things as the wedding house, the gifts sent for the groom, even the baksheesh given to our men, and had therefore decided that as regards dowry, such a man's words should not be taken at face value. So he had brought along our family goldsmith with him. When I went into the next room, I found my uncle sitting on a cot and the goldsmith on the floor ready with his scales and touchstone.

Shambhunath-babu said to me, 'Your uncle says that right before the ritual begins he would like to have all the bride's ornaments examined. What do you say to this?' I kept silent, my head hung low.

'What can he have to say?' my uncle intervened. 'What I say is final'.

Shambhunath-babu looked at me and asked, 'Is that right then? What he says is final? You have no say in this?'

I slightly tilted my head to signify that I had no right whatever to interfere in such things.

'All right', he said. 'Then I must go and pluck the ornaments off the bride's body'. He got up.

My uncle said, 'What will Anupam do here? Let him go and sit in the assembly'.

'No, not in the assembly. He must stay right here', said Shambhunath.

After some time, bringing the ornaments wrapped in a piece of cloth, he displayed them on the cot. They were heirloom from his grandmother's time, in heavy, solid gold—not the tawdry things of these days. The goldsmith picked a piece and said, 'What's there to test? There's no alloy in it. Such pure gold is rarely used these days'. He pressed a thick bangle between his fingers to show that it bent.

My uncle at once made a list of the ornaments in his notebook in case one or the other from the tally was eventually missing. Making a quick calculation he found that in number, weight and price, they were far in excess of his demand.

There was a pair of earrings in the lot, which Shambhunath-babu handed to the goldsmith. 'Just test this one'.

'This is cheap foreign stuff', said the goldsmith. 'There's very little gold in it'.

Shambhunath-babu handed the earrings to my uncle and said, 'Keep it to yourself'. Taking them in his hand, my uncle recognised them as the very item they had gifted the bride for the blessing ritual.

My uncle blushed scarlet. He had been deprived of the pleasure of the poor man trying to cheat him and his refusing to be cheated; moreover, he had received something else in the bargain. With a very grave face, he said, 'Anupam, go sit in the assembly'.

Shambhunath-babu said, 'Not now. Come along; let me treat you to dinner first.'

'What are you saying? The wedding hour –' said my uncle.

'Don't worry for that', said Shambhunath-babu. 'Now please come.'

The man was a very innocent type, but inwardly, seemed to have considerable spirit. My uncle had to comply. The bridegroom's party too had their dinner. It was no elaborate menu, but the food was tasty and neatly served; everyone enjoyed it. When they had finished, Shambhunath-babu asked me to eat. 'How can that be?'

my uncle objected. 'How can a bridegroom take any food before the ritual is over?'

Ignoring whatever my uncle might have had to say in the matter, Shambhunath-babu turned to me and said, 'What do you say? Is there any harm in it?' As the embodiment of my mother's command in person, my uncle was present: going against him was impossible for me. I could not sit down to eat.

Shambhunath-babu then said to my uncle, 'I've given much trouble to you all. We are not rich people and could not make arrangements worthy of you. Please forgive us. It is already late. I would not like to give you any more trouble. Now then –'

'Well, of course, let's go to the venue', said my uncle, 'We are ready'.

'Shall I then send for your carriages?' asked Shambhunath-babu.

My uncle was stunned. 'Are you making a joke?'

'Aren't you the one to have made it already?' retorted Shambhunath. 'I have no wish to perpetuate the jocular relation.[13]'

My uncle stood stupefied, staring at him with his eyes wide open.

Shambhunath-babu said, 'I can't marry off my daughter into a family that thinks I can filch her ornaments.' He did not consider it necessary to speak a single word to me, because it had been proved that I was a nonentity.

What happened thereafter, I do not wish to recount. Smashing the chandeliers, wrecking the furniture and leaving a complete mess, the bridegroom's party finally trooped out of the venue.

On the way back home, there was no concert of band, flute and shehnai. The decorative mica lamps, after handing over charge to the stars in the sky, vanished forever no one knew where.

3

Everyone in the house was furious: a girl's father to have such hubris! The Kaliyug[14] was almost over! Everyone said, 'We'll see how he manages to get his daughter married'. Nevertheless, how was a man to be punished, one who was not dismayed by the prospect that his daughter would not get married?

I must be the lone bachelor in all Bengal to have been bundled out of a wedding venue by the bride's father himself. On the brow of so enviable a groom, what evil star could have branded so great a stigma amidst so much light, so much fanfare of trumpets? The bridegroom's party kept beating their foreheads, deploring, 'There was no marriage, and they tricked us into eating. Only if we could throw up the stomach, food and all right there, would our disappointment have been assuaged.' 'I must sue them for breach of contract and defamation.'

My uncle made great noises blustering like this. 'In that case', explained his well-wishers, 'whatever is still left of the tamasha[15] will have been completed.'

Obviously, I too had been very much angry. 'Somehow Shambhunath-babu is mortally harassed and eventually will fall at our feet!' Tweaking my hint of a moustache, this is what I kept praying for.

Alongside this dark current of rancour, flowed another, which was far from black. Ah, my heart had gone out to that unknown girl! I was still not able to drag it back howsoever I tried. Alas, she remained behind the wall; her brow decked with sandalwood paste, her body draped in a red sari, her face blushing in embarrassment, and her heart—well, how could I tell what state it was in? She embodied the fancy creeper of my dreamland that bowed down with the offerings of its vernal blossoms—gentle breezes wafted their fragrance and the murmur of their leaves. She was just a step away from me, when suddenly that small distance had merged into infinity.

How I had frequented Binu-dada's house every evening until now, pestering him for tips on the girl! As his language was laconic, each word of his description was like a spark that ignited my heart. I understood that the girl was amazingly beautiful, but neither did I see her with my mortal eyes nor did I see her photograph—everything remained forever vague. Not only did she not give herself unto me, she remained elusive in imagination, as well. Hence, my mind hovered with deep sighs like a phantom around the walls of that wedding venue.

Harish told me the girl had been shown my photograph. Well, she must have liked me; there was no reason why she would not. I believed that she still had the photograph with her put away in one of her boxes. Sitting behind closed doors on lonely afternoons, did she not take it out and have a look, loose strands of her hair falling on it as she leaned over to see? If someone tapped on her door, did she not hide it in her scented sari folds?

Days went by. It had been a year since. My uncle had lost his face to talk marriage again. My mother wished to start afresh only after people would have forgotten about my humiliation.

Meanwhile, I came to know that the girl's father had found a good match for her, but that she had vowed not to marry. I felt a tingle of ecstasy at the news, and sat down to build up my world of fantasy. I imagined she ate sparingly; evening came and she forgot to do up her hair. Her father looked at her face and wondered what she might be languishing for day after day. Suddenly one day, he came into her room and saw her eyes full of tears. 'Tell me, dear', he would say, 'what's the matter with you'. Quickly wiping her tears, she would say, 'Nothing is the matter, Baba'. She was the only child of her father, the most beloved in his life. So, when she drooped like a bud withering for lack of rain, her father could bear it no more. He forgot his pride and came at our door. And then? Then the black stream of vengeful resentment that flowed in my heart mutated into a serpent and hissed at me, 'That's fine! Let there be another wedding arrangement; let there be lights; let there be people from far and near. Then you can trample on your wedding crown and stomp out of the assembly with your retinue.' But the undercurrent, which was as pure as tears, formed into a swan that told me, 'Let me fly to her as I once did to Damayanti's[16] flower garden. Let me whisper the good news to your pining sweetheart.' And then? Then the night of sorrow ended; the first drops of rains fell; the withered flower peeped up. This time, the rest of the world stayed outside that wall, and only one person entered. And then? Then my story ends.

4

But the story did not end the way I would have liked. Let me recount it briefly until the point where it became never-ending.

My mother and I were going on a pilgrimage. I had to be her escort by default, because my uncle had yet not overcome his fixation about crossing the Howrah Bridge. I dozed off in the train; the rocking of the carriage set off snatches of incoherent dreams; its chugging sounded like a child's rattle in my mind. Suddenly I woke up at a certain station. In the dim light it also looked like a dream—everything was hazy and unfamiliar except only the stars. The pale lamps burning from tall posts served to create a mysterious ambience in which the world seemed strange and the things around it, distant. Inside the carriage, my mother was asleep under a lamp with a green screen under it. Our baggage was dumped carelessly like the confused litter of furniture in a dream, suspended between reality and hallucination in the green twilight.

Suddenly in that strange world, on that mysterious night, someone spoke, 'Hurry up; there is room in this carriage.'

It was music to my ears. You can appreciate how sweet the mother tongue sounds, when spoken by a girl, if only you come to hear it like this—suddenly, at an out-of-the-way place, at an unearthly hour. But this was a voice you could not just class as a female voice: once you heard it, you felt you have never heard anything like this before.

I have always held a person's voice as supreme. Beauty is no mean thing, of course. But I feel that the voice is the embodiment of all that is innermost and inexpressible in a person. At once, I opened the window and looked out, but could see nothing. The guard waved his one-eyed lamp from the dark platform, and the train began to move; I kept sitting at the window. I had no image before my eyes, but in my heart, I visualised the image of another heart. It was like this star-lit night that envelops one but remains inaccessible. Hail the music, the music of some unknown voice! In a moment, you have occupied the seat I have set apart for the ever-familiar. How amazingly perfect you are! You have blossomed like a flower on the fidgety time's ruffled heart, yet its waves have not knocked off a single petal, nor dented its infinite tenderness.

The train moved on, keeping time on the iron drum. I listened to my heart's song whose refrain was: there is room here. Room here? I wondered: is there indeed any room? Does one ever give another any room? Possibly not, because no one knows the other. Yet they do not know that this unfamiliarity is but a mist; it is an illusion; once it is dispelled, there is no end to knowing. O my mellifluous voice, am I not forever familiar with the heart, of which you are the exquisite form? Indeed, there is room; you asked me to come quick, and I have come quick, not a moment too late.

I slept badly that night. Almost at every station, I looked out of the window, lest the person I had not seen should get down that very night.

Next morning we were to change trains at a big station. We had first-class tickets and had hoped there would not be any rush. When we got down, we found that a general of the army was travelling by that train and his orderlies were waiting with his luggage on the platform. Soon the train arrived. I realised there was no hope of travelling first-class and was at a loss which coach to board with my mother. Every coach was crowded. As I was peeping inside from door to door, a girl called out to my mother from a second-class coach, 'Why don't you come here? There is room here.'

I was startled. It was the same strange sweet voice with the same refrain: there is room. Immediately we boarded the carriage. There was not enough time for the luggage to be lifted. There is none as incompetent as me in the world. The girl hauled up our goods from the heads of the porters, even as the train started to move. My camera was left behind, but I could not care less.

And then? I do not know what to write. There is an integral picture of bliss in my mind, it is in one piece—where shall I begin and where end? I do not like just to kill time by writing sentences endlessly.

Now I could see the music personified; she still was music to me. I looked at my mother and noticed that she too was gazing at her. The girl was sixteen or seventeen, but her sprouting youth did not seem to have encumbered her in body or mind. Her movements were easy; her brilliance, subdued; the chastity of her beauty, extraordinary. Everything about her was free and unimpeded.

I find myself quite inept at details. I cannot even say exactly what colour her sari was or what style she wore it. One thing is certain, however, that there was nothing about her dress or ornaments that might overshadow her. She overshadowed everyone around her. Like a white tuberose on its stalk, she stood tall even superseding the branch on which she bloomed. There were two or three very young girls with her; she talked and laughed incessantly with them. I was pretending to read a book with my ears turned in their direction. What I picked up were but exchanges of childish talk. The remarkable thing about it all was that it was uninhibited despite difference of age; easily and merrily, she had become a child herself with the children.

The children had some illustrated story books with them; they were urging her to read them a particular story from one of the books. They must have heard that story several times over, yet were so eager to hear it again. I realised why: every word was turned into gold by the golden wand of her mellifluous voice. Her body and her soul were brimming over with the joy of life; all her gestures and movements radiated life. When the girls heard her telling stories, they seemed to listen to her rather than to her story: the fountain of her life poured forth over their hearts. The radiance of her life made the sun's rays brighter for me that day. Nature that enveloped me with its sky seemed to be a universal extension of this girl's tireless and undiminished vitality. At the next station, she purchased some spiced snacks from a vendor and fell to eating without hesitation along with the girls, laughing and clamouring like children. I pitied myself for my fettered mind: why could I not overcome my awkwardness to ask the girl for a handful of the snacks; why could I not admit my greed by stretching out my hand?

My mother was in two minds about the girl: whether to like or dislike her. The girl showed not the least shyness in her conduct before me, a male. Moreover, she was eating so voraciously that my mother did not quite approve of it. Nevertheless, she did not regard her as a brazen girl, either. She decided that the girl had not received adequate training as she grew up. My mother was incapable of striking up a conversation with strangers; she was used to keeping aloof from company. Though she was very eager to know about the girl, she could not overcome her natural inhibition.

Meanwhile, the train had stopped at a junction station. A group of retainers, apparently of that general, were making as if to board the train. Every coach was fully occupied. They were peering particularly into ours; my mother shrank in fear and I too felt a little uneasy.

A while before the train's departure, a native railway official came and pegged two name-tags to our berths. 'These two seats are already reserved for two Englishmen,' he told me. 'You have to find place elsewhere.' I stood up immediately, but the girl took on the official, in Hindi, 'No, we're not going anywhere.'

'But you have to,' insisted the official arrogantly. When the girl still showed no signs of moving, he called in the stationmaster. An Englishman, he said to me, 'I'm sorry, but...'

This was enough for me to turn tail and shout for a coolie. But the girl took over, her eyes blazing. 'No, you must not move out of here. Stay put,' she told me. Then she turned to the stationmaster and said in English, 'It's a lie. There's no reservation.' She pulled off the tags and threw them on to the platform.

Meanwhile, a uniformed Englishman had arrived, orderly in tow. He had earlier motioned to the orderly to lift his luggage, but when he looked at the girl, heard her words and saw her determination, he apparently put off his move; he signalled to the stationmaster and took him aside to say something. The train was detained, and eventually left with an extra bogey attached. The girl and her company sat down to enjoy another round of spiced nuts while I pretended to see the landscape from the window to fight off my discomfiture.

The train reached Kanpur, and the girls were ready with their luggage to get off there. A Hindustani servant waiting at the station ran up to their help. My mother could not hold her reserve any longer. 'What's your name, dear?' she asked.

'Kalyani.'

My mother and I started together.

'And your father...?'

'He is a doctor here; his name is Shambhunath Sen.'

And they got down.

EPILOGUE

Only after defying my uncle's advice and ignoring my mother's command did I come to Kanpur. I happened to meet Kalyani and her father. To them I folded my hands and bowed my head. Shambhunath-babu relented. Kalyani said, 'I will not marry.'

I asked why.

She said, 'My mother's command.'

Good Heavens! Is there a maternal uncle on this side, too? I then realised she meant motherland. After that wedding fiasco, she had made the education of girls her mission.

But I could not give up hope. That tune, which was still ringing in my heart—which seemed to be the flute of another world coming from beyond my own world—beckoned me outside all worlds. And those words: 'there's room here'—that had seeped into my ears on that dark night, have remained my life's refrain. I was twenty-three then; now I am twenty-seven. I have not given up on her yet, but I have given up my uncle. Since I am my mother's only child, she could not give me up.

Do you think I hope ever to marry her? No, never. What sustains me is the melodious promise of an unknown voice of a single night: there's room here. Room there must be; where else shall I go? Thus, years roll by, but I am still here. I see her; I hear her voice, and I help her in some way when I can, and then my heart says: this is the room I desired. O my unknown woman, I have not yet known all there is to know of you; I never will. But I am fortunate, I have found my room after all.

Kartik 1321 (1914)

NOTES

1 Silk-cotton flower, showy but without smell.
2 A beautiful, small, red fruit with a foul taste.
3 The Bengali phrase translates literally to: Gajanan's younger brother in Annapurna's lap (see Glossary).
4 A subterranean river at Gaya in Bihar, rarely used in the original meaning; metaphorically, an undercurrent of any feeling.
5 In Bengali *gurguri,* hubble-bubble was the long-stemmed, sometimes silver-plated, variety of the hookah using costly brands of tobacco, and was a symbol of social status, compared to the ordinary variety offered to unimportant guests.
6 Lakshmi, goddess of fortune is supposed to carry a pitcher of wealth (see Glossary).
7 The Howrah Bridge spans the river Hooghly, on one bank of which is Calcutta, and on the other, Howrah town and the districts of

Howrah and Hooghly. Konnanagar is a small town in the latter.

8 According to Hindu mythology, the fourteenth son of Brahma, father of mankind and lawgiver; author of *Manusamhita,* the original Hindu code of conduct.

9 In confirmation of the betrothal.

10 Obviously, a reflection on the penny-pinching uncle who wanted to save money and avoid the usual hassles, going contrary to the custom (see Glossary).

11 A unit of measurement, very nearly equivalent to 11.6 gm.

12 *gayehalud* (see Glossary).

13 In Bengal, a married couple's fathers are traditionally held to bear such relationship.

14 *Kali Yug* (see Glossary).

15 Farcical show, cheap roadside entertainment.

16 Damayanti, princess of Vidharbha; legend has it that a swan carried the word of love from Nala, king of Nishadha, to Damayanti who was languishing for him in her garden, and they finally married. The episode is from the Mahabharata.

The Royal Mark
(*Rajtika**)

When Nabendushekhar[1] married Arunlekha[2], god *Prajapati* must have smiled wryly from the haze of the sacrificial fire. But alas, what is play to gods is not always amusing to us.

Nabendushekhar's father Purnendushekhar[3] was a celebrity in the British Raj. He had navigated the sea of life only by means of brisk salaams to arrive at the high desert shores of the title of Roy Bahadur. He had the resources to negotiate more arduous paths of honours; patronised by the Raj, he had eyed the rarer title of Raja. But on reaching his fifty-fifth year, all of a sudden he left for the world of no titles, his piteously longing eyes staring at the not-too-distant misty hilltop of that title. And his neck-joints, slackened by his infinitely many salaams, finally found rest on the pyre.

But as science says, energy is transformed or transported; it is never destroyed. The energy conceived in the salaam, which is the constant companion of the inconstant goddess of wealth, descended from the father's shoulders on to the son's, and Nabendu's novice head kept bobbing up and down before the British officials like a pumpkin on the waves.

Nabendu's first wife having died childless, he married a second time, into a family that had a history of a different nature. That family's eldest son Pramathanath was an object of love to his friends, of fond affection to his relations; his family and neighbours considered him worthy of emulation in every respect.

Pramathanath was formally a graduate, and practically, a man of astute judgement, but he cared neither for a lucrative job nor for a career in powerful writing. He did not enjoy much patronage either, simply because he used to give the British as wide a berth as they did him. As a result, Pramathanath was brobdingnagian only among his lilliputian friends and family; he totally lacked the skill to attract people outside his familiar domain.

This Pramathanath had once been in England for about three years. There he had been so fascinated by the courtesy of the English that forgetting India's suffering and humiliation, he returned home in an Englishman's attire.

Initially, his brothers and sisters had felt some embarrassment, and then in a couple of days, came round to say that no one would look as good in English dress as their elder brother. The vanity of English apparel gradually insinuated itself into the family psyche.

Pramathanath had planned while in England that once back home he would set up a unique example of himself in dealing with the English on equal terms. In his view, to think that one must demean oneself to socialise with Englishmen betrayed one's lack of self-respect, and moreover, laid an unfair imputation on the English as a whole.

By flaunting several testimonials obtained from eminent personalities in England, Pramathanath earned some standing among the Anglo-Indian circles, to the extent that he started enjoying the privilege of joining them, with his wife in tow, in their teas, dinners, sports, and amusemants. Drunk with the pride of his privileged status, he began to feel a slight tingling in his veins.

About this time, invited by the railway company to mark the inauguration of a new railway line, along with the Lieutenant-Governor, a number of dignitaries priding themselves on royal patronage rode down the new iron path. Pramathanath was among them as well.

On their return journey, a British police officer very disgracefully ejected the native personages on board a particular compartment. Pramathanath, who was dressed in English apparel, was also made to get down to avert any possible humiliation, when the officer said, 'Why are *you* getting up? *You* can sit.'

Pramathanath at first felt somewhat flattered by this selective honour. But after the train had steamed off, when from the edge of the grey grassless western field, the pale glow of the setting sun spread seemingly all over the country like a pitiful blush of shame, and when sitting alone he began to contemplate, looking fixedly from the window at the diffident face of Bengal hidden behind the cover of woods, his heart was sundered by self-reproach, and scalding tears kept rolling down his eyes.

An allegory[4] came to his mind: a donkey was pulling a chariot carrying an idol. Passers-by prostrating themselves before it in the dust were making *pronam*s to the idol, and the stupid donkey was thinking, 'It is me they are paying homage to.'

Pramathanath said to himself, 'My only difference with the donkey is that today I have realised that the respect that was shown was not to me but to the trappings on my shoulders.'

Coming back bome, Pramathanath called up the children of the house, lit a holy fire, and threw into it all his English garb one after another as offerings. The higher the flames leapt up, the more enthusiastically the boys kept dancing.

From that day onwards, he renounced all hobnobbing at English households—tea, toast and the rest--and retreated into the impregnable citadel of his domestic seclusion, while the other insulted dignitaries continued as before to doff their turbans at Englishmen's doors.

By an odd conjunction of stars, the hapless Nabendushekhar ended up marrying one of the younger daughters of this family. The girls were as much educated as they were good-looking. Nabendu thought: 'It's been a good bargain.'

But he lost no time getting down to prove: 'You have struck a good bargain in me.' Pretending as if this was a sheer mistake, inadvertently taking out letters from his pockets written once upon a time by different Englishmen to his father on different occasions, he used to pass them over to his sisters-in-law. When a sharp shrewd smile began to play around their delicate ruddy lips, like a glinting dagger drawn from a bright red velvet sheath, the poor fellow woke up to the gravity of the situation: he realised, 'It's been a great blunder.'

Labanyalekha, the eldest as well as the most beautiful and accomplished of his sisters-in-law, on a prescribed auspicious day, laid two pairs of English-cut boots anointed with vermilion in a niche in Nabendu's bedroom wall, and in front of them placing flowers, sandalwood paste, and two lighted lamps, completed the ritual by igniting incense in a thurible. As soon as Nabendu entered the room, two of his sisters-in-law holding him by the ear from two sides, said, 'Bow down to your tutelary deity. May you prosper with his blessings.'[5]

His third sister-in-law Kiranlekha having worked assiduously for long had embroidered a fabric in red thread with one hundred common English names like Jones, Smith, Brown, Thomson, etc., and one day with great ceremony presented it as a *namabali* to Nabendu.

The fourth, Shashankalekha, still too young to be counted, chipped in, 'Brother, I'll make you a rosary, so you can mention the names of Englishmen in your prayers.'

Her elder sisters snubbed her, 'Don't you talk like a matron.'

Nabendu felt peeved as well as embarrassed, yet could not give up the company of his sisters-in-law, especially because of the eldest one who was indeed very beautiful. Of honey and thorns, she had equal measure; both the intoxication and the piquancy of her company lingered permanently in the mind. An insect with injured wings keeps buzzing angrily, and yet, goes round and round blindly to death.

Eventually, under inexorable infatuation with the sisters-in-law's company, Nabendu began to openly deny his fascination for Englishmen's favours. Thus, when he went to pay court to *Barosaheb*[6], he would tell them, 'I'm going to hear Suren Banerjee[7]'s speech.' When he went to Sealdah station to receive *Mejosaheb*[6a] who was returning from Darjeeling, he would leave the message, 'I'm off visiting my *Mejomama*[6b].'

It was a critical situation for the wretched fellow trying to sail by two boats: the sahib's and the sister-in-law's. The sisters vowed to themselves, 'We'll not rest until we have wrecked that other boat of yours.'

There were rumours that on the Queen's ensuing birthday, Nabendu would be designated Roy Bahadur, the first step on the flight of stairs to the celestial world of honours. But the cowardly fellow could not bring himself to break that euphoric news of probable decoration to his sisters-in-law; however, one bright lunar autumn evening, under the unsettling spell of moonlight, in an ecstatic mood, he ended up revealing it to his wife. The next day, in daylight, his wife went by palanquin to her elder sister's house and started a tearful wail over the matter. 'So where's the harm in it?' Labanya said, 'After all your husband won't be growing a tail by becoming a Roy Bahadur. What makes you so ashamed?'

Arunlekha kept protesting, 'No, sister, no. Let them call me anything but a Roy Bahadur's wife.'

The inside story is that one of her acquaintances, Bhutnath-babu, was a Roy Bahadur, that's why she was especially prejudiced against the title[8]. Labanya assured her, 'Well, you don't have to worry about that.'

Labanya's husband Nilratan worked at Buxar. From there, at the close of autumn, Nabendu received an invitation from Labanya. An exhilarated Nabendu lost no time to take the train to Buxar. When he boarded the train, his left side did not twitch, but this merely proves that it is nothing but a baseless superstition that the twitching of one's left side forebodes an impending peril.[9]

Blossoming with the mixed pink and pallor of health and beauty heralded by the north Indian winter, Labanyalekha was sparkling with ripples and laughter like the ever joyous *kaash* fields thriving on quiet river shores under the pellucid autumn sky. Upon Nabendu's bemused face a full-bloomed *malati* creeper, as it were, was showering sprays of cold glistening dewdrops of an early winter morning.

A cheerful mind and bracing climate cured Nabendu of his dyspepsia. Powered by the ecstasy of good health, rapture of beauty, and thrill of tender ministrations at the hands of his sister-in-law, he seemed to be walking on air leaving the earth. The brimming Ganga, as if embodying the uncontrollable turbulence in his mind, flowed past their garden riotously with intense passion for an unknown destination.

On his way back from a stroll on the riverbank, the bracing sunlight of the winter morning satiated Nabendu's whole being as if with the warmth of a lover's embrace. Thereafter, on return, he used to run errands for his sister-in-law's cherished cookery, only betraying his ignorance and clumsiness at every step, but the infatuated tyro did not show the least inclination to remove them gradually through practice and attention, because he could never have enough of her scowls and reprimands which he took pains to earn with his contrived blunders. Proportioning the spices, draining the rice-water, controlling the oven so as not to burn the curry, and so on: striving to prove that in any department of cookery he was as incompetent, incapable and helpless as a new-born baby, he used to enjoy his sister-in-law's condescending smiles and amused reproofs to his heart's content.

At midday meals, with the driving hunger on the one hand and the solicitous sister-in-law on the other, his own avidity and a dear one's eagerness, the excellence of cooking and the charming ministrations of the cook in conjunction, he found it hard to keep within gastronomic limits.

Even in the simple card games which they used to play after lunch, Nabendu could never prove his talents. He would cheat, peek, snatch and wrangle, but still could not win. Though he did not win, he would forcibly deny defeat and thereby earn her rebukes everyday. Even so, the rascal was completely indifferent to self-rectification.

Only in one matter, he had redeemed himself completely: he had forgotten for the time being that the sahib's patronage was the ultimate aim of life. Now he realised wholeheartedly how happy and proud it felt to be loved and respected by one's kith and kin.

Apart from that, he seemed to find himself in a new climate. Labanya's husband Nilratan, despite being a senior advocate in the court, never made courtesy calls on sahibs and officials, which was a talking point in his fraternity. He would tell them, 'Why should I do that, brother? In case they do not return my courtesies, can I take back what I have given them? Only because the desert sand is shining white, can one be happy sowing it? One would sow even black soil if it promised to yield crops.'

Nabendu found himself in this circle, heedless of the consequences. The budding chances of his becoming a Roy Bahadur continued to thrive spontaneously on the soil prepared by his father's endeavours as well as his own; no fresh watering or manuring was necessary. Nabendu had gifted a whole race course made for the British at a huge cost in a particular town of their choice.

Meanwhile, the annual session of the Indian National Congress fell due. Nilratan got a letter asking him to collect subscriptions.

One day, when Nabendu was playing cards with Labanya, in a carefree happy mood, Nilratan came in, bill-book in hand, and said, 'Please sign for your subscription.' Nabendu went pale, as he was wont to in such situations. Labanya hurriedly interposed, 'Be careful! Don't do that. Your race course will be a complete washout.'

'As if I don't sleep at night worrying over it!' Nabendu said boastfully.

Nilratan assured him, 'Your name won't be published in newspapers.'

Labanya said, 'Even so, you shouldn't, in case during conversation –' She pretended to be worried and serious.

Nabendu retorted with some irritation, 'My name won't wear out if it is published in newspapers.'

With this, he snatched away the bill-book from Nilratan's hand and signed up for a thousand rupees at one go, still hoping that after all it won't come out in the newspapers.

Labanya slapped her forehead and wailed, 'What have you done?'

'Why, what wrong have I done?' Nabendu said haughtily.

'A railway guard at Sealdah station[10], an assistant at Whiteaway's[11], the coachman at Hart Brothers[12]—supposing such officials take offence and do not come to drink champagne when you invite them home during the *puja*? Supposing they don't give you a pat on the back when they come across you?'

'In that case, going home I'll feel mortified,' Nabendu said indignantly.

A few days after this, Nabendu was reading the paper over his morning tea, when he stumbled upon a letter in which the correspondent, signed 'X', had thanked him profusely for his subscription to the Congress, and admitted his inability to estimate the extent to which his membership had enhanced the Congress.

Pooh! Enhancing the Congress! O heaven-borne father Purnendushekhar! Did you bring this wretch upon the hallowed soil of India only to enhance the Congress?

With sorrow, however, there is promise of happiness as well. That Nabendu was no ordinary man, that the Anglo-Indian community on the one hand, and the Congress on the other were fishing for him avidly with unblinking eyes on the float, each trying to haul him up on to its side were certainly not something to be kept secret.

A smiling Nabendu therefore took the paper to Labanya. Feigning surprise, as if quite ignorant about the letter, Labanya said, 'My goodness, I see he has divulged everything! Aha! Who could be such an enemy of yours? Let his quill be infested with mite, his ink clogged with sand, his paper eaten away by moth.' Nabendu laughed and said, 'Enough! Do not curse him any more. I forgive my enemy and wish him a gold quill and gold inkpot.'

Two days later, an anti-Congress English newspaper edited by an Englishman reached Nabendu by post. It had published a rejoinder to the earlier letter, written by someone signed *One Who Knows.* The correspondent wrote that people who knew Nabendu could never believe such libellous gossip about him. It was just as impossible for Nabendu to join the Congress as it was for a leopard to change its spots. Babu Nabendushekhar was a man of considerable substance. He was neither an unemployed hanger-on nor a briefless barrister. He was not one who had just touched England, ludicrously aped the dress and manners of the English, then trying to strut proudly in their society had finally come back upset and let down. So why after all should he –? etc. etc.

O heaven-borne father Purnendushekhar! You died only after winning such recognition and such credibility with the British!

This letter too deserved to be fanned out like a peacock's tail before his sister-in-law: it had made the point that Nabendu was no obscure, inconsequential, miserable wretch, but a man of worth.

Labanya had once again to pretend surprise. She said, 'Goodness, who is this dearest friend of yours to have written this time round? Which ticket collector, or tannery agent, or drummer in a band, pray?'

Nilratan joined in, 'After all, this one you ought to protest.'

'What's the point?' retorted Nabendu in a dignified tone, 'Must I protest against whatever anyone says?'

Labanya burst into an uproarious laughter.

'What makes you laugh so much?' asked an embarrassed Nabendu. In reply, Labanya exploded in a fresh fit of hysterical laughter, the full-bloomed vine of her youthful body throbbing violently.

Doused all over with squirts of banter, Nabendu was thoroughly discountenanced. Somewhat offended, he said, 'You think I am afraid to protest?'

'Not at all,' said Labanya, 'I find you have not yet given up trying to salvage your race course of many hopes and promises. Well, while there is life, there is hope.'

'You think that is the reason I am not willing to write?' Looking very angry, he sat down with pen and ink. But what he wrote did not quite reflect the tone of his anger, and so it fell on Labanya and Nilratan to revise it. The process now looked somewhat like the way *luchi*s[13] are made: Nabendu made cool, soft dough, leavened with water and ghee, and rolled out as flat as possible; his two assistants at once deep-fried it until it was crisp, brown and puffed-up.

This was the revised text: a kin turned an adversary is more dangerous than an external enemy. The Pathans or the Russians are not so potentially dangerous enemies of the Indian government as the arrogant Anglo-Indian community. They are the most formidable impediment to a friendly bond between the government and the people. The Anglo-Indian newspapers are like thorns strewn across the highway laid by the Congress to an amicable understanding between the king and the subjects. And so on.

Nabendu had a sneaking feeling of apprehension, yet felt rather delighted at times, thinking, 'After all, it's been an excellent piece.' Such good writing was beyond his capacity.

For quite some time after this, a storm of protests and counter-protests raged in various newspapers, and Nabendu's controversial subscribing to and joining the Congress became a talking point everywhere.

A desperate Nabendu now carried himself like a very brave patriot in his sister-in-law's circle. Labanya laughed quietly to herself and said, 'Your acid test[14] is yet to come.'

One morning before his bath Nabendu, having just finished rubbing oil on his chest, was manoeuvring to oil the inaccessible parts of his back, when the servant brought him a card with the magistrate's name written on it. Labanya was watching the fun secretly with gleeful curious eyes.

It was out of the question meeting the magistrate with an oil-smeared body: Nabendu kept fidgeting unnecessarily like a marinated climbing fish waiting to be fried. He rushed through his bath within minutes, and hastily putting on his clothes, ran to the drawing room. The servant told him, 'The sahib waited for a long time, and then left.' How much of the sin of this outrageous falsehood is to be apportioned to Labanya, and how much to the servant is an intricate problem of moral philosophy. Just as a lizard's severed tail writhes involuntarily, Nabendu's agitated heart kept thrashing about inwardly. He could not eat or sleep peacefully all day.

After wiping all traces of her secret laugh completely from her face, Labanya said, 'Whatever has happened to you today? You aren't ill, are you?'

Forcing a smile Nabendu hazarded a reply appropriate to the situation, 'What illness would enter your domain? You are my cure-all physician[15].'

But the next moment, his smile had vanished. He thought: on the one hand, I subscribed to the Congress, wrote a strong letter in newspapers. On top of that, when the magistrate himself came to see me, I kept him waiting. I don't know what he might be making of the whole mess.

'O father, O Purnendushekhar! By a strange quirk of fate, I have been made out to be what I am not!'

Next day, decked out in his best clothes, his watch in his pocket with a pendant chain and an imposing turban on his head, Nabendu went out of the house. 'Where are you going?' Labanya asked him.

'I have some urgent work.'

Labanya said nothing.

As soon as he brought out his visiting card at the entrance of the sahib's residence, the latter's orderly said, 'You can't see him now.'

Nabendu took out two rupees from his pocket. The orderly made a cursory salaam and said, 'There are five of us.' Nabendu at once gave him a ten-rupee note.

The sahib called out his name. In his morning gown and slippers, the sahib was then busy reading and writing. Nabendu made him a salaam. The magistrate motioned to him to sit down and without so much as lifting his face from the papers, said, 'What do you have to say, babu?'

While fingering his watch-chain, Nabendu said in a cringing, tremulous voice, 'It was so kind of you to have gone to visit me yesterday. But –'

Knitting his brows and raising one eye from his papers, the sahib said, 'Went to visit you! *What nonsense are you talking, babu?*'

Nabendu kept saying, '*Beg your pardon!* It was a mistake. I must have got mixed up,' and somehow made his exit, drenched in sweat. That night, as he lay in bed, one single line kept coming into his ears like a chant heard in a distant dream, '*Babu, you are a howling idiot!*'

On his way home, he convinced himself that only to express his displeasure did the magistrate deny that he had come visiting him. He uttered in his mind, 'Mother Earth, split asunder.'[16] But the Mother refusing to comply with his request, he reached home safe.

He came to Labanya and said, 'I went to buy rosewater for my native home.'

Even as he said this, six liveried bailiffs from the Collectorate had arrived. After making salaams, they kept standing silently with smiling faces.

Labanya said jocosely, 'I hope they haven't come to arrest you for subscribing to the Congress?'

The bailiffs grinning from ear to ear said, 'Baksheesh, Babu Sahib!'

Coming out of the next room, Nilratan said petulantly, 'Baksheesh! What for?'

The men, still grinning, said, 'Because babu went to see the magistrate.'

Labanya said with a smile, 'Has the magistrate been selling rosewater these days? Why, he was never known to deal in such cool things!'

Trying to reconcile rosewater with his meeting the magistrate, what gibberish the poor wretch muttered was beyond anybody's comprehension.

Nilratan said, 'Nothing has happened for baksheesh. You won't get any.' The last words he said in Hindi.

Nabendu hesitantly took out a currency note from his pocket and said, 'They are poor people. What's the harm in giving them something?'

Taking away the note from his hand, Nilratan said, 'There are poorer people on earth. I'll give it to them.'

Having been denied the opportunity to appease even the ghoulish retinue of the angry Shiva[17], Nabendu found himself in a bit of a spot. When the sepoys left casting angry looks, Nabendu looked back in abject pity, appealing silently, 'Fellows, you know it was not my fault.'

The Calcutta session of the Congress was due shortly. Nilratan came to Calcutta with his wife to attend it. Nabendu too returned with them.

As soon as he reached Calcutta, the partymen just mobbed him and started a frenzied activity. There was no end to the honours, ovations and flatteries. Everybody said, 'If leaders like you do not take up the national duty, the country can never come out of the rut.' Nabendu could not deny the truth of it, and in the hurly-burly became a leader of the nation. When he set foot on the dais in the conference, he was given a standing ovation and was cheered uproariously in the alien British chorus of *Hip, hip hurrah.* Our motherland blushed scarlet to the roots of her ears.

The Queen's birthday came and went with Nabendu's prospect of the Roy Bahadur appellation disappearing like a fast receding mirage.

That evening Labanyalekha invited Nabendu to a ceremonial dinner. She presented him with a new set of clothes, and with her own hands, painted a mark of red sandalwood paste on his forehead. Each of his sisters-in-law placed a garland round his neck. Dressed in scarlet, Arunlekha was then sparkling in her jewellery, joviality, and blushes from behind the curtain. Pressing a thickly set wreath into her perspiring hands frigid from bashfulness, her sisters egged her on. But she was in no way to be persuaded, and that principal garland kept waiting secretly for Nabendu's neck in the privacy of night. His sisters-in-law told Nabendu, 'Today we have anointed you king. Nobody else in India can earn this honour.'

Whether this coronation was consolation enough for Nabendu was known only to his heart and the One who abides there, but we are entirely doubtful about this. We firmly believe that he will earn the title of Roy Bahadur in any case before his death. We also believe that the Englishman and the Pioneer will definitely mourn his death in one voice in their obituary notices. Till then *Three cheers* for Babu Purnendushekhar. *Hip, hip, hurrah!*

Ashwin 1305 (1898)

NOTES

The English words in italics appear in the original text.

* Rajtika: Derived from Sanskrit *tilaka,* 'tika' means mark; a spot or mark of sandalwood paste worn on the forehead as a sign of allegiance to a particular sect or creed, or of a status like that of a king as in this story.

1 *Nabendu* is crescent, and *shekhar* is crown; hence 'crowned with the crescent': Lord Shiva.

2 Charioteer of the sun; the crimson sun at dawn.

3 The full moon, hence crowned with the full moon.

4 The allegory may have inspired Tagore's short poem on a similar theme: *Rathjatra lokaranya maha dhumdham / Bhaktera lutaye pathe karichhe pranam / Path bhabe ami deb, rath bhabe ami / Murti bhabe ami deb, haase antarjami.*

5 The Bengali *padabriddhi* means 'an enhancement of rank', that is, a promotion or lift in one's career; it can, as a pun, also mean 'increase of feet'. Nabendu's loyalty to the British was comparable to that of a domestic quadruped; the second meaning seems not improbable as indicated by the two pairs of shoes.

6, 6a & 6b The seniormost official; the official second in hierarchy; second eldest maternal uncle, respectively.

7 Surendranath Banerjee, one of the founder-members of the Indian National Congress, and a formidable orator; celebrated more for oratory than for political acumen.

8 *Bhutnath* is another name for Lord Shiva who drinks, and roams the burning ghats with his retinue; *bhut* means 'ghouls and spirits', and *nath* means 'master or lord'; since ghouls are the retainers of Shiva, the association of his name to Roy Bahadur was repugnant to Nabendu's wife.

9 The Bengali superstition is that when the left side twitches in a man it is a bad omen; and the right side, in a woman.

10 One of the two terminal railway stations in eastern India, the other being Howrah.

11 Whiteaway, a famous departmental store in Calcutta.

12 A stable company, which accommodated and hired out horses and coaches.

13 A roti-like preparation of the refined flour of wheat leavened with and deep-fried in synthetic or animal ghee; a special item of breakfast or dinner, and occasionally, to entertain guests with.

14 *Agnipareeksha,* ordeal by fire, was enforced on Sita to prove her virtue in the context of her abduction by Ravana, towards the end of the Ramayana.

15 In the text, Nabendu hails Labanya as *Dhanwantarini,* the feminine of *Dhanwantari,* the physician of the gods; the word has come to mean 'a never-failing healer', and hence to imply utmost faith in someone as a physician.

16 This is what the earth did to shelter Sita during her ordeal (See Notes to the story The Exercise Book).

17 The magistrate is likened to Shiva, and his retinue to that of Shiva.

The Wife's Letter
(*Streer Patra*)

My submission at your lotus feet–

We have been married for fifteen years now, but never once have I written a letter to you. All along under the same roof, you have heard numberless words, and so have I; there has never been an occasion to write a letter.

Today, I have come on a pilgrimage to Puri; you are stuck up with your work at office. You relate as inherently to Calcutta as a snail inheres in its shell; the city has impregnated itself into your being. That is why you did not apply for leave from office. God must have willed so; He granted my prayer for leave.

I am the second daughter-in-law[1] in your joint family. Today, standing on the seashore, I feel for the first time in fifteen years that I have another relation as well with my world and the Lord of the world. This has encouraged me to write this letter; this is no letter from the second daughter-in-law of your family.

In my infancy, when no one except the Lord who had ordained my relation with your family should have been aware of that eventuality, my brother and I together fell ill with typhoid. I survived, but my brother did not. The girls of the neighbourhood kept saying, 'Isn't Mrinal a female? That's why she survived; would any male have been spared?' *Yama* is a past master of the art of stealing; he eyes only precious things.

I am not going to die any time soon. I will presently explain why.

A distant maternal uncle of yours came with your friend Nirad to inspect the bride. I was twelve then. We lived in a remote village, where jackals howled even at day. To reach it from the railway station, one had to cover nearly fourteen miles by hackney carriage and another three of dirt track by palanquin. What harassment it must have been to them that day! On top of that, there was the meal—East Bengal style—your uncle is yet to forget the farce of it.

Your mother always insisted that her *mejobou's* beauty must make up for *barobou's* lack of it. Otherwise, you would never have taken the trouble of going as far as that village. In Bengal, has anyone ever to search out enlarged spleen, dilated liver, gastric colic and brides? They visit you on their own, refusing to go.

My father waited with bated breath and mother kept telling the name of *Durga*. What could a rustic worshipper offer to appease an urban deity? They had pinned their hope on their daughter's beauty. But the daughter, practically, took no pride in that beauty: whatever price the person who had come to see her would stipulate was her value. This is the reason why women never get rid of their diffidence, whatever their beauty or accomplishment.

This anxiety of my parents, indeed of the entire neighbourhood, bore down on my heart. It seemed all the light of the sky and forces of the world were working as footmen for the two examiners by holding up a twelve-year-old country girl firmly to two pairs of probing eyes; I had nowhere to hide.

The flute poured out strains leaving the sky inundated with its tearful wails: I stepped into your house. Even after close scrutiny of my imperfections, the crowd of housewives acknowledged in one voice that overall I was beautiful. My elder sister-in-law became crestfallen to hear the verdict. But I wonder what if any was my need for beauty. If beauty was something an ancient pundit were to make out of *Ganga* silt, it would have been adored; but it is something born purely out of Lord's own pleasure, so it has no value in your righteous world.

That I had beauty did not take you long to forget, but what all of you had to remember at every step was that I do have intelligence. And that one thing is so exceptionally natural for me that even after slogging through fifteen years of domesticity, it has survived until today. My mother was particularly concerned about this good brain of mine: for women it is rather an encumbrance. If you are required to abide by constraints, yet want to go by your brains, you must meet with disaster. But what can I do anyway? God has unwittingly given me intelligence far in excess of what is just enough for a woman of your family. To whom do I return the extra bits now? All of you have been abusing me day and night as a female-elder-uncle[2]. Harsh words are the sole comfort for deficient people. I forgive them.

I had one thing outside the pale of domesticity, which none of you ever knew. I used to write poems secretly. Trash or ash, whatever it was, the walls of women's quarters had not encompassed it. There I found my freedom; there I was myself. Whatever qualities in me overshadowed the stereotype of a mejobou you never liked, nor did you recognise it. That I was a poet you could not discover even in fifteen years.

Of the first memories of your house, what is most prominent is the cattle-shed. It was next to the stairs leading to the inner quarters; except for the slice of courtyard in front, the cattle had little room to move about. In a corner of that yard, there lay the wooden trough for their fodder. In the morning while the servant was heavily busy with other chores, the hungry cows kept licking and chewing the insides of the trough, leaving it deeply dented. My heart wept for them. As I was a country girl, the two cows and their three calves seemed to be the only relatives I knew in the whole city when I first came to your house. When I was a new bride, I would often starve myself to feed them secretly. When I grew up, noticing my fondness for cows my jesting partners started expressing doubts about my lineage.

My only daughter died immediately after birth; she had almost taken me as well with her. If she had lived to this day, she herself would have brought me whatever is great, whatever is true in life; from just a daughter-in-law, I would have been promoted to a mother. A mother is universal, even as she belongs to a particular family. I suffered the pangs of motherhood, never got the liberty it brings.

I remember how the visiting English doctor was surprised to see the women's quarters, and annoyed at the plight of the lying-in room, even rebuked you. There is a facade of elegance to the outer house with a small garden in the front and no dearth of frills and furniture in the rooms. In contrast, the entire inner house looks like the reverse side of a woollen garment: there is no decency, no grace, and no decoration. There lamps burn dimly; air creeps in furtively; rubbish in the courtyard refuses to budge; stains on the walls and floors stay on indelibly. However, the doctor must have made one mistake: he had supposed that this was a constant suffering. Far from it. Neglect is something like ash; while it covers a smouldering fire, it keeps the heat from permeating through it. When self-respect is on the wane, no neglect seems unfair. That is why it causes no suffering. That is why women are ashamed even to acknowledge their sorrow. So, if this is your decree that a woman must suffer, she is best left neglected as far as possible; any care only aggravates the pain of sorrow.

In whatever manner you may have kept me, even the perception of sorrow, if any, never occurred in my mind: in my labour room, death stood staring right behind my head; there was not a trace of fear in my mind. What precious thing is our life after all that we have to fear death? The ones who recoil from death are those whose attachment to life has been fortified by comfort and care. If Yama had snatched at me that day, I would have been yanked off, roots and all, like a clump of grass from loose soil. A Bengali woman, as you know, seeks death at every breath;

but what glory is there in such death? For us it is a shame; so easy is death to us!

My daughter, like the evening star, had disappeared soon after rising briefly. I went back to my routine work, cattle and the rest. Life would have rolled on just like that until the end, and this letter would have been totally redundant. But then, a tiny wind-borne seed germinates into a peepul tree in a brick-house and eventually ruptures the rib case of bricks and wood; a speck of life flew in from somewhere into my settled household. Thereafter began the cracks.

After the death of her widowed mother, when my elder sister-in-law's sister Bindu, thrown out by her tyrannous cousins, found refuge with her sister in our house, all of you must have wondered whence did this nuisance come? It is my wretched nature, and you know I just can't help it: I felt everyone of you was getting irritated, and so my mind went all out to stand by the homeless girl. To take shelter with strangers against their will: what a disgrace it is! How could I have turned away one who under compulsion had to acknowledge even so much of dishonour?

Then I noticed the plight of my elder sister-in-law. She had given her sister shelter out of sheer pity. However, when she saw her husband was demurring, she began to pretend that the girl was a great nuisance to her personally, whom she would have liked to get rid of, to her great relief. She could not summon up the courage to show her affection openly to her orphaned sister. She is a devoted wife.

Her quandary was even more painful. When I found that she demonstratively arranged the coarsest of food and clothes for Bindu, and engaged her in the meanest of chores, I felt not only pain, but shame as well. To everyone she was anxious to prove that our family got Bindu fortuitously at a bargain price, who turned out work in volumes, but cost very little.

My elder sister-in-law's paternal side had little to boast of except its lineage; they had neither wealth nor good looks. How importunately they pleaded with my father-in-law for her marriage into your family, well, you know everything. She has always considered this as a grievous wrong done to this family. For this reason, she has demeaned herself in every matter as far as possible to occupy the barest minimum of space in your family.

But this honest example of hers is an embarrassment for women like us. I cannot lower myself on every point so abjectly. What to my mind is good I am not the kind to come round for anyone's sake to acknowledge as bad. You too had enough proof of this.

Into my room I drew Bindu for shelter. My sister-in-law remarked I was going to spoil the girl of a poor family, and went around complaining that I had brought about a disaster of sorts. But I know for sure that she felt quite relieved: the onus of any fault now lay squarely on me; at the same time, getting me to show her sister the affection she herself could never have shown, she found a great deal of comfort.

My sister-in-law always tried to understate Bindu's age by a couple of years. But privately speaking, her age was no less than fourteen. As you know, she was so plain looking that if she had cracked her head by falling on the floor, people would have been anxious for any damage to the floor, rather than her. Naturally, in the absence of her parents, there was no one to take the responsibility of her marriage. That apart, how many had the fortitude to marry her?

Bindu came to me, very nervously though: as if, I would shrink from her touch. As if she was not supposed to be born, she was always careful to avoid brushing against anyone or meeting anyone's eyes. In her father's house, her cousins were not willing to spare even a corner where an unwanted thing could lie. Unwanted refuse easily finds space around the house because people forget them. But an unwanted woman who is unwanted in the first instance and moreover difficult to forget has no place even in a dump. It is not as if Bindu's cousin brothers are by any means indispensable to the world. But they are doing fine. So when I brought Bindu into my room, her heart began to tremble. Her fear made me feel sad. I showered her with profuse love to convey that there was a little space for her in my own room.

But my own room was by no means my sole preserve and so my task was not easy. After a couple of days, she developed a rash, perhaps a heat rash, or something else. All of you said it was small pox: it had to be, because she was Bindu. An inexperienced doctor from the neighbourhood said he could not fix it before observing for one or two days. But who was prepared to bear that one-or-two-day wait? Bindu was dying of shame for her illness in the first place. I declared, 'If it is small pox, let it be; I'll move with her to the labour room. No one else need be bothered.' At this, when all of you were furious with me, and even my sister-in-law putting on a pretence of great annoyance, proposed to have the wretched girl despatched to hospital, the rash disappeared completely. You were now even more concerned. You said the pox must have been suppressed: it had to be, because she was Bindu.

One great benefit from growing up in neglect is, it makes one almost ageless and imperishable: there is no question of any sickness; the highways to death are permanently closed. So her sickness just played a joke on her; nothing happened. But one thing was clear enough: to give shelter to a most inconsequential person was a most difficult thing to do. One who most needs shelter most faces the obstacles.

When Bindu had overcome her fear of me, she got into another fix. She began to love me so comprehensively that I was quite alarmed. Such manifestation of love I have never seen in real life; fiction of course has such stuff and that too between man and woman. That I had beauty I had practically no reason in many years to remember consciously; now so long after, it fell to this ordinary-looking girl to make all sorts of fuss over that beauty. Her eyes never stopped gazing at my face; she would say, 'Didi, nobody except me has seen this face of yours.' She would very much resent my ever doing my own hair: she was exceedingly fond of caressing my masses of hair with both hands. Except when going out on invitation, as you know, I hardly at all needed any make-up. But

Bindu would keep pestering me until I agreed to do some. The poor girl was just crazy about me.

In the inner precincts of your house, there is nowhere an inch of land. A *gaab* tree has somehow grown by the compound wall near the gutter in the north. The day its new leaves turned a dazzling red heralded the advent of spring on earth. In my household, when the heart of that neglected girl took on a similar colouring, I realised that in the realm of the heart as well there is something like a spring breeze—a breeze from some undefined paradise, not from the turn of the lane.

Bindu's unbearably passionate love had nearly driven me mad. Though I was angry with her at times, nevertheless, through this love of hers I discovered an aspect of my identity which I had never seen before, and that was my free aspect.

Yet, a girl like Bindu being so much pampered seemed an egregious excess to you. There was no end of complaints and frayed tempers because of this. When my armlets were stolen from my room, you were not ashamed to throw a hint that Bindu might have had a hand in it. When the police started house-to-house raids during the Swadeshi movement[3], you people simply suspected Bindu to be a female informer in the payroll of the police; the only proof was she was Bindu.

The maidservants of your house were reluctant to do any personal chore for her. If they were ordered to do something for her, she was such a girl she shrank in embarrassment herself. On this score alone, my expenditure on her went up: I employed a maidservant especially for her, which you did not like. The sort of clothes I gave her to wear made you so angry that you went on to stop my allowance. From next day, I started wearing five-quarter-rupee-a-pair coarse, unbleached, mill-made dhotis[4]. Furthermore, I forbade Moti's mother to pick up the dishes after my meals. I went personally to the courtyard washery feeding the calves with the leftovers and then washing my dishes myself. When you suddenly found me doing this one day, you were not too pleased. You don't necessarily have to please me, and I do willy-nilly have to please you: this home truth I have never really learned.

Meanwhile, as your anger was growing, so was Binu's age, regardless. You got abnormally flustered about that normal phenomenon. One thing I still find puzzling: why did you not throw her out in the first place? I feel certain that you all fear me, even if not openly; you simply cannot resist admiring me in your minds for the brains God has gifted.

Finally, when you failed in your capacity as humans to get rid of her, you fell back on Lord *Prajapati*. A bridegroom was found for Bindu. My sister-in-law said, 'Thank God, the fair name of our family is saved.'

I knew nothing about the groom; you said he was good in every respect. Bindu fell at my feet weeping, 'Didi, what's the point of my sort of girl getting married?' I tried to persuade her. 'Have no worry, Bindu. As far as I know, your groom is a good man.'

'If so,' said Bindu, 'What is there in me to make him like me?'

The groom's family, as you know, did not even mention inspection of the bride, to the great relief of her sister.

But there was no stopping Bindu's weeping; I knew how excruciatingly it tormented her. I had fought many battles for her in the family, but to demand her marriage to be cancelled proved beyond my courage. Besides, what were my resources to demand it? What would happen to her when I was dead? A girl in the first place, and then a dark girl: whose home she was going to make and what fate awaited her were better not worried about.

Bindu said, 'Didi, there are still five days to the wedding. Shall I not die in the meanwhile?' I gave her a good rebuke, but my good Lord knows that if she could have died an easy death, I would have felt relieved.

The day before the wedding, Bindu went to her sister and said, 'Didi, throw me into the cattle-shed; tell me whatever to do. I beg of you, Didi, do not throw me away in this manner.'

Her sister had been shedding secret tears for the last few days and so she did on that day. But emotions are not all that matter; there are scriptures as well. 'Don't you know, Bindi[5],' she said feelingly, 'Husband is the be-all and end-all to a woman; her fate, her salvation, her everything. If it is your lot to suffer, there is no averting it.' The bottom line is that there was absolutely no way in any direction: Bindu must marry; come what may thereafter.

I had wished the wedding to take place in our house[6]; but you declared it had to be performed in the groom's house, because that was their family custom. I realised that if your family had to incur expenses on something like Bindu's marriage that would be terribly upsetting for your family deity. Therefore, I had to go silent. However, one thing I did which you do not know. I would have liked to tell my sister-in-law, but refrained, because she would have collapsed in fear: I had decorated Bindu with part of my jewellery. Perhaps her sister had noticed it, but she overlooked it. For heaven's sake, forgive her.

On the eve of her departure, Bindu embraced me and said, 'So then you have finally abandoned me, Didi!'

'No Bindi,' I assured her, 'Whatever happens to you, ultimately I'll not abandon you.'

Three days passed. A tenant of your estate had gifted a lamb to make your dinner. I rescued it from the fire of your stomach, and sheltered it in a corner of the coal-shed on the ground floor. I would feed it with gram the first thing in the morning. Initially I tried to rely on the servants, but found that they were interested more in eating it than in feeding it.

That day when I went into the shed, I found Bindu sitting huddled in a corner. As soon as she saw me, she slumped at my feet, weeping silently.

Bindu's husband was a lunatic.

'Is it true, Bindi?' I was stunned.

'Do you believe I could utter such an appalling lie before you, Didi? He is indeed mad. My father-in-law had not approved of this marriage; but he is mortally afraid of my mother-in-law. He left for Varanasi even before the wedding, and she carried on with her stubbornness.'

I collapsed in a heap on the mound of coal. A woman never shows pity on another woman. For her 'The poor wretch is a mere woman. What does it matter to her even if the groom is mad? After all he is a man.'

Bindu's husband did not look a lunatic at first sight; but at times, he grew so violent that he had to be locked up. On the wedding night, he was normal, but night watching and other hassles turned him completely berserk from the following day. Bindu had sat down to her meal, served on a brass platter, when suddenly her husband snatched the platter and threw it, rice and all, into the courtyard. He had somehow come to believe that Bindu was *Rani Rasmani*[7] herself, and the servant had replaced her gold platter with his own brass plate. This was the reason of his anger. Bindu was nearly dead with fear. On the third night, when Bindu's mother-in-law bade her to go to sleep in her husband's room, she froze in fright. Her mother-in-law was a terrible woman; when in a fit of anger, she had no control of her senses. She too had insanity, but was not stark mad, and hence even more dangerous. Bindu had to comply. Her husband was cool that night, but Bindu stiffened in fear like a log. Late at night, after he had gone into deep sleep, Bindu managed to run away, the details of which are unnecessary.

I was smarting all over from hate and anger. 'Such a fraudulent marriage is no marriage at all,' I decided. 'Bindu, you shall stay with me as you did. I dare anybody to take you away.'

All of you said in one voice, 'Bindu must be lying.'

'She has never lied,' I protested.

'How do you know?' You challenged.

'I know this for certain.'

You tried to frighten me. 'If Bindu's in-laws file a criminal case, we will be in trouble.'

'They cheated us by getting a mad man married to her,' I argued. 'Won't the court accept our plea?'

'Do you suppose we must go to court over this? Why, what's our obligation?'

'I'll do what I can by selling off my own jewellery.'

'So you mean for us to rush to lawyers' chambers? Why, what forces us to do it?'

There could be no answer to this. All I could do was privately give vent to my feelings of frustration.

Meanwhile, the elder brother of Bindu's husband had arrived. He was making great noises and even threatening to go to the police.

I do not really know what the secret of my strength is; but I could not bring myself to accept that the cow that had run away from the slaughterer and taken shelter with me must be sent back for fear of the police. 'Let them go to the police,' I said defiantly.

I then decided to take Bindu into my bedroom and together stay locked up. When I went to fetch her, she was gone. While I was exchanging words with you, she had gone out on her own to turn herself over to her brother-in-law. She had realised that if she stayed in this house, she would have put me in great trouble.

In the process, Bindu, by running away, had aggravated her miseries. Her mother-in-law argued that her son had not after all gone to swallow her up. Instances of bad husbands were not rare in the world. Compared with them, her son was pure gold.

My elder sister-in-law bemoaned, 'She is a most unfortunate wretch. What's the point of lamenting it? Mad man or donkey, whatever he may be, he's her husband all the same.'

While glorifying the traditional husband, you seemed to have been inspired by that instance of wifely devotion, where a woman carried her leprosy-stricken husband on her back to the brothel. You males never felt embarrassed to proclaim this worst tale of cowardice in all history. That is why you could resent Bindu's conduct; you didn't hang your head in shame, contrary to humanity. My heart was bleeding for Bindu, but my shame was endless because of you. I was a mere country girl, moreover, thrown into your family: whence did I acquire this sensitivity? I could never come to terms with your pious talks.

I knew that Bindu would rather die than come back to our house. But had I not assured her the day before the wedding that I would not abandon her till the end? My younger brother Sharat was at college in Calcutta. As you know, he was so passionately involved in all sorts of voluntary service from rat killing in plague quarters to relief in the Damodar[8] floods that even though he had failed his First Arts examination twice in succession, his enthusiasm had not flagged a bit. I called him in and said, 'Sharat, I want Bindu's news. You must arrange it. She is afraid to write me any letters; even if she does, I won't get it.'

If instead of such request, I had asked Sharat to kidnap Bindu or break her insane husband's head, he would have been far happier.

In the midst of our talk, you walked in and said, 'What fresh trouble is this you have started?'

'The same trouble that I started the first day: I arrived into your family; but you have yourselves to blame for that.' I stood my ground.

'Have you brought her back and hidden her?'

'If Bindu were to come, I would certainly have kept her secretly with me. Don't worry. She won't come.'

When you saw Sharat with me, you became even more suspicious. I knew you had never liked Sharat visiting our house. You were worried that the police were keeping watch on him; some day he might be involved in a political case, dragging the whole lot of you into it. That is why even on the *brother's day*, I would not invite him, and instead, dispatch my gifts and blessings through a messenger.

I heard from you that Bindu had run away once again, and so her brother-in-law had come to enquire. I was shattered. I realised how terribly the wretched girl must be suffering, yet there was little I could do.

Sharat hurried off to bring news of her. He came back in the evening to report, 'Bindu had gone to her cousin's house; but they were furious and promptly deposited her back to her in-laws' house. They are still feeling the pinch of the travelling and other expenses on this count.'

Your aunt had stopped over at your house on her way to Puri on pilgrimage. I insisted I would go with her, too. You were so much delighted to see this sudden turn of my mind to piety that you raised no objections. You considered another point also: if I stayed back at this time in Calcutta, I might again create some problem concerning Bindu. I was indeed a problem woman.

We were set to leave on a Wednesday; I had decided on the preceding Sunday what I would do about Bindu. I called Sharat in and said, 'Anyhow, you must bring up Bindu on board the Puri Express on Wednesday.'

Sharat's face lit up; he said, 'Don't worry, Didi, I'll not only put her on board, but accompany you as well so I can see Jagannath for free.'

That evening Sharat came again. I was disheartened to see his face. 'What news, Sharat?' I said, 'Couldn't you manage?'

He said, 'No.'

'Couldn't you persuade her?" I asked.

'There's no need either,' he said, 'she killed herself last night by setting fire to her clothes. Their nephew, whom I had befriended, told me she had left a letter for you, but they have destroyed it.'

Peace had come at last to everyone!

People were angry; they said it was now a fashion with girls to set fire to their clothes and burn to death.

You said, 'It's all cheap drama!' Maybe it was. But have you ever thought why the *tamasha* always happens at the cost of the saris of Bengali women, and never the dhotis of the brave Bengali males?

Poor Bindi! Such was her misfortune indeed! In life, she was never known for her beauty or talents; even when it came to dying, it had not occurred to her to take her time devising a novel method so males across the land might rejoice with applause. In death as well, she left people fuming!

My sister-in-law wept secretly; but therein she had some consolation: whatever may have happened, nevertheless it was to everyone's relief. And what else has happened to her except that she died? Were she to survive, who knows what could not have happened?

I have come on pilgrimage. Bindu had outlived her need; but I have not.

What is generally perceived as misery I had nothing of the kind in your household: food and clothes were never in short supply; whatever your elder brother's character may be, you have no such vices for which I can curse my lot. Even if you had been like your brother, my days might perhaps have dragged on more or less like this, and unlike my loyal sister-in-law, I would have blamed the Lord of the universe, instead of the lord of woman. Therefore, I do not wish to make any complaints against you; this is not the purpose of my letter.

In any case, I will never go back to No. 27, Makhan Boral Lane. I have seen Bindu. I have seen what really the status of a woman is in a male-dominated world. I have had enough.

Apart from that, it was my perception that a woman as she was, Bindu was not abandoned by God. Whatever the extent of your dominance over her, there was a limit: she was grander than her miserable life on earth. Your feet were not long enough to trample her life underfoot with your customs arbitrarily forever. Death proved superior to you. In death lies her greatness. There Bindu is no mere Bengali girl, no mere sister to cousins, and no mere cheated wife of an unknown, insane husband. There Bindu is infinite.[9]

In the beginning I felt as if an arrow pierced my heart the day that strident flute-call of death emerging from the broken heart of this girl rang on the Yamuna-bank of my life[10]. I asked God why the pettiest of things in life were the sturdiest of all. Why is the tenuous bubble of walled-in gloom within this lane a most formidable obstacle? Why can I not cross even this low threshold of my quarters for a moment no matter how bewitchingly Nature may beckon me with her nectar-bowl of seasons? With such a life in so wonderful a universe, why must I die every minute of it cooped up within that most trivial work of wood and brick? How trivial is the routine life of mine! How trivial are its set rules, fixed habits, stock phrases, and familiar adversities! Yet ultimately, what triumphed was the stranglehold of all that meanness, and Your own universe of joy was overshadowed!

But the flute of death continued to jeer: where are thy walls of brick and mortar? Where is thy spiked fencing of domestic regimentation? With what suffering, what humiliation can they imprison human beings? Look there! Death is waving the triumphal flag of life! O thou second daughter-in-law, have no fear! It takes not even a blink for thy wifely veneer to be shattered.

I am no longer afraid of your lane. The vast blue ocean lies before me; monsoon clouds have gathered overhead.

The darkness of your habits and customs had shrouded me all over. In the brief while that Bindu came, she had caught sight of me through the pores of that shroud. That very girl with her death tore that shroud apart. Today, having come out free, I find myself brimming over with glory. The one, that Beauteous One, in whose eyes lies this neglected beauty of mine, is beholding me through the whole sky. Now at last, the second daughter-in-law is dead.

You think I am going to kill myself? Don't worry; I won't make such stock jokes with you. Wasn't *Mirabai*[11] a woman like me? Were her fetters any lighter? Nevertheless, did she have to die in order to survive? Sang Mira: 'Let father, let mother, let everyone abandon her. O Lord, but Mira shall hold fast forever, whatever befall her.'

This holding fast is life.
I too shall live. I live.

Bereft of the shelter of your feet,[12]
Mrinal

Shravan 1321 (1914)

NOTES

1 *Mejo* means 'second', hence wife of the second son (see 'Punishment').
2 Literal English equivalent of *meye-jyatha: jyatha* (father's elder brother) is a word of disapproval for a precocious child, which word does not rightly apply to married woman; hence the modifier *meye* (female).
3 A nationalist movement to use only homegrown goods, discarding everything foreign, triggered by the 1905 partition of Bengal.
4 Cheaper than handloom cloth. However, it defies comprehension why she should have chosen 'dhoti' rather than 'sari', even given the other criteria. No Hindu woman would wear dhotis while her husband is still living, *white* cloth by social decree being the traditional sign of widowhood.
5 An affectionate variation on 'Bindu'. The Bengalis are characteristically fond of altering, either by shortening (see 'The Silent Girl') or by euphonic variation, the names of their beloved ones in conversation.
6 Mrinal need not have particularly wished so, because it had always been and still is the custom for the groom to come to the bride's house for the wedding.
7 A beautiful, dignified woman, heir to a huge estate, later turned a philanthropist and social worker.
8 A river of Bengal, notorious for floods in those days, now reined in with barrages.
9 The English equivalent of *Bindu* is *point*; thus the Bengali translates to: there the *point* is *infinite.* An obvious epigram.

10 The 'flute' and the 'Yamuna' are reminiscent of Krishna and Radha. Mrinal may somehow have related herself to Radha.

11 Wife of a Rajput prince, she was persuaded by an inner urge to renounce the world, a minstrel, finally to become a minstrel composing and singing *bhajans* famously named after her.

12 *Mrinal* means the stalk of a lotus, and to a lotus, she has likened her husband's feet, in the salutation. Since she has now severed herself from her husband, she aptly subscribes *as bereft of* etc. Beneath this apparently innocent metaphor, there is a deep undercurrent of subjugation, as opposed to equal treatment, of women by their husbands in the male-dominated society at the time. They were brainwashed or browbeaten into worshipping their husbands as the living manifestation of their gods. There is no reason why a wife should otherwise have been so obsequiously submissive in addressing her husband just for writing him a letter.

An Unapproved Story (*Namanjur Galpo*)

We had been at our revolutionary best during the inflammatory days of political ferment[1]. Having arrived at the quiet aftermath[1] of contemporary times, we still did not quite retire, but we had shouted ourselves hoarse; those arsonist activities were over as well.

The revolutionist drama began on the stage of the partition of Bengal[2]. Everyone knows that Act V was played not at Alipur[3], but at the shores of the Andaman Islands[4]. I had certainly had enough to my credit to earn a deportation, but thanks to my stars, my suffering had ended with a prison term on this side of the Bay of Bengal. Offering my homage to the few of my comrades-in-arms who had been awarded the highest promotion to the gallows, I set up a good practice as a homoeopath in a small town of western India.

My father was then a public prosecutor in a large subdivisional town of Bengal. He enjoyed the title of *Ray Bahadur*. He made no bones about declaring me persona non grata at home. Whether my bond with his heart had severed God only knows, but that with his pocket certainly had; not even a money order came from him. My mother had died while I was still in prison; she, in a way, bore the punishment that I deserved.

A doubt persists in some as to whether the woman known as my aunt was paternal or self-acquired, because my relation to her had remained a complete secret before I moved westward. Let them speculate what relation she was to me; all I know is that but for her affection in those anarchical days of kinship, I would have suffered immensely. She had spent all her life in western India; there she had been married, there she had been widowed, and there she held the landed property her late husband had made. And that tied her down.

She had another tie: a girl called Amiya. The girl was the husband's daughter, of course, but not his wife's. Her mother was a young maidservant of my *Pishima*'s, from the *kahar*[5] caste. After her husband's death, my aunt had brought the girl over, and had been raising her since. She did not even know that my aunt was not her mother.

At this point, she developed an additional tie: I mean myself. When there was little room for me outside the prison, this widowed woman was the one to give me shelter in her home, and in her heart. Thereafter, when on my father's death we learned that in his will he had not deprived me of his property, pishima's eyes filled with tears of joy as well as sorrow. She realised that I had outlived my need for her. Even so, I had certainly not outlived her affection. 'My son,' she said, 'wherever you be, my blessings will be with you.'

'Not only your blessings,' I insisted, 'you must be present as well; I cannot afford to lose you. My mother whom I never found after coming out of prison must have herself led me unto you.'

Pishima wound up her settled home and household of so many years in the west to live with me in Calcutta. I quipped, 'I have carried the *Ganga* of your affection from the west to the east. So I must be *Kali Yug*'s Bhagirath[6].'

Pishima smiled and wiped her tears. She had some hesitation, too. 'I have been contemplating for long,' she said, 'once I've made some suitable arrangement for Amiya, I'll spend the rest of my life on pilgrimage. And now, son, you're dragging me the opposite way!'

I said, 'Pishima, I am myself your pilgrimage on the move. In whatever shrine of sacrifice you offer yourself, your god will appear personally to accept it, a holy soul that you are!'

One argument weighed most with her: she feared that because my natural disposition was Andaman-oriented, if there were no one to bridle me, I must eventually land in the embrace of the police. Her plan was to find me a tender embrace that was far more rigid and lasting, and only then go out on pilgrimage. Unless I was tied down, there was no freedom for her.

There she had miscalculated about my nature. According to my horoscope, my guiding star of captivity and casualty, though not reluctant to consign me to vultures, was vehemently opposed to delivering me to *Prajapati*. Brides' fathers had spared no pains, and they came in large numbers as well. Everyone was aware of the tremendous affluence of my inherited property. Naturally, if I had wished, I could have laughed my way amid tunes of Sahana[7] in the bridal concert to earning twenty to twenty-five thousand rupees along with the bride, leaving the prospective father-in-law bankrupt. I did not. My future biographer may please take note of this one-time sacrifice of twenty to twenty-five thousand rupees to my vow of service to the nation. Just because the transaction was penned in invisible ink, let him not forget to include this in the record of my plaudits. This trait of my noble character happens to be in common with Grandfather Bhishma's[8].

Pishima had not given up hope till the end. Around this time, the political firmament witnessed a post-martial ambience of conciliation[9]. As already mentioned, we were no longer the principal characters in the present drama, though far behind the footlights our lethargic movement was going on occasionally, so sluggishly that pishima had ceased to worry about me. Once for my sake she had wanted to perform propitiatory rites at Kalighat[10]. Now that in my firmament there was no trace of ominous clouds of the redcaps, she forgot about it altogether. That was a mistake.

That day, there was a picketing in the *puja* market in favour of khaddar[11]. I had gone there just as a spectator; my heat of enthusiasm was below fever point, and pulse not too fast. That I could have any cause for concern that day was beyond everyone's knowledge except the star in my horoscope. Suddenly a police sergeant roughly pushed away a picketing Bengali woman. Instantly my image of non-violent non-cooperation[12] changed into one of violent opposition. Soon enough I landed up in the police station, then in due course from the avid jaws of a lock-up into the dark underbelly of a prison. To pishima I said before parting, 'Now you'll have respite for some time. There is no lack of guardians for me. Take this opportunity to visit holy places. Amiya is in her college hostel, and there are people to take care of the house. If you now devote yourself one hundred per cent to your gods, neither any god nor any human can reasonably object.'

I accepted prison life as such without demur. I never raised any cavil or demands, never tried to be hostile. I was not too surprised at the lack of comfort, compliments, courtesy, companionship, and comestibles[12a]. I obeyed the strict rules rigidly. To raise any objection whatever was a matter of shame to me.

I was released even somewhat before completion of my term. There were claps of applause everywhere, their 'Encore! Excellent!' apparently reverberating throughout Bengal. I felt demoralised. He who suffers, suffers alone, I reflected, but to taste the fruits of suffering there are thousands.[13] That too does not last long. The curtain falls, the light goes out, and then all is forgotten. The bearer of the handcuffs and fetters alone remembers their marks on the limbs forever.

My aunt was still on her holy tour then. Where she might be at that point of time was not known. Meanwhile the *puja* festival was round the corner. One morning, my editor friend came on a visit. He said, 'Hullo, I want a contribution from you for our festival number.'

'You mean poems?' I asked.

'No, no. The story of your life.'

'That would be too long for a single number.'

'Why must it be single? It'll be a serial.'

'You remind me of Sati whose body was sliced by Lord Vishnu's disc and strewn around[14]. I don't like the idea of your editorial disc mincing my biography and then scattering them each in the numbers. If ever I write it, I'll publish it in one piece.'

'In that case, why not write about one particular event of your life?'

'What kind of event?'

'Your harshest experience—something very pungent.'

'What's the point ?'

'People want to know these things, my friend.'

'Are they so curious? Fine, I'll write.'

'Remember, it has to be your harshest experience.'

'You mean what hurt me most will please people most. All right, but the names have to be changed extensively.'

'Quite naturally. It's risky not to replace historical giveaways in explosive stories. And some such desperate thing is what I want. We'll pay you–per page –'

'Let me first finish it, and then we'll fix up the rate.'

'But you must not give it to anyone else, ok? No matter what he offers, I'll beat it –'

'All right, all right, that's agreed.'

Finally, before leaving, he said, 'Er, Mr So-and-So—you know whom I mean, I won't name names—ah, that fellow you call a literary great—boasts he is a great writer. But whatever you might say, your style compares with his as Dawson's boots with Taltala[15] slippers.'

I understood that upgrading me was just a ploy; to dwarf the giant in comparison was the purpose.

So much for the preface. Now for the story of my harshest experience.

Ever since I had started reading the revolutionary journal 'Sandhya', I had been practising austerity in food and physical comforts, a drill you can call a rehearsal for prison life. I had become inured to persistent neglect of the body. Consequently, the first time they threw me in jail, my spirit remained unperturbed, and thereafter, when I had come out, I never tolerated anyone volunteering to nurse me. This hurt my aunt. 'Pishima,' I said, trying to assuage her, 'in affection you find freedom; in service, bondage. Moreover, to impose one's personal regimen upon the body of another is some sort of diarchy[16]—which is what our non-cooperation movement is against.'

With a sigh she said, 'All right, son. I won't bother you any more.'

A fool that I was, I had thought the crisis was over. I had forgotten that affection and service have a covert aspect; their charm is difficult to escape. When the destitute *Shiva* went begging with his bag for alms, drunk with pride in his mendicancy, he was not aware that *Lakshmi* had woven the sack in soft silk, its golden threads worth more than the sun and the stars. And when the ascetic Shiva blissfully ate what he flaunted as alms, he did not know that *Annapurna* had cooked it with such salivating spices that even *Indra* was tempted to whisper into *Nandi*'s ears for a helping. I was in such a condition. Pishima's affectionate hand secretly worked its magic on my daily ritual from eating through sleeping, which the patriot in me was too preoccupied to notice. I was secure in my conviction that my austerity had not been compromised.

The spell broke once I went back to prison. No tenet of non-dualism could reconcile the difference between pishima's system and that of the police. I kept reciting from the Gita: O Arjuna, rise above the three attributes[17]. Poor ascetic! When it was that pishima's various designs aided by various subterfuges had wormed their way across my heart into my stomach I had never known. Dysfunction set on in the latter organ while in prison.

As a result, the body, which nothing except a thunderbolt could once overpower, fell ill; although the prison term eventually ended, that of the diseases contracted refused to. I had headache at times, indigestion often, and afternoon fever regularly. Even when the garlands and applause had dwindled into a trickle, the symptoms persisted dominantly. To myself I said: 'pishima is away on pilgrimage, and there is no grudging it. Does Amiya not have any sense of propriety?' But then, could I really blame her? Earlier, during my illness or health, pishima had often encouraged her to look after me, but it was I who had dissuaded her, saying I did not like it. Pishima had said, 'I sent her so she could learn these things, not for your comfort.' I had said, 'Why don't you send her to any hospital for nursing, then?' Aggrieved, she had not carried the point further.

Today as I lay, I argued to myself: 'I may have restrained her at some point of time, but did she have to go by that order forever? So much devotion to elder's orders in this day and age!'

Most household matters, big or small, normally escape a patriot's notice. Now that I lay sick, my eyes were most keen. I observed that in my absence, Amiya too had developed a far greater patriotic fervour than before. My examples and precepts had never worked so wonderfully on her. Now thanks to the tremendous impulse of non-cooperation[18], she ended up a college dropout. While she had no trepidation in addressing a crowd, she used to knock at unfamiliar houses as well for donations to an orphanage for girls. I further noticed that her friend Anil worshipped her as a goddess for this dogged perseverance of hers. On her birthday, he presented her with a verse on this very theme set to halting metre and printed in gold lettering.

I felt I had to do something of the sort or there would be problems. In Pishima's regime, servants used to work on schedule: someone or the other was always close at hand. Now if I wanted a glass of water, I had to wait like a *chatak*[20] for an accidental appearance of Jaladhar[19], my servant from Midnapur; for taking medicine on time I had to rely absolutely on my forgetful mind. Even though it was contrary to my established principle, I sent for Amiya once or twice to attend at my sickbed; but I noticed that every time she heard footsteps at the door, she looked back with a start and fidgeted in her seat. I felt pity and said, 'Amiya, you must have a meeting today, don't you?

Amiya would say, 'Never mind, dada. There's still time to –'

'No, no. How can that be?' I would protest, 'Duty first.'

But I often saw that Anil turned up far ahead of duty. His arrival sent a gust of wind to the sails of her enthusiasm for duty, and she needed no more persuasion from me.

Not only Anil, but also a good number of inspired youths, all school dropouts, assembled in my ground-floor room in the afternoons for imbibing tea and motivation. They called Amiya Yugalakshmi or the goddess of the new age. There is a kind of title, such as 'Rai Bahadur', which is like a neatly folded chuddar: whoever gets it can go about unmindfully flaunting it across his shoulder. There is another kind: the poor fellow who is unfortunate to get it is in perpetual anxiety to make himself befit it. Clearly, Amiya's position was the latter kind; unless she appeared always glowing with excessive enthusiasm, it did not do justice to her status. To have little or no time to eat or sleep happened with ostentatious regularity. The news went across the neighbourhood. When someone expressed concern over her health she just smiled weakly—a strange smile it was. Her admirers said, 'You must take some rest. We'll somehow manage,' and she took umbrage: was it very important to spare her the exhaustion? Was it any small affliction to be deprived of the glory of suffering?

The list of her self-denials included myself as well. No less a person than her jailbird dada who belonged to the same constellation of revolutionaries as Ullaskar-Kanai-Barin-Upendra[21], one who having read the second chapter[22] of the Bhagabad-Gita was making good progress towards the last[22]—she could not spare enough time to take adequate care of even so great a dada! So great a sacrifice! When occasionally for some reason, fewer people of her group were present, I provided her with a dose of heady flattery, saying, 'Amiya, individual relationships aren't for you. You're made for the new age.' She accepted it quietly and seriously. Since my prison days, my laughter had been flowing like a subterranean river. Those who did not recognise me certainly regarded me as a very solemn personality.

As I lay alone on my bed, staring at the ceiling, I thought friends were turning away their faces. Then suddenly I remembered that the other day a limping dog from somewhere was trying to find shelter in a corner of my veranda. Its body was almost shorn of hair, and the skeleton had barely any covering beneath its withered skin; it was half-dead. I had shooed it away with utmost disgust. Now I figured out why I had driven it away with such vehemence: not because it was a stray, but because it showed signs of decay all over. In the concert of life, its existence was a discordant note, its sickliness an affront. I found a parallel between our states. In the stream of life around me, my sickness lay as an immovable boulder, an impediment to the flow. Sickness demands: stay quietly by the bedside. Vitality demands: move around and explore. Someone who is tied down by illness wants to detain someone else who is healthy; that is a kind of crime. So I decided to forego my demands altogether on any living being, and fell back on the Gita.

When I had almost attained perfect equipoise transcending the dialectics of affliction and bliss, I felt someone touch my feet in the traditional expression of reverence. Lowering my eyes from the Gita, I saw she was a girl from pishima's bevy of dependants. So far, I had known her casually from a distance and knew nothing specifically about her; even her name was unknown. She covered her head in a veil and began to massage my feet gently.

Now I recalled that she had often crept up like a shadow at the outside corner of the door and went back each time, perhaps because she could not summon up the courage to enter. She must have secretly gathered a good deal of information about my headache and body ache, without my knowing it. Today she had overcome her shame and fear to come into my room and touch my feet. This girl now came perhaps to repay me by falling at my feet on behalf of the women of Bengal for the suffering I had once undergone for saving a woman from disgrace and offered as a tribute to womankind. When I had been released from prison, I had received plenty of floral tributes at numerous receptions; but today this humble tribute from unknown hands in a corner of my room went straight to my heart. An aspirant of freedom from worldly pleasures, this hardened jailbird's long-dried-up eyes were on the point of becoming moist. As I have already said, I was not used to taking any personal service: if someone offered to massage my feet, I would feel disgusted and drive her away with a rebuke. Today, the insolence of refusing this service did not even occur to me.

My aunt's in-laws were originally from Khulna district. She had brought over a couple of girls from there and given them shelter. They assisted her in her chores and prayers; they were indispensable to her in all her rites and rituals. Amiya had free access to the whole house, except the prayer room. Amiya did not know, nor did she seek to know, the reason. My aunt wanted Amiya to get a good education and marry into a family free from rigid orthodoxy, where deities and Brahmans alike were treated unceremoniously before being sent away empty-handed. It is a matter of regret, but that was her destiny: how could a girl entirely escape the consequences of her father's transgression? Hence, my aunt had given her enough rope to be slack in her ways, and did not care if the laxity finally led her into a welter of modern-day aberrations. Since childhood, Amiya had come first in her class in English and mathematics. She had walked away jubilantly in her skirt and swinging plait with four to five prizes from her missionary school every year. If ever by chance she came second, she would closet herself in her bedroom and weep away until she got swollen eyes, stopping just short of going on a fast. She had taken the vow of fulfilment before the reigning deity of examinations, and remained absorbed in its worship all these years. Then she took her oath in the diabolical creed[23] of the Non-cooperation Movement and took a first class at the test of forsaking the aforesaid deity. She was not the sort to lag behind others either in getting passes or in missing passes at examinations.

The fame she had earned by studying she far exceeded now by giving up studies. The prizes she now secured walked; they talked; they melted away in pools of tears; they even wrote poems.

Naturally, Amiya had scant regard for the adopted village girls of my aunt's. At a time when in the Women's Homes, inmates were rarer than donations, Amiya had strongly pleaded with pishima to dispatch the girls there. Pishima had said, 'How can you say that? They are not orphans. What am I here for then? Whether orphans or not, what girls want is a home. Why must they be branded and dumped in an orphanage? Well, if you really feel for them, why don't you give up your own home for them?'

Be that as it may, as the girl kept rubbing my feet with her head bent low, I picked up a newspaper in front of my face and kept browsing through the advertisements, embarrassed yet flattered. Suddenly then, at a most inopportune moment, in came Amiya; she had written a new interpretation of the brothers' day in the context of the new age. She wanted to circulate it in English as well, and I was to help with the translation. Her followers were very much excited over the originality of the idea and waiting eagerly to give it wide publicity.

The sight of the girl waiting upon me stiffened her expression. Her celebrated brother had just to throw a hint and a whole lot of girls would fall at his feet in attendance. And he had finally opted for this–

She could not restrain herself. 'Dada, did you ask Harimati to– '

Cutting her short, I came out with 'My feet were aching severely.'

Once trying to save a woman from humiliation by a sergeant, I had landed up in jail. Today trying to shield one woman from the wrath of another, I had lied. Punishment came this time as well. Amiya sat down near my feet. Harimati tried to make an excuse by saying something meekly, which Amiya ignored with a contemptuous tilt of her face. Harimati slipped out of the room. Now Amiya took charge of my feet leaving me in real trouble. How could I tell her that I did not need it, that I disliked it from my heart? I seemed to be losing my autonomy over my feet!

Hurriedly, I sat up and said, 'Amiya, give me your article. Let me translate it.'

'What's the hurry, Dada, with your feet aching? Let me carry on for some time.'

'No, no, why should they be aching? I mean yes; they are, slightly. At any rate, Ami, this brothers' day idea of yours is wonderful. How could it come into your head after all? Take this one—it's terrific. 'The forehead of the brother in this age is very broad, extending over the whole of Bengal; no single home is big enough for it.' Well, let me see how it goes in English: *With the advent of the present age,* [*the*] *Brother's brow, waiting for its auspicious anointment from the sisters of Bengal, has grown beyond the narrowness of domestic privacy, beyond the boundaries of the individual home.* [Tagore's own words. Ed.] Really, if you get an idea worth its salt, there's no stopping the pen.'

Amiya's interest in pressing my feet vanished. I had a nagging headache and no interest in writing; still I got going after taking an aspirin tablet.

Next day, when Jaladhar was taking his afternoon siesta, the doorman was in his cubbyhole reading *Tulsidas's*[24] Ramayana, the entertainer with dancing bears was clattering his small drum at the street corner, when the untiring Amiya had gone out on her duties as the goddess of the New Age, there appeared the timid figure of a girl on the empty veranda away from the door. She dithered for a while, then suddenly came in, picked up a fan and began to wave it sitting beside my head. Obviously, yesterday's frown on Amiya's face deterred her from touching my feet again. I guessed that the meeting on the publicity of New Bengal's Brothers' Day must now be in progress, and Amiya must be occupied there. I was contemplating telling the girl at my peril that my feet were aching badly, but luckily, I did not. As I dallied over the lie, in came Amiya, the quarterly report on the Women's Home in her hand. Harimati's fanning got a jolt. I could easily guess the flutter in her heart and the pallor in her cheeks. Her fan beats decelerated considerably at the inhibiting presence of the Home's secretary.

Amiya sat down on the edge of the bed and said in a very stern voice, 'You know, dada, so many homeless girls of our country have found shelter with rich families and are growing up happily, but they are least useful there. They merely stand in the way of other really needy girls' earning their livelihood. If instead they are employed in public work, for instance, in running our Home, I think –'

I could see that I was merely a dummy, and Harimati was the target of this lashing declamation. 'So you mean,' I said, 'you will go by your own fancy, and the homeless girls are to go by *your* orders. You will be the Home's secretary, and they will be its servants! Rather than that, try doing their work yourself and you will soon learn it is too hard for you. To harass the destitute is easy; to serve them is not. Make demands on yourself, not on others.'

I was of martial temperament, and sometimes forgot the dictum: 'Conquer anger by not getting angry.' The fallout of my reaction was that Amiya fetched another girl from among my aunt's adoptees. Her name was Prasanna. Amiya posted her at my feet and said, 'Dada's feet are aching; massage them.' The girl started doing her job diligently enough. How could the poor wretch of an elder brother now admit without loss of face that there was nothing wrong with his feet? How could he convey that such massaging only embarrassed[25] him? I sensed that sooner or later, I was going to lose the privilege of my sickbed. It was better to become chairperson of the Brothers' Day Society of New Bengal. The fanning slowly came to a stop. Harimati got the message, loud and clear: Prasanna had been set up to eject Harimati. Set a thief to catch a thief.[26] After a while, she put down the fan and got up to leave. She bowed her head over my feet, wiped them softly, and left.

I sat down with the Gita once again. In the gaps between the verses, my eyes pried into the gap in the doors, but could nowhere locate that speck of shadow again. Instead of her, Prasanna came often, and inspired by her instance, some other girls also came in attendance upon Amiya's nationally-acclaimed patriotic brother. Amiya made a roster for the girls to work in shifts in my service.

One day, we heard Harimati had left Calcutta without a word to anyone and gone back to her village home.

My editor friend appeared on the twelfth day of the month and said, 'What's this? Is it a joke? Is this what you call your harsh experience?'

I smiled and said, 'Won't it sell in the Puja market?'

'Absolutely not. It's most trivial stuff.'

The editor was not to blame, though. Ever since my prison term, I have been sorrowing inwardly. People judge me from my exterior for a very shallow-minded person.

The editor returned me the manuscript. Just at that moment, Anil came in. He said, 'I wouldn't say myself, but please read this letter.'

In it, he had expressed his wish to marry Amiya, his idol, the goddess of the new age. He had also mentioned that Amiya had consented.

Then I had to tell him the facts about her birth. I would not have told it so easily, but I knew that Anil had a condescending, though respectful, attitude towards the lower castes. I told him, 'The stigma of forefathers is washed away by birth. This you can see clearly in Amiya's life. She is like a lotus, without a trace of mud on her.'

The meetings of the Brothers' Day Society never came about in right earnest thereafter. The ceremonial sandalwood paste was ready, but the intended foreheads had been on the run. Moreover, I heard that Anil had left Calcutta for Kumilla on a propaganda mission on self-government.

Amiya prepared to get readmitted to college. Meanwhile, my aunt returned from her pilgrimage, and now finally, my feet had been freed from the shackles of humble service aimed at the marriage altar.

Agrahayan 1332 (1926)

NOTES

1 The text has *Yuddhakanda* and *Uttarakanda;* War canto and Aftermath canto of the seven-canto Ramayana. They respectively signify the heady days of political conflagration, and the later low-key non-violent phase of the Indian Nationalist Movement.

2 Partition of Bengal effected by Lord Curzon in 1905 that acted as a trigger for the first open hostility between occupying Englishmen and Indians through what is called the Swadeshi Movement.

3 Freedom-fighters were tried chiefly at the sessions court at Alipur in Calcutta, and upon conviction, jailed there or deported, if not hanged.

4 Those deported for life were lodged at the infamous Cellular Jail in the Andaman Islands under cruelly oppressive conditions.

5 Derived from Sanskrit it means 'one who carries (someone) on his shoulders': palanquin-bearer, of a low caste.

6 A progenitor of the Surya dynasty, said to have redeemed his accursed ancestors by bringing down the holy Ganges from heaven to earth by his meditation. His name traditionally symbolises (i) selfless service, (ii) tenacity and perseverance, and (iii) noble cause. Such comments, as in this instance, where none of the criteria is met, are often made humorously.

7 A midnight raga that excites joy and passion, a favourite wedding tune.

8 The grand old patriarch, valiant fighter, and a noble character of the Mahabharata; held in esteem for his repudiation of succession to the throne and for his vow of celibacy. His inviolable vow has been acclaimed down the ages by the phrase: *Bhishmer pratijna* (as firm a resolution as Bhishma's).

9 A pointer to the turn in the Freedom Movement from the violent phase to the non-violent under Gandhi.

10 A pilgrimage spot in Calcutta, famous for its shrine of the goddess Kali, which devotees visit for two purposes: (i) to redeem a pledge after supposedly receiving the boon they had prayed for, and (ii) to perform ritual worship to ward off the evil effects of astronomical conjunction.

11 *Khaddar* or *khadi* is hand-woven coarse cotton cloth made of hand-spun threads, introduced and popularised by Gandhi; campaigning

for khadi and other indigenous goods was at fever pitch in the initial days of the Swadeshi movement after the partition of Bengal.

12 Non-violent non-cooperation was Gandhi's political credo.

12a Please mark the alliteration in 'c' (corresponding to the Bengali equivalent of 's' in the text).

13 Quoted in the context of a marriage, the Sanskrit saying is: *Mishtannam itare janah,* which literally means, 'common men want sweets': the bride cares for the groom's looks; her mother, his wealth; her father, his education; relatives, his lineage; *the ordinary guest wants a grand feast.*

14 The fact of the simile has already been stated in the text; the context was Sati's father Daksha's abusing her mendicant husband Shiva publicly at the *yajna* which she had gone to attend uninvited. She collapsed in mortification, and Shiva went berserk ransacking heaven and earth, carrying her body. Vishnu salvaged the situation with his *sudarshan-chakra*. The fifty-two pieces into which the body is said to have been severed made as many *peethas* or holy places for Hindus.

15 Taltala, a central Calcutta district known for manufacturing ordinary shoes.

16 The system of dual provincial administration introduced by the Government of India Act 1919, under which the provincial list of subjects was divided into (i) Reserved subjects to be administered by the Governor with the help of Executive Council, and (ii) Transferred subjects to be dealt with by the Governor with the help of his ministers. The Indians were dissatisfied with the project of diarchy.

17 In the Bhagavad-Gita, Ch. II, Sl. 45, Krishna exhorts Arjuna to abjure the collective attributes of the three *gunas*: *sattva* (the highest virtue of pure knowledge), *rajas* (the normal instincts of desires and passions), and *tamas* (the basest instinct of vice), which are advocated by the Vedas through their prescriptive rituals. Krishna advises Arjuna to strive to attain equanimity in pleasure and pain, acquisition and preservation.

18 The Congress under the leadership of Gandhi decided in 1920 to take a revolutionary step by launching a programme of total non-cooperation. This consisted in boycotting government offices,

schools and colleges, legislatures and law courts, and finally non-payment of taxes. The movement served as a baptism by fire which initiated the people to a new faith and confidence.

19 Literally, 'one who or which carries water', or a cloud, or the sea. Since the servant appears just once in the story, Rabindranath seems to have taken this opportunity to give the scarce servant this unusual name, as Tagore often does with names.

20 A rain bird, popularly, if wrongly, called swallow, soars high up to the clouds and is believed by poets to call '*phatik jal*' (crystal water). Hence proverbially, a person awaiting something eagerly is said to be waiting like a *chatak.*

21 Ullaskar Datta, Kanailal Datta, Barindrakumar Ghosh and Upendranath Banerjee were revolutionaries involved in the Alipur Bomb Conspiracy Case of 1908, in which Kanai was sentenced to death and the other three to life. Incidentally, Kshudiram Bose, one of the accused, was hanged, too.

22 The second chapter, *Sankhya Yoga,* preaches the indestructibility of the soul and the frailty of the body, and advocates renunciation of desire; the eighteenth and last chapter *Moksha Yoga* advocates repudiation of all religious creeds and complete surrender to the Almighty. Though the narrator professedly strove to follow the preaching of the second chapter, ironically, he still desired comfort and fell way short of the final goal.

23 The Bengali has *yoginimantra,* literally, the psalms of praise of the *yoginis,* the sixty-four companion goddesses of Durga. However, *yogini* has another meaning: woman sage. Since Amiya has been *initiated* into the *creed* of *asahayog* (non-cooperation), Rabindranath seizes the opportunity to use a pun; otherwise, the choice may not be particularly apt.

24 Hindi version of the Ramayana by Tulsidas.

25 Though the Bengali word *pada* means 'foot', *apadastha* in the text never means 'without feet'. It carries an untranslatable pun; the humour is lost in the bland but real meaning in translation, 'embarrassed'.

26 The proverb, *kantakenaiba kantakam* literally means '(to remove) a thorn with a thorn'.

House Number One
(*Poila Nambar*)

I don't even smoke. I have one overweening passion which has weeded out the possibility of any other addiction taking root: it is my obsession for reading books. The motto of my life was: no matter how long you live or whether you live / Read books and buy books even if you need to borrow[1].

In my younger days of inadequate resources, I used to read catalogues of books the way those with wanderlust lacking the wherewithal travel vicariously through timetables. My elder brother's uncle-in-law used to buy Bengali books indiscriminately, as soon as they were published. It was his particular pride that he had not lost even one copy to this day. In Bengal, no one else perhaps was as lucky. Of all the things in the world which are subject to dispossession—be it wealth, life or umbrellas of forgetful people—Bengali books are the most vulnerable. It can be deduced from this that the keys to my brother's uncle-in-law's bookcases were inaccessible even to his aunt-in-law. In those days, whenever I accompanied my brother to his in-laws' house, 'like a pauper going to the king of kings[2], I used to spend my time gazing at the locked bookcases, as I eyed them covetously! Suffice it to say that right from my childhood I had read such an incredible lot that I simply could not pass my examinations, because I had never found the time for minimal reading essential to passing.

One great benefit of having been a failed student is that I do not have to bathe[3] with the limited water of learning stored in the university pitcher; it has been my habit to dip in the running stream. Many BAs and MAs come to me these days. Whatever their claim to modernity, they are still under restrictive surveillance of the Victorian age. Like the geocentric universe of Ptolemy, their world of learning is firmly screwed to the antiquated ideas of the eighteenth and nineteenth centuries, as if generations of students in Bengal are supposed to revolve round that world. The carriage of their intellectual trip trundled arduously beyond Mill and Bentham eventually to break down at the Carlyle–Ruskin post. They dare not go out to walk in the open air outside the fence of their teachers' cant.

But in the country whose literature we have been cultivating by pegging our minds to it is by no means static, but keeping time with the pulse of that land. I may not have that pulse, but I have tried to follow its pace. I learnt French, German, and Italian all by myself; I started learning Russian a few days ago. I am travelling by the superfast express of modernism. Hence, neither did I get stuck at Huxley and Darwin, nor do I hesitate to examine Tennyson. I even recoil from the idea of plying the safe trade of easy fame in literary monthlies by riding the boat designated Ibsen–Maeterlinck.

That a certain class of people might one day seek out a person like me was something beyond my expectation. I have noticed that in Bengal, a handful of youths are still found who do not drop out of college, and are at the same time excited by the strumming of *Saraswati's veena* outside the ambit of college. These very young men began to trickle into my room.

Thus I picked up a second addiction––talking, or discoursing in chaste language, if you like. The literature we find in the books and periodicals across the country is so shallow on the one hand, and stale on the other, that at times I want to blow away its asphyxiating stuffiness with the open air of liberal thinking. Yet, when I think of writing, laziness grips me. Therefore, I eagerly look forward to some avid listeners around me.

My crowd of admirers started swelling. I lived in house Number *Two* of our lane, while my first name is *Adwaita*charan[4]. Hence, our group came to be known as Dwaita-Adwaita Sampraday[5] or 'Sect of the Dualist and the Non-dualist'. No member of our sect had any sense of time. Someone might turn up right in the morning, a recently published English book in hand with a punched tram ticket flagged between pages. Discussions would run into hours and would not end until after one in the afternoon. Another fellow might turn up in late afternoon, day's college notes in his hand, and would show no sign of leaving even at two in the night. I asked him very often to dine with me, for I had observed that the eclectic keenness of literary aficionados was not limited to the brains, but extended to the palate as well. But I never bothered about the plight of the person on whose help I relied for this scheduled and unscheduled hospitality. Enormous potter's wheels of world thoughts and ideas are shaping human civilisation, partly baked to permanent set, partly half-baked and crumbling: how could one engrossed in it notice the bustle of the household and fire of the kitchen?

Shiva alone can read the frowns of his consort, say the epics. But Shiva has three eyes; I have only two, and their vision too had been dimmed by constant reading. Naturally, how my wife's eyebrows arched when asked to prepare extra meals at extraordinary hours escaped my notice. By and by, she had realised that untimeliness and indiscipline were the order of my house. My domestic clock ticked aperiodically, and every nook and cranny of my household was a gaping hole of penury. Nearly all my money and energy went down a single drain—in buying books. My wife must have known better the mystery of how our other needs were met,—like a stray dog licking and sniffing the leftovers of my pedigreed pet.

To talk on diverse branches of knowledge is an imperative need for a person like me. Not to exhibit learning, nor for the benefit of others; it is a way of thinking: thinking through talking, just an intellectual exercise for digesting knowledge. If I had been a writer or a professor, talking at large would have been a redundant exercise. People with some regular manual work don't have to find out other means of digesting food; those who stay at home need at least to walk briskly for some time on the terrace. I belonged to the latter category. Obviously, until my Dualist Sect was floated, my only double had been my wife. She had silently borne this eloquent process of intellectual digestion for long. Although she used to wear coarse mill-woven saris, and her gold ornaments were neither pure nor solid, whatever she got from her husband by way of lecture—be it Eugenics or Mendelism or mathematical logic—had nothing cheap or spurious about it. She was deprived of this lecture when my sect grew in number; but she had no complaints about it.

My wife's name is Anila[6]. I do not know what the word means, neither perhaps did my father-in-law. The word sounds sweet, and when heard for the first time seems to carry some meaning at least. Irrespective of the dictionary, what it really meant was—that my wife was her father's darling. When my mother-in-law died leaving behind her two-and-a-half-year old son, my father-in-law, as a gratifying means of caring for the boy married a second time. How far his purpose had been fulfilled will be clear from what he had told Anila two days before his death holding her hand: 'Now that I am going, dear, there is no one left but you to take care of Saroj.' I do not exactly know how he had provided for his wife and the children by her. But to Anila's care he secretly left his savings, nearly seven thousand five hundred rupees. 'This money need not be invested at interest,' he suggested. 'Spend it in cash to pay for Saroj's education.'

This was somewhat surprising to me. My father-in-law was not merely intelligent; he was what is called prudent. In other words, he never acted on impulse, but proceeded with calculated moves. Therefore, if he ought to have entrusted his son's education and welfare to anyone, it was me, and I entertained no doubt about it. But how he came to believe that his daughter was abler than his son-in-law is beyond my comprehension. Even so, unless he had been convinced about my trustworthiness, he could not have left so much money in cash with my wife. In fact, he was a philistine of the Victorian era; he could not recognise me finally.

Out of pique, I had tentatively decided not to make any comment on this. And I did not either; I believed that Anila would have to come forward herself, for she had no choice except take my refuge. When she did not approach me for any advice, I thought she might be lacking the courage. Then one day, I asked her casually, 'What have you decided on Saroj's education?' Anila said, 'A tutor has been engaged. He is going to school as well.' I gave her indications that I was willing to take charge of teaching him myself. I tried to explain some of the new methods of learning currently in vogue. She was non-commital.

After all these years, I suspected for the first time that Anila did not respect me. I had no university degree; perhaps that was why she thought I had neither the competence nor the moral right to advise her on education. I was certain, Anila had not comprehended a bit of the significance of whatever I had told her so long on eugenics, evolution and radio waves. Perhaps she thought even boys of the Second Class[7] knew more than this. Reason: each tweak of the ear at their teacher's hand screwed each bit of knowledge firmly into their minds. With some irritation, I said to myself: let no one whose principal asset is knowledge and wisdom ever hope to prove his worth to women.

Most of the pivotal dramas of life continue to be enacted behind the scenes until after the fifth act, when the curtain suddenly lifts. While discoursing with my associates on Bergson's philosophy and Ibsen's psychology, I had thought that no fire had ever been lit on the sacrificial altar of Anila's life. But today, looking in retrospect,

I clearly see that the Maker who forges living images by means of heating in fire and hammering was very much active in Anila's heart: there, owing to the conjunction of a younger brother, his elder sister and her stepmother a play of interactive impulses was going on perpetually.

The mythical earth poised on the mythical Vasuki[8] is of constant shape. But for the woman who has to bear a world laden with pain, her world is continually reshaping itself every moment with every fresh blow. With her heart weighed down by that changing load of pain, if she has to undergo the travails of domesticity, who but the All-knowing would fully appreciate what she feels? At least, I did not. What anxiety, what slighted efforts, what secret turmoil of wounded affection were brewing so near me behind a veil of silence was entirely beyond my cognition. All I knew was that the principal occupation in Anila's life was to be preoccupied with holding feasts for our group on the scheduled dates. Today, I understand quite well that it was through her extreme suffering that this younger brother had grown to be the closest person to his sister in the world. Since they had spurned my advice and assistance in Saroj's upbringing as entirely unnecessary, I had never given the matter further thought, and never cared to ask how he was doing.

Meanwhile, the house Number One in our lane got residents. This house had been built by the famously rich moneylender of yesteryear, Uddhab Baral. Over the following two generations, the family lost nearly all its wealth and men, leaving one or two widows who did not live there leaving the house in a state of complete disrepair. Occasionally, it was rented out temporarily for the purpose of a wedding or some such function; for the rest of the year such a big house almost went without tenants. This time round there came someone whose name was, let us suppose, Raja Sitangshumouli, and let us assume he was the zamindar of Narottampur.

So great an arrival, so near my house might well have gone unnoticed. For, like Karna[9] who came to the world only after wearing a natural armour, I too had a god-gifted one for myself: my congenital absent-mindedness—a very thick and durable shield indeed, which gave me protection from the scramble, commotion, and cursing continuously going on in the world.

But rich men of modern times are worse than ordinary pests; they are extraordinary pests. Two hands, two feet and a head are all that constitutes what is called a human being. Creatures who have suddenly grown some extra limbs and heads are called demons[10]. They go on breaking their barrier with continuous whooping and thudding, and with their unmitigated excesses drive heaven and earth to distraction. It is impossible not to take notice of them. Those who do not deserve the least attention, yet are too compelling to ignore, are the bane of the world, of whom even *Indra* is scared.

Clearly, Sitangshumouli was this type. I had never known that an individual could be so tremendously excessive all by himself. With men and attendants, horses and carriages, he seemed to be playing the regular demon king of the Ramayan. His depredations started to infringe on my scholastic paradise everyday.

I first met him at the corner of our lane. The main advantage of the lane was that a self-absorbed person like me could walk on safely even without looking in front or minding the back or glancing on the right or left. Even while walking, one could cogitate critically on Meredith, Browning, or some modern Bengali poet, yet avert an accident. But that day, alerted by a sudden howl of 'Hey! Beware!' from behind, I turned to find a pair of brown horses drawing a hoodless brougham about to land their hooves upon me. The owner himself was driving, the coachman sitting beside him. The babu pulled hard at the reins. I managed to skirt the car by pasting myself to a tobacco shop on the narrow lane. The babu seemed very angry with me, because one who drives carelessly can never pardon a careless pedestrian. I have already mentioned the underlying reason: a pedestrian has two legs; he is a human being, whereas one who rides a coach has eight; he is a demon. With these unnatural appendages, he creates nuisance on earth. The Maker of the two-legged creature had not foreseen this eight-legged phenomenon.

By virtue of the salubrious rule of nature, I would have forgotten the horse-carriage, rider and all, in course of time, because they were not especially worth remembering in this marvellous world. But these people have forcibly occupied far more than an individual's normal right of creating disturbance. Hence, even if I could remain oblivious of my neighbour at house Number Three for months together, I could not forget the one at Number One even for a moment. The arrhythmical stamping on the wooden stable floor by eight to ten horses at night severely hampered my sleep. Moreover, when early in the morning, eight to ten grooms massaged as many horses with whacking raps, it was impossible to maintain decorum. Add to this his retinue of upcountry footmen and gate-keepers from Orissa and Bihar, none of whom were soft-spoken or men of few words. Thus, even though the person was just one individual, many were his noise-making tools. This is the revealing feature of a demon, which may not be disturbing to himself, though. Ravana may not have disturbed his own sleep while snoring from his twenty nostrils, but consider the plight of his neighbours! The principal feature of paradise is the beauty of its proportions, whereas that of the demons who once laid waste to its aesthetic beauty was the lack of them. Today, that very monster of excessiveness riding the wings of money has laid siege to human habitation. Even if we try to brush past him, he stumbles upon us riding his four-horse carriage, and gives a nasty look into the bargain.

That afternoon, none of my colleagues had arrived yet. I was reading a book on the theory of tides. Suddenly, a memento from my neighbour flew in over the compound-wall, across the door, and banged against my widow-pane with a clang. It was a tennis ball. Lunar pull, earth's pulsation, the perpetual prosody of a universal lyric and such things—pushing everything to the background, what came to my mind was that I had a neighbour who was larger than life; for me he was a total siperfluity, yet inevitable. The next moment, my old servant Ajodhya came in running and panting. He was my only attendant, whom I could neither find by calling, nor stir by shouting. When asked about his absences, he would plead he was one man, but his chores were many. That day I saw him pick up the ball unasked and run off to the neighbour's. I gathered that each time he returned the ball fetched him four paise in remuneration.

I discovered that not only was the window-pane broken and my peace shattered, but the morale of my followers was undermined as well. That Ajodhya was growing increasingly contemptuous of my insignificance was not so surprising; but even the flag-bearer of my Dualist Sect, Kanailal, became most keen about the neighbour. I had been secure in my belief that his devotion to me was heart-based, not matter-based. At that point, one day I noticed that overtaking my Ajodhya he reached for the tennis ball and picking it up ran off to the next house. Obviously, he wantd to make acquaintance of my neighbour on this pretext. I suspected his disposition was not exactly like the Brahma-seeking Maitreyi's; ambrosia alone would not satiate him.

I tried to severely deride the sybaritic life of the Number One Babu. Attempts to cover up the hollowness of the mind with the trappings of body, I argued, were like colourful clouds trying in vain to shroud the sky: a mild breeze, and they disperse exposing slices of the sky. Kanailal interrupted me one day to say that the man was not entirely hollow after all; he had a BA degree. Kanailal himself had one, so I could not make any comment at least on the degree.

Number One's chief accomplishments were acoustical. He could play three instruments—cornet, esraj, and cello. I had its demonstration too, often enough. I am no master of music, but music to my mind is no exalted art. music evolved when man had no articulate language: since he could not think, he would only scream. Even today, tribes who are still in the primitive state love to scream for no apparent reason. But I noticed that there were at least four members in my group who were diverted even from the latest chapter on mathematical logic once Number One began to play his cello.

When quite a few of my boys had inclined towards house Number One, Anila told me one day, 'We've got a nuisance of sorts next door. Isn't it better to move to some other house?' I was very much pleased. 'Have you noticed,' I told my boys, 'how women have a natural perception? Things that require comprehensive proof they cannot comprehend at all; what is beyond proof is readily grasped.'

Kanailal smiled and said, 'For instance, spirits, Brahmin ghosts, holy dust of Brahmin's feet, virtues of husband worship, etc., etc.'

'Not at all,' I said. 'Just see how we have been overwhelmed by Number One's ostentation while Anila remains unimpressed.'

Anila pressed her proposal a couple of times, but I lacked the tenacity to foray into the lanes of Calcutta looking for a house. At last, one day I saw Kanailal and Satish playing tennis at house Number One. Then I heard the rumour about Jati and Haren: in the musical soirees at Number One, one played on the box harmonium and the other on the tabla, as accompanists, while Arun had earned quite a bit of fame by singing parodies. I had known them for five to six years, bur never suspected they had these accomplishments. Arun, in particular, was known to be mainly interested in comparative theology. How could I have guessed he was skilled in parodies?

Honestly, I envied this Number One fellow secretly, even as I spoke slightingly of him. I can think, I can judge, imbibe the essence of everything, crack difficult problems: it is impossible to imagine Sitangshumouli as my equal in intellectual wealth. Even so, I envied the man. If I explain why, people will laugh.

Every morning, Sitangshu went out riding his robust horse. With what amazing skill he controlled the animal by the rein!

This scene I watched everyday and wished, 'Oh, if I could ride with such effortless ease!" I nourished a secret envy towards what is called competence that I totally lacked.

I do not understand music too well. But I would very often look furtively from my window to watch Sitangshu play the esraj. His effortless, graceful control of the instrument seemed enthralling. I thought the esraj loved him like a sweetheart who had willingly surrendered all her music to him. The ease of his dominance over everything from goods and furniture to beasts and men exuded an elegance in his ambience. This was something ineffable, which in my view was exceedingly rare. I felt here was a man who did not need to ask for anything; things would come to him of their own; a great reception awaited him wherever he chose to go.

So, when most of my Dualists, one after another, had become regular visitors at house Number One, some to play tennis, others to play in concerts, I could contemplate no other way to reclaim these fascinated souls than shift from the place. An agent brought in the news that a suitable house was available in the vicinity of Baranagar or Kashipur. I agreed. It was half past nine in the morning. I went to tell my wife to start packing up. I found her neither in the kitchen nor in the pantry. She was in the bedroom, sitting quietly at the window, her head resting against the bars. As I entered, she stood up. I told her, 'We can shift the day after tomorrow at the earliest.'

'Let us make it a fortnight later,' she said.

'Why?'

'Saroj's exam results will be out by then. I'm anxious about it. I don't feel like stirring right now.'

This was one matter among a host of others that I never discussed with my wife. The shifting was therefore put off for the time being. In the meantime, I came to know that Sitangshu would soon be out on a trip to south India, hopefully removing his imposing shadow over house Number Two.

The drama of life being enacted behind the curtain suddenly becomes visible towards the end of the fifth act. My wife had gone to her father's house. She came back the next day and shut herself in her room. She knew it was the scheduled date for our group's full-moon day feast. To discuss the arrangements with her, I knocked on the door. There was no response; then I called her by her name. She opened the door after a while.

'Are the arrangements ready?' I asked.

She nodded without uttering a word.

'Don't forget they are fond of your fish *kachuri*[12] and *amra*[13] chutney,' I told her.

Saying this, I came out and saw Kanailal waiting; I said, 'Come a little early tonight, Kanai.'

Kanai was surprised. 'What are you saying? Are we having a meeting tonight?'

'Yes, of course,' I said, 'Everything is ready—Maxim Gorky's new novel, Russell's appreciation of Bergson, fish pie, and even amra chutney.'

Kanai, still surprised, kept looking at me. After a while he said, 'Adwaita-babu, rather drop it today.'

At last, asking specifically I learnt that my brother-in-law Saroj had killed himself the previous afternoon. He had failed his examination and was severely reproached by his stepmother. He could not bear it and had hanged himself with a chuddar.

I asked him, 'Where did you hear this?'

'From Number One,' he said.

From Number One, of all places! Then I heard what had happened. When the news came towards the evening, Anila, not waiting for a carriage to be brought in, had gone out[14] with Ajodhya as escort, hired one on the way, and gone to her father's house. As soon as he learnt it from Ajodhya at night, Sitangshu had at once arrived there, silenced the police, and personally supervised the cremation.

I hurried into the inner rooms. I had expected Anila to have again retreated to her bedroom. But I found her in the verandah in front of the pantry, making preparations for the amra chutney. When I observed her face carefully, I realised that her life had turned topsy-turvy in the course of a single night.

'Why did you not tell me anything?' I accused her.

She lifted her large eyes and looked at me once, but said nothing. I felt small in shame. If Anila had said, 'What use would that have been?' I would have had nothing to say. Did I at all know how to carry myself in the face of these upheavals of life, the joys and sorrows of the world?

I told her, 'Anila, put these things aside. We are not going to meet this evening.'

'Why not?' she said keeping her eye on the amra she was peeling. 'You must have it. I have taken so much pains to make all these things; I can't let it go to waste.'

'By no means. It is impossible for the meeting to be held tonight,' I said.

'Meeting or no meeting, I invite them to dinner today.'

I felt somewhat relieved, and persuaded myself that her bereavement was not too great after all. That I had once given her many highly intellectual discourses, I explained to myself, had detached her mind a great deal. Though she had neither the background nor the ability to comprehend everything, nevertheless, there is such a thing as personal magnetism.

In the evening, two or three Dualists did not come. There was no question of Kanai coming; neither did any one of those who had joined the tennis group at house Number One. I was told Sitangshumouli was leaving by the early morning train, and so they had gone there to attend the farewell dinner. At the same time, the dinner Anila had arranged was such a grand one as she had never done before. Even a spendthrift like me had felt the expenses were rather extravagant.

It was one or one-thirty in the morning when the group dispersed after their dinner. I was tired, so went to bed at once and asked Anila if she would not.

She said, 'I have to clean up the dishes.'

It was about eight when I woke up next morning. On the teapoy in my bedroom where I used to leave my spectacles before going to sleep, I found a piece of paper under it where Anila had written, 'I am going away. Don't try to find me out. Even if you do, you won't succeed.'

I failed to make anything of it. She had left a tin box on the teapoy. In it I found all of her ornaments, even the bangles and bracelets she always wore—everything except the conchshell and iron bangles, her marriage insignia. In one compartment was her bunch of keys, in others were coins of all denomination in paper packets. This accounted for whatever money she had saved from the monthly budgeted expenses. A notebook contained a list of utensils and other household goods, as also of clothes sent to the washerman. Also noted were the milkman's and grocer's dues. Only what was not there was her own address.

All I understood was Anila had left. I looked for her in every room, enquired at her father's house; she was nowhere. I was never wise enough to figure out what particular step had to be taken in a particular situation. I felt hopelessly forlorn. Suddenly my eyes turned to house Number One: its doors and windows were shut; the doorman at the gate was smoking his hookah. Their Raja Babu had left early in the morning. My heart missed a beat. I suddenly realised that while I was preoccupied with the latest treatises on logic, one of the original sins of human society was spreading its tentacles in my house. When I had read of such incidents in Flaubert, Tolstoy, Turgenev and other great novelists, I had very lustily analysed the nuances of their underlying philosophy. That this could happen ultimately in my own house I had never even dreamt.

After I had overcome the initial shock, I tried to philosophise on the whole thing and dismiss it as of no consequence. I remembered my marriage day and allowed myself a wry smile. How much desire, how much effort, how much emotion go to waste, I rued. So many days and nights, so many years had rolled by: I knew a living thing called a wife did exist, and blissfully I had kept my eyes shut. Now suddenly, opening my eyes I found the bubble had burst. Well, if she had gone, so be it: after all, not everything in the world was a bubble. Had I not learnt to recognise things that have lasted through the ages transcending life and death?

But suddenly, I discovered that the modern day philosopher in me had collapsed in a faint, and the primitive creature had woken from its slumber, hungry and crying. I paced about on the terrace and the balcony, roamed through the empty rooms until one day, I went into my bedroom, where I had often seen my wife sitting quietly by the window, and started rummaging frantically through her personal effects. As I opened the drawer of her dressing table, out came a bunch of letters tied with a red silk ribbon. They were from house Number One. My heart was afire. My immediate reaction was to burn them. But tension is felt most where it hurts most. There was no holding me back from reading the letters, one and all.

And I read them for the umpteenth time. The first letter was in fragments. Apparently, the reader had torn it up immediately after reading it, and then as an afterthought, pasted the whole thing carefully with some adhesive on a sheet of paper. It ran thus:

> Even before reading this letter of mine, if you tear it up, I will still not be sorry. But what I have to say, say I must.
>
> I have seen you. I have been walking all these years in this world with my eyes wide open. But something worth seeing has happened for the first time in my life only now, at thirty-two. There had been a curtain of sleep over my eyes. You touched them with your magic wand[15], and today, through my reawakening I saw you: you who defy all description, your Creator's beloved object of wonder. What I wanted I have found. I want nothing else, except only recount my eulogy of you. If I had been a poet, there would have been no need of writing this in a letter; I would have set it to lyric to

> be sung by the entire world. I know that you will give no reply to this letter; in any case, please do not misunderstand me. Wiping away any trace of suspicion from your mind that I am capable of causing you harm, accept my worship silently. If you can respect my adoration for you, you will benefit by it as well. Who I am I do not need to write, but certainly it will not remain secret to your heart.

There were twenty-five such letters, none of which had any indication that a reply had ever gone from Anila. Had it gone, it would have at once struck a discordant note, or instead, the spell of the golden touch would have broken, silencing the hymn of eulogy with it.

How strange! The woman, whom Sitangshu had visualised from momentary glimpses, I saw now for the first time in eight years of intimate association, from the letters of a stranger. How thick could the pall of slumber over my eyes possibly have been? I had received Anila just as she was given over by the priest, but I had paid little price to acquire her as her Creator had shaped her; I had valued my sect and my new logic far more than I did her. So, one whom I had never really seen, never really possessed for a moment, if someone else had won by dedicating his life, what and to whom could I complain?

This was the last letter:

> Outwardly, I know nothing of you, but with my mind's eye I have seen your pain. And here I face a crucial test. These my virile arms refuse to remain passive. They want to defy all mortal and divine injunctions to liberate you from your futile life. But then, I reflect that your suffering is the seat of your own god; I have no right to seize it. I have permitted myself to contemplate until dawn. If an oracular voice by then dispels my hesitancy, something whatever will happen. Gusts of desire blow out the lamp that is the beacon on our path of life, so I will keep my mind under control and only recite earnestly, 'May God bless you.'

Clearly, his doubts had been dispelled; their paths had merged. As an offshoot, Sitangshu's letters grew into my own letters, my own heart's paeans of praise.

Many years have passed by. Books no longer interest me. I felt such an intense longing for a glimpse of Anila that I could not restrain myself. I came to know that Sitangshu was in the Mussouri hills then.

When I went there, I saw Sitangshu often enough walking on the street; but I never saw Anila with him. I was dismayed to suspect that she might have been disgraced and deserted. I grew restless, and finally went straight up to him. The details of the meeting are not necessary. Sitangshu said, 'I got only one letter from her; here it is.'

He took out from his pocket a card-case of enamelled gold, and picked out a piece of paper. In it was written, 'I am leaving. Don't try to find me. You can never find me out, even if you try.'

The same hand, the same script, the same date. And the piece of paper was the other half of the blue note-paper, half of which I retained.

Asharh 1324 (1918)

NOTES

1 A comic adaptation of the dictum from sage Charvaka's atheist and hedonistic philosophy, which sought to demolish the Vedas and shashtras as apocryphal and to preach: literally, *As long as you live, live merrily / Borrow money to drink ghee* (Live luxuriously/ Drink life to the lees).

2 A line from the nineteenth century Bengali poet Michael Madhusudan Dutt's *Meghnadbadhkavya.*

3 According to the ancient Hindu order, an *ashramite* Brahman, after completing his studies, was ritually bathed (*snata,* hence *snatak*) before being permitted to launch on the *domestic* order (the subsequent two orders being *anchorite* and *mendicant*). Ancient Indian universities, following this tradition, ceremonially bathed their students to award their first degree, *graduate,* which tradition has been handed down to the modern universities. 'To bathe in

the limited water etc.', therefore means 'to have graduated', which the narrator had not done.

4 The name derives from Shankaracharya's Advaita philosophy, according to which, only Brahma has reality, while the whole phenomenal world is the outcome of illusion (maya).

5 *Dvaita* means 'dual or dualism' referring to the 'Number Two' of his house. Since his own name is *Advaita*, he has wittily combined the two.

6 *Anil* means 'wind', *Anila* has no meaning. Since many female Bengali names end with a long *a* or *i,* parents often innocently choose such names, if only as a euphonious word in affectionate adaptation.

7 According to the then current system of numbering classes, the highest class X was called the First class, class IX the Second, and so on.

8 The king of serpents, according to mythology, holds the earth upon his hood.

9 Son of the sungod, born to a virgin Kunti, discarded at birth, later to fight heroically with his younger brother Arjuna in the Mahabharata.

10 *Asuras,* the mythological giants who, after being deprived of the ambrosia (*sura*) churned out of the sea, fought for it with the gods, but were eventually defeated by *Durga* and came to be called so, the prefix *a* meaning 'without'.

11 A woman sage, wife of Yajnavalkya, author of scriptures, who realised the futility of the material life and meditated all her life in pursuit of immortality.

12 *Luchi*-like flour preparation (see 'Royal Mark'), stuffed with some spiced mash of dal or fish or meat.

13 A slightly sweet sour fruit, seldom used except for chutney.

14 Bengali women of respectable families, except under compelling circumstances like this, never went out in the streets on their own in tnose days, unchaperoned.

15 A fairy-tale imagery; gold wand and silver wand are almost a sine qua non. Usually, the prince would awaken the princess.

In Quest of a Bride
(*Patra o Patri*)

1

Hitherto, the Butterfly[1] had never alighted on my brow, indeed, but once on the lotus of my mind it had. I was sixteen then. Thereafter, my condition was like one startled out of inchoate sleep, which just refuses to return. Some of my friends, in the matter of taking on wives, had graduated to twice or even thrice married status. Sitting on the last bench of the bachelors' class, I spent my days counting out the joists of the empty house.

I had passed my Entrance Examination at the age of fourteen. In those days, there was no age factor in marriage or entrance examination. I had never crammed textbooks, and therefore never had to suffer any kind of physical or mental indigestion. Just as a mouse nibbles away at whatever it gets to sink its teeth into, whether consumable or not, right from my childhood I had been inclined to go through any printed matter I came across. Non-textbooks far outnumber texts; in my bibliographic solar world, therefore, the non-curricular sun was fourteen hundred thousand times as massive as the earth of curricular books. Even so, in spite of the grim prediction of my Sanskrit *pandit-mashai*[2], I got through the examination.

My father was a deputy magistrate. We were then living at Satkshira or Jahanabad or some such place. At the outset, let me point out that any specifically mentioned time, location or person in this account is patently false; readers with more of curiosity than of wit will be disappointed. My father had been away on investigation then. My mother one day wanted to perform the ritual of a religious vow, for which she required a Brahmin to be feted and remunerated[3]. On such occasions of spiritual need, my pandit-mashai was her principal benefactor. Hence, my mother was especially grateful to him, although my father had just the opposite feelings.

That day, the list of gifts supplementing the feast included myself. The discussion they had had in the matter was essentially this: It was about time I would be going away to Calcutta for studying in college. In this condition, it was necessary to make some proper arrangement for ameliorating her estrangement from her son. If there were to be a child-bride on her lap, then by bringing her up and caring for her she could spend her days. Pandit-mashai's daughter Kashishwari was ideally suited for this purpose: she was as much a child as she was docile, and according to the family compatibility code, we matched each other perfectly. Besides, the spiritual reward of relieving a Brahmin of the liability of his daughter was no less an inducement.

My mother grew eager. As soon as she hinted that at least the girl should be inspected for once, pandit-mashai informed that the previous night his wife had arrived at his residence here bringing along their daughter. My mother did not delay approving of the girl, because the spiritual gain had lent its weight to her discriminating taste in making the decision. 'The girl has auspicious signs,' said my mother. The implication was that even though the girl was not sufficiently beautiful, there were reasons for consolation.

The word reached my ears through the grapevine. The very pandit-mashai I dreaded most for his lessons on conjugation of Sanskrit verbs was father of the girl with whom my marriage was proposed: the sheer incongruity of it was the first thing to fascinate me powerfully. Magically, as happens in fairy tales, the declension of nouns casting away its trappings of case-endings[4] suddenly turned into a princess, as it were.

One evening my mother called me into her room and said, 'Sanu, these mangoes and sweets have come from pandit-mashai's family. Have some.' My mother knew that if I was fed twenty-five mangoes and that was complemented[5] with another twenty-five, only then did it round off my rhythmic metre. It was therefore through the succulent route of the tongue that she appealed to my heart. Kashishwari was sitting on her lap. My memory has almost faded, but I still remember that her hair was wrapped with tinsel and she wore a satin jacket from a Calcutta shop, which was a visual delirium of red and blue and lace and ribbons. As far as I remember, her complexion was dark, her eyebrows were thick, the two eyes without shyness staring like a pet's. The rest of her face I have completely forgotten; perhaps it was still in the process of moulding in the Creator's workshop with just the first layer of clay[6] put on. At any rate, she looked quite innocent.

My heart swelled with pride. I said to myself: this tinsel-plaited, jacket-encased creature is entirely mine; I am its lord, I am its deity. For any other rare object one has to endeavour arduously, except for this singular thing: all I had to do was lift my little finger in condescension, and the Lord would feel obliged in blessing me with this boon. From what I had seen of my mother for so long, I knew what it meant to be a wife. I had observed that my father was ill-disposed to all other religious observances, but when it came to *Savitri-brata*[7], no matter what he might openly say, in his mind he felt quite elated. My mother did love him, I know, but what might anger my father, what might annoy him, were things that utterly dismayed her, and just the flavour of this perception my father relished most of all with his manliness. Worship, perhaps, does not matter much to gods, for it is their rightful due. But for humans, it is an illegitimate due, so they lose their head hankering after it. The appeal of that girl's looks and virtues had not reached me that day, but the notion that I deserved to be worshipped fermented in the manly blood of a fourteen-year-old. That day very proudly indeed did I eat the mangoes, I even left three unfed, boastfully, which had never happened in my life. I regretted it all afternoon.

That day Kashishwari had not been told what kind of relation she was going to be to me, but soon after going back home perhaps came to know of it. Thereafter, whenever she came across me, she became flustered, hurriedly looking for a place to hide. This nervous hurry on sighting me I enjoyed very greatly. The bio-chemical message that my presence generated a tremendous impact at some place of the world in some form was highly gratifying to me. That at the sight of even one like me, someone did feel scared, did feel abashed, or did do something whatever was simply unique. By her disappearance itself did Kashishwari indicate that in the world she was especially, entirely, and intimately mine alone.

From the inconsequentiality of so many years, suddenly in an instant attaining such extremely glorious position made my head begin to reel. I kept emulating in my mind the way my father was constantly badgering my mother with his nitpicking about her culinary or domestic lapses. In my imagination, I found Kashishwari follow the path of my mother who while pursuing an object undesirable to my father, realised it in cautious and intriguingly tactful ways. In my mind, I started giving her ungrudgingly and suddenly at intervals gifts ranging from bank notes of high denomination to diamond jewellery. On some days, sitting down to eat, she left her meal half-eaten and sat by the window wiping tears with her sari-end: I could see with my mind's eye even such a pathetic sight, and I cannot say that it seemed extremely pitiable to me. My father was extremely careful about the self-reliance of little boys. Keeping one's own room in order, putting away one's clothes and so on, all these things I had to do myself. Nevertheless, in my mind the pictures of domesticity that surfaced in prominent lines were somewhat different, of which here I mention one. Needless to say, in my father's history, just such an incident had happened one day; I had no *originality* at all in this imagination. This was the picture: after the midday meal on a Sunday, I am reading the newspaper reclining against a pillow, my legs stretched out and the hookah tube in my hand. As I become drowsy, the tube slips down. Kashishwari, sitting in the veranda was keeping notes of the items with the washerman. I call her; she comes running and puts back the tube in my hand. I tell her, 'Look, in the cupboard on the left in my sitting room, on the third shelf, there's a thick English book with a blue cover. Go fetch it.' Kashi brings me a blue-covered book. I tell her, 'Oh, not this one. That one is thicker, and on its spine is the name written in gold lettering.' This time she brings up a green book, which I throw on the floor angrily and get up. Kashi looks thoroughly abashed and her eyes brim with tears. Going myself, I find that the book is not on the third shelf; it is on the fifth. I return with the book and go back quietly to my bed without telling Kashi anything about my mistake. Hanging her head, looking sad, she goes on handing out the clothes to the washerman, and she is unable to forget her fault in disturbing her husband's rest by her stupidity.

My father was investigating a robbery, and this is how I was passing my days. Meanwhile, concerning me, pandit-mashai's language and conduct had instantly switched from imperative to the intransitive passive mode of speech[8], and that was an extremely friendly mode of communication.

The investigation being over, my father returned home. I know that my mother had prepared herself to bring up the talk of my marriage little by little to my father taking care to make it agreeable to him in the way she sautéed his favourite curry with spices. My father despised pandit-mashai for his avarice: mother would certainly have introduced the matter by criticising the man mildly, and at the same time, praising his wife and daughter profusely. Unfortunately, thanks to pandit-mashai's exhilarated garrulity, the news had received wide publicity. There was no one in the town whom he had not told that the marriage had been settled and that the date and time were being decided. He had even completed a round of discussion with the appropriate authorities that he would be requiring the *sheristadar's*[9] brick and mortar house for a couple of days for the purpose. Everyone had assured him of helping him to the best of his ability for the auspicious ceremony. The lawyers at my father's court had also agreed to raise funds to finance the wedding. The secretary of the local Entrance school Bireshwar-babu's third son read in class VIII; using the simile of moon and lotus, he had already composed a verse in tri-syllabic metre on marriage. The secretary, taking that verse, after stopping whomever he met on the way, read it out. People of the village had grown optimistic about the boy's potential.

Naturally, as soon as father returned from his tour, he heard the good news even before entering our portals. The immediate fallout: mother weeping and fasting; everyone in the house fear-stricken; servants getting undue punishment; at his court, cases being summarily dismissed and sentences rigorously pronounced; pandit-mashai dismissed from service disappearing along with the tinsel-haired Kashishwari—and even before the end of vacation detaching me from my mother's company for my forcible banishment to Calcutta. My mind deflated like a collapsed balloon; its frisking and rollicking in the skies, in the air stopped altogether.

2

On my matrimonial path, this was then the obstacle right at the commencement. Several times thereafter, the butterfly fluttered its wings over me, but never settled on my brow. I do not wish to give an elaborate account, but will leave one or two brief notes on the history of my failure.

Well before I was twenty, having honourably passed my MA I had come out flamboyantly sporting spectacles on my eyes, and twirling[10] my hint of a moustache. My father was then posted at Rampurhat or Noakhali or Barasat or some such place. Now that my years of churning the ocean of words had turned out the gems of degrees, it was the turn of the ocean of money being churned. My father, going to recall influential patrons among the sahibs found that his principal benefactor had passed away; the next in importance had been pensioned off to England; a lesser third had been transferred to the Punjab, and the only one left in Bengal was a man who promised much at the introduction and reneged on it in the end to most candidates. When my grandfather had been a deputy magistrate, patrons had never been so scarce that candidates from the same family could not be ferried between the shores of employment and pension perpetually. Now these were bad times, so when my father was contemplating whether the scion of his family would alight from the lofty cage of government service on the lowly perch of a mercantile firm, the only daughter of a rich Brahmin came to his notice. The Brahmin was a contractor, whose avenue of income was much wider in the clandestine underworld than on the open surface of the earth. Because of Christmas, he was then busy distributing oranges and other kinds of gifts to appropriate slots when I appeared on the scene. My father was then staying just opposite his house across the road. For obvious reasons, a deputy magistrate's MA-passed son was like the 'inaccessible fruit of the tallest tree'[11] for a father with a marriageable daughter. The contractor therefore stood on tiptoe 'with his arms stretched out' to me. I have already mentioned that his arms were long enough to reach up to the dust; they at least reached the Deputy-babu's heart easily enough, but mine were then perched on a loftier branch.

All this had happened when I was barely past twenty when I coveted no jewel other than the gem of a wife. Not only that, my heart still burned bright with idealism. That is to say, the perception of a true wife[12] that I had in my mind was not in vogue in the market. In the present time in our country, the world is shrunken on all sides. In intellectual pursuits, extending the mind to the liberal fields of wisdom and idealism, and in practice, attenuating it to the size of that narrow world was a contradiction I could not tolerate even in my mind. If the wife I wanted to make a fellow traveller on the path of idealism were to hobble me like a shackle in the prison of domesticity, at every movement pulling back with jangling of irritation, I was unwilling to acknowledge such an evil star as my partner. In fact, after coming out fresh from college, I had turned into a thoroughly modern person such as those who are lampooned as modern in the satires of our country. This brand of modern people was far more numerous in our times than they are now. What is surprising is that they truly believed that conforming to society was retrogressive, and dragging it along progressive.

Such a person like this, I, Sanatkumar, Esquire, found myself in front of the gaping mouth of the money-bag of a powerful Brahmin burdened with a daughter. 'No dithering for what augurs well,'[13] said my father. I kept silent, but decided to see with my own eyes, and hear with my own ears to judge it for myself. I kept my eyes and ears open: I saw a little and heard a great deal. The girl was small and beautiful like a doll. She appeared not to have been moulded in the usual cast: she seemed to have been hand-made by someone with consummate care with each strand of hair neatly stuck in and the eyebrows tidily painted. She could recite Sanskrit hymns to the Ganges. Her mother used to wash everything down to the coal in Ganges water[14], only then could she cook. Since Mother Earth, the sustainer of living creatures, bore various races, that lady always shrank from contagion with the earth. Most of her associations were exclusively with water, because fish, which is aquatic, is not Muslim by birth, and onions do not grow in water[15]. The principal preoccupation of her life was cleansing and purifying her body, her house, her clothes, her furniture, and her utensils. By the time she had finished all her duties, it would be half-past two in the afternoon. She had personally brought up her daughter to such a purified state in every respect that she never had to bother about any such thing as the girl's own wishes or opinions.

No matter how inconvenient a certain arrangement is, it is easy to carry out as long as no reasonable ground has to be explained to the person. At mealtime, she never wore good clothes, lest they should be contaminated[16] with food. She had even learned to be discriminating about the shadows of people. On the one hand, she even used to bathe in the Ganges sitting inside a palanquin; on the other, all her movements were circumscribed by the eighteen *Puranas.* For religious laws and injunctions, my mother too had ample regard, but that anyone else should have even greater regard than her and should boast of it tacitly was something she could not tolerate. So when I said to her, 'Ma, I'm no match for this girl,' she laughed and said, 'Yes, it's hard to find such a match in this age.'

I said, 'Let me then take your leave.'

'Why, Sonu?' said my mother. 'Don't you like her? She's quite pretty!'

'Ma, a wife is not just a thing to keep looking at; she has to have intelligence, too.'

'Now, just listen to him! What proof of her deficiency have you had till now?'

'No one with a modicum of intelligence can survive with such nonsensical trifles day and night; they simply suffocate one to death.'

My mother was crestfallen. She knew that my father had virtually committed himself to the other party on this marriage. She also knew that father often forgot that other people as well might have their own wishes. In fact, if my father had not been excessively hot-tempered and domineering, perhaps eventually marrying that Puranic doll, devoutly observing rites and rituals, vows and fasts I too might have attained salvation one day on the banks of the Ganges. That is, if my mother had been entrusted with this marriage, she would have taken her time finding opportune moments, sometimes instilling counsels into my ears, sometimes shedding tears, until finally realising the goal. But when my father kept blustering and thundering, I became desperate and told him, 'Ever since childhood, you've taught me self-reliance in everything from eating through sleeping. Is it only in marriage that self-reliance has no role to play?' I have never seen anyone being successful with the sheer force of logic except passing the subject at college examinations. Rational arguments never act like water to the fire of sophistry; rather, it acts like oil. My father had convinced himself that he had given word of mouth to the other party and there could be no greater proof of acceptability of the marriage than this. On the other hand, if I had reminded him that my mother too had once given her word to pandit-mashai, yet because of that word, not only did my marriage fall through, but his livelihood perished with it as well, a regular criminal case might have ensued. That piousness, mantras and rituals were far superior to intelligence, judgement and discernment, that their poetic appeal was profound and beautiful, that their holiness was sublime, that their results were benign, that *symbolism* itself was *idealism* were some of the topics my father had been discussing within my earshot at all times for some days. I held my tongue; but how could I silence my mind? The rejoinder that came to the tip of my tongue but receded was: 'If this is your faith, then why do you raise chickens, of all things?' Yet another point came to my mind: it was my father again, who once used to chastise my mother for the futility of her religious ceremonies, her observances of rites and rituals, restrictions and injunctions, her gifts and remunerations to priests whenever he found them to his disadvantage or detriment. My mother, then acknowledging her insignificance, and because the weaker sex is irrational by nature, bowing down her head, overcame the impact of his annoyance, and engaged as usual in making elaborate arrangements for the ritual feeding of Brahmins. But *Bishwakarma* did not craft human beings by casting them in the perfect mould of logic. Therefore, you cannot win someone over by pointing out the inconsistency in his words and actions; all you do is infuriate him. To appeal to anyone's logic is to aggravate the virulence of his wrong: those who have any faith in political or domestic agitation ought to remember this. When a horse kicks at the cart behind, thinking it an injustice, the injustice does persist all the same; all it gets gratuitously is injured hoofs. In the exuberance of youth, going to do a bit of argument, I too was in a similar plight. Of course, I escaped the clutch of the Puranic girl, but forfeited the security of my father's modern day bank balance as well. 'Well then,' said my father, 'go and practise self-reliance.'

I touched his feet and said, 'As you please.'

Mother sat weeping.

My father's right hand had retracted[17] from me, but thanks to the intervening mother, bearers of money orders visited me off and on. Clouds stopped giving rain, but secretly on cool nights, dewdrops kept moistening me. Armed with those resources, I launched upon a business. The initial capital was just seventy-nine rupees. Today the total capital, though far short of the sum on the envious grapevine, is no less than twenty lakh rupees.

Agents of the marriage-god followed me about. I unbolted the doors that had been kept closed earlier. I remember one day in the irrepressible optimism of youth, my heart was bent upon a girl of sixteen (for fear of the pious readers of these days, I have given a more or less tolerable age), but I heard that her mother was eyeing a civil servant; her sight did not reach below a barrister at the lowest. I was below the zero-point of her attention meter. But later in the same house on another day, I was treated not only to tea but lunch as well, and after dinner at night, played whist with their daughters, listened to their conversations in English, which was straight out of the aristocratic quarters of England. My problem is that I had picked up my English by reading *Rasselas,* 'The Deserted Village', and the essays of Addison and Steele. It was beyond me to match these girls. Exclamations like '*O my, O dear O dear!*' just refuse to come out of my mouth with the proper accent. As far as my learning goes, I can at best carry on transactions at market places in abject pedestrian English. But if I think of a romantic conversation in twentieth-century English, romance itself evaporates. Yet, given the absence of Bengali language on their lips, if I had tried to exchange romantic words in true Bankim style,[18] I would have to regret; it would not have been the labour's worth. In any case, once, such girls with a coating of Englishness had been easily accessible to me. But the dreamland I had seen through the chinks of the door later disappeared altogether from view when the door opened wide. Then the thought kept coming back to my mind: just as that vow-keeping doctrinaire girl used to delight her imbecile mind turning day and night in the swirl of recurrence of meaningless rituals, these girls too with the same frame of an indefatigable mind observing every triviality of British manners and customs were blissfully spending their time day after day, year after year. In the same way that those orthodox girls shuddered in indignation at someone's slightest deviation in the observance of touching and bathing norms, these modern girls, when they noticed a slight fault in accent or a small slip in table manners, became suspicious about the offending person's genuineness as a human being. Those were country-made dolls, these foreign-made ones. Neither kind moved under the force of will; a clockwork mechanism wound by habit moved them. The consequence of this musing was that towards the entire female race itself I grew irreverent in my mind: I deduced that since they had only limited intelligence, they had necessarily to indulge in the ritual trivia of bathing, purging, fasting and all that, to find any meaning of life. I have read there is a particular variety of bacterium that keeps going round and round in circles. But man does not go round and round; he moves forward. Is it then with the magnified version of that microscopic organism that God decreed the unfortunate male of the species Homo sapiens to enter into conjugal relations?

Meanwhile, the older I grew, the stronger became my hesitation about marriage. Up to a certain age, man can get married even without any thought; after that age, marriage requires extraordinary courage. I do not belong to that reckless band of men. Besides, why a sensible girl should marry me all at once without rhyme or reason is something I have never figured out. Love is blind, they say.

But that blinding quality has nothing to do in this case. Worldly wisdom has more eyes than two: when those additional eyes look at me dispassionately, what they discover in me is what I wonder. My qualities are certainly many, but they can be detected only in course of time, and are not discernible at a glance. I know that the stubbiness of my nose has been compensated for by the superiority of my brain; but the nose is what sticks out conspicuously, whereas the Almighty kept intelligence formless. However, when a mature girl does not make the least objection to marry me even at the shortest notice, my regard for the female race dwindles even further. If I had been a girl, the long sighs from Sri Sanatkumar's own short nose would be blowing away her hopes and vanity into the dust.

Thus, my yet-to-be loaded matrimonial boat foundered at times at the sandbanks, but never made it to the *ghat.* The ingredients of home-making, except for a wife, kept increasing in step with the prosperity of business. One thing I had forgotten: I was growing older. Suddenly an incident reminded me of this.

Going to inspect a mica pit at a town in Chhotanagpur district, I came across my pandit-mashai who was living comfortably in his own house in a *shal*-grove by the side of a small river. His son worked there. I had pitched my tent at the end of that shal-grove. I was now widely known for my wealth. He said he knew it from the outset that I would grow in course of time to be an outstanding person. Possibly true, but he had astoundingly kept it secret. Apart from that, by what signs he had known it I am not supposed to know. Perhaps outstanding persons are short of understanding the nuances of homophonous spelling[19] in their student days. Kashishwari was at her father-in-law's house, so there was no hindrance to my growing into a member of pandit-mashai's family. His wife had passed away a few years before, but he was accompanied by a crowd of granddaughters. Not all of them were his own; two belonged to his deceased elder brother. With their company, the old man had made the afternoon of his old age colourful with various hues. The flow of his Sanskrit *slokas* from

Amarashatak and *Aryasaptashati* kept circling round the girls with gurgles of laughter like the foamy current of a mountain stream round pebbles.

With a smile I said, 'Pandit-mashai, what's all this I see?' He said, 'It says in your English books that Saturn wears a string of moons; this is my string of moons.'

This scene of that poor family suddenly reminded me that I was alone. Then I realised that I had grown weary of dragging my own weight. Pandit-mashai was not aware that he had grown old but I realised distinctly that I had. That I had grown old means I had surpassed my surroundings, which slackening on all sides were showing gaps: gaps which neither money nor fame could fill. From the world I was drawing no vital fluid, was only accumulating things; to the frustration of it, one can remain oblivious as a matter of habit. But the scene at pandit-mashai's house revealed that my days were arid, my nights deserted. He must have convinced himself that I was more fortunate than he was: a thought at which I laughed to myself. There is an invisible realm of delight around this material world. If our life has no link with that realm of delight, we hover in the air like Trishanku[20]. Pandit-mashai did have that link, I did not, and that was the difference.

Sprawling over the hand-rests of my armchair, smoking a cigarette, I kept musing that the four stages in the life of a male have four presiding deities: mother in his childhood, wife in his youth, daughters and daughters-in-law in middle age, granddaughters and granddaughters-in-law in old age. This is how through women, a man attains his own completeness. This realisation in the distraction of the rustling shal-grove captivated me. In my mind, I looked out at my future old age to the farthest end: at the utter barrenness of it, my heart gave out a wail of desolation. Carrying the burden of profit on my shoulder through that desert path, where was I going to drop down dead in the end? No, there was no delaying any more. I had recently crossed forty; fifty was waiting down the road, stick in hand, to thresh the last reserve of youth out of me. With no further concern for money, let me now think of life instead. But there was no going back to that part of life which had been kept in abeyance. Nevertheless, the time to patch up the discontinuity had not passed yet.

From here, my work took me to a city in western India. Bishwapati-babu was a rich money-lender there, and I had some business with him. He was a shrewd fellow, so clinching a deal with him took much time. One day, when I was just fed up and thinking, 'He is going to be no use to me,' and had even told my servant to pack up my things, Bishwapati-babu turned up in the evening and said, 'You must have acquaintance with a lot of people. If you take some interest, a widow can be saved.'

This is what had happened:

Nandakrishna-babu had first gone to Bareilly as headmaster of an Anglo-Bengali school. He had done a very good job of it. Everyone had wondered why such a competent and well-educated person leaving his hometown had come so far away for a job that carried no decent salary. Not that he had a reputation only for getting his students successfully through the examinations; he had devoted himself to much good work as well. Then somehow, it was revealed that his wife was indeed beautiful, but of poor lineage: a woman of a very low caste; even her touch defiled the potability and other hidden sublime qualities of drinking water. When people demanded an explanation from him, he said, 'Yes, she is of low caste, nevertheless she is my wife.' Then someone questioned how such a marriage could be valid. To him Nandakrishna said, 'Well, you have taken two wives in succession in the presence of *shalgram*[21] and have given ample proof that two is not enough. I can't say what shalgram would say, but God knows my marriage is more valid than yours, valid every day, every minute of the day. I don't want to discuss the matter with you any further.'

The man at the receiving end of Nandakrishna's diatribe was far from pleased. Besides, his ability for doing mischief to others was extraordinary as well. So, compelled by the persecution that followed, Nandakrishna, leaving Bareilly, came over to this town and began to practise law. The man was extremely fastidious about professional ethics; even if he had to starve, he never took up an unfair litigation. Whatever difficulties he may have had in the beginning, thereafter success started coming, because the judges trusted him completely. He had built a house and just settled down to a comfortable life, when the great famine struck. Masses of people were wiped out. Among those who had been entrusted with the distribution of relief material, some were pilfering; when Nandakrishna reported this to the magistrate, he said, 'Where do I find an honest person?'

Nandakrishna said, 'If you trust me, I can take up part of the responsibility.' He was duly entrusted, and while executing that trust one day at noon he dropped down dead under a tree in an open field. The doctor said he had died of heart failure.

So much of the story had been already known to me. Somewhat in a vein of idealism citing this very person, one day I had said at our club, 'People like this Nandakrishna who have failed in the world and withered away—have left neither fame, nor money—they are the ones who are working for God to elevate the world –'

I had hardly finished when, like a full-sailed boat being suddenly grounded by a sandbar, I was cut short. One of the members, a man of great wealth and standing, was reading the newspaper; peering at me from over his spectacles, he exclaimed, 'Hear! Hear!'

Be that as it may. Bishwapati said Nandakrishna's widow lived along with her daughter in the same neighbourhood. The girl had been born on the night of *Diwali*[22], so her father had named her *Dipali.* Since the widow had been thrown out by the society, she lived completely alone raising and educating this daughter all by herself. The girl was over twenty-five now. Her mother was in poor health and was growing old as well. She might die any day when the girl would be left utterly helpless. Bishwapati requested me very earnestly, 'If you could find her a match, that would be a virtuous act.'

I had thought somewhat disdainfully of Bishwapati as an insensitive, selfish and worldly fellow. His concern for the orphaned girl of a widow moved my heart. I thought of the extinct mammoth of the prehistoric age: seeds of food grains extracted from its stomach had been planted and found to germinate; perhaps human qualities too, even remaining buried deep under mounds of the dead, never completely perish.

I told Bishwapati, 'I know of a bridegroom. There will be no problem. You finalise the matter and fix up the date.'

'But without seeing the girl –'

'That will not be necessary.'

'But if the bridegroom wants property, there's not much. When the mother dies, he'll get only her house and the little savings, if any.'

'The groom has property. You need not worry about that.'

'His name and other details –?'

'Not now. If people come to know, the marriage may fizzle out.'

'At least the girl's mother should have a description of him.'

'Tell her that the man is a mixture of faults and virtues like other ordinary men. The faults are not grave enough to cause any worry, and the virtues are not enviably great either. As far as I know, parents with unmarried daughters have a special liking for him, though the daughters' minds are not quite known.'

When Bishwapati-babu was very much grateful in the matter, I grew more respectful to him. For the business deal I had not previously found profitable enough to agree on, I felt eager to sign the registration documents even acknowledging loss. At the time of departure, he said, 'Tell the groom that whatever the other considerations, such an accomplished girl is rarely found.'

If the girl, who had been deprived of the patronage and respect of society, was enthroned in the heart, would she stint in the least from dedicating herself? That girl who entertains high hopes is the one who has no end of hopes. This Dipali's lamp was earthen, so in a corner of an earthen house like mine, the flame of her lamp would of course be treated with no neglect.

That evening, I sat reading an English newspaper when I was told that a girl had come to see me. There was no woman in my house, so I was flustered. Before I could think of some formal reception, coming into the room she made a *pronam.* People would not believe from my outward appearance that I am a very shy type: neither did I look her in the face nor did I say anything to her. 'My name is Dipali,' she introduced herself.

Her voice was very sweet. Summoning up my courage, I looked at her face, which was imbued with intelligence and tenderness. She had no veil over her head, her sari white and ordinary, worn in the fashion of the day. I was wondering what to say when she said, 'Please do not try to arrange my marriage.'

Whatever else she might have said, such objection from Dipali's lips was beyond my expectation. I had convinced myself that she would be thoroughly grateful for the proposal.

I asked, 'Whether known or unknown, won't you marry anyone?'

'No, none.'

Even though I was more experienced in the theory of matter than in the chemistry of the heart, and especially, feminine psychology was far more difficult for me than Bengali spelling, nevertheless, the obvious meaning of the word did not seem to me to be the true meaning. 'The groom I have chosen for you does not deserve your scorn,' I said.

'I mean him no scorn,' she said, 'but I will not marry.'

'That man also respects you from his heart.'

'But no, please don't ask me to get married.'

'All right, I won't. But can't I be any use to you and your mother in some way?'

'If, by finding me a teaching assignment in a girls' school, you take me away from here to Calcutta, it might be a great help.'

'There are openings. I can find you one.'

This was not entirely true. What did I know about girls' schools? But certainly there was no harm in founding one.

'Will you come to our house,' Dipali said, 'and discuss it with my mother?'

'I'll go tomorrow morning itself.'

Dipali left. I stopped reading the newspaper. After walking on the terrace, I sat on a stool. I asked the stars, 'From millions of miles away, are you really weaving the threads of actions and relations of human life, sitting silently?'

Just then, without notice, Bishwapati's second son Shripati appeared on the terrace. The gist of our conversation was this:

In his eagerness to marry Dipali, Shripati was prepared to renounce society. His father had said he would disown him if he did such an atrocious act. Dipali said she was not worth anybody's sorrow, humiliation and sacrifice of this magnitude. That apart, Shripati had been brought up in a wealthy family since childhood; in Dipali's view, after being cast away by society and from his house, he would not be able to bear the hardship of poverty. They had argued long without reaching a conclusion. Right at this critical moment, interposing gratuitously, foisting another bridegroom in between them, I had complicated the matter enormously. Shripati was therefore telling me to bow out of this drama like the deleted portion of a proof sheet.

'Once I've come,' I said, 'I'm not quitting. And if I do quit, I'll do so only after disentangling the knots.'

The wedding date did not change. Only the groom changed. Bishwapati's request I had kept, but he was not pleased. Dipali's request I had not kept, but from all appearances, she was pleased. I do not know whether a teacher's vacancy existed at school, but in my home, a daughter's place was vacant and that vacancy was filled up. That a worthless fellow like me was not a useless[23] fellow, my money alone proved to Shripati. The lamp that was to light his home was lit in my home instead. I had been considering completing my deferred marriage, but discovered that with the higher authority condescending, one could receive promotion even beyond his next higher class. Today at fifty-five, I am happy with a swarm of granddaughters and a grandson too. But Bishwapati-babu snapped his business ties with me—because he did not approve of the bridegroom.

Paush 1324 (1918)

NOTES

English words in italics appear in the original text.

1 *Prajapati* (literally, butterfly) is another name for Brahma, who being the Creator, is believed to predestine the couples; divine matchmaker (see Glossary).

2 At the time, teachers were generally called *pundits*, irrespective of the subjects they taught; *mashai* is a respectful suffix (see Glossary).

3 In Bengali, *bhojan-dakshina* is the customary gift of small amounts of money (sometimes, even as small as a token coin) to a Brahmin who is believed to have obliged the host spiritually by partaking of the food *(bhojan)* and accepting the fee *(dakshina)* as remuneration. Usually non-Brahmins, to consummate funeral rites of parents, and devout women, to keep a vow, perform this ritual.

4 According to Panini Grammar, forming Sanskrit words in different case endings by adding inflectional affixes to root nouns is called 'Declension' *(Subanta Prakaran)*, while forming verbs in the different tenses in this way is called 'Conjugation' *(Tinganta Prakaran)*.

5 A Sanskrit rhetorical device of completing *(puran)* a quarter part of a verse *(Pada)* with additional, often meaningless, inflexion is called *Padapuran*.

6 In clay modelling, the initial step consists in mounting a layer of clay on the raw bamboo and straw structure. This is called *Ekmete* or 'the first layer of clay', and is used in reference to images of gods and goddesses.

7 A *brata* or vow in honour of Savitri, wife of King Satyavan, and one of the five traditional Hindu women held as models of chastity and wifely devotion; the ritual is performed on the fourteenth lunar day of the dark fortnight of *Jyaishtha*.

8 If, for example, he had previously said, 'Bring the book', he now

said, 'Let the book be brought.' Strictly, what is *Bhab-bachya* (a mode of speech where the speaker's intention is expressed in the third person present tense of the verb: for example, *Let it be done/ Let him go/ He can go,* etc., the person being present before the speaker) has no corresponding mode of voice in English grammar, which does not admit of a passive voice of intransitive verbs.

9 Record-keeper/ office superintendent;

10 The Bengali *ta* derives from the Sanskrit *tar* meaning 'string'. Hence, to twirl the moustache is to twist the untrimmed bristles at the ends so that they curve up in a string like the prow of a boat. It signifies idling away the time in careless abandon or having superior airs.

11 The Bengali phrase literally means 'attainable only to a man with the highest stature'. Note how the metaphor is sustained until it reaches its logical conclusion in the last sentence.

12 The Bengali word literally means 'co-religionist'. It is enjoined on the wife by the sacred vow of marriage to adhere to the same beliefs and practices as the husband's.

13 The first half of a Sanskrit couplet (*Shubhasya shighram/Ashubhasya kalaharanam*) most uttered by the Bengalis fearing that an unforeseen snag might delay or even mar a happy event. The other half means, 'Procrastinate with what augurs evil.'

14 The Ganges water is most sacred to the Hindus. It has become synonymous with purity. Though a hyperbole, it points to the ridiculous extent of superstition of orthodox women.

15 This brings into sharp focus the hatred among orthodox Hindus against Muslims and low caste Hindus. Onion is a chief ingredient of Muslim cookery.

16 In that case, she would have to change and wash the defiled clothes all over again, if not discard them altogether!

17 In Bengali parlance, the work of the right hand refers either to eating food or to giving money. Obviously, the latter meaning is suggested here.

18 High-flown Bengali replete with euphonic Sanskrit combination words (sandhi), compounds (*samasa*), and rhetoric (*alankara*) with unmitigated vigour (see Glossary).

19 The Bengali idiomatic phrase *natwa-shatwa-jnan* derives from

Sanskrit grammar distinguishing between two pairs of homophonous letters of the alphabet: the dental 'n', and the cerebral 'nd'; the dental 's', and the cerebral 'sh'. A particularly complex set of rules for students (and teachers as well). Hence the phrase means the power of discerning.

20 A legendary king, father of King Harishchandra. When sage Bashishtha and his sons thwarted the king's move to ascend to heaven in his mortal frame by virtue of his penances, the omnipotent sage Vishwamitra created a whole stellar abode in between heaven and earth, to rehabilitate King Trishanku. Hence, the name has come to mean 'a state of suspension'.

21 A stone image of Vishnu, found in the bed of the river Gandaki; it is known in sixteen different names depending on the pores, lines and wheels carved on it; Vishnu is worshipped in this form as household deity by devout Hindu males; the name derives from the legendary land by that name in the riverbed; the stone is traditionally held as the most sacred, incontrovertible and inviolable witness to a Hindu marriage.

22 Diwali < Dipabali < Dipali: a row of lamps. A major Hindu religious festival honouring goddess Kali (outside Bengal, goddess Lakshmi), celebrated all over India on the new moon day of the month of *Kartik*, marked by lighting of lamps, feasting and gifts. The second day following this in Bengal is the brothers' day (see Glossary).

23 The text has *nirarthak* or 'meaningless, useless, unnecessary', but since the word is a compound of *nih* (no) and *artha* (money), the author has used a pun which, however, is untranslatable, because *nirarthak* never means 'moneyless'.

The Laboratory
(*Laboratory*)

1

Nandakishore was a qualified engineer from the University of London. He was a perfect model of a brilliant student, or *Dedipyaman*[1] in chaste Bengali. Beginning from school, he always rode first class in his academic journey until the last examination.

His intellect was outstanding; his necessities were extensive; but his financial resources were limited.

He had managed to enlist in two giant bridge-construction projects of the Railway Company. There is ample scope in such projects for enhancing one's income and saving on expenditure, never mind the unedifying example it sets. When he wielded his hands, both right and left, he had never felt a prick of conscience. It is widely believed that such transactions pertain to an abstract entity called company, and hence any stigma does not attach to the personal account of an individual's morality.

In his own sphere, his superiors called him a genius; he had consummate skill in calculation. Only because he was a native Bengali did he never receive his due recognition. When his British colleagues of lower calibre, standing astride with their hands in their stuffed pockets, patronised him with a pat on the back, saying, 'Hallo, Mr Mallik,' he did not like it the least bit, particularly because all the responsibility was his, while the money and fame fell to their lot. Necessarily, he had to make his private estimate of his legitimate dues, which he knew perfectly well how to make good.

He never lived foppishly with the money he had made legitimately and otherwise. He lived in a one-and-a-half-storey house in a lane in Shikdarpara. He had no time to change out of his grimy factory clothes. If anybody tried to pull his leg, his repartee was, 'Well, this livery of Labour Master is my dress!'

But he had built a huge mansion specially designed for his scientific collection and research. So engrossed was he in his scientific hobby that the gossip doing the rounds did not reach his ears: 'For such an enormous building to spring from thin air, where had he found the Aladdin's lamp?'

Some kinds of hobby preoccupy man obsessively; it is of the nature of drunkenness; he is oblivious to people eying him with suspicion. Nandakishore was an unusual character; he was mad about science. While flipping through the catalogue, he would impulsively clutch the arms of his chair from shivers of thrill. He used to import such expensive instruments from Germany and America as had no parallel even in the greatest universities of India. This lack of facilities was what troubled the mind of this seeker after knowledge. This wretched country had to eke out an intellectual living out of the leftovers from the feast of learning. Lacking the opportunity to use sophisticated instruments, which is available in those countries, our students only forage for second-hand knowledge from bland textbooks. 'We are not lacking in brains,' he would boast, 'What we lack is funds.' His mission was to open up the highway of science enough for the youth.

His colleagues' sanctimonious protestations became intolerably louder in proportion to the costly instruments he continued to collect. At this point, the senior sahib rescued him from his predicament. He had great respect for Nandakishore's competence. Besides, he was aware of his ingenuity in siphoning off fat fistfuls in railway assignments.

Nandakishore was obliged to resign his job. With the blessings of his boss, he bought up scrap from the Railway Company at a bargain price and set up his own foundry. That was during the First World War, when there was a boom in the market economy. The man was extraordinarily resourceful; he found new ducts and channels of making money through which came a deluge of profits.

At this time, he acquired another passion.

Nandakishore had once stayed for some time in the Punjab in connection with his business. There he picked up a female companion. One day he was sitting in his veranda, sipping tea, when this woman, then of around twenty years, came up to him without inhibition, her long skirt swinging; her eyes were bright, a smile as sharp as a freshly honed knife dangled from her lips. She sat close to his feet and said, '*Babuji*, I've been watching you morning and evening over the last few days. I'm simply amazed.'

Nandakishore laughed and said, 'Why, isn't there a zoo in this area?'

'Why need a zoo?' she said, 'Those that were to have been there, are roaming free. I'm looking for man.'

'Found any?'

'Here is one.' She pointed to Nandakishore. Nandakishore laughed. 'Tell me what virtues you have found in me,' he asked.

She said, 'Big businessmen of these parts, thick gold chains round their necks and diamond rings in their fingers, had all closed in on you. They had found you a newcomer, a Bengali, who did not understand business. They had thought you an easy prey. But none of their tricks clicked; on the contrary, they've fallen in your trap. I think they haven't yet realised that, but I have.'

Nandakishore was startled to hear this. He concluded: a no-nonsense girl this, by no means easy and simple!

'Let me tell you about myself. Listen now,' said the girl. 'There is a famous astrologer in our locality. He examined my horoscope and said I would make a big name one day. He said that my birth planet had an aspect of Satan.'

'Strange!' exclaimed Nandakishore, 'Saturn, surely?'

The girl said, 'Don't you know, babuji, Satan is the predominant power in the world? People usually speak ill of him, but he is genuine. Our Lord Shiva is always inebriated[2]; he is no good for running the show. Just see how our rulers have conquered the world by satanic power, not by the Christian power. But they are true to their word; that's why they have retained the empire. The day they go back on their word, they will perish at the hands of Satan himself.'

Nandakishore was amazed. The girl continued, 'Don't mind, babu, if I say there's a streak of devilry in you too, so you'll certainly succeed. I've charmed a lot of men, but this is the first time I've met a man who can go one up on me. Don't let me go, babu, or you will regret it.'

Nandakishore smiled and said, 'What do I have to do?'

'My grandmother has incurred some debts; she is going to sell her house to repay it. You have to pay up.'

'How much?'

'Seven thousand rupees.'

Nandakishore was stunned by her presumptuous demand. 'Well,' he said, 'All right, I'll pay, but what then?'

'Then I will never leave you.'

'What will you do?'

'I'll see that no one can ever cheat you, except myself.'

Nandakishore laughed. 'Very well,' he said, 'that's settled then. Here is my ring; wear it.'

His mind was like a touchstone, which registered the hallmark of a noble metal. He saw the effulgence of strength of character radiating from this girl; that she was aware of her own worth there was no doubt. He did not hesitate to say, 'I'll give the money,' and gave her old grandmother seven thousand rupees.

The girl was called Sohini. She had firm, beautiful features of the north Indian mould. But Nandakishore was not the kind to fall for appearance; he had not the time to gamble on hearts in the market of youth.

The situation from which Nandakishore had reclaimed her was neither quite pure nor entirely private. But this stubborn and self-willed man had scant regard for the conventional codes and strictures of society. Asked whether he had married her, Nandakishore's reply was an unusual, 'Not a great deal, only to a tolerable extent.' People laughed in their sleeves to see him try overzealously to train her after his own educational model. 'Is she going to become a professor?' they would ask. 'Not exactly,' he would reply, 'but she has to be a she-Nandakishore, which no ordinary girl can ever wish for.' He declared, 'I do not support unequal marriages.'

'Would you clarify?'

'An engineer husband and a kitchen-bound wife do not make a match sanctioned by moral laws[3]. Such unequal marriages are to be seen everywhere, but I'm trying to match our kinds. If you should have a devoted wife, make sure you devote yourselves to the same mission.'

2

Nandakishore died in middle age in an accident from a daring scientific experiment.

Sohini closed down all his enterprises. Conmen given to cheating propertied widows began to swarm round her. Whoever had any remote connection by blood filed property suits. Sohini got down to picking up the fine points and loopholes of law. Moreover, she cast her female charm at the right places in the legal community. She had perfected that art and had no pretence of modesty about it; she had no scruples for propriety, either. She won one case after another, and a distant cousin-in-law was sent to jail on charges of forging documents.

They had a daughter whom they had named Nilima[4]. The girl herself changed it to Nila[4]. Let no one think that their daughter's dark skin made the parents devise a euphemistic cover-up for the stigma of complexion. The girl was extremely fair. Her mother said the girl's ancestors were from Kashmir. Her features had the lustre of the white lotus of Kashmir; her eyes were like the blue lotus; her hair was a sparkling golden-brown.

As for getting her married, there was no fussing over caste, creed or lineage. The only way was to insinuate into someone's heart, the magic of which excelled the seductive ploys prescribed by the shastras. A young Marwari boy, whose wealth was paternal and education modern, was caught unawares in the imperceptible trap of the god of love. One day, Nila was waiting at the school gate for the pick-up car, when the boy happened to see her. Several times thereafter, he sauntered down the street, and the girl, motivated by her female instincts, made a habit of waiting at the gate far ahead of schedule. Not the Marwari boy alone, youths of several other communities as well did the rounds of the place with no apparent reason. Out of them, it was that boy who plunged headlong into her dragnet, never to resurface. They were married under civil law, beyond the jurisdiction of society. The marriage did not last long. Fate had ordained him a bride first, typhoid next to terminate their conjugal life, and eternal freedom in the end.

Young hopefuls persistently courted her by various means, fair or foul. The girl's restlessness was all too apparent to the mother, who recalled the volcanic fire raging in herself at that age, and was deeply anxious. She penned her in with a fence of education. Male tutors were ruled out; a learned woman was engaged instead. The glare of Nila's youth singed her mind as well, working her up with the steam of indefinable desire. Lovelorn admirers hovered around, but remained shut out. Girls desirous of Nila's friendship invited her to tea, tennis, or the cinema; but the invitations never reached the addressee. Swarms of greedy suitors buzzed around in her honey-scented surroundings, but none of the wretched beggars got the endorsement from Sohini. The restless girl, on the other hand, seized every opportunity to peep into unapproved places. She read books not approved by the textbook committee, smuggled in pictures which were deviously certified as conducive to art lessons. Her learned tutor herself was distracted. One day, on her way back from the Diocesan school, a handsome boy, with tousled hair and the hint of a moustache, had flicked a missive into her car. It had made her blood race wildly. She had hidden it in her wardrobe. Her mother happened to find it. Nila was locked up in her room the whole day without food.

Sohini tried to choose a groom from among the bright students who had received scholarship from her husband. She found that almost all of them obliquely eyed her purse. One of them went as far as to dedicate his thesis to her. Sohini said to him, 'Alas, it's so unfortunate! You embarrass me. I hear your postgraduate term is nearly over; yet you have offered your tributes[5] to an improper place. Look, you have to exercise greater care in settling for whom you're worshipping, or it won't get you anywhere.'

For some days now, Sohini had set her eyes on a particular young man. He was an obvious choice as a match. His name was Rebati Bhattacharya. He was a Doctor of Science, and some of his papers had been critically acclaimed abroad.

3

Sohini was well versed in the art of socialising. Manmatha Choudhuri was one of Rebati's earlier professors. She reached up to him and floored him with her charm. She treated him often to tea with toast or omelette, or sometimes fried hilsa roe, until she brought up the matter one day. She said, 'You may perhaps be wondering why I ask you over to tea so often.'

'I assure you Mrs Mallik, that doesn't bother me at all.'

Sohini said, 'People believe we befriend people to serve our selfish ends.'

'Well, Mrs. Mallik, I feel whoever's end may be served, it's the friendship that counts. Besides, it's no small thing that an ordinary professor like me can be of any use to anyone. The intelligence of this tribe has turned pale for lack of open-air exercise outside books. I can see you are amused to hear me say so. Well, I'm a teacher, but I've a sense of humour too. Note this for the next time you decide to call me over for tea.'

'I've noted, and I'm relieved. I've seen a number of professors who need to be tickled in their ribs to laugh.'

'Excellent! You're my kind, I see. Let's get down then to business.'

'Perhaps you know that my husband's laboratory was the only source of joy in his life. I don't have a son, so I'm looking for a young man whom I could put in charge of the laboratory. I have heard of Rebati Bhattacharya.'

'He fits the bill, no doubt. However, the field he is researching in will need a great deal of resources to be carried through till the end.'

Sohini said, 'I have heaps of money gathering fungus. Widows of my age spend their money on the commissioned agents of gods and goddesses to buy their passport to heaven. You may be offended to know that I don't believe in all this.'

Choudhuri looked in wide-eyed surprise. 'What do you believe in then?' he asked.

'If ever I find a man truly worth his salt, I would pay off all that he deserves as far as I can. This is what I mean by religious work.'

Choudhuri said, 'Hoorah, a stone floats in water! It seems even women can sometimes be intelligent, if rarely. I know of a dull-headed Bachelor of Science, whom I saw the other day touching his guru's feet and turning reverse somersaults; it seemed his brains were tumbling out and flying like silk cotton bursting out of its seed.—Well, do you want to plant him in the laboratory right in your house? Wouldn't it do to place him at some distant place?'

'Make no mistake, Mr. Choudhuri, I'm a woman. This laboratory here was my husband's place of worship. If I can put the right person to keep the light aflame at his altar, he will be pleased, wherever he may be.'

Choudhuri said, 'By Jove! It's a woman speaking at last. Not unpleasant to hear after all. But remember, if you want to fully support Rebati until the end, it may run into more than a lakh.'

"Even if it does, I'd still have something left.'

'But would it not offend the person in the other world whom you want to please? The dead are known to possess anyone they like and play havoc.'

'You surely read newspapers where they list out over several paragraphs the virtues of a departed soul. There certainly can't be anything wrong in having faith in that deceased person's generosity. A man who has made tons of money has also accumulated loads of sin with it. What are we here for if not for lightening their sacks of money—and the sins along with it? Let the money go; I don't need it.'

The professor said excitedly, 'What can I say? Gold that is taken out of mines is pure gold, even if mixed with other material. You are such a nugget of gold in disguise. I now know your real self. Now tell me what I have to do.'

'Get that young man to agree.'

'I'll try, but it won't be easy. Anyone else would have jumped at your offer.'

'What stands in the way?'

'A female planet has been guiding his destiny right from childhood; lack of good sense is blocking his path immovably.'

'Strange! After all a male –'

'Whom would you blame, Mrs Mallik? Do you know what matriarchal society means? A society where women are superior to men. The wave of that Dravidian culture once swept over Bengal.'

'But those happy days are gone,' said Sohini, 'There still may be an undercurrent, muddling one's senses; but the rudder is in the hands of men now. It is men who whisper counsel in our ears—and tweak them, often so hard that they nearly come apart.'

'Oh, how very artful you are with words! If matriarchal society were to come back, where women like you were in charge, I wouldn't mind keeping inventory of your saris sent to the laundry, and sending our college principal off to work the husking pedal. Psychologists say that in Bengal, matriarchy doesn't exist physically, but runs in our psyche. Have you heard of the males of any other race lowing 'Ma-Ma', calf-like, so wretchedly? Let me inform you that a difficult woman is sitting atop Rebati's wisdom.'

'Is he in love?'

'Had it been so, that would have meant he has an ounce of life in his veins. His kind is born to lose his head over a young woman, which is what it should be at his age. He has instead at this young age become a bead in the hands of a rosary bead-counting woman. What can possibly rescue him? Nothing, not his youth, his brains, his science.'

'Well, how about inviting him to tea one day? Would he take food from unholy persons like us?'

'Unholy! If he refuses, I'll give him a good laundering[6] that will cleanse the brahmanical sanctimony thoroughly out of him. By the way, I suppose you have a beautiful daughter.'

'Yes, I do. And the wretched girl is indeed beautiful. But again, what can I do about that?'

'Oh no, don't misunderstand me. As for myself, I prefer beautiful girls rather too much. It's like a disease with me. But Rebati's relatives are devoid of humour; they may panic.'

'Don't worry; I've decided to marry her into our own caste.'

This was a gross lie.

'But you yourself have married outside your caste.'

'And I have been harassed no end for that. I've had to fight a series of legal battles over possession of property. What it took to win is best left unsaid.'

'I've heard bits of it. There was a gossip associating you with the articled clerk on your opponent's side. You won the case and ditched him, and the poor man was about to hang himself.'

'Or how else could women have survived through the ages? Seductive tricks too need planning, no less than strategic rules, except that it also needs topping up with some honey. That's a woman's natural technique of fighting.'

'There! You misunderstand me again. We are scientists, not judges. We observe the play of nature quite dispassionately, while its results follow naturally. In your case, the outcome was just as expected, and I said, "Hats off to you!" One other point: that I was a professor, not an articled clerk, is what has saved me. Mercury's distance from the sun is just enough to keep it from being burnt out; it's a mathematical truth with nothing good or bad about it. You must have learnt these things by now.'

'That I have. Planets follow the law of attraction, and avert it as well, which is something worth learning.'

'I must confess to one other thing. I was making a mental calculation as I was talking; that is also mathematical. Come to think of this: if I had been at least ten years younger, I would have courted trouble today needlessly. I've averted collision by the skin of my teeth. There ended the matter. However, the steam is nevertheless rising in the breast. Imagine what mathematical clockwork the entire creation is!'

Having finished, Choudhuri burst into a hearty laugh with slapping of his knees. However, he had failed to notice that Sohini had put on make-up—spending a good two hours before encountering him—to look younger than her age, cheating her Creator Himself.

4

Next day, when Choudhuri came, he saw Sohini washing a skeletal, mangy dog and wiping it with a towel.

'Why such princely treatment to this inauspicious creature?' he asked.

'Because I've rescued him. He fractured his leg in a car accident. I bandaged it up and cured him. Now I've a share in his life.'

'Won't you be disgusted to see this repulsive figure every day?'

'Have I kept him to admire his figure? The way he is recuperating after cheating death is inspiring. Because I provide him his daily necessities for survival, I don't need to run to the Kali Temple to offer goats for acquiring virtue. I've decided to build a hospital for the maimed dogs and rabbits of your biology laboratory.'

'The more I see you, the more I'm amazed, Mrs Mallik.'

'The amazement will wear away, if you see even more. You said you would give me news of Rebati-babu, so let's begin.'

'Rebati and I are distantly related; so I know all about his family. His mother died soon after he was born. His father's sister has brought him up since then. This aunt is fanatically devoted to rites and rituals: the slightest lapse made her stir up the whole household. There was not a soul in the family who did not fear her. Rebati's manly pride took a severe beating at this aunt's hands. If he was late by five minutes from school, he would have to explain himself for a good twenty-five minutes.'

Sohini said, 'My impression is that disciplining is to be done by men; women are to do the pampering. That keeps the balance.'

The professor said, 'Women with a gait like swans are not poised to keep their balance; they sway from side to side. Don't mind, Mrs Mallik, but even among them there are exceptions who can keep their heads up and walk straight, like –'

'You need not say more. But I too have enough of the woman about my roots. Don't you see this recent obsession: catching young men? Otherwise, would I have bothered you?'

'Now, don't keep saying that. Just for your information, I've come here today without preparing for my classes. That shows how I'm enjoying neglecting my duties.'

'Perhaps you are a bit soft on the whole female race.'

'Not impossible at all. But distinctions have to be made there too. Anyway, we could discuss that some other time.'

Sohini said with a smile, 'We may as well not discuss that at any time. Now finish what you were saying. How did Rebati-babu make so much progress?'

'No where near what he could have. His research required him to go high up to the mountains. He had decided to go to Badrinath[7]. Shocking coincidence! His aunt's aunt had died, of all places, on that very road to Badrinath. His aunt said, "No mountains for you, as long as I'm alive." Therefore, what I've been sincerely wishing since then is best left unsaid. Let's drop it.'

'Why blame the aunts alone? Why spare their pampered nephews? Won't their bones ever mature?'

'I've already told you why. Matriarchy infuses in their blood the urge to moo, and muddles the calves' brains. I don't know how to deplore it. That was folly number one. Later, when Rebati was all set to go to Cambridge on a government scholarship, it was his aunt again throwing a spanner in the works with her whining. It had got into her head that he was going there to marry a memsahib. I said, "What if he does?" My God! It had been in the surmise stage but this seemed to clinch it. She said, "If he goes overseas, I'll hang myself." Being a nonbeliever, I didn't know which particular god to swear by for tying the rope; the rope was not found. I gave Rebati a good haranguing in English, calling him stupid, dunce, imbecile. That was the end of the matter. Now the darling Rebati is occupied with extracting drops of oil from the Indian mill.'

Sohini impatiently cut in, 'I feel like banging my head against the wall. Well, one woman has sunk Rebati. Another woman will pull him back to shore. It is my vow.'

'To be frank, madam, you're quite adept at taking these beasts by the horns and drowning them; but I'm afraid you're not quite practised at pulling them up by the tails. Better, start practising from now. Incidentally, how did you pick up such interest in science?'

'To every branch of science my husband had dedicated all his life. His only addictions were Burma cheroots and his laboratory. He made me a regular in smoking cheroots, almost like a Burmese woman. I gave it up eventually because people seemed to find it odd. He made me the subject in his pursuit of another passion. Other men fool the women whom they want to enchant; he enchanted me by imparting knowledge day and night. You know, Mr Choudhuri, a husband's vices can never remain secret to his wife; but let me tell you I never detected a trace of impurity in him. When I saw him from close quarters, he appeared to be a great man; now seen from a distance, he seems even greater.'

'What do you find to be his greatest strength?'

'To tell you the truth, it was not his learning, but his dispassionate devotion to learning. There was an awe-inspiring atmosphere of worship around him. We women cannot do without a visible, tangible object before us to worship; his laboratory is my deity. Sometimes I feel like lighting incense, blowing a conch, beating gongs; I fear my husband's revulsion at all this. Every day when he worshipped, college students crowded round these instruments to listen to his lecture, and I sat down too.'

'Could the boys concentrate on the theories?'

'Those who could were marked out. I've seen some among them with almost ascetic devotion. There were others too who would pretend to take notes while actually honing their literary skills, writing letters to their neighbour.'

'How did you like that?'

'Frankly speaking, I rather liked it. My husband would go off to work, and the romantic ones would hang around here.'

'Don't mind if I ask this—but I like to study psychology: did they get any favours?'

'I don't like to say it: I'm an immodest woman. I came to know a few of them; I still feel a wrench in my heart to think of them.'

'A few of them?'

'The mind is greedy. The greed smoulders under flesh and bone, only to flare up with a little stoking. I had begun by sullying my name; so I have no hesitation in speaking frankly. We women are not ascetics all our lives. We slog away trying to keep up appearances. Draupadis and Kuntis have to pretend to be Sitas and Savitris[8]. One thing you must remember, Mr Choudhuri: since childhood, I have never had a clear notion of right or wrong. I had no guru to teach that to me. So I plunged into filth quite easily, and negotiated it easily too. I've stained my body in the process, but not my mind. Nothing could get hold of me. Anyway, when my husband departed, he set fire to my desires with the flames of his funeral pyre, which is burning away my accumulated sins one by one. That fire is burning like sacrificial fire in this very laboratory.'

'Bravo! You've such courage to speak the truth.'

'It's easy when there is one to get the truth out of you. You're so simple, genuine yourself; that's why.'

'Well, do those correspondents favoured by you still pay visits?'

'They did, of course, and thereby purged my heart of its filth. I realised they were gathering with an eye on my purse. They thought women's infatuation dies hard, so they would burgle their way through romancing into my coffers. They didn't seem to know that I don't have so much passion in my prosaic Punjabi heart. I don't mind flouting the injunctions of society on carnal pleasure, but never for my life will I betray another. They couldn't lessen my laboratory funds by a single paisa. My stony heart is impregnably guarding the treasure chest of my deity. They don't have the strength to melt it. The man who had hand-picked me made no mistake.'

'I would have liked to bow to that man, and tweak those boys' ears.'

Before taking leave, the professor made a round of the laboratory along with Sohini. 'Here, in this laboratory,' he said, 'womanly wisdom has been sublimated, uprooting the evil spirit and distilling the pure spirit.'

'Say what you like, but I can't stop worrying,' said Sohini. 'Womanly wisdom is God's original creation. When women are rather young and have strength of mind, it lies low, hiding in bushes; when their blood cools down, out comes the traditional aunt in them. I would like to die before that.'

'Don't worry. Take it from me you'll die with full control over your senses,' said the professor.

5

Wearing a white sari and dabbing powder on her greying hair, Sohini managed to give an impression of undefiled virtue to her face. Along with her daughter, she took a motor launch and arrived at the Botanical Gardens[9]. The girl was dressed in a bluish green Benarasi sari transparent to a light yellow inner garment. She had a spot of scented red powder paste on her brow, a faint touch of the eye-liner, her hair gathered in a loosely tied chignon at her shoulder, her feet shod in black leather sandals embroidered in red velvet.

Sohini, armed with clues to Rebati's whereabouts, captured him in the neem grove where he normally spent his Sundays. She made her obeisance, dipping her forehead right down to his feet. Rebati jumped up in embarrassment.

Sohini said, 'Don't mind, my son, but you're a Brahman[10]'s son, and I'm a Kshatri[11]'s daughter. You may have heard about me from Mr Choudhuri.'

'I have, but where do I tell you to sit?'

'Why, here is lush green grass; what better seat can you find? Perhaps you're wondering what brings me here. I'm here to keep a vow. I shan't find another Brahman like you.'

'A Brahman like me!' Rebati was surprised.

'Of course! My guru said that the greatest of the Brahmins is the one who has mastered the best learning of our times.'

Embarrassed, Rebati said, 'My father was a priest, but I know nothing of his mantras[12] and rituals.'

'Why do you say that? The mantras you've learnt are the ones that man has used to tame the universe. You must be wondering how a mere woman could say such things. I learnt it from one who was truly a man. He was my husband. Promise, my son, you'll visit the holy seat of his worship.'

'I'm off duty tomorrow morning; I'll go.'

'I see you have a liking for plants. Very glad to see that. My husband went all the way to Burma in quest of plants, and I did not leave his side.'

She had not left his company indeed, but not because of any urge for science. The grossness that surfaced in her mind, she could not help suspecting in her husband's nature too. Suspiciousness existed in her very pores. Once when Nandakishore was hopelessly ill, he had told her, 'The only consolation in death is that you can never track me down to bring me back.'

'But I might go along with you,' Sohini had said.

'Horrors!' Nandakishore had said with a smile.

Talking of plants, Sohini told Rebati, 'I brought back a sapling from Burma. "Kozaitanieng" the Burmese call it. It had lovely flowers, but it didn't survive the transplant.'

She had hunted up the name from her husband's library for the first time that morning. She had never even seen the plant. She just cast a net of learning to trap a learned man.

Rebati was impressed. 'Do you know its Latin name?'

'It's *Miletia,'* Sohini said with an expert's ease. 'My husband did not believe in traditional lore, yet he had a blind faith. He believed that if women in a special state of body and mind meditatively looked at whatever was beautiful in nature, its fruits, its flowers, then their children were certain to be born beautiful. Do you believe that?'

Of course, this was none of Nandakishore's beliefs.

Rebati hemmed and hawed. 'We haven't found sufficient proof as yet.'

'But I've found at least one proof—in my own home. How else did my daughter get her amazing beauty? Like the choicest parts of all spring flowers—well, you have to see for yourself to believe.'

Rebati grew eager to see her. Sohini had spared no pains to dramatise the event.

She had brought along her Brahman cook dressed up like a priest in a short-length silk dhoti, with a sandalwood tilak on his forehead, a flower tied to his topknot, the thick sacred thread across his chest scrubbed with wood-apple resin. She called him and said, '*Thakur*, it's time now, bring Nilu[13] up here.'

Her mother had kept her waiting inside the steam-launch. She had been instructed to enter with a basket of flowers, so she could be inspected for quite a while in the mellow morning light and shade.

All this time Sohini was examining Rebati in threadbare detail. His complexion was a smooth darkish brown. His forehead was broad, with his hair swept back with his fingers. His eyes were not large, but they shone bright and clear, and were his most prominent feature. The curve of his face was smooth, like a woman's. Of all the information she had gathered about Rebati, she had especially marked one point. His childhood friends had a tear-filled, sentimental affection for him. He had a delicate charm that could fascinate immature males.

This one point jolted Sohini. She believed a man should not necessarily be handsome to be able to moor at a woman's heart. Learning and intelligence too were of secondary importance. What mattered most was his male magnetism. It was like radio signals transmitted by his nerves within his muscles, which was manifest in the suggestive arrogance of desire.

She lapsed into retrospection of her own youthful days of turbulent flirtation. The man she was drawn to, or maybe, it was the other way round, was neither handsome nor learned, to say nothing of ancestry. But he radiated some strange heat that had captured and enabled her to feel with all her body and mind his vigorous masculinity. She was constantly worried about when Nila would begin to experience that inevitable visitation of turmoil. The last phase of youth is the most dangerous phase, which Sohini had largely tided over with her relentless pursuit of knowledge. Sohini's mind just happened to be fertile ground. But abstract knowledge does not appeal to every girl. Nila's mind was opaque to enlightenment.

Nila showed up from the landing platform and drew up slowly. The sunlight fell on her forehead, on her hair; the gold threads in her sari glittered. Rebati's eyes took a snapshot of her. The next moment he had lowered his eyes; that was the etiquette he had been taught from childhood. Beautiful girls, who are but infatuating manifestations of the Mother-goddess's[14] mysterious pleasure, had remained hidden from his view behind his aunt's forbidding finger. Therefore, when he did get a chance, he had to take in the visual nectar with a quick furtive draught.

Sohini, censuring him silently, said, 'Look, look; do look up once.'

Rebati looked up with a start.

Sohini said, 'Don't you see, Doctor of Science, how splendidly the colour of her sari matches the colour of the leaves?'

'Splendid!' said Rebati hesitantly.

'Oh, it's impossible,' said Sohini to herself. To him she said, 'Light yellow peeping through greenish blue—now, which flower has got this contrast?'

Encouraged, Rebati now took a good look and said, 'There's one flower I can think of, but its outer petals are brown, not blue.'

'Which flower?'

'*Melina,*' said Rebati.

'Ah, I know. It has five petals; one bright yellow, four darkish.'

Rebati was staggered. 'How did you know so much about flowers?'

Sohini smiled. 'I shouldn't have known, my son. Any flowers that are outcast in the worship of gods are like unrelated males to us.'

Nila approached slowly with her basket of flowers. 'Don't keep standing so shyly,' encouraged her mother. 'Come and touch his feet.'

'Don't, don't,' said Rebati, extremely embarrassed. He was sitting cross-legged. Nila had to grope for his feet. Rebati's whole body shivered. There were rare species of orchid in her basket, and in a silver platter, delicacies: coconut, cashew, pistachio, and milk preparations of various shapes and solidity complete with squares of steamed yoghurt.

As these were laid, Sohini said, 'Nila has made them all by herself.'

This, of course, was an utter lie. Nila had neither skill nor interest in such work.

'You must take some, my son,' Sohini insisted. 'It's all home-made, only in your honour.'

They had been made to order by a reliable shop at Barabazar.

Rebati said, joining his palms in apology, 'Sorry, I don't eat at this hour of the day. Rather I can take them home if you permit.'

'That's fine,' said Sohini, 'My husband forbade pressuring anyone to eat. He would say, "People are not pythons, are they?"'

She parcelled the entire fare neatly in a large tiffin carrier. 'Now dear,' she told Nila, 'arrange the flowers in a basket. Don't mix up the kinds, mind you. And take that silk scarf from your hair and spread it over the flowers.'

The avidity of a thirsting art-lover shone in the scientist's eyes. What they saw was something outside the physical world of weights and measures. Nila's well-shaped fingers were meandering rhythmically in various modes into the nosegay of flowers: Rebati could hardly take his eyes off them, looking up at her face now and then. Her face was framed on one side by a slender chain of an array of rubies, pearls and emeralds, arching her hair like a rainbow; on the other, by the red piping of her light yellow garment showing through. Sohini was doing up the sweets, but she had a third eye, as it were; the magic being woven in front of her did not go unnoticed.

Going by her own experience with her husband, she believed that the securely fenced-in pasture of scholars was immune from infiltration by common cattle. Today she realised that the fences were not equally close-knit for all. It did not please her, though.

6

Next day Sohini called the professor over. She said, 'I keep bothering you like this for my personal needs. I'm afraid I disturb your work too.'

'Call me more often, please. If there's a need, well and good; if there's none, it's all the better.'

'You know my husband lost his head when it came to acquiring costly equipment. He used to cheat his employers out of this dispassionate greed. His would be the finest laboratory in all Asia: he was crazy about this one passion, which I picked up for myself as well. Thanks to this, I got going, or my spirituous blood would have fermented and spilt over. There's evil still clinging to my nature. You're the only friend, Mr Choudhuri, to whom I can speak unreservedly about that. A window to one's shady side brings great relief to one's mind.'

Choudhuri said, 'It's pointless trying to keep the truth from someone who can see a person inside out. Half-truths are shameful. We scientists are inured to seeing things in their entirety.'

'My husband used to say, "People try desperately to protect life, but life doesn't last. Hence, to satisfy the urge for living, they look for something much more valuable than life itself." That something he found in his laboratory. If I can't keep this going, that'll mean his death, and I'll go down as one who murdered her husband. I want someone to safeguard it. That's why I was looking for Rebati.'

'Did you try?'

'I did, and I'm hopeful of instant result; but he'll not last.'

'Why?'

'Once his aunt comes to know I've drawn him near, she'll snatch him away in a swoop. She would think I set up a trap to get him married to my daughter.'

'What's wrong with that? It wouldn't be bad at all. But didn't you say you wouldn't get her married outside your own caste?'

'I didn't know your views then, so I lied. In fact, I dearly wanted them to marry. But I've given up the idea.'

'Why?'

'I've realised that she is a potentially destructive girl; nothing that she touches will remain whole.'

'But she's your daughter, isn't she?'

'My daughter, of course, and hence I know her fully.'

The professor said, 'But don't forget women can greatly inspire men.'

'I know it all. Meat and fish is all right for men's diet; add alcohol, and you ruin them. My daughter is a veritable decanter filled to the brim.'

'What'd you like to do then?'

'I'd like to gift my laboratory to the public.'

'Depriving your only daughter?'

'My daughter! If she were to get it, who knows to what depths it will sink? I'll make Rebati president of the trust. His aunt can't possibly object to that?'

'If I could find out why women might object, why should I have been born a man? But one thing I don't understand. If you won't have him as your son-in-law, why make him president?'

'What good are the machines if left to themselves? You need a man to give them life. There's another point. We haven't acquired a single new instrument since my husband died. It's not for lack of funds. You have to have a definite objective of purchase, you know. I'm told Rebati is working on magnetism. Let purchases be made in that direction. Never mind the cost.'

'What can I say after this? If you were a man, I would have held you aloft on my shoulders. Your husband had misappropriated Railway funds, and you appropriated his male cast of mind. Really, I'm yet to find another instance of such wonderful grafting of mind. And, surprisingly, you think it necessary to consult the likes of me.'

'That's because you are a very genuine person. You can say what is right.'

'You make me laugh. I'm not that stupid to risk getting found out telling you something wrong. Well, let's then get down to brass tacks. We've to begin by making an inventory of assets and getting them valued, then get a good lawyer to settle your rights, frame the regulations, and complete many other formalities.'

'You must take charge of all that please.'

'That'll be in name only. You know very well that I'll say just what you'll tell me to say, and do just what you'll ask me to do. What I gain in the process is that I get to see you twice a day. You don't know with what eyes I look upon you.'

Sohini, suddenly rising from her stool dashed to Choudhuri, and putting an arm round his neck kissed his cheek, and then retreating quickly, went back primly to her stool.

'My goodness! That's the beginning of my end, I see.'

'If I feared that, I wouldn't go near you at all. You'll have this allowance now and then.'

'Really?'

'Of course! It costs me nothing, and you don't appear to expect much more either.'

'You mean it's like a woodpecker pecking on dead wood. Well, I'm off to the lawyer's.'

'Just come this way tomorrow.'

'To do what?'

'To liven up Rebati.'

'And give away my own heart besides.'

'Are you the only one with a heart?'

'Do you have anything left of yours?'

'Yes, a lot of leftovers.'

'That's enough to set a lot of monkeys hopping around you.'

7

The next day Rebati arrived at the laboratory at least twenty minutes too early. Sohini was not ready; she hurriedly came into the room in her ordinary sari. Rebati realised he had made a gaffe. 'My watch doesn't seem to be keeping correct time,' he said, trying to be polite.

'Of course,' replied Sohini tersely.

There was a slight sound, and Rebati looked at the door starting inwardly. Sukhan the servant entered the room to deliver the keys to the glass case.

'Shall I get you a cup of tea?' Sohini asked.

Rebati thought he should accept the offer. 'Not a bad idea,' he said.

The poor fellow was not used to having tea. At the signs of a cold, he would take sips of hot water boiled with wood-apple leaves, but no tea. He had hoped Nila herself would bring him the tea.

'Do you like your tea strong?'

'Yes,' he blurted out.

He thought that was the expected answer. The tea arrived, and it was no doubt strong—dark as ink, bitter as neem. The Muslim cook brought it. This too was designed to test him[15]. He could not utter a word, though he demurred silently. Sohini did not approve of such hesitancy. She said, 'Why don't you pour out the tea, Mobarak? It's getting cold.'

Rebati had come here twenty minutes ahead of time surely not expecting a Muslim cook to serve him.

How mortified he felt at having to sip the tea the Almighty alone knew, and so did Sohini. Being a woman after all, she took pity on his plight and said, 'Leave that cup. Have some milk instead, and some fruits with it. You came so early, possibly without eating anything.'

That was a fact. Rebati had expected a repeat of the Botanical Gardens fare. This was a total let-down, with only the bitter taste of black tea on his tongue and bitter experience of battered hopes in his heart.

In walked the professor. Slapping Rebati on the back, he said, 'What's happened, young man? Sitting frozen! Sipping milk like a little girl! Are these children's toys you see around you? Intuitive men have seen Lord Shiva's entourage come visiting and performing the dance of destruction here[16].'

'Oh! Why are you scolding him? He's come on an empty stomach this morning. He was looking rather pale.'

'Now, Aunt the Second's come; one aunt to slap this cheek, another to kiss the other. Between them, the poor fellow will crumble like damp clod. You should know, Sohini, when the goddess of wealth visits gratuitously, she's not perceptible; he who moves heaven and earth to hunt her down, she is his. There's no easier way of being disappointed than getting something unasked for. Well, tell me Mrs–oh, hell with the 'Mrs', I'm going to call you plain Sohini, whether you're angry or whatever.'

'Heavens! Why should I be angry? Call me Sohini[17]. And if you call me Suhi[18], that'll be music to my ears.'

'Let me tell you a secret. There's is a word (*kinkini*)[19] that rhymes with your name; it brings to mind the jingle of anklets and makes me play the tambourine in my mind.'

'You're used to matching things in your chemical research; this must be an offshoot of that.'

'Matching things sometimes proves fatal, too. Such things are best not disturbed too much—they're highly inflammable stuff.' And he laughed heartily.

"No, we shouldn't be discussing such things in front of this young man. He is not an apprentice yet in the gunpowder factory. His aunt's sari-end is screening him, and that's non-combustible.'

Rebati's girlish face was growing red.

'By the way, Sohini, have you given him any opium this morning? Or why is he looking so drowsy?'

'If I have, I have done it unwittingly.'

'Now Rebu, wake up, I say. You shouldn't be sitting tongue-tied before women; it makes them even more daring. They're like a disease, prying for any weak spot in a man. Once they locate it, they burrow into him and make his temperature shoot up. I've knowledge of the subject; so I am obliged to warn the young fellows. They've got to take the lesson from people like us, who've been battered short of death. Don't take it to heart, Rebu dear, but those who don't speak, the silent ones are the most dangerous. Now come along, let me show you around. Look at those two galvanometers—the latest model. Here's a high vacuum pump, and this one's a microphotometer. These are not floats of plantain leaves to negotiate the sea of exams. Just set yourself up here firmly, and let's watch how wan that baldpated professor of yours looks. I name no names. When you started out as my student, didn't I tell you that the future, so-called, was dangling before your nose? Don't ruin it through your negligence. If I am mentioned even in a footnote to the first chapter of your biography, I'll consider it a great honorarium paid to your guru.'

The scientist promptly responded to the wake-up call. His eyes glowed. His whole expression now spoke of a great transformation within. Thrilled, Sohini said, 'Everyone who knows you expects the highest achievement for you, something out of the ordinary, and timeless. But again, the greater the expectation, the stronger the obstacles, both within and without.'

The professor gave Rebati an even more encouraging slap on the back. His spine tingled. Choudhuri said in his booming voice, 'Look Rebu, the great future we've set for you should come riding Indra's elephant; but the niggardly present despatches it by a bullock-cart that gets stuck in the mud and remains immobile. Do you hear me, Sohini, Suhi? No, no, don't worry; I'm not going to slap you on the back. Tell me, did I not put it across succinctly?

'Wonderful.'

'Write it down in your diary.'

'I will.'

'Did you get the meaning, Rebu?'

'I think I did.'

'Remember, great talent means great responsibility. It's no one's personal property. One has to account for it to eternity. Do you hear, Suhi? How was that for pithiness?'

'Excellent, again. In olden times, kings would have taken off their necklaces to –'

'They're all dead, but –'

'That "but" hasn't died. I'll remember it.'

Rebati said, 'Don't worry, nothing will weaken my spirit.'

Rebati made to touch Sohini's feet. Sohini hurriedly stopped him.

Choudhuri said, 'Now, why did you stop him? If you don't perform a pious act, it's a moral lapse; to prevent someone from doing it is even more so.'

'If he must bow down to anyone, it's there.' She pointed to a platform with a portrait of Nandakishore; there was incense burning and a tray of flowers there.

'I've read in the Puranas about reclamation of sinners,' she continued. 'That great man has reclaimed the sinner in front of you. He had to stoop very low before he could pull me up; not to sit beside him—I would be lying if I said so—but at his feet. He instructed me to redeem man through learning. He warned me not to fritter away the gems he had mined all his life to enhance the vanity of our daughter and the son-in-law. He said, "Therein lies my salvation, and the salvation of my country."'

'Did you note that, Rebu?' said Choudhuri, 'It'll be a trust property, and you'll be the chief trustee.'

Rebati quickly protested, 'I don't think I'm worthy of trusteeship. I could never manage it.'

'Can't manage! It's a shame on a man to say so,' prodded Sohini.

'I've always been preoccupied with studies. I've never taken on such responsibility.' Rebati tried to reason with her.

Choudhuri argued, 'Can a duckling swim before it is hatched? Today you shall break out of your shell.'

Sohini said, 'Do not fear. I'll always be with you.'

Rebati left, reassured. Sohini looked at the professor. He said, 'Of all kinds of fools, male fools are exemplars of foolishness. But you must remember that one can't grow worthy of responsibility until one's entrusted with it. Man is man because he's got two hands. If he'd got hooves instead, he'd have grown a tail as well to be twisted. Have you seen hooves on Rebati instead of hands?'

'I can't quite accept this anyway. Men who have been brought up by women alone never lose their milk teeth. It's my bad luck. Why should I have thought of anyone else when you're around?'

'I'm glad to hear that. But tell me what qualities you've spotted in me.'

'You're not in the least covetous.'

"That's insulting! Do you presume I don't covet what is covetable? Of course I do. –'

Sohini stopped him short by kissing him on both cheeks, and withdrawing quickly.

'To which account is it credited, Sohini?'

'I can never repay the debt I owe you; that was only the interest.'

'I got one the first day; today it's two. Will it go on increasing?'

'Of course, it will, like compound interest.'

8

Choudhuri said, 'Sohini, did you have to make me priest to preside over your husband's obsequies? That's a terrific responsibility: to please someone who doesn't have a palpable existence. It's not the usual kind of offering, so that –'

'You're no usual kind of priest either. Whatever you think best will set the standard. Offerings are ready, I hope.'

'That's just what I've been doing all these days. I had to do a good deal of scouring the market. The goods for offering are all laid out in the hall downstairs. The living souls who are supposed to ingest them will surely have their fill.'

Sohini went downstairs with him, and saw the gifts meant for science students: various instruments, models, costly books, slides for microscopes, biology specimens. Each item had a tag with name and address. Cheques had been written out for two hundred and fifty students in advance payment of a year's stipend. No expenses had been spared. The expenses all told were several times that incurred on propitiating Brahmans at rich men's funeral ceremonies; yet they were not conspicuously lavish.

'And what will be the priest's remuneration? You haven't mentioned that.'

'Your satisfaction will be my remuneration.'

'Satisfaction plus this chronometer: I've kept it aside for you; my husband had bought it from Germany, and it aided his research all through.'

'I've no words for what I feel. I don't like to utter any nonsense. I consider my priesthood amply recompensed.'

'There's one other person whom I can't forget today—our Manik's widow.'

'Who is Manik?'

'He was the head mechanic of this laboratory. He was a wonderfully skilled hand. In work requiring extreme accuracy he would not waver an inch. He had an uncanny knack for machinery. My husband looked upon him as a family friend. He took him along in his car to visit big factories. But he was an alcoholic, and the laboratory assistants looked down on him because of his lowly origin. My husband said, "His talent is the sort that you can't hunt out or acquire by training." Manik got his due respect from him. You'll understand from this why he gave me such honour after all. To him, the bad was negligible compared to the good that he discovered in me. The one sphere where he reposed his utmost trust in a waif like me, I've never betrayed the least bit of that trust, and to date I am trying to preserve it heart and soul. He sure wouldn't have got this devotion from anyone else. He ignored my pettiness and accorded full honour to my virtues. If he hadn't identified my worth, it's anyone's guess to what depths I might have sunk. I'm a fallen woman, but I'm also a very good person, even if I say this myself, or he could never have tolerated me.'

'Look, Sohini, I can boast that I knew from day one that you were an essentially good person. Had your goodness been just skin-deep, any stain on you would never have washed out.'

'Anyway, whatever other people may think about me, the honour he gave me remains undiminished to this day, and will last my life.'

'The more I see of you, Sohini, the more I am convinced that you're not the soppy kind of woman who swoons over mention of the word husband.'

'Of course not. I saw the strength in him; I knew from the first day that he was a real man. I never felt the urge to act the devoted wife enjoined by the scriptures. I'll say this proudly that the jewels I have in me are worthy to wreathe round his neck, and no one else's.'

At this point Nila entered. 'Excuse me, Professor,' she said, 'I'd like to talk to mother.'

'By all means, dear. I was just going to the laboratory. Let me check how Rebati is doing.'

'Don't worry,' said Nila, 'He seems to be going ahead with his work quite well. I've watched him through the window a few days. He has his head buried in his books, writing away, taking notes, biting his pen and thinking. I'm not allowed in, or Sir Isaac's gravitation might go haywire. Mother was telling someone the other day that he's working on magnetism. That's why his needle gets deflected if anyone passes by, particularly women.'

Choudhuri burst into loud laughter. 'The laboratory is inside us, my dear girl. Work on magnetism is a continuous process there. We've necessarily to watch out for people who deflect the needle, because that makes one lose one's sense of direction. I'll be off now.'

Nila said to her mother, 'How long will you keep me tied to your sari-end? You can't for any length of time; you'll only end up being sorry.'

'Tell me what you would like to do.'

'You know, a Higher Study Movement[20] for girls has been launched. You've made a substantial donation to it. Why don't you engage me there?'

'I'm worried in case you won't go the right way.'

'Is a ban on all movement the road to go the right way?'

'Of course not. I know it, and that's what worries me.'

'Why don't you let me do the worrying instead of doing it yourself? Ultimately, you'll have to. I am not a child now. You seem to think those public places are haunts of different kinds of people, and that's dangerous. Well, people aren't going to stop moving just to do you a favour. And you can't prevent me meeting them under any law.'

'I know; I do know that my fear won't hold back the cause of fear. So you want to join their Higher Study Circle[20]?'

'Yes, I do.'

'All right! I know you'll send the male professors there to damnation one after another. But you must promise me one thing: you mustn't go anywhere near Rebati. Neither shall you enter his laboratory on any pretext.'

'Ma, I have no idea what you think of me. Go near that diminutive Sir Isaac Newton? Such is my taste? I'd rather die.'

Nila caricatured the way Rebati squirmed in times of embarrassment, and said, 'That's not the style I like in a man. Let him be kept for the kind of woman who likes babying adult boys. He's no game worth hunting.'

'You exaggerate, Nila. So I suspect you're not speaking your mind. Anyway, whatever your feelings are about him, if you try to ruin him, you'll do that at your own peril.'

'I never know what you really want, Ma. When you were decking me up as a doll, did you think I couldn't see that you wanted to get me married to him? Is that why you forbid me to get too close to him, in case I lose my gloss by the contact of familiarity.'

'Look Nila, I tell you this straight and simple: you'll never ever get to marry him.'

'Should I marry the prince of Motigarh then?'

'If you so please.'

'It has advantages too. He has three wives already; that'll leave me with a lesser charge to bear. And he is known to carouse and behave scandalously at night clubs—so I'll get much respite then.'

'Very well, that's approved. But I won't let you marry Rebati.'

'Why, do you think I'll addle Sir Isaac's brains?'

'Let's not argue about that. Just keep in mind what I've told you.'

'And if he comes on his own to hang around me?'

'He'll have to quit the place then. You can feed him out of your own resources; he won't get a paisa of your father's money.'

'That's alarming! Then good-bye, Sir Isaac Newton.'

That was the day's action in brief.

9

'Everything is running smoothly, Mr Choudhuri, except that my daughter is giving me worries. I can't make out whom she is targeting.'

'And what about the people who are targeting her? That's a matter of concern too. Now, it's already rumoured that your husband left a fortune for preserving the laboratory. And the rumour mill keeps the figure increasing. So everyone has staked his life on the kingdom and the princess.'

'The princess will sell at a throwaway price, I know. But as long as I'm alive, the kingdom can't be bought at a bargain price.'

'But people have started coming. I saw our Professor Majumdar the other day, coming out of a cinema hand in hand with the princess herself. He looked the other way when he saw me. He is found lecturing around on all noble topics; he is very eloquent about the good of the country. But by turning his head away, he left me despairing about our motherland.'

'Mr Choudhuri, the doors have given way.'

'They indeed have. Now this poor fellow will have to guard his own goods and chattels.'

'Let Majumdar and his tribe be stricken by plague for all I care. All I'm concerned about is Rebati.'

'There's at present no cause for worry,' said Choudhuri, 'He's absorbed in his work. It's going perfectly well.'

'His problem lies elsewhere, Mr Choudhuri. He is a great expert in science, all right. But when it comes to what you call matriarchy, he's a novice.'

'Very true. He hasn't been vaccinated even once. If he gets infected, it'll be hard to save him.'

'You must come this way and check him once every day, please.'

'Hope he doesn't carry a germ from somewhere. If he does, and I catch it at my age, I'm done for. But you need not fear, and even though you're a woman, I do hope you can understand a joke. I'm out of bounds of the epidemic zone; now I don't get infected even by contagion. But there's a problem. I've to leave for Gujranwala the day after tomorrow.'

'Is that a joke too? Spare this woman, please.'

'It's no joke. A good old friend of mine, Amulya Addy, was a doctor there. He practised for some twenty or twenty-five years, made some property too. He died recently of coronary thrombosis, leaving his widow and children. I've to sort out his affairs, dispose of his property and bring the family back here. I can't say how long that'll take.'

'One can't say anything after that.'

'One can say nothing about whatever happens in this world, Sohini. One just has to have the courage to take things as they come. Those who believe in destiny are not wrong. We scientists too say that what is inevitable can't be modified even by a whisker. Do what you can until there's nothing you can do, and then call it quits.'

'Well, I'll abide by that.'

'The Majumdar I've just spoken of is by no means the most virulent of the lot. They suffer him only to borrow his respectability. The others I've heard about are, as Chanakya[21] would say, potential dangers even at a hundred cubits' distance. There's Bankubihari the attorney; associating with him is the same as embracing an octopus. Such men relish the hot blood of wealthy widows. Save this information and use it if and when necessary. And above all, remember my philosophy.'

'Keep your philosophy aside, Mr Choudhuri. If anyone dare intrude into my laboratory, I shan't go by your fatalism, your immutable law of cause and effect. I'm a Punjabi woman; I can wield a knife at the least provocation. I can kill anyone, even my own daughter or any aspiring son-in-law.'

She had a knife tucked into a waistband under her sari. She drew it out with a sweep of her arm and brandished its shining blade. 'He hand-picked me,' she said, referring to her dead husband. 'I'm not a Bengali woman who only blubbers over love. I can give my life for love, and take life too. My laboratory and the heart within me: in between, I place this knife.'

Choudhuri said, 'Once I wrote poetry. Today I feel I can do it again.'

'Write if you please, but take back your philosophy. I'll never accept what is unacceptable. I'll stand my ground and fight alone. And I'll say proudly I'll win, win, win.'

'Bravo! I take back my philosophy. From now on, I'll be the drummer in your victory procession. For the time being, I'll take leave of you for some time. I hope to come back soon.'

It's a wonder that Sohini's eyes filled with tears. 'Hope you don't mind,' she said, and flung her arms round Choudhuri's neck. 'No ties are everlasting in this world; this too is a momentary one.'

With this, she withdrew, fell at his feet and made a *pronam*.

10

What in newspaper parlance is called 'juncture' comes all of a sudden, and never comes alone. The story of life punctuated by joys and sorrows proceeds haltingly, until the last chapter, when a sudden collision shatters everything, and then all is quiet. The Maker builds up His story little by little, only to demolish it with a single blow.

Sohini's grandmother lived in Ambala. She sent her a telegram, 'If you wish to see me, come soon.'

This grandmother was her only living relation. From her hands had Nandakishore bought Sohini in lieu of her debt.

To Nila, her mother said, 'You too must come with me.'

Nila said, 'That's impossible.'

'Why impossible?'

'They're preparing to give me a reception.'

'Who are they?'

'The members of the Jagani (Awakener) club. Don't be alarmed; it's a respectable club. You'll know it from the register of members—very select.'

'What are its aims and objectives?'

'It's hard to tell precisely. The name itself embodies them. Underlying it are all possible meanings–spiritual, literary, artistic. Nabakumar-babu gave a very cogent interpretation the other day. They're planning to ask you for a donation.'

'But I find they've already taken a donation to the maximum degree. You've fallen completely into their hands. But that's all. They have had what I consider dispensable. There's nothing else they can get from me.'

'Why are you getting so angry, ma? They want to serve the country quite selflessly.'

'Let's not talk about that. Your friends must have told you by now that you are independent.'

'Yes, they have.'

'Those selfless people must have also told you that you can freely use your share in the money my husband left.'

'They have.'

'I've heard that you're planning to get a probate on the will. Is that true?'

'Yes, it's true. Banku-babu is my solicitor.'

'Has he given you any more advice, any more hopes?'

Nila kept silent.

'I'll purge your Banku-babu of his crookedness[22] if he makes any move to enter my territory. If I can't do it lawfully, I'll break the law. I'll return via Peshawar. Four Sikh sentries will guard the laboratory day and night. And let me show you this before I go—I'm a Punjabi woman.'

She drew out a knife from her belt and said, 'This knife is no respecter of my daughter or her solicitor. Let this be stored away in your memory. If I need to settle scores on my return, I will.'

11

Vast tracts of land around the laboratory remained vacant, screening it from sounds and vibrations as much as possible. Rebati found this quiet atmosphere congenial to his work, so he often came back at night to work.

The clock downstairs had struck two. For a while, Rebati was gazing through the window at the sky thinking on his work, when he suddenly noticed a shadow on the wall.

He turned to see that Nila was in the room. She was in her nightwear, a thin silk chemise. Rebati was startled and almost leaped up from his seat, when Nila overtook him and sat on his lap clasping his neck with her arms. Rebati started trembling and heaving violently. He said in a thick, choking voice, 'Go away. Do please go away from this room.'

'Why?' she asked.

'I can't bear it,' said Rebati, 'Why did you come here?'

Nila clasped him even harder and said, 'Why? Don't you love me?'

'I do, I do,' said Rebati, 'But you must go now.'

Suddenly, a Punjabi guard came into the room. 'It's a matter of shame, Maiji[23]. Please leave the room.' He told Nila in a chastising tone.

Rebati had pressed the electric bell unwittingly in a state of daze.

The guard turned to Rebati. 'Babuji, don't betray your trust.'

Rebati pushed Nila off his lap and stood up. The man now warned Nila, 'Please go away, or I'll have to carry out the mistress's orders.'

He meant he would be obliged to throw her out bodily. Nila moved towards the door, addressing Rebati tauntingly, 'Look here, Sir Isaac Newton, you're invited to tea at our place tomorrow afternoon—at a quarter to five sharp. Did you hear that? Or have you fainted away?' She stood for once turning to look at him.

'Yes, I heard,' said Rebati in an emotional undertone.

Nila's immaculately formed body, like a sculpted statue, was prominently outlined by her thin nightwear. It was impossible for Rebati not to look on, spellbound. Nila left. Rebati slouched in his seat, resting his chin on the table. Such amazing beauty was beyond his imagination. An electric discharge was coursing through his veins like a stream of sparks. He kept repeating to himself clenching his fists that he would not go to tea the following day. He wanted to make a strong vow, but couldn't utter it. 'I won't go, won't go, won't go,' he wrote the vow on the blotting paper on his table. Suddenly he observed a scarlet handkerchief lying on the table with 'Nila' embroidered in one corner. He pressed it to his face. The perfume went to his head, and a shiver of intoxication went down his body.

Nila came back into the room. She said, 'I have a business with you, which I forgot.'

The guard tried to stop her. 'Don't worry,' she told him, 'I haven't come to steal anything,' and then turning to Rebati, said, 'I just want a signature. I want to make you president of Jagani Club; you're widely known.'

'But I know nothing about the club,' protested Rebati very humbly.

'You don't need to. It's enough for you to know that Brajendra-babu is a patron.'

'I don't know Brajendra-babu either.'

'Suffice it to say he's the director of the Metropolitan Bank. Now be a good man, my darling—just one signature, nothing more.'

She took her right arm round his neck to hold his hand pointing on the dotted line. 'Sign here.'

And he signed, like one in a dream.

Nila was folding up the paper when the guard came up and demanded, 'I must see this paper.'

'But you won't understand what's written,' said Nila.

'I don't have to.' He snatched the paper out of her hands and tore it to pieces. 'If you must make out any document, do it outside, not here.'

Rebati stifled a sigh of relief. The guard said, 'Come, Maji[23], I'll take you home.' And he led her out.

After a while, the man entered once again. He said, 'I keep all the doors closed. You must have opened one to her from inside.'

What suspicion! What an insult! He said repeatedly, 'I did not open it.'

'How did she come in then?'

That was equally true. The scientist started looking around the rooms for any clues. Finally he found a window facing the road which had been latched from inside. Someone had unhooked the latch sometime during the day.

The guard had never held Rebati in such esteem as to attribute any cunning to him, dismissing him off as a simpleton who was clever enough to handle his books. He struck his forehead, seeming to have found out. 'Woman! She's destined to be diabolic.'

The little that was still left of the night ticked away with Rebati resolving repeatedly that he was not going to the tea party.

The crow called at dawn. Rebati left for home.

12

The next day there was no mistaking the appointed time. On the dot at 4-45, Rebati arrived at the tea party. He had expected it to be a private meeting for two.

He had never bothered about a fashionable dress code. Today he was wearing freshly laundered dhoti and kurta, with a folded chuddar across his shoulder. He realised it was a garden party, a gathering of fashionable people unfamiliar to him. His enthusiasm dipped; he wished he could hide somewhere to his relief. When he was about to take a corner seat, the entire crowd stood up in a body. 'Welcome, Dr Bhattacharya, this seat is for you.'

He was shown to a high-backed chair upholstered in velvet, right at the centre of the gathering. He realised that he was the principal focus of the assembly. Nila came forward, placed a garland round his neck, and a dot of sandalwood paste on his forehead. Brajendra-babu proposed that he be made president of the Jagani Club. Banku-babu seconded the proposal, to loud cheers from everyone. Haridas-babu the writer gave a speech on the international fame of Dr Bhattacharya. He summed up thus, 'Propelled by the winds of Rebati-babu's fame, our Jagani Club will sail from port to port along the coasts of the western ocean.'

The organisers whispered to the press reporters to take particular note of each metaphor for their story.

When the speakers rose one after another, each saying essentially: 'It was left to Dr Bhattacharya to finally put the victory mark of science on the forehead of Mother India', Rebati's heart filled with pride; he imagined himself blazing in the high noon of western civilisation. The scandalous rumours he had heard about Jagani Club he condemned in his mind as malicious propaganda. When Haridas-babu said, 'Rebati-babu's name gives to this gathering a protective amulet, indicating how very noble our aims are', Rebati savoured the glory of his name and became acutely conscious of the onus it laid upon him. He shed the shell of diffidence covering his mind. The women lowered cigarettes from their lips before leaning over his chair to say with sweet smiles, 'Sorry to bother you, but you must not refuse to give us your autograph.'

Rebati felt as if he had been evolving within the cocoon of a dream all these years, and now emerged a full-grown butterfly.

The invitees left one by one. Nila held Rebati's hand and said, 'You mustn't go just now.'

It was like an intravenous shot of some heady wine.

The day shaded into evening plunging the bower in a greenish haze of dusk. They sat close to each other on a bench. Taking Rebati's hand in hers Nila said, 'Dr Bhattacharya, being a man, why are you so afraid of women?'

'I'm afraid? Never!' said Rebati sounding confident.

'Aren't you afraid of my mother?'

'Far from it. I respect her.'

'And me?'

'Of course I'm afraid of you.'

'That's good news. My mother said she would never let us be married. If she has her way, I'll kill myself.'

'I'll stop at nothing. We'll certainly get married.'

Nila, leaning her head on his shoulder said, 'Perhaps you don't know how much I want you.'

Rebati drew her head close to his chest and said, 'No power on earth can snatch you away from me.'

'What about caste?'

'Not bothered about caste.'

'Then you must file a notice with the registrar tomorrow itself.'

'All right. Tomorrow I will, by all means.'

Rebati had begun to display male vigour.

The consequences were to follow quickly.

Sohini's grandmother had developed symptoms of paralysis. Death seemed imminent, and she would not let Sohini leave her until the last. Nila seized this opportunity with both hands to unleash her riotous youth.

Rebati's masculinity had lost its verve under the weight of his scholarship. Nila did not find him attractive enough. Nevertheless, he was a safe bet as a husband: he lacked the strength to stop her extra-marital excesses. Not only that. The enviable property associated with the laboratory was immense. Her well-wishers told her nowhere would she find anyone better suited than Rebati to take charge of the laboratory. Shrewd men were of the opinion that Sohini would never let him go.

Meanwhile, swallowing the taunts of his colleagues, Rebati finally consented to the newspapers announcing his presidency of the Jagani Club. When Nila teased him, saying, 'Are you getting nervous?' he said, 'I don't care.' He was determined to disabuse her of any doubts about his manliness. 'I'm in regular correspondence with Eddington, you know. I'm going to invite him to the Club one of these days,' he said. 'Bravo!' said the members of the club.

Rebati's primary work had stopped. The thread of his scientific quest had snapped. He would now intently look forward to the moment when Nila would arrive, suddenly press her hands over his eyes from behind, or sit on the arm of his chair with her left hand round his neck. He tried to assure himself that the halt to his work was only temporary, that the continuity would be restored once his mind had calmed down a little. There were no immediate signs of its calming down. That the damage to his work was in any way affecting the interests of the world did not alarm Nila the least bit. She thought it was all an elaborate joke.

Day after day the net was closing in. Jagani Club spread its tentacles round him, and they were making a complete male of him. He still could not bring himself to utter the unspeakable, but he forced himself to laugh when he heard obscenities. Dr Bhattacharya had become an object of great amusement to them.

Rebati often felt stings of jealousy. Nila lit her cheroot from the one on the bank director's lips. This was something Rebati would never be able to imitate. A puff of cigar made his head reel, but this obnoxious sight nauseated him even more. Besides, he could not refrain from objecting to all kinds of pulling and nudging that went on. Nila would argue, 'We have no fascination for the body of ours; what is its value to us? What is really precious is love, which we will never squander away.' With these words, she would clutch Rebati's hands, and Rebati would look condescendingly upon others as a pitiable lot: they were content to get the coir, not the kernel.

Outside the laboratory doors, there was round-the-clock vigil. Inside, the work lay unfinished; nobody was to be seen.

13

Nila was sitting in the drawing room, resting her feet on the sofa and reclining against the cushion. On the floor, Rebati was sitting near her, leaning against the sofa, with written foolscap pages in his hand.

Nodding his head, Rebati said, 'The language is too ornate. I'll feel embarrassed to read this exaggerated citation.'

'As if you're an authority on language. This is not your chemistry formula. Don't complain, just memorise. Do you know it's been written by the author Pramadaranjan-babu himself?'

'All those long sentences and high-flown words: I'll never manage them.'

'What's so unmanageable? Having to prompt you several times, I almost entirely have it by heart. Here goes: "At this most auspicious moment of my life, the garland of celestial flowers with which the Jagani Club has decorated me—" Grand! Don't worry. I'll be just around; I'll whisper the cues.'

'I'm not quite familiar with Bengali writing styles, but somehow I feel the entire piece is taunting me. Whereas it sounds so cogent in English—*Dear Friends, allow me to offer you my heartiest thanks for the honour you have conferred upon me on behalf of the Jagani Club, the Great Awakener,*—etc. Just one or two sentences, that's all.'

'That won't do. It'll be so amusing to hear Bengali from your lips. Just take the bit where you address, "O you youth of Bengal, who steer the chariot of independence, pioneers on the road strewn with the broken chains of bondage"—whatever you may say, can it be duly rendered in English? Such words from the lips of a scientist like you will make the youth of Bengal dance like snakes with their hoods swaying. There's time yet. Come, let me get you to read with me.'

Dragging his massive and tall body noisily up the stairs, the bank manager Brajendra Haldar in sahib's attire walked in with his creaking boots. 'This is intolerable,' he grumbled. 'Whenever I come, I find you holding Nila in your custody. Don't you have anything else to do, always standing like a hedge of thorns keeping Nili from us?'

Rebati said diffidently, 'I've an important work today, that's why –'

'I know you've work, and I took that opportunity to come here. Today you've invited the members over; assuming you'd be busy with that, I took time off for half an hour or so and dropped by on my way to office. Now I hear this is the place where he's tied to his work. Wonderful! When he has no work, this is where he spends his leisure, and again, when he has work, this is where he works. How do we busy people keep up with such a tenacious type? Nili, is it fair?'

Nila said, 'Dr Bhattacharya's weakness is that he can't come out with the truth plain and simple. It is not true that he has come because he has work. He's come only because he can't stop himself from coming. That itself is something worth hearing, and that's the truth. He has taken over all my time by enforcing his obstinacy. That speaks for his manliness. All of you have had to concede defeat to that yokel.'

'Well then, we'll show our manliness too. From now on, the members of the Great Awakener will practise the art of abducting women. We'll bring back the Puranic Age.'

'That sounds rather interesting,' said Nila, 'Abduction is better than marriage. But how does one go about it?'

'Shall I demonstrate?' asked Haldar.

'Right now?'

'Yes, right now.'

At once, he swept her up in an arc off the sofa. Shrieking and giggling Nila clung to his neck.

Rebati's face darkened. His problem was that he was too weak physically to imitate or resist. He was angry much more with Nila: why did she encourage these uncivil boors?

'The car's ready,' said Haldar, 'I'm taking you off to Diamond Harbour[24]. I'll bring you back in time for the dinner party. I had some work at the bank; let that go to hell. I'll be doing a good turn in its stead, giving Dr Bhattacharya a chance to work all by himself. It's advisable to remove a big hindrance like you. He'll thank me for it.'

Rebati noticed that Nila showed no signs of struggle to free herself from Haldar's hold. Rather, she lay snugly close to his chest, putting her arms around his neck rather passionately. 'Don't worry, Scientist-Sahib,' she said as they were going out, 'This is just a rehearsal of abduction. I'm not going across to Lanka[25]. I'll be back in time for your party.'

Rebati tore off the citation.

Compared to Halder's strength of arms and confident authority, today his own pride in learning paled into insignificance.

The dinner that evening was hosted at a renowned restaurant. The host was Rebati Bhattacharya himself; beside him sat his honoured guest Nila. A famous film actress had come to sing. Bankubihari had risen to propose a toast. Rebati's praises were being sung, and Nila's too, associated with his. The women were puffing very hard at cigarettes, if only to prove that they did not lag behind. Mutton dressed as lamb was much in evidence as middle-aged women disported themselves wildly to outsmart the younger girls in nudging and prodding, gestures and postures, in their boisterous laughter and loud voices.

All of a sudden, Sohini entered the hall. Everyone fell silent. Turning to Rebati, Sohini said, 'I don't seem to recognise you. Is it Dr Bhattacharya? You had asked for money for necessary expenses, which I sent last Friday. But I can clearly see you're not at all short of funds. Now you have to come along right away. I want to take stock of the items of the laboratory tonight itself.'

'You distrust me?'

"I did not distrust before. But if you have some shame left in you, make no mention of trust ever again.'

Rebati was about to get up, but Nila made him sit down tugging at his clothes. 'He's invited his friends tonight. Let them take their leave. He'll go after that.'

There was a cruel insinuation in Nila's words. Sir Isaac was her mother's favourite: there was no one more trustworthy. So he had been preferred over all others in being entrusted with the charge of the laboratory. To rub it in even more, Nila said, 'Ma, did you know sixty-five people have been invited this evening? All of them couldn't be accommodated here, the rest are in the next room; can't you hear the hubbub? Twenty-five rupees per head flat, whether you drink or not. The penalty for empty glasses is going to be quite high. Any other person would have blanched at the sum. The bank director was amazed at his spending spree. Do you know how much the film singer had to be paid? Four hundred rupees for just one night!'

Rebati's heart was fluttering like a catfish just cut up. His parched mouth did not utter a word.

Sohini asked, 'What's today's celebration for?'

'Why, don't you know that? It's already reported by Associated Press. He's become president of the Jagani Club; the dinner is to celebrate it. The six hundred rupees for life membership he'll pay at his convenience later.

'Perhaps, it won't be convenient any time soon.'

Rebati felt a steamroller lumbering in his heart.

'So it won't be possible for you to come along now?' Sohini asked him.

Rebati looked at Nila. Her angry frown excited his manly pride. 'How can I, with the guests—?" he said.

'All right,' Sohini said. 'I'll sit here until then. Naserullah, you go and guard the door.'

'That can't be, ma,' said Nila, 'We have some private matter to discuss. You shouldn't be present.'

'Nila, you're just an apprentice in the game of wits; you can't outwit me yet. Do you think I don't know what it's all about? I tell you, Nila, for that discussion of yours it's my presence which is most required.'

'What have you heard, and from whom?'

'The trick of getting news lies in the money-bag, like a snake in the hole. You have gathered three lawyers here to look among the documents for any loopholes concerning the laboratory funds. Isn't it so, Nilu?'

'I'll tell you the truth. It's unnatural for a daughter to have no share in the huge sum of money her father has left. That's why everyone suspects—'

Sohini rose from her seat. 'The real reason for suspicion goes much further back in time,' she said, 'Who's your father? Whose property do you claim to share after all? Aren't you ashamed to say you're the daughter of such a man?'

Nila jumped up. 'What are you saying, ma?'

'That's the truth. It was no secret to him; he knew it all. He got everything he expected from me, and will get even now. He cared for nothing else.'

Barrister Ghosh said, 'Your word is no proof, is it?'

'He was aware of that, and hence he put everything down clearly in a registered document.'

'Banku, it's getting late. Why wait any longer? Let's go.'

The stance of the Peshawari guard made all sixty-five guests beat a retreat.

Just then, Choudhuri entered, suitcase in hand. 'I received your telegram and hurried back. What's up, Rebi? Your face looks as white as parchment. Is there anyone around—where's the child's bowl of milk?'

Pointing to Nila, Sohini said, 'There's sitting the one to supply it.'

'So you're a milkmaid now, dear?'

'Not exactly,' cut in Sohini, 'She was hunting for a milkman. There's her quarry.'

'Who, is it our Reby?'

'This time my daughter has saved my laboratory. I couldn't judge the man. But my daughter noticed that I was turning my laboratory into a cattle shed. A little longer in detection and the whole thing would have sunk in a cow dung pit.'

'Since it's you,' said the professor, 'who've spotted this cowherd, my dear, you must take charge of this creature. He has all the qualities, except intelligence. When you are beside him, no one will notice the lack. It's easy to lead stupid males by the nose.'

'What do you say, Sir Isaac Newton?' asked Nila, 'You've already notified the marriage registrar. Would you like to withdraw the notice?'

'Not on my life,' said Rebati with a show of determination.

'The marriage will be at an inauspicious moment, then.'

'It will happen anyway, it must.'

'But it has to be far away from the laboratory,' said Sohini.

The professor said, 'Nilu, dear, he's stupid, but not incompetent. Once he comes out of his spell, you don't have to worry about his subsistence.'

'Sir Isaac, you must dress in a smarter way then, or else I'll have to wear a veil in your presence publicly.'

Suddenly another shadow fell on the wall. Rebati's aunt came and stood before him. 'Rebi, come along,' she said.

Rebati did as he was bid, quite meekly, without looking back once.

Ashwin 1347 (1940)

NOTES

English words in italics appear in the original text.

1 What is *dedipyaman* in chaste Bengali is explained as *brilliant* in the text.

2 The Bengali *byombholanath* refers to Shiva, and *bho* [nasalised] means a state of intoxicated abstraction in which he blissfully remains.

3 *Manab* (human) *dharmashashtra* (religious code) is an ironical reference to Manu's code of conduct for humans, the basis for the traditionally neglected status of women.

4 *Nilima* is the noun form of *Nil* or 'blue', which especially refers to 'an azure sky'. *Nila*, unless it means sapphire, is mistakenly thought to be the feminine form of *Nil.*

5 *Mala-chandan* or 'flower and sandalwood paste' is used for prayer or worship offered to gods and goddesses.

6 In the text, there are two closely related words: *achhre* and *shuchi* meaning 'by beating' and 'clean' respectively. Hence 'laundering'

7 A famous spot of pilgrimage on the bank of the river Alakananda at the foot of the Himalayas in Garhwal.

8 In the Mahabharata, Draupadi was married to all five Pandava brothers. Kunti, Pandu's wife, had a son, Karna, by the Sun god, while still a virgin. Contrarily, Sita was inviolably devoted to her husband Rama, and Savitri, daughter of king Ashwapati, married king Satyaban heedless of his foretold death within a year. Sita and Savitri are held among the five chaste wives (*panchasati*), the other three being Sati, Damayanti and Arundhati. Incidentally, Draupadi, Kunti, Ahalya, Tara and Mandodari are the five virgins (*panchakanya*) to be remembered in the morning.

9 A sprawling garden at Shibpur in Howrah across the river Hooghly from Calcutta.

10 *Bhattacharya* is a Brahman's surname.

11 *Chhatri* < *kshatri* < kshatriya, the second highest Hindu caste; a warrior caste.

12 *Mantra* is part of Vedic literature, which consists of metrical psalms in praise of gods and goddesses chanted during prayers; *tantra* refers to those mantras especially devoted to Shiva. In fact they combine to mean the same thing: ritual slokas, in a Bengali rhetorical device somewhat like 'hendiadys' (e.g., 'nice and warm').

13 *Nilu* < *Nila.* See notes to 'Subha'.

14 The supreme impersonal form, mother of the Trinity; the power that produces time, space, and causation, as also the phenomenal appearance, which exists on the relative plane. A lesser meaning is 'the grand illusion', which in this case, refers to the seductive spell of a woman.

15 Orthodox Hindus, especially the Brahmans, would not touch food prepared and/or served by a Muslim.

16 *Mahakaal* is another name for Shiva or Rudra; the reference is to Shiva's destructive dance (*tandava nritya*) (see Glossary), suggesting the inherent power of the atom. Put simply, it refers to the instruments in the laboratory meant for carrying out chemical experiments involving interaction of atoms.

17 An oft-repeated melodious raga in the stories.

18 An even more melodious adaptation.

19 A girdle or an anklet with small bells jingling sweetly at every movement.

20 'Movement' at one place and 'Circle' at another; a discrepancy in the text.

21 A very able and unscrupulous, almost Machiavellian, political advisor to Chandragupta Maurya of the fourth century BC, called variously also as Kautilya and Vishnugupta, credited with the authorship of 'Arthashastra' or 'Treatise on Polity' and 'Chanakya-shloka', a compendium of distilled worldly wisdom.

22 'Banku' signifies bent, curved or crooked. The literal translation would be 'I'll straighten out your "Banku"-babu', which has been avoided. The pun in Bengali could have been preserved if the name was rendered into 'Bent'-babu, which would be absurd.

23 '-Ji' (as in 'Maji' or 'Maiji') is a respectful suffix to names of persons.

24 A sub-divisional town in south Bengal, near the mouth of the Hooghly; a tourist resort.

25 The demon-king Ravana abducted Sita to his kingdom in Lanka (present-day Sri Lanka) in the *Ramayana*.

Throttling Progress
(*Pragatisanghar*)

In this college, mixing of boys and girls was rather brazen. They were mostly from affluent families and loved to squander money. By behaving like wastrels, the boys earned the appreciation of open-handedness from the girls. They would set their hearts aflutter and the latter would say proudly, 'Such are the boys of our college!' *Saraswati puja* used to be celebrated so ostentatiously that markets ran short of marigolds. Besides this, furtive glances, jokes and banter were rampant. In this atmosphere of camaraderie, an association sprung up all of a sudden, threatening to demolish the esprit de corps.

Suriti was at the helm of the association. She named it 'Nari-pragati Sangha' (association for the advancement of women), where no males were allowed entry. The impulse of Suriti's strength of mind eventually set off a wind of revolt against the males. It was as though the males were lowbred: all kinds of social interaction with them were forbidden, so nasty was their behaviour.

This year's Saraswati puja was a fairly tame affair. Suriti had forbidden every girl to give any contribution towards the revelry of pomp and splendour. Suriti's nature was strict; the girls feared her. Moreover, she made the members forswear all wasteful expenditure on festivals. Those who could afford might instead contribute their mite towards the poor fund, she had suggested.

Boys became furious at this revolt. 'Just wait and see how we parade the groom riding on a donkey at your weddings,' they threatened.

'Such a pair of donkeys, one upon another,' the girls retorted, 'is of no use for us. We'll despatch them to your court, with garlands round their necks and red sandalwood paste on their brows. Welcome them cordially into your band.'

Anyway, a rift between the males and the females seemed imminent. Whenever a boy approached and tried to pick up a conversation, the girls, turning up their noses, would say, 'This guy is too intrusive.' Earlier, some boys used to smoke cigarettes, sitting with girls: now the girls, snatching them away from their mouths flicked them away. To behave harshly with boys was seemingly self-glorifying to girls. While in a public vehicle, if a boy came forward to accommodate a girl, the rebel in her would burst forth, 'What was the need to do this little favour? We don't want the privilege of different treatment in a crowd.'

A pet slogan of their association was: males are inferior to females in intelligence. This used to be proved very often in examination results. If ever a boy happened to come first, it would be a matter for tears. They would not even hesitate to complain openly that he had been shown special favour.

Earlier on, girls used to clip some flowers to their hair and invariably display some variety in dress and make-up. Nowadays, they cried shame over it in their society. To charm men, women would make themselves attractive with dress and ornament: the humiliation of it they had willingly accepted for long. But no more. They started wearing ill-matched khaddar. Suriti gave away all her ornaments to her grandmother, saying, 'Keep them for your charity; I no longer need them. You can earn some virtue.' It was barbarous to dab cosmetics on one's God-gifted looks, whatever they were. All this was befitting to central Africa. If the girls were to tell her, 'Look Suriti, you're carrying it too far. You must have read Tagore's *Chitrangada*. Chitrangada knew how to fight, but did not know the art of beguiling men, and that spelt her defeat.' Suriti would flare up, 'I don't accept it. Nothing can be more insulting.'

Some of these girls started revolting. They said, 'To drive a wedge between men and women in this way goes against the modern trend.' Those who held an opposite view said, 'Males will be particularly cordial to us, offering us chairs, picking up our handkerchiefs, and that's what it should be. Why should Suriti call this an insult? We would rather say this is honour to us. We must exact service from males. Time was when women were mere nurses and servants. Now men come forward on their own to eulogise us: this reception, no matter what Suriti says, we would not forgo. Today males are our slaves.'

Such conflicts were brewing up inwardly among them all. Particularly, Salila did not like this dry wrangling over classification. She was from a rich family; exasperated, she took transfer to a missionary college in Darjeeling. In this way, other girls too had started dropping off in ones and twos. But Suriti did not budge from her stand.

This hubris of the girls, especially of Suriti, was intolerable to the boys. They began to harass her in any way they could. The mathematics teacher was a very strict person; he did not tolerate any frivolity. Yet it was in his class that a great disorder was created one day. On Suriti's desk was found an envelope written in her father's hand. As soon it was opened, out came a cockroach fluttering its wings. A great clamour started. The scared insect flitted its way on to the chignon of the next girl. It was utter pandemonium. The mathematics teacher Beni-babu tried to look serious, but the cockroach was no respecter of his browbeating. The prestige of the class was in jeopardy. Another day, page after page of her notebook was smeared with snuff and it was a very strong stuff. As soon as the book was opened, a severe infectious bout of sneezing started, leaving everyone with a runny nose and eyes. And the frequent noisy bursts almost drowned the lecture. The teacher took furtive glances and he too found it difficult to suppress a laugh.

One day, news came that some Maharaja was coming on a visit to the college, particularly the girls' class. A gossip did the rounds: this was a reconnaissance mission for brides. A group of girls pretended that they felt insulted. Even so, the day he came visiting, it was found that there was some intricate style in their coiffure, some gaudy colour in the border of their saris. He was no ordinary man but a millionaire. They vied with one another to attract his attention. The lecture was spoilt. A messenger came to announce that the Maharaja had taken a fancy to Suriti, of all girls. Suriti knew that the vast wealth of this king could sweep away all the meanness of the male race. But she pretended that not only was she unwilling to accept the proposal, but she felt rather slighted as well. Her argument was that a girls' college was no cattle market for the merchant to come, inspect and take his pick. But inwardly, what she had hoped for was a little more cajoling. Just then, news came that the Maharaja had departed, with his puggree and fineries. He had left the message that among the Bengali girls he had found no one worthy of his choice. Compared to them, he had further observed, even the upcountry gypsy girls in his native land were far better.

The whole class was aflame. Who had told him to come to fling this gratuitous insult at them? The thought of special care they had taken that day in their dress and make-up put them to shame. At that point, it was revealed that the Maharaja was an alumnus of this college. Having squandered away all his paternal property in gambling, he was now on the look out for a moneyed girl. Girls hung their heads. Suriti repeatedly said she had not believed it one bit. Not only had she not believed from the outset, but she had even been prepared to complain to the principal about this disturbance in their studies. Perhaps, she had been, but definitely, there was no documentary proof of this.

This was by no means the last of such troubles. The mastermind behind all this was Nihar.

Once, Suriti was going to the convocation, when Nihar accosted her and said, 'O proud lady, thou art too proud to tread on the ground!'

With a grimace Suriti said, 'Please don't ever joke with my name.'

'You're so learned and you call this a joke? Don't you know this is a *quotation* straight out of pure *classical* literature? Could any other name do you this honour?'

'You don't have to do me any honour.'

'I can't do without it. O full-bloomed lotus-eyed one, your face the full moon of autumn, your smile the beaming moonlight, no epithet is just enough for my satisfaction.'

'Look, if you keep teasing me like this publicly, I'll report you to the principal.'

'Do so if you must, but let me know your definition of insult. Which of these words do you find insulting? Rather, I can heighten them, should you like. For instance, O you maddener of all hearts.'

Red with anger, Suriti hurriedly left the place. A roar of laughter rose in her wake, with a train of addresses: 'Look back, O you red-eyed-in-anger, drunk-with-youth elephant –'

Next day, before the class began, a noise arose: 'O you bumble bee humming and honey-seeking at the lotus feet of *Saraswati*, your face resembling the full moon –'

A furious Suriti went straight to the superintendent, Gobinda-babu, and said, 'Sir, if they keep insulting me like this, I shall not stay in this college.'

He came and told the boys, 'Why are you teasing her in this way?'

Nihar replied, 'Would you call this teasing? If anyone could at all complain, it was the full moon who could have said I had jested with her. Jogesh of our class says: discarding all else, plain Nibhanana[1] would do, because her mouth is as sharp as the nib[2] of a pen. I protested, "For shame, Jogesh, you shouldn't have said so. They are all learned women." I downplayed his remark. But I didn't find anything wrong in "Purna-chandra-nibhanana" or "Your face resembling the full moon".'

Other boys said, 'Just consider this, sir. We recited delightedly, "O you bumblebee humming and honey seeking at the lotus feet of *Saraswati*"! Firstly, the word is not condemnable. Secondly, how did she presume the pride of thinking that it was directed at her? There were other girls too in the room. They didn't seem perturbed.'

The superintendent said, 'Such greetings hurled at the wrong place, at the wrong hour are generally looked upon as jest. Why must you utter this at all?'

'Sir, when the mind is agitated, can it judge the time or place? Apart from that, if our greeting really has been a jest, anyone could have laughed it off without taking offence. Moreover, there are so many scholars in your college. Do they not even know how to return a jest? Would their white-as-moonbeam teeth not show in their charming smiles? How then do we males who are thirsting for nectar survive?'

Such exchanges were frequent. Suriti was at the end of her patience: her natural gravity was at stake. She had no flair for banter, yet she was not capable of any riposte either. She only seethed with rage. There were males who took pity on her plight, but they were of no consequence.

Another day, when Suriti was on her way to college, Nihar on an impulse called out from across the road, 'Hail to thee, Golden-champak *Gouri*[3]!'

The man was widely read, seemingly having a passion for languages. He used to recite Sanskrit verses at any hour without any apparent reason; it sounded so sweet in his voice. In textual matter, Suriti was way ahead of him; she was a master in cramming. But Nihar had vast studies outside the texts. Suriti, almost in tears, went straight to Gobinda-babu. 'I can't stand such greetings; he has not even a sense of place,' she moaned.

Nihar said, 'I'm at fault, sir. From now on, I'll call her "Inky-complexioned". But would that not be too *realistic*?'

Suriti ran away, almost weeping.

Nihar had a streak of unrelenting cruelty in his character. It took adequate bribing to placate him, as was known to all.

One day he brought a Japanese toy—a wooden croaking frog—in good numbers and kept them with the boys. When it was time for Plato's philosophy to be expounded, croaking started all over the class. It was difficult to ascertain just which direction the sound was coming from. That day, Plato's words were completely drowned by croaking frogs. In the end, a search yielded ten wooden frogs from Suriti's desk.

She burst out crying, 'These can never be mine. Someone wickedly shoved them into my desk.'

The boys burst out furiously, 'We won't tolerate such unfair charges against us. Never can males have a fancy for such childish pranks. All this is in the girlish nature of women.'

For a while, the classroom was silent. Thereafter, from the other corner rose a bizarre noise: all the boys had started dragging their feet simultaneously on the concrete floor. A grotesque concert was created by so many shoes rubbing together. Gradually it exceeded the limit when Suriti could not take it any longer silently. Still she waited patiently for a while until there was a booming sound after which the boys started imitating the sound of the *shehnai*.

It was then that Suriti spoke forth, 'Sir, would you please tell them to stop making a noise? We are here to study; this is no place for practising music. If someone finds no interest in the lessons, he'd better leave the class.'

At once, there rose a cry of 'Shame!', 'Shame!' from all sides and the boys marched out of the room. The mood of the class was lost. After the class, when the girls had retired into the common room, a peon came to announce that the secretary was calling Suriti. The girls started whispering. In the secretary's room, Suriti saw their professor was sitting, and Nihar was standing beside him. 'The boys have complained,' said the secretary. 'They felt insulted at your conduct today. If you have anything to say in your behalf, say so.'

Suriti said, 'Sir, they behaved insultingly with the professor, behaved rudely with us: does it not mean that if anyone has been insulted, it is we?'

The secretary and the professor, after hearing both sides and considering their merits, told Nihar, 'So it is conclusively proved that you are the person to have begun troubles in the class and you were the leader of the group. It is you who ought to apologise.'

Nihar said, 'That is impossible for me, sir. If you so permit, I would rather leave the college.'

'Take your time. Think it over carefully.'

'So be it,' he said and got up to leave. That day the students found a notice hung up on the notice-board: The puja vacation begins today.

Nihar had special intimacy with Salila. She proposed to Nihar, 'Why don't you too come over to Darjeeling?'

Nihar said, 'But my father is no millionaire like yours. How can I afford the expenses of studying there?'

'All right. I will bear your expenses,' she said.

Nihar had this quality: whatever you offer him, he does not hesitate a moment to accept it. He decided to go to Darjeeling at the expense of his rich classmate.

Now, for all her vanity, Suriti felt a twinge in her heart that all Nihar's affection was for Salila. Assured of a rich girl's shelter, Nihar started passing comments at Suriti indiscriminately. He said, 'Women who can expect any courtesy from males are the ones who have not discarded their femininity.' This neglect from males Suriti pretended to ignore defiantly. That is not to say that she did not nourish a desire to win over the same Nihar. Nihar used to take his monthly allowance from his rich girl friend: at this, some of the boys out of jealousy, some others out of hatred, called him 'Ghar-jamai'[4]. Nihar paid no heed; what he needed was money. As long as he found some girl to sponge off for partying with his friends at Firpo's and buying his regular supply of necessaries and fancy goods, he had no compunction to remain her parasite. Whenever he felt the need, he sent word to Salila asking for money. Here was a male dependant of whose talents Salila had a high esteem. She had thought that one day Nihar would make a big name. He never desisted from suggesting that he had an unhesitating demand from the entire world, and Salila too accepted it.

While in Darjeeling, Salila had *double pneumonia*; there was no neglect in her treatment, but *Yama's* messenger was not to be resisted. Salila died. Nihar had expected until the last moment that perhaps she would allocate something in his name in her will. But when no sign of it could be found, he felt great anger against Salila. Particularly, when he heard that she had provided one hundred rupees for her maidservant, crying shame on Salila he burst out, 'What *meanness*!'

The girl Nihar used to worship as 'Jagaddhatri'[5], after ending her mission of fostering males, departed for ever dealing Nihar a jolt of despair. With the funds at Darjeeling no longer forthcoming, he had to wind up and come back to his mess in Calcutta. The boys had a hearty laugh at his expense. Nihar did not let it touch him; he hoped that a second Jagaddhatri could be sought out. A renowned Oriya astrologer had divined that he would receive the favour of a very rich girl. He eagerly looked forward to the result of that divination: there was no knowing along which road Jagaddhatri would be making her visitation. He found himself in a financial crunch.

Sudddenly finding the Darjeeling-returned Nihar at college, Suriti too was astonished. She asked him, 'When did you return from the Himalayas?'

Nihar smiled and said, 'Just returned, after taking in some fresh air. Kalidasa says: *Mandakini-nirjhara-shikaranam bodha muhuh kampita-debadaruh*[6]. That wind shook my thin Bengali bones far more severely than it did that deodar tree; look at this, how I am swathed in blankets like a Bhutanese.'

Suriti said with a smile, 'Why, it's fine! Your health has picked up too and you look quite well in the Bhutanese dress.'

'Glad to know it. Now that I no longer have to worry how to escape from the cold, the problem is how to charm the eyes of you all; that's more difficult.'

'Well, why must you seek to charm our eyes? What carries weight about males is their learning, of which you know you have no dearth.'

'Here you are mistaken. Newton said he had collected pebbles on the seashore of knowledge, whereas I have picked up mere grains of sand.'

'Good heavens! I can see this time you've brought back a great deal of humility from the hills. I don't remember you ever had any.'

'Look, this I've learnt from Kalidasa himself who said: *Prangshulabhye phale lobhad-udbahuriba bamanah*[7].'

'All the time hearing your Sanskrit slokas, I am almost suffocated. Would you speak some pure Bengali for a change, please?'

Most amazing is that he did not even mention Salila's death. Meanwhile, the bell rang and both had to go to their class; but the slokas kept reverberating in Surita's mind every moment like the deodar. She had noticed that nowadays other girls very much appreciated Nihar's joking and reciting slokas; they praised him for it and so she too had realised that in it there was no pungent taste of mockery and therefore of late had been trying to love his sudden bursts of Sanskrit recitation.

Around that time, there occurred an incident, which opened up an opportunity for the students to work in tandem. A scholar in Indian archaeology from Sorbonne University was to visit on an invitation from Calcutta University. The students had decided that they would usurp the glory of formally receiving him en route to the university: they invited him in advance on behalf of their Pragatisangha[8]. The scholar, out of his characteristic French sense of courtesy, accepted it right away. Thereafter, they could not decide who would read the felicitation address. Someone said he would speak in Sanskrit; someone said English would be just right; but neither medium was found acceptable. Finally, they settled for French as the suitable medium to pay respects to a French scholar. But who was to do it? External readers were available, but that would hardly be prestigious. At this point, Niharranjan broke in, 'If you entrust it to me, I can manage and manage it well enough.'

Some of the girls were present. Those who had a special feeling for Nihar, said, 'We might give him a chance.'

Suriti was particularly opposed: 'That would amount to tomfoolery,' she said.

All the other girls said, 'Our language is different from the visitor's. Even if a fault occurs in our diction or pronunciation, the French scholar will have the grace to ignore it. They are no Englishmen: the English cannot tolerate any lapse in their manners even by foreigners. Such is their pride. Not so with the French. On the contrary, if there is any inadequacy they will accept it graciously. Why don't we see how far Niharranjan's learning goes? One hears he studies French all by himself at his home.'

Niharranjan's native home was in Chandannagar[9]. During his early years, he had studied at a French school where he had won wide reputation for his command over the language. All this was unknown to his friends in Calcutta. Anyway, he stood his ground. And lo, as he went on reading the felicitation, the French scholar and the associates who accompanied him were amazed at the brilliance of his language. They had never heard such chaste language anywhere outside France, they said. They further said that the boy should go and earn a degree from Paris. The professors at his college were all praise. They observed that he had preserved the name of the college, even outshining the University of Calcutta in reputation.

Hereafter it was impossible for anyone to ignore Nihar. The college was abuzz with 'Nihar-da', 'Nihar-da'. Pragatisangha's primary code of conduct was violated. They had abjured colourful saris and make-up meant to charm the males. Suriti was the first to break that rule: her sari-ends began to display colour. She felt embarrassed to befriend Nihar overcoming her previous antagonism, but that embarrassment seemed unlikely to last much longer.

She found that all other girls were trying to outsmart her: if someone invited him to tea, some other girl, unnoticed, tucked a bound set of Tennyson into his desk. Suriti fell far behind them. When a girl presented him a nice table-cover embroidered with her own hands, Suriti felt a twinge in her heart for the first time. She thought, 'Had I acquired such women's skills!' She had never threaded a needle; all she had done was study. That pride of learning today began to dwindle within her. 'If I had been able to do something whatever that could enchant Nihar's eyes!' That was not to be. How freely the other girls exchanged courtesies with him! Suriti fondly wished she too had enlisted herself in that enterprise, but she just did not fit in. Consequently, her dedication seemingly grew even stronger than that of the other girls. She would feel obliged to be able to inflict some harm upon herself on any pretext for the sake of Nihar. Now the wind in the sails of Pragatisangha started to blow from the opposite direction.

While the other girls gradually resumed their studies in right earnest, Suriti could not manage to do that. One day, Nihar's fountain pen slipped from his desk on to the floor; Suriti forestalled others by picking it up and handing it to him. Lower than this, she had never stooped. On one occasion, Nihar had said in his address—and it included a quotation from a French playwright—'Every beautiful thing has a veil of its own; if males eye it, it loses its tenderness. In our country, the age-old custom of women as far as possible avoiding direct encounter with males owes its origin to the perception that encounters keep diminishing women's value and tarnishing their delicate charm.' Other girls passionately argued against it. They said it was a mockery trying to preserve delicacy by guarding it so jealously. Male contact is equally essential to everyone, whether male or female. Surprisingly, Suriti, of all, rose in support of Nihar.

Under the impact of this one Sorbonne episode, Suriti's conduct and demeanour changed altogether. Now she went to take advice from Nihar. When a film based on one of Shakespeare's plays was shown, could the girls not go to see it together with a male guardian? Nihar's strict order was: no, they could not. If somehow there was a deviation from the rule, it was not possible to preserve the sanctity of rules.

Earlier, every time a good movie came, Suriti used to go to the cinema. Whatever happened to her now? Such noble self-sacrifice was unimaginable. She even gave up attending altogether the social occasions where nowadays men and women invitees participated together. The adherents of tradition praised her generously. On her own, she had her name struck off the rolls of Pragatisangha.

Suriti proposed to take up a job: she asked Nihar whether she could not teach male students at school, even if they were of a very young age.

Not even that could be done, said Nihar. Suriti struck a balance: she accepted the job at half the salary and offered the other half for a separate teacher to be appointed exclusively for boys. The secretary was astonished.

Suriti's intensity of passion became increasingly unbearable. At one point, she somehow communicated her feeling: could they not get married? According to the rules of the very society she once refused to recognise, she learnt that their marriage was by no means permissible. Yet, there was no fault in her owing loyalty to this man and surviving with her head bent low forever, because that was the decree of the Almighty.

She often heard that Nihar's financial condition was not good; he had even to borrow his textbooks. Suriti then started helping him sufficiently from out of her tiffin allowance. Nihar felt no shame in it. It was as if males had the right of getting offerings from women. Yet there was no end to his pride in learning. Once in a college, a professor's post for teaching Bengali fell vacant. At Suriti's request, the proposal to appoint Nihar to that post was being discussed favourably. His name being considered in the committee, Nihar's vanity was wounded.

Suriti said, 'This is your false sense of hurt. Even the Vice Chancellor's appointment is discussed among the council members.'

Nihar said, 'Maybe, but wherever they are to accept me, they have to do so unanimously without debate. Short of this, I cannot keep my prestige. I was the first to be awarded the degree of MA in Bengali. I can't accept a post at the committee's condescension.'

If he had taken this post, he would have overcome the need to take allowances from Suriti. He ignored the post, but not the need. Suriti's intake of refreshments gradually shrank. Her family members grew anxious at her demeanour and appearance.

Ever since her childhood, her health was not good; on top of that, she had this present suffering. When they discovered who it was for whom she was observing this austerity, they accosted Nihar, 'Either you marry her or you give up her company.'

Nihar said, 'Marrying her is out of the question, and as for giving up her company, why ask me? She can do so at her pleasure; I have no objection.'

Suriti knew this. She knew that she had no value whatever to Nihar, except for his own benefit. If she were to stop providing it, he could easily throw her out like a stray dog. Even so, by giving as many facilities as possible—buying books, presenting entire sheets of new khadi cloth–any way she could, she kept him bound up in ties of self-interest. Having no other option, Suriti had to acknowledge this disgrace.

Once, Suriti had joined a mofussil college as its principal at a good salary. Then it kept crossing her mind, 'Here I am living in great comfort while he keeps rotting there like a poor man. How can I put up with this?' In the end, one day without showing any reason, resigning her post she took up the post of a teacher at a nominal salary in Calcutta. Three-fourths of that salary went to feed Nihar and cater to his fancy. In this self-denial alone did she find her joy. She knew that none of the arts of alluring the mind was at her disposal. That is why her sacrifice became so unlimited. With this sacrifice alone, she had tried to outsmart other girls. Moreover, nowadays she had been continually hearing of reverse progress: that women should dedicate themselves to men was the decree of Providence. The girl who did not dedicate herself for males was no girl worth her name. Such opinions took hold of her.

In Calcutta, the room she took at a very low rent was a damp breeding ground of diseases. There was no question of going to the terrace; the tap was continuously leaking. On top of that, what she had never done with her own hands she had to do now: she began to do her own cooking. She knew many arts, but not the art of cooking. With the inedible unhealthy stuff she managed to prepare, she merely filled her stomach. This completely broke her health. She was compelled to skip her duties with a medical certificate. So frequent was her absence that the authorities could no longer grant her any leave. At last, it was detected that she had been insidiously attacked with tuberculosis. It was necessary to shift her from her rented house. Her friends and relations admitted her into a private hospital. Nobody knew that she had kept apart some money secretly; from it, her due allowances reached Nihar regularly. He was aware of everything, yet he used to accept it as his due. And yet he never found the time to pay her a visit at the hospital. Suriti lay eagerly straining her ears towards the window, but never once could hear the sound of any familiar feet. At last one day, her purse was emptied out and with it came her ultimate sacrifice.

Ashwin 1348 (1941)

NOTES

1 *Nibha* is a Bengali suffix meaning 'like or similar to or resembling', obviously requiring another word to make it meaningful, as in Girinibha, 'like mountain'; *anan* means face or mouth. Therefore, *Nibhanana* lirerally means 'face (here mouth) resembling' which is not a sensible word, though the Bengalis were fond of keeping such names for their daughters.
2 The text has 'nibh' for 'nib', an ill-conceived pun.
3 Another name for goddess Durga.
4 One who lives in his father-in-law's family as a sponger.
5 The foster-mother of the world, an appellation for goddess *Durga*.
6 The literal meaning of the sloka: in the wind bearing the sprays of the fountain, the deodar is trembling incessantly.
7 The meaning of the sloka: in the wind the dwarf stretches out his arms to reach the fruits hanging high.
8 Association for advancement.
9 A French-occupied settlement in pre-Independence India.

Sunday
(*Rabibar*)

The main character of my story comes from a traditional Brahman-pundit family. In worldly matters, his father was steeped in the lawyer's profession; in religious belief, pickled in the strong enzyme of *Shakta*[1] ritual. Now he no longer practised in court. Sitting in his home, side by side doing his prayers and giving legal counsel, he was very cautiously maintaining a balance between his worldly and other-worldly interests.

If from beneath the crack in such a rock-solid, ritual-bound traditional house, by chance, a bristly atheist springs up, his iconoclastic mind keeps impinging severely on the old brick-and-mortar juggernaut. Thus, in this orthodox Vedic Brahman family, there was the emergence of a formidable heretic[2] in the hero of our story.

His real name was Abhayacharan. He obliterated completely whatever imprint of family custom was inherent in this name; he changed it to Abhikkumar. Moreover, he knew that he was a type out of the ordinary. He hated the idea that his name should wallow in sweat by rubbing shoulders with the plebeian names in streets and markets.

Abhik's physical features were strikingly in a British mould. With a stout, tall, fair figure, brownish eyes, sharp nose, his chin was curved as if in a gesture of protest against any opponent. His fisticuffs were powerful deterrents; of his classmates, whoever had suffered his mauling considered him worthy to be kept a hundred yards away.

His father Ambikacharan was not particularly worried about his son's ungodliness. Ambikacharan's glaring precedent was Prasanna Nyayaratna[3], his father's elder brother. Old Nyayaratna was a gunner of logic; sitting in the chatushpathi[4], he used to fire cannon balls of suffixes and prefixes at the dialectics of God. The Hindu society said with a snigger, 'Cannon balls eaten up!' No dent was left on the society's edifice. If the bird of religious faith is allowed to soar into the sky, leaving the cage of customs and rituals hanging in the veranda, no communal disturbance can ever take place. But Abhik, on the slightest pretext discarded orthodox customs as good riddance to bad rubbish. The constant cackle of chickens waddling around the house proclaimed the eldest son's inner attraction for them. Word of all this irreligious practice very often reached his father's ears; he paid no heed. Even if some well-meaning friend came to report against it, he would be thrown out most unceremoniously. Unless an offence is self-evident, society sidetracks it in its own interest. But eventually Abhik ended up doing such a blatant excess as was impossible to overlook: Bhadrakali[5] was their family deity; she was reputed to be a living deity. Abhik's colleague, poor Bhaju, was mortally afraid of incurring her wrath. Therefore, out of impatience to demean his faith, Abhik had done such an ungodly thing in the worship room that his father, being furious, burst out, saying, 'Get out of my house. I shan't see your face again.' Such instant severity was possible only in the character of an orthodox Brahman-pundit family.

The disowned son went to his mother and said, 'Ma, you know I have abandoned gods long since; so it is quite redundant for gods to abandon me. But I know that if I stretch my hand through the hole in the fence of your kitchen, surely I'll get your leftovers. That is one place where no ordinance of god works, no matter however living that god may be.'

His mother, while wiping her tears, untying her sari-end took out a banknote and offered to him. He said, 'When I shall no longer feel the acute necessity of that note, only then shall I take it from your hand. To deal with the goddess of misfortune, all one needs is strength; banknotes are of no avail in grappling with her.'

One or two more words about Abhik need to be told. He had two hobbies in his life, which were of opposite nature: one, dabbling with machine tools; another, painting. His father had three cars, which were his means of transport for excursions to the mofussil[6]. Abhik had his initial training in engineering through handling those models. Besides that, a client of his father had an automobile factory, where he had worked voluntarily without wages for a long time.

Abhik had gone to learn painting at the government art school. Before long, he was firmly convinced that too many days of further training would make his hand work like a piece of machinery, his brain cast in a die. That he was an artist he got down to establish with sheer publicity. He sponsored an exhibition of his paintings. Newspapers carried his advertisement: the greatest artist of modern India, Abhikkumar, the Bengali Titian[7]. The more he kep't thundering, 'I am an artist,' the more it kept echoing in the cave of the vacant minds of a certain class of people; they were simply overwhelmed. Admirers—females outnumbering males—gathered round him in large numbers. They branded the opponents as *philistine*, called them *bourgeoisie*.

At last, in trying times, Abhik discovered that his fame owed much of its brilliance to the lustre of silver, which emanating from his affluent father's funds used to reflect from his name. At the same time, he had also discovered that his financial deprivation had made little difference to women's devotion to him. Ultimately, their eyes bulging with wonder, they had hailed him as '*artist*' in their sharp sweet voice. They had always confided to one another that barring one or two, none of them understood a thing of art; they were given to pretensions—simply irritating!

The subsequent history of his life is long and vague. He had not minded wearing a soiled hat and grimy blue-coloured shirt and shorts working first as a mechanic and later as the head mechanic in Burn Company's factory. Befriending the Muslim labourers, eating four-paisa worth of parathas[8] along with them with less costly forbidden meat he had spent his days blithely quite cheap. To people's remark, 'He has become a Muslim', he had retorted, 'Is a Muslim even greater than an atheist?' When he had saved quite a sum, he emerged from his life incognito, and once again, began to practise *bohemianism* as a full-fledged artist. Male students enlisted; so did the females. In his studio, bespectacled young girls kept discussing in the modern shameless fashion selected topics of nudist psychology, the stigma of which was overlaid with thick layers of cigarette smoke. Glancing and pointing fingers at one another they had said, '*Positively vulgar*'.

Bibha was entirely outside this group. Her acquaintance with Abhik had begun at the very first step of the college. Abhik's age was then eighteen, sparkling with the vigour of new youth; even the senior students had acknowledged his leadership quite naturally.

Having been raised in the Brahma Samaj[9], Bibha had no inhibition in mixing with males. But it was at the college that she encountered an impediment. Some of the boys had been behaving indecently, with titters, glances, gestures and hints. But one day, the incivility of an urban boy was conspicuously a bit too obtrusive. As soon as it came to Abhik's notice, he hauled him up to Bibha. 'Ask her forgiveness,' he bade him. Forgiveness he had to ask, with his head hung low, his speech faltering. From then on, Abhik took up the responsibility of Bibha's protection. For that, he had been the target of many sarcastic remarks, which however had rebounded from his broad chest; he had not cared to take any notice. Bibha had felt very much embarrassed at the whispering campaign, but at the same time, it had given her a thrilling sensation as well.

In Bibha's appearance, gracefulness rather than beauty was the dominant feature. There is no explaining how one gets attracted. One day, Abhik had told her, 'In the feast of the uninvited, the common man wants sweets.[10] But your beauty is not common man's sweets. It is for the artist only; it compares with Leonardo da Vinci's portrait alone—*inscrutable*.'

Once in a college examination, Bibha had outshone Abhik. On that score, she had shed copious tears and expressed profound resentment, as though it had been her own disgrace. 'You keep painting day and night, and hence lag in the exams; I feel small,' she had grumbled.

By chance, overhearing it from the adjoining veranda, one of Bibha's friends, with a twinkle in her eye, had quipped, 'Bravo! Proud am I of your pride, beauteous by your beauty.'

Abhik said, 'Those who are pundits by cramming do not even know what "no marks" examination I have been passing. My obsession with painting brings tears to your eyes, whereas your bland pedantry has dried up the tears of my eyes. You'll never ever realise it, because all of you stay with your eyes shut wallowing at the feet of celebrities and we keep shining as the crown of the infamous.'

In the matter of painting, there was a great discord between the two. In fact, Bibha could not at all comprehend Abhik's works. When other girls made much of whatever he painted, and convening a felicitation garlanded him, Bibha thought it was mere pretension of the uncultured and felt ashamed. But starved of Bibha's compliments, Abhik was restless and deeply distressed. All the country considered his work as sheer madness: it was most intolerable that Bibha too concurred with them, if not expressly. His constant thought was that one day he would go to Europe and there he would win tumultuous applause when Bibha too would sit down to weave his victory garland.

It was Sunday. In the morning, Bibha, on returning from her worship at the Brahma-shrine, found Abhik sitting in her room. There was a brown paper parcel cover of a book in the wastepaper basket. Retrieving it, he was scrawling some picture with his fountain pen.

'What brings you here at this hour?' Bibha asked.

'I can cite a fair reason,' said Abhik, 'but that will be secondary. If I come out with the primary reason, that will perhaps not be fair. Whatever else you may think, do not suspect that I have come to steal.'

Bibha took her seat at the desk and said, 'If you feel the need, you had rather steal. No question of informing the police.'

'It is in front of the gaping mouth of needs that I have been perpetually standing. Stealing is in many cases a virtue; but I have to refrain from it, afraid that the calumny should stain my sacred atheistic views. For the sake of keeping the prestige of our non-existent god, we have to tread far more cautiously than the virtuous.'

'Have you been waiting very long?'

'Indeed so. Sitting all this while I was trying to solve an intricate problem of psychology: you're well-read and apparently fairly intelligent too; then how it that you believe in God? I haven't been able to crack it yet. Perhaps, I'll have to make frequent visits to this room before I can complete this research.'

'So you're again going after my belief?'

'That's because your belief is going after me. The wedge it has driven between us is heart-breaking. This I cannot forgive. You cannot marry me, because being sensible I do not believe what you do. But I really have no difficulty in marrying you, no matter whatever true or false you believe thoughtlessly. You cannot make an outcaste of an atheist, can you? Therein lies the greatness of my religion. No gods but you alone are the perceptible truth to me, which none of your gods can make me debunk.'

Bibha sat there silently. A little later, Abhik spoke forth, 'Is your god very much like my father? Has he disowned me?'

'Er, yes? What are you prattling?'

Abhik knew wherein lay the difficulty of her not getting married. He wanted it admitted by Bibha. She kept silent.

Bibha had always been her papa's child. So much love, so much respect she could never offer to anyone else. Her father Satish too had showered her with copious affection. On that score, her mother harboured a tinge of jealousy in her mind. Bibha had once raised geese. Her mother had often complained petulantly, 'They cackle too much.' Bibha had bought a sky-blue sari and jacket for herself. Her mother had remarked, 'They don't match Bibha's complexion at all.' Bibha had a special love for her maternal uncle's daughter. When she expressed her wish to attend the latter's marriage, her mother protested, 'There's malaria there.'

Having been cold-shouldered at every step by her mother, Bibha's dependence on her father had grown even deeper and ingrained in her marrow.

Her mother passed away first. For a long time thereafter, tending her father was Bibha's singular mission of life. All the wishes of this affectionate father she had identified with her own. Satish had bequeathed all his estate to his daughter, but had left it to the care of a trustee providing for a regular monthly allowance to her; the entire cash was allocated to a suitable groom. Bibha knew who according to her father's norm this suitable groom was. At least, she had no doubt as to who was unsuitable. One day, Abhik had raised the topic. 'The one you do not wish to hurt is no more, whereas another who is most cruelly hurt is alive and kicking. You feel pain to stab at air, and feel no compassion for this body of flesh and blood.'

Hearing this, Bibha went away weeping. Abhik realised that she could suffer even her god to be controverted, but not her father.

It was about ten in the morning. Bibha's niece Susmi came and said, '*Pishima*, it's quite late for the kitchen.'

Bibha handed her the bunch of keys and said, 'Go, take out the provisions. I'm coming.'

Since the unemployed have no fixed schedule of work, household work multiplies on their score. Bibha's household was just like that. Because domestic obligation was lighter for the relatives, it was extensive for the non-relatives. Lest the servants should ignore anyone, she had made it her habit to work all by herself for the house she had built up with personal care. Abhik said, 'It will be wrong for you to go right now, not only to me, but to Susmi as well. Why don't you give her scope for independent authority? *Dominion status* at least for today? Besides, I wish to perform an experiment on you. I have never told you to do anything; today I want to test you. It will be a new experience.'

'So be it,' said Bibha, 'Why don't you do it?'

Abhik took out a leather case from his pocket, and displayed it before her. It held a wristwatch: platinum dial, gold band inlaid with chips of diamond. 'I want to sell it to you,' he said.

'Strange! Sell it?'

'Yes, sell. Why are you surprised?'

After a moment's silence, Bibha said, 'Isn't this the one Manisha presented you on your birthday? I think her pangs of the heart are still ticking in it. Do you know what sorrow she had had, what slander she had suffered and what an absurd sum she had wasted only to make the gift suitable for you?'

Abhik said, 'Of course it was she who had given this watch, though she had never let it out who it was. But I am no idolater so that mounting it on an altar, I'll keep blowing conchs and ringing bells day and night in my mind.'

'Really, now you surprise me. It's been only a couple of months since she contracted typhoid and –'

'But isn't she now beyond all happiness and sorrow?'

'Until the last moment she had held fast to her belief that you loved her.'

'She wasn't wrong in her belief.'

'Then?'

'What then? She is no more, but if her gift of love can bear me fruit even today, what can count more than that?'

The signs of a severe affliction appeared on Bibha's face. After remaining silent for a while, she said, 'When you are free to roam anywhere, why did you come to sell it particularly to me?'

'Because I know you won't haggle over the price.'

'You mean in all of Calcutta, I am the lone customer ready to be short-changed?'

'I mean love is happy to be short-changed.

Such a person is hard to be angry with. What may be called authoritatively boastful childishness! He was seemingly not aware that there could be any cause for shame in anything. This, his candid imprudence, this easy surmounting of the fence of social impropriety was what made women's affection draw him inexorably; it abstracted the strength to reprimand. Women take the dust of the feet of those who carry their sense of propriety very carefully about them. And those wild, turbulent souls who are not bothered about right or wrong, women bind them with the snare of their arms.

After scrawling for some time with her blue pencil in the blotting paper on the desk, Bibha said, 'All right, if I can manage, I'll give you the money just like that, but I won't buy that watch of yours. By no means.'

In an excited voice, Abhik said, 'Charity! Had I been as rich as you, I would have accepted your charity as a gift, and returned with an equally costly gift. All right, let me rather be chivalrous: here is my watch, take it. I won't take a single paisa.'

Bibha said, 'Women are meant only to accept, aren't they? There's no shame in it. But that does not include accepting this watch. Well, tell me why you want to sell it in the first place.'

'Listen then. As you know, I have a very insolent Ford car. The laxity of its manners is intolerable. Only because it is me its tenth stage[11] has been kept in abeyance. With a mere eight hundred rupees, it can be exchanged for an old Chrysler model of its father's age. Then I can give it a new look with my own expertise.'

'What will you do with a Chrysler?'

'Won't go to marry.'

'It's not possible that you'll do such a civil thing.'

'Quite right. Well then, let me first ask you: have you seen Shila, Kulada Mittir's daughter?'

'Seen her only beside you, at any hour, at any place.'

'Yes, beside me, she has proudly made her own place resisting several others. She has to show she is progressive. She delights in shocking the gentry.'

'Is that all? By no means. The hearts of the bevy of girls will be pierced by shafts—no less delight in that either.'

'That point was in my mind too; coming from you, it sounded nice. Well, tell me, isn't that girl's beauty rather unfair? You might call it God's excess.'

'I see! Only when talking of beautiful girls, you believe in God.'

'When you need to disparage something, you have to put up an opponent. In his days of sorrow, when Ramprasad[12] needed to vent his resentment, he projected a mother goddess and moaned, 'No more shall I call you mother.' Whatever fruit so many days of calling mother had borne him would not be surpassed even after desisting from calling: even so, the devotee satisfied his urge to disparage. So too with me: to cast aspersion, I've taken the name of God.'

'What aspersion?'

'I'll tell you. I was taking Shila along in my car rattling all the way from the football ground, exhaling fumes into the nostrils of pedestrians behind. At that time, Mrs Pakrashi—you know her; one hesitates to call her tolerable even by the most liberal measure of exaggeration—she was coming from somewhere in her new Fiat. Motioning our car to stop, she had a hearty exchange of pleasantries for quite a while blocking the traffic. Every now and then, she kept glancing furtively at the hood of my chipped car and its decrepit footboard. If your God had been egalitarian, He would not have created such a gulf of difference in the appearances of women setting our hearts afire on the streets.'

'Is that why you –'

'Exactly. That's why I have decided that as soon as possible, with Shila in the Chrysler I will drive away honking past Mrs Pakrashi. Well, let me ask you one thing; tell me frankly whether a slight pang of –'

'Why drag me into this? As for my beauty, I don't think God has been unstinted. Besides, my car too is not worthy of outshining yours.'

Abhik, at once leaving his stool, sat on the floor near Bibha's feet and pressing her hands, said, 'What a comparison! Amazing, you're amazing; I say you're simply amazing! As I keep looking at you, I suspect that some day I will end up believing in your God. Ultimately, there will be no salvation for me. I have entirely failed to excite your jealousy. At least that much you did not reveal to me. Yet, you know –'

'Stop it. I know nothing, only know that you are strange! You are like God's burst of laughter!'

Abhik said, 'You won't so much as tell me expressly, but I can correctly guess that you want to know my *psychology* about Shila. I am growing intensely used to her, just as I was addicted to smoking at an early age. I felt giddy, yet would not give up the habit. It tasted bitter on the tongue, but made me feel proud at heart. Shila knows how to build up the intoxication day by day. The wine in women's love is my *inspiration*. I am an artist; she is but the wind in my sails. Without her, my paintbrush runs aground in sandbanks. When Shila sits by my side, I can feel that in her heart blazes a bright red fire, *danger signal*; its heat transmits into my veins. Don't take offence, austere woman, you are thinking that it is my recreation. No, dear, no; it is my necessity.'

'That's why you're so much in need of a Chrysler car!'

'That I admit. Whenever Shila feels proud, she dazzles more brightly. This is exactly why women need to be supplied with so many dresses and ornaments. What we want in women is grace; what they want of males is wealth. The golden fullness of that very wealth sets the *background* for displaying themselves. This trick of nature is merely for the sake of aggrandising the males. Tell me isn't it true?'

'May be true. But what do you call wealth? That's the point of debate. In my view, those who call the Chrysler car wealth only lower the esteem of males.'

Abhik cut in impatiently, 'I know, I know, you could have placed me on the top of what is wealth by your reckoning. But your God came and stood in between.'

Retracting her hand from Abhik's hold, Bibha said, 'Don't repeat the same thing over and again. I have all along heard just the opposite. Marriage for an artist is a noose; it stifles *inspiration*. If I had been able to make you great, if I had that power, then –'

'Why speak hypothetically?' Abhik exploded. 'You have done it. My only regret is that you could not recognise that wealth in me. If you did, you would have stood beside me as my partner snapping all ties of religion and custom, and you would not have cared for any obstacles. The ferry arrives at the shore, yet the pilgrim cannot locate the *ghat* to reach his desired shrine. My condition is like that. Bee[13], my bumblebee, tell me when you will discover me completely.'

'When you will no longer need me.'

'Those are all empty words, inflated with the air of much untruth. Admit that your entire being is keenly anxious because "you cannot do without me." Can you conceal it from me?'

'What difference will it make even if I admit it and why should I conceal it either? Whatever my feelings may be, I do not wish to hanker piteously.'

'I do wish, I am a supplicant. Day and night I will keep saying, "I want, want, want only you".'

'And with it say, "I want the Chrysler car too".'

'There you are! That is only *jealousy*. *Parbato bahnimaan dhoomat*[14]. Better, let the smoke of jealousy billow out at times, so it would prove the existence of the hidden fire of love. Your mind is no extinct volcano. It's active Vesuvius.'

With this, Abhik stood up raising his hands and cried out, 'Hurrah!'

'What childishness is this! Is that why you came this morning after planning in advance?'

'Quite so. I admit it. Otherwise, there are a few, who, I know, are so enamoured of me that I can at once sell this watch without any pretext even at an unfair price. But it is not merely to ask for the price that I have come to you; I wanted to solicit your favour by striking at the spot which is the source of your anguish. Poor me, nothing happened; neither this, nor that.'

'How did you know? Does fate always play card games? Let me tell you one thing. You have often asked me whether your flirtations with others hurt me. To be honest, they do.'

Impatiently Abhik said, 'That is indeed good news.'

'Don't be so elated. I didn't mean *jealousy*; I say it is insult. This hobnobbing with girls, this indecent shamelessness only betrays your disrespect for the entire race of women. I don't like it.'

'What a thing to say! Is respect not individualistic? You mean, to the entire race, wherever and whomsoever I encounter, I will keep paying my respects? No testing of the material, *wholesale* respect right away? That is nothing but *protection*, which in business parlance means enhancing the price by loading artificial cess on the commodity.'

'Don't argue for argument's sake.'

'Which means you will argue, I will not, is it? This is what is meant when they say, "Dangerous days these / women will prattle; men, silence please."'

'Abhi, you're merely looking for pretexts to keep arguing. You know very well what I wanted to say: it is only civil for men naturally to maintain a distance from women.'

'Naturally maintain or not naturally maintain a distance? We have no regard for the *modern* artificial civility; we respect genuine human nature. With Shila by my side, I drive the jerky Ford; what is natural is our being side by side. If for the sake of form, one and a half arms' length of space were to be left in between, that would amount to showing disrespect to one's nature.'

'Abhi, you males by gratuitously paying a special price to women had once made them costly, had not belittled them solely in your own interest. Today, if you take back that price, you'll only be rendering your own discretion cheap and be deceiving yourself of your own dues. But all this talk is useless: the *modern* time is itself cheap.'

'I would not say cheap; I would say shameless. The hoary old Shiva sits in meditation; the modern Nandi-Bhringis[15], with mirror in their hands, are taunting their own images–what is called *debunking*. Born to these times, I can't be a disciple of Bholanath and keep sitting with upturned eyes[16]. Rather, if one can imitate the grotesque grimaces of Nandis and Bhringis, one can make a name now.'

'Well, well, go make a name by making grimaces all around. But before that, tell me one thing honestly. With your indulgence, girls everywhere madly scramble for you. Does it not blunt the edge of your sense of feeling good? What you frequently call *thrill*—does the scrambling not trample it underfoot?'

'Let me tell you honestly, then. Bee, what is called *thrill*, what is called *ecstasy* is a first-rate commodity, luckily found by chance. But what you call scrambling in a crowd is the stuff of a *second hand* shop: stained at places, torn at others, but in the market they also sell—though at a low price. How many of the rich can pay for the best stuff?'

'You can, Abhi, surely you can; you can afford the full price. But strange is your behaviour: you artists are amused by and curious about what is torn, what is dirty. Perfect things are not *picturesque* for you. Anyway, let us stop all these squabbles. For now, let us advance the Chrysler episode as far as possible.'

Saying this, Bibha rose and went into the next room. On returning, she handed Abhi a bunch of notes and said, 'Here is your *inspiration*, bearing the Company government's seal. But don't ask me to take that watch of yours in exchange.'

Abhik kept sitting on the floor, resting his head on the stool. Bibha drew back her hand and said, '"Don't misunderstand me. You are in need now; I have no want. In this case –'

Cutting her short, Abhik said, 'I do have want, severe want. In your hand lies the opportunity to satisfy it. What will money do?'

While stroking Abhik's hand soothingly, Bibha said, 'My inability to do what I cannot do will torment me forever. Why should you deprive me of the happiness of doing whatever I can do?'

'No, no, no, by no means. Taking money from you, I'll go riding with Shila? I had thought you would cry shame on this proposal, had expected you to be angry.'

'Why should I be angry? Do I not know you'll be naughty only for a while? This is terrible for Shila, not at all for you. How often I have seen such childishness of yours! I was secretly amused. I know that for a few days you cannot do without playing this game. I also know that if it becomes steady, you cannot do with it at all. Perhaps you want to get something, but it is unbearable that something should get you instead.'

'Bee, you know me only too well; that's why you're so terribly careless about me. You've realised that I do have fascination for girls, but that fascination is just an atheist's fascination; there's no bonding in it. I will not confine that worship within a stone temple. I have sometimes seen the ecstatic spectacle of intimacy with girl friends; I feel sick at that bemused uxoriousness. For me, girls are the gods of an atheist, that is, of the artist. An artist does not drown, gasping for breath; he keeps swimming and easily gets across. I am not avaricious; avaricious is the girl who indulges in jealousy over me. You are not greedy; the greatest gift of your detached mind is freedom.'

Bibha smiled and said, 'Stop your hymn now. As an artist, you're all mature children; this time I'd prefer you take the toy for the play you've devised from my hand.'

'No, no, never. Well, let me ask you one thing: how did you extract the money from the clenched fist of your trustees?'

'If I told you candidly, that wouldn't perhaps delight you. You know I'm learning mathematics with Amar-babu.'

'So you want to surpass me in every matter, now in learning too?'

'Stop your chatter, listen. Aditya Uncle is one of the trustees. He is himself a *first-class medallist* in mathematics. He believes that given adequate opportunity, Amar-babu will become a second Ramanujam. Uncle had referred a problem solved by him to Einstein. I have seen the reply he received. If you must help such a person, you have to be careful to preserve his honour. So I said I would learn mathematics from him. Uncle was very happy. As educational grant, he has kept a lump sum from the trust fund at my disposal. From that I give him scholarship.'

Abhik's face took on a strange look. Trying to smile, he said, 'Perhaps there is such an artist as well who, given suitable aid, could reach at least up to the chin of Michelangelo.'

'Perhaps, even without any aid he will be able to reach there. Now tell me whether you will or will not take the money from me.'

'The cost of the toy?'

'Yes, dear, we women have forever been giving you the cost of toys only. What's the harm in it? After all, there is the rubbish dump.'

'The Chrysler is hereby given a burial. Let the progressive woman's impetus of progress riding the ramshackle Ford chug down its wobbly path. Anyway, I no longer find those talks interesting. I've heard Amar-babu has been saving money for going to England. From there, he will prove that he is no ordinary person.'

Bibha said, 'I sincerely hope it may happen so. It will make the country proud.'

Abhik declared loudly, 'I will have to prove so, too, whether or not you hope for me. For him to prove himself is rather easy, along the thoroughfare of *logic*: art has to prove its worth along the path of taste, which is the *private* path of the aficionados. That is no Grand Trunk Road. This blinkered, oil mill-turning land of ours is no good for me. Those who are perspicacious, theirs is the land where I will go. Let that day come when your uncle will be obliged to say I am no trifling man either, and his niece too have to –'

'Don't worry about the niece. She did not have to wait to know whether you were or were not of the same calibre as Michelangelo. To her, even without proof you are extraordinary. Now, do you want to go to England?'

'That is my only dream day and night.'

'Then take this gift of mine. At the feet of genius, this is my humble revenue to the king.'

'Stop it; stop that topic. Doesn't sound quite in tune. May the glory of the maths professor be meaningful! For me, even if it is not possible in the present life, the next life is still there; *posterity* will keep waiting. I tell you—a day will come when waking in the middle of the night burying your face in the pillow you will have to regret that fame could have been attached to name for ever, but that did not happen.'

'You don't have to wait for *posterity*, Abhi; my cruel punishment has begun.'

'I do not know which punishment you mean, but I know that your greatest punishment is that you could not appreciate my work. The new age has come; you miss the opportunity to witness me on the modern chair in the felicitation ceremony of that age.'

With this, Abhik got up and made for the door.

Bibha asked, 'Where are you going?'

'There's a meeting.'

'What meeting?'

'With the students who will stay back in the vacation, I will organise *Durga-puja*'"

'You'll do *puja*?'

'Yes, I will. I do not believe in anything. In the emptiness of that non-belief, there will be no scarcity of space for the accommodation of the three hundred thirty million gods and demigods. To accommodate all the childish games of the universe, there is the empty sky.'

Bibha realised that it was against her God that his sarcasm was directed. Without going into any argument, she sat silently, her head bent low.

Abhik turned back from the door to say, 'Look Bee, you're a staunch nationalist, dreaming of establishing unity in India. But in a country which is constantly ravaged by religious fanaticism, the sacred vow of unifying all religions behoves only an atheist like me. I am the saviour of India.'

Bibha knew why Abhik's atheism had grown so savagely cruel. So she could not get angry with him. She was unable to surmise what it would ultimately lead to. Bibha could give him whatever else she had; she had to stop short only at her father's wish. That wish was not just a matter of opinion or faith or argument; it was part of her nature. There was no protesting it. Often, she had thought she would surmount that barrier. But at the last moment, her feet refused to move.The bearer came to announce that Amar-babu had arrived. Abhik at once rushed down the stairs. Bibha's heart was in turmoil. At first, she had thought she would send word to the professor that she would take no lessons that day. The next moment, she hardened her mind and said, 'All right, bring him in here. Tell him to wait. I'll be coming in a short while.'

She flung herself on her bed and lay face down, sobbing inconsolably clutching the pillow. After quite a while, composing herself and freshening up, she came back, smiling, and said, 'Today I had planned to play truant.'

'You aren't well, I suppose?'

'No, I'm fine. In fact, the Sunday-off habit has been ingrained in my marrow; off and on it rears its head.'

The professor said, 'The microbe of holidays has so far found no time to infect me. But today, I too shall take leave. Well, let me clarify. The international mathematics conference is scheduled for this year at Copenhagen. I do not know how they picked up my name. I am the only one from India to have been invited. Surely I can't afford to miss the opportunity.'

'Of course, not. You must go,' said Bibha encouragingly.

The professor smiled and said, 'The authorities who could have sent me on deputation are not willing, because they fear I may lose my head. Obviously, all their anxiety is only for my good. I'll go out today in search of some friendly person who is not shrewd enough. What I can promise to mortgage in lieu of the loan can neither be weighed in a balance nor be tested on a touchstone. We scientists always look for some tangible evidence before accepting any proposition; so do the business-minded: there's no deceiving anyone.'

'I must find out one, whatever it takes,' said Bibha excitedly. 'He may not turn out to be shrewd enough. Anyway, don't worry about that.'

The problem was not solved in a few words; for that day, an understanding of sorts was reached.

Amar-babu was medium-built, dark-complexioned, lean-bodied, broad-browed with a receding hairline. The geniality of his face gave the impression that he had never had the opportunity to make enmity with others. What his eyes suggested was not exactly absent-mindedness; rather it was perspicacity. In other words, when he was on the street, looking after his safety was other people's concern. Of friends, he had very few, but the few he had entertained very high hopes about him; the rest of his acquaintances turned up their noses and called him *highbrow*. He spoke few words, which people interpreted as a lack of amicability. Overall, the public had virtually no presence in his life. It was compatible with his *psychology* that he was completely ignorant of what others thought of him.

That Bibha had offered Abhik eight hundred rupees on a moment's decision was a desperate act out of blind impulse. Bibha's uncle had firm faith in her devotion to rules; there had never been an exception to it. Her uncle for all his practical knowledge could not even imagine when and from which direction a sweeping deviation from rules can suddenly come over a woman's life. The castigation and shame of this rashness Bibha had pondered over before she presented her offering to Abhik in a momentary surge of passion. That spurned offering had now returned within the ambit of rules. In the present case, there was no impulse of the arrogance of love in her mind. She could not dare to bring to mind the thought of lending money to anybody transgressing her rights. Therefore, Bibha had *planned* to sell off her mother's jewellery received as heirloom and dedicate the money to her motherland on the pretext of giving it to Amar.

Bibha helped the children who were growing up under her care with their lessons also. That day was Sunday. After lunch, she had been taking her class with them till now; she dissolved it earlier than usual.

Taking out her casket, spreading a rug on the floor she was laying out the ornaments one by one. Their family jeweller had been sent for.

Then she heard Abhik's footsteps on the staircase. Her first impulse was to hide the ornaments, but she left them as they were: to conceal anything from Abhik for any reason whatever was contrary to her nature.

On entering the room, Abhik stood watching; he realised what the matter was. 'So it's passage money for the extraordinary man! When dealing with me, you're *Mahamaya*[16], the great illusionist, to keep me distracted. To the professor, you're *Tara*[16], the great rescuer. But does the professor know that a frail woman has arranged to send him across with the lotus-stalk of her hands?'

'No, he doesn't.'

'If he comes to know it, won't the scientist's masculine pride be hurt?'

'All I know is that great men have an unrestricted right to respectful gifts from lesser people. With that right they do us favour; they oblige us.'

'That I admit; but the ornaments on a woman's body are only

meant to entertain us, however small we may be, not to pay for someone's passage to England, however great he may be. From the very beginning, this is women's standing offer as a treat to the eyes of men like us. This necklace of matching rubies and pearls I saw one day on you when we had just begun to know each other. It is intermingled with the memory of that first acquaintance. Can it be only yours? Is it not mine as well?'

'All right. Let it be yours alone.'

'It is meaningless tearing the necklace away from your whole being; that'll amount to stealing. I'm waiting with the hope of taking it along with you and all you have. If in the meantime you transfer that necklace, you'll be deceiving me.'

'These ornaments my mother gave me as dowry for my prospective marriage. If the marriage does not happen, how am I to define them? Anyway, do not expect to see the bejewelled image of this girl at any hour whether auspicious or not."

'The bridegroom has been settled elsewhere, perhaps?'

'Yes, on the bank of the *Baitarani*.[17] Better, I can do one thing: I'll leave some of these ornaments for the bride you'll marry.'

'Do you think I've no prospect of a bride on the bank of the Baitarani?'

'Don't say that. The living brides are all clutching your horoscope.'

'To tell you honestly, the prediction of the horoscope is not altogether improbable. By the curse of the evil star, if the lack of a female partner proves disastrous, it portends evil days for males.'

'Maybe. But soon after that, it is the presence of a partner that proves disastrous, when the portent becomes one of predicament, or what is called circumstance.'

'"Or what is the same as forced hanging. Even though the context is *hypothetical*, it is so near the borderline of possibility that any argument over it is pointless. So, one day when the Benarasi-wearing bride will find me to have become another person's property, then –'

'Don't frighten me any more; then I too shall suddenly discover that I do not lack other men either.'

'For shame, Bee. It did not sound modest coming from you. Males worship women as goddesses, because when they give up the ghost, you are willing to wither away to death. Nobody cares to think of males as gods, because whenever the latter are scarce, they are intelligent enough to fill up the gap. That is the problem with prestige. You women have to stake your life to prove your devotion. Let us drop *psychology* for the present. My proposal is that you'd rather give us the responsibility of earning immortality for Amar-babu. Do we not recognise his worth? Why must you put the males to shame by selling your ornaments?'

'Do not say so. The fame of males is the greatest treasure for women themselves. In the country where men are great we women are blessed.'

'Let this country be so. This is what I sincerely hope for when I look at you. Anyway, keep aside my views in this context; we'll discuss it later. Mean-minded fellows who are jealous of Amar-babu's success are by no means few in Bengal. The people of this land are like pestilence to great men. But for heaven's sake, do not club me with that band of dwarfs. Listen then to what a big *criminal* virtuous deed I've done: the entire subscription for Durga-puja was with me; I've donated it to the *fund* for Amar-babu's foreign trip. And I did it without anybody's knowledge. When it comes to their notice, the devotees of the goddess won't have to look elsewhere for the sacrificial victim[18]. I do not believe in gods, so I know what true worship means. They are virtuous; what would they know?'

'What's this you've done, Abhik? Is this worthy of what you call your holy atheism? This is nothing but treachery.'

'I agree. But let me tell you what had weakened the foundation of my religious belief. My followers had been very enthusiastic about celebrating the puja with much pomp. But the subscription that was collected was as ridiculous as it was miserable. It would hardly have made the tragic drama of sacrificial goats sufficiently interesting; the red in Act V would have been pale. I had decided that we would ourselves beat the drum without rhythm in mad enthusiasm and hack gourds and pumpkins with a hatchet. This is enough for a non-believer, but not for the pious. In the evening, unknown by me, one of them made himself up as a sadhu with five others as his disciples and going to a rich old widow said: goddess *Durga* had told him in his dream that unless she was offered sufficient goats and a full-scale *puja*, she would devour the widow's son, who worked in Rangoon. They extorteded five thousand rupees out of her. The very day I came to know this, I put the money to good use. Thereby I lost my caste, but the stigma of the money was removed. To you, this is my *confessional*. By confessing to sin, I'm washed clean of the sin. Outside of the five thousand, all I have is a mere twenty-nine rupees, which has been set apart to pay up the dues in the vegetables market.'

Sushmi came to say, 'Bachchu the bearer's temperature has risen; he has cough too. The doctor has left a prescription. You come and tell me what to do.'

Pressing Bibha's hand firmly, Abhik said, 'You well-wisher of the world, you're busy looking after the afflicted. And for those unfortunate souls who are terribly healthy, you find no time.'

'Not for the good of the world, dear, it is merely to keep a certain extremely healthy wretch out of my mind that I have to invent so much work. Now let me go. You wait a bit. Keep an eye on the ornaments.'

'And who is to keep watch on my greed?'

'Your atheist belief.'

Abhik had not been seen for a long time. Neither had any letters been received. Bibha's face had grown pale. She was in no mood for work. Her thoughts had all mixed up. She could not ascertain just what had happened or might happen. Her days seemed like an unbearable load. Her recurring thought was that Abhik had left her in a state of pique. He was a run-away boy; he had no ties, so he disappeared, perhaps never to return. She kept pleading to him in her mind, 'Don't be angry. Come back. I'll never ever make you unhappy.' All Abhik's childishness, his lack of consideration, his demands—the more she remembered them, the more the tears streamed down her eyes: she kept reproaching herself for a stone-hearted woman.

At that point of time came a letter bearing the seal of a steamship company. Abhik wrote:

'I am going to England as the *stoker* of a ship; my work is to feed coal into the engine. I would tell you not to worry, but I would have liked you to worry. Even so, for your information, I am inured to suffering the heat from the engine. I know that you will take umbrage against me for not claiming the passage money from you. The sole reason is that you do not have the least regard for my identity as an artist. This is my perpetual grievance. But I would not blame you for this. I am sure one day the aficionados of that culturally sensitive country whose acceptance is truly valuable will give me recognition.

'Many ignoramuses have praised my work. Again, some liars have prevaricated. You never tried to deceive me with false homage. You were aware, though, that a little praise from you is nectar for me. The unwavering truth of your character has given me immense sorrow, yet I have held that truth in high esteem. One day when I will be acclaimed by the world, it is you who will accord me the highest honour, together with the nectar of your heart. As long as your conviction does not attain the indisputable truth, you will keep waiting. Keeping this in mind, today I am on my way to achieve the impossible.

'By now, you know that your necklace has been stolen. The thought that you were going to sell it in the market was unbearable. You were going to break through my ribs to find a passage into my heart. In lieu of that necklace, I left a bunch of my works beside your casket of ornaments. Spare me the silent laughter.

Nowhere in Bengal will those paintings sell dearer than a scrap of paper. Do wait Bee, my dear bee, you won't lose, never. Just as hidden treasure is suddenly struck by the pickaxe, boastfully I tell you, likewise the priceless lustre of my work will be revealed all of a sudden to you. Until then, you can smile, because to every woman, every male—whom she loves—is but a child. That benign amused chuckle I have stuffed in my imagination and am carrying across the sea. And along with it I have taken from your honeyed house a sweetly bad name. I have seen that to your god you keep praying with so many demands: from now on, please make this prayer—may the severe pangs of coming away from you be fruitful one day.

'I do not know whether you have ever envied me. It is true that I love girls. Even if not all that passionately, I do like them. They all loved me, and their love makes me feel grateful. But you certainly know that they are but a cluster of nebulae; in their midst you are the singular Pole Star. They are just hint; you are truth. All this may sound *sentimental*. There's no helping it; I'm no poet. My language is like a raft made of the banana tree; as soon as a wave comes, it keeps rocking until it vibrates in resonance. I know that where pain is profound, it calls for restraint, or else, the dignity of truth is violated. Weakness is fidgety; often you laughed at my weakness. In this letter, finding the same indication you may say with a slight smile that this was just like your Abhi. But this time, perhaps no smile will come to your face. I grumbled often enough that I had not possessed you, but nothing can be more unjust than to say that you stint on the bounties of the heart. In fact, in this life my complete identity could not be revealed. Perhaps, never will it be. This acute lack of contentment has left me a beggar forever. That is why, no matter whether I do or do not believe in anything else, I may have to believe in rebirth. You have never clearly confessed your love, but from the depth of your silence, what you have gifted me every moment, this atheist could never give any definition to that; he called it miraculous. Under its very spell, perhaps in my closeness with you, somehow I have roamed near your god himself. I do not know for sure; maybe, all this is a figment of my imagination. But in our hearts, unknown to ourselves there is an inner sanctum, which given a violent blow sets off spontaneous words, maybe it is some such truth I have so far not known.

'Bee, my dear Bee, you are the one I have loved most. If that love is assumed to have some infinite role of truth and if that truth you call your God, then His door and yours are united for this atheist. I will return again when my opinions, my beliefs, my all I will surrender without a thought to you; you will deliver them to the ultimate address of your pilgrimage so that never again because of intellectual shortcoming does a moment's separation occur with you. Today as I have come away from you, the incredibility of love has become bright in my mind; it has transported me across the barbed wire fencing of logic and reason: I behold you in transcendental glory. So long, I tried to understand you with my brains; now I wish to win you over with my whole being.

Your atheist devotee,
Abhik'

Ashwin 1346 (1939)

NOTES

English words occurring in the text have been shown in italics.

1 Relating to Shakti or the female aspect of creation.

2 The text has *Kalapahar*: historically, a Brahman, after embracing Islam turned into a notorious iconoclast; an awful religious renegade.

3 Literally, jewel of a logician; a title awarded to an erudite logician.

4 Sanskrit school where the Vedas, grammar, poetry and philosophy were taught.

5 An aspect of goddess *Durga*; materialising from the goddess's ire, along with Birbhadra, Shiva's charnel house aide (hence the name, *Bhadrakali*), she rampaged through King Daksha's sacrificial ceremony.
6 Areas outside towns and metropolises; urban sprawl.
7 Italian painter of the Venetian school, noted for his religious and mythological works.
8 Hand-made bread of wheat flour folded twice over, rolled into a triangular shape and fried in ghee or vegetable oil.
9 A *Brahmo* is one who followed the cult of monism introduced by Raja Rammohan Roy in the nineteenth century, which preached worship of Brahma, discarding the worship of images; the place of their congregation was called S*amaj*. Inclusion of women as members, abolition of early marriages of girls and polygamy, sanction of widow marriages, and inter-caste marriages were some of its achievements.
10 The text has: *mishtannam itare janah*. See Note (13) in 'An Unapproved Story'.
11 The last of the ten conditions or stages of human life; death.
12 Ramprasad Sen, an eighteenth-century religious poet and composer, ardent devotee of goddess Kali, with whom in his fanatic piety he believed he had established a mother-son relationship of love-hate and even visualised the goddess incarnate.
13 'Bee' for Bibha is an affectionate adaptation, like a nickname, as evident from the epithet, bumblebee.
14 A Sanskrit aphorism meaning: smoke reveals that the mountain is afire. The significance is brought out by the next sentence in the text.
15 Charnel house retinue of Shiva (see Glossary).
16 Bholanath is another name for Shiva whose eyes are upturned in meditation like those on the eve of one's death.
17 An aspect of goddess Durga (see Glossary).
18 Hindu mythological river corresponding to the river of Hades, Styx. The implication is that her marriage will come about in the other world, the land of the dead.
19 It was and still is, though on a lower scale, customary to sacrifice animals like goats and buffaloes as part of the ritual.

The Story of a Muslim Woman (*Mussalmanir Galpa*)

A DRAFT*

That was a time when secret anarchical agents were stalking the body politic. People were perpetually on tenterhooks from the apprehension of unexpected persecution. Every sphere of household activity was ensnared by nightmares: all a householder could do was to look up in supplication to gods; people lived in consternation from the imaginary fear of evil spirits. Whether god or man, it was hard to trust anyone, and tears were the only resource to fall back upon. The dividing line between the consequences of good deeds and bad deeds was barely discernible. In life's journey, people stumbled at every step and fell into misery.

In this state of affairs, the arrival of a beautiful daughter at one's home was like a curse of God. When such a girl was born, the members of her family used to say, 'The sooner the poor wretch departs, the better for us.' Just such a jinx had visited the Teen-Mahala Talukdar[1] Bangshibadan's house.

Kamala was remarkably beautiful; her parents had died; if only she too had gone with them the family would have had no cause for worry. But that had not happened, and her uncle

Bangshi had brought her up very affectionately, very carefully for so many years.

However, her aunt often grumbled to her neighbours, 'You will agree that her parents left her only as an impending doom on our heads. Nobody can tell what might happen and when. I have my own children in the house, and she has virtually kept a torch of disaster burning in its midst; wicked people are always looking this way. Because of her alone, I will come to utter ruin any day; for that fear I cannot sleep properly.'

So far, the days had been passing in some sort of way, but now came a proposal of marriage. In the hurly-burly of it, there was of course no hiding her away. Her uncle would say, 'That's why I've been looking for a family that is capable of protecting their women.'

The bridegroom was the second son of Paramananda Sheth of Mochakhali. He was sitting pretty over a bulging bag of money that was all set to go to waste once his father died. The boy was extremely fashionable: flaunting his wasteful flings in falconry, gambling and *bulbul* fights[2], he had quite unrepentantly cleared the path for squandering his money. He was inordinately proud of his wealth, of which he had plenty. He had a complement of formidable *pehlwan*[3]s from Bhojpur[4], all skilled in fighting with lathis[5]. 'Whoever[6] is there across the district,' he would go about bragging, 'that can lay hands on me?' As for his taste in women, he was a bit of a connoisseur : he had his wife; another, a younger one, was what he was now looking for. Word on Kamala's beauty had reached his ears. The Sheth family was very rich, very powerful. They were determined to get her married into their family.

Kamala wept and said, 'Uncle dear, why are you letting me loose from my moorings?'

'If I had the strength to protect you, dear child,' said her uncle, 'I'd have safeguarded you all my life, don't you know?'

The marriage was settled. The groom walked jauntily into the wedding assembly; there was no end of pomp and splendour.

Kamala's uncle pleaded, joining his palms, 'My son, I feel it isn't wise to make so much fanfare; these are not good times.' At this, again throwing a challenge at any likely miscreant, the groom said, 'All right, we'll see how he dares come near me.'

The uncle said, 'The girl was our responsibility until the wedding. Thereafter, the girl is now yours; you take the responsibility to reach her home safely. We are not competent to do this, we are weak.'

'Don't fear,' he said puffing out his chest.

The Bhojpur pehlwans twirled their moustaches and stood up, lathi in everyone's hand.

So the bridegroom set out with the bride on his way home through that famous area, the Taltori field. Madhu Mollar was the brigand leader. At about midnight, he and his men with lighted torches in their hands, battle cry on their lips, swooped down on the bridal party. Most of the Bhojpuris were put down. Madhu Mollar had formidable reputation in his line; there was no escape from his hands.

Leaving her palanquin in fear, Kamala was about to hide in the bushes when the old Habir Khan came and stood behind her. Everybody venerated him as a prophet[7]. Habir stood tall and ordered, 'Clear out, boys. I am Habir Khan.'

The dacoits said, 'Khan Sahib, of course we cannot override you, but why did you spoil our trade?'

Anyway, they had to disperse.

Habir came to Kamala and said, 'You are like my daughter. Have no fear. Now come away with me from this dangerous place to my house.'

Kamala cringed and squirmed. Habir said, 'I can understand. You are a Hindu Brahman's daughter, so hesitating to go to a Muslim's house. But remember this: those who are true Muslims honour devout Brahmans as well. In my house, you will stay just like the girl of a Hindu family. People respect my name. My house is nearby. Come with me; I'll keep you safe.'

Kamala was a Brahman's daughter; it was not easy for her to

overcome her hesitation. Realising that, Habir said, 'Look dear, as long as I am alive, there is nobody in the area who can outrage your modesty. You come with me, do not be afraid.'

Habir Khan took Kamala to his house. Most surprisingly, of the eight-wing house in the Muslim home, in one wing, there was a Shiva temple along with all arrangements for practising the Hindu way of life.

An old Brahman appeared and told Kamala, 'My child, this place is just like a Hindu home; here you can preserve your caste.'

Kamala cried and pleaded, 'Please send word to my uncle; he will take me back home.'

Habir said, 'You are mistaken, my child. Once you have been here, they won't take you back again. They will abandon you on the way. You can test it for yourself if you like.'

Habir Khan took Kamala to her uncle's house, and leaving her at the postern said, 'I'll be waiting right here.'

Kamala went inside, and clasping her uncle's neck said, '*Kakamani*, do not desert me, I beg you.' Tears rolled down her uncle's eyes.

Her aunt came and screamed, 'Throw her out! Throw out the ominous wretch! You ruinous girl, aren't you ashamed to come back from a heathen's house?'

Her uncle said, 'I am helpless, my child. We are a Hindu family; here nobody will take you back. If we do, we'll lose our caste ourselves.'

Kamala stood there for a while with her head bent low, then slowly stepped out of the door and went away with Habir. The doors of her uncle's house closed forever behind her.

In Habir Khan's house, she was at liberty to practise her rites and rituals. Habir Khan said, 'My sons won't come to this wing which is yours; with the help of this old Brahman you can do your prayers and worship following the custom of a Hindu house.'

Now, the house, specifically this wing, had a history. The wing was called 'Rajputani's Wing'[8]. A certain Nawab had brought home a Rajput woman, but he had accommodated her in separate quarters to preserve her faith. She worshipped Shiva, and sometimes even went on pilgrimage. Aristocratic Muslims of that time used to respect devout Hindus. The Rajput woman sheltered all Hindu begums in this wing, who were thus free to follow their customs and beliefs. Legend has it that Habir Khan was the son of that Rajput woman herself. Though he had not adopted his mother's religion, he worshipped her in his heart. His mother was long gone, but after her death, he had taken a vow for preserving her memory to provide special shelter for Hindu women oppressed or ostracised by society.

What Kamala received from them she had never had at her own home. There her aunt used to shoo and curse her; she was used to hearing only castigations against herself: she meant evil; she meant ruin; she had brought misfortune with her; only her death could save the family. Her uncle sometimes bought her clothes and other necessaries secretly, but she had to hide the fact from her aunt. Coming into the Rajputani's wing, she seemed to have ascended a queen's throne. There was no end to the care she received here; she had a large retinue around her, all from Hindu families.

Eventually, she felt the surge of youth in her body. A boy of the family started visiting Kamala's wing secretly, to whom she was drawn and developed an attachment for.

Then one day, she told Habir Khan, 'Baba, I know no other religion; the fortunate soul whom I love is alone my religion. I never found any divine grace in the religion that deprived me of all love, and discarded me beside the garbage vat of neglect. Their gods brought me only disgrace everyday, which is still fresh in my memory. It is in your home, Baba, that I first tasted love. Here I have discovered that life has a value even for a wretched girl. I worship that god alone who has given me shelter, which means love and honour to me. That deity alone is my god; he is neither Hindu nor Muslim. Your second son Karim is the one whom I have accepted in my heart; with him my work, my religion, my being has become identified. Convert me to a Muslim; I have no objection. I think I can preserve both religions.'

Life went on in this way with the two; there were no chances of any further meeting with Kamala's relatives. Meanwhile, Habir Khan tried to expunge any vestigial memory of her family: Kamala was renamed Meherjan.

In course of time, it was the turn for her uncle's second daughter to get married. Her marriage too was arranged as gorgeously as before. Once again, that old disaster struck: the same bandits waylaid the bridal party roaring thunderously. They had once been deprived of their quarry and had since been smouldering. This time they were determined to retaliate.

But their howling was immediately followed by another intimidating roar, 'Take care!'

'Damnation! It's Habir Khan's hounds come to spoil it again.'

When the bride's men, deserting the bride in the palanquin started running desperately, there appeared in their midst a spear with Habir Khan's crescent-marked[9] ensign tied to it. Holding it aloft was a woman standing fearlessly.

To Sarala she said, 'Don't be afraid, sister. For you I have brought shelter from someone who gives shelter to everyone; he is not concerned with anyone's caste or religion.'

'Uncle, my *pronams* to you. Don't worry, I won't touch your feet. Now take Sarala back home; no one has defiled her by touch. Tell aunt that when I had been growing up on the food and clothes she grudgingly gave me, I never dreamt that I would be able to repay my debts in this way. I have brought a red silk sari for Sarala; take this, and this brocade cushion. If my sister ever falls in distress, remember she has a Mussalman sister to protect her.'

24–25 June 1941

NOTES

* This is the last of the four stories dictated during May-June 1941, barely a month and a half before Tagore's death. There is no manuscript written by him, nor is there any revision in the transcript. First published fourteen years after his death in the Monsoon Number of *Ritupatra* from the copy in Pratima Thakur's hand preserved at Rabindra Sadan, Santiniketan. It is not a full-fledged 'short story', but a 'draft', and his last attempt to write a story [from the Note to Bibliography in the Appendix to *Galpaguchchha*, Visva-Bharati].

The draft is significant, apart from its historical interst, as another document of Rabindranath's ruthless attack on social ills and communal conflict.

1 Landlord of an estate named Teen-Mahala.

2 Idle pastime of wealthy, prodigal, often profligate, dandies representing the decadent culture of nineteenth-century Bengal (cf. *Babus*).

3 A Persian word meaning 'wrestler'.

4 A district in present-day Bihar; city (*pur*) of King Bhoja of ancient India. Incidentally, the king was so renowned for his skill in the art of illusion and legerdemain that his name eventually became synonymous with the art itself. The males are especially nurtured for undertaking jobs requiring physical prowess, such as fighters and bodyguards.

5 Long, heavy, wooden or bamboo sticks used as weapon especially by the police, and earlier by paid fighters of zamindars.

6 The word in the text is 'son of brother-in-law' (*shala*), often used as an expletive (see Glossary).

7 The text has *paigambar* or Allah's emissary.

8 Perhaps the allusion is to Emperor Akbar's Rajput Hindu wife Jodhabai to point to his religious tolerance, which is the central theme.

9 Emblem of Islam.

The Epilogue
(*Shesh Katha*)

In the turbid flow of life's abracadabra, long before the moment when the plot suddenly begins to thicken, the hero and heroine had been spinning the yarn of knowing each other. One has necessarily to follow the course of the prologue to that story. I will therefore take some time clarifying my identity. But I will need to assume a false name, or else it will be difficult coping with the show-cause notices from my circle of acquaintances. What name to take is a problem: I do not wish to attune the mood of the story from the outset to raga Basant[1] by *romantic* nomenclature. Perhaps the name of Nabinmadhab[2] will do. The real-life darkish colour of its owner could be whitewashed to Nabarun[3] Sengupta. But that would not have sounded genuine: the story would have lost its credibility while boasting its name; people would have thought that wearing a borrowed *jamiyar*, it had come to show off in the literary conference.

I was one of the revolutionaries of Bengal. The gravitational force of the British government had pulled me very close to the Andaman Islands. Taking devious routes, I had managed to give the CID the slip up to Afghanistan, from there as a shipmate finally reaching America. With the characteristic stubbornness of East Bengal ingrained in my marrow, I had not forgotten for a single day that I would have to file away at the fetters on India's hands and feet day and night as long as I lived. But just a few days of staying abroad had convinced me that the way we had started our revolutionary activities was like throwing a cracker at fireworks, whereby we had burnt our fingers several times, leaving the British throne unscathed. For fire, insects have a blind inclination. When we were proudly taking the plunge, scarcely had we realised that thereby we were lighting no historic sacrificial fire, but small personal pyres. Meanwhile, the grim destructive image of the great European War with its immense military display had appeared before our eyes: the illusory hope of instituting this epoch-making cataclysm in the sanctum of our thatched huts was obliterated from our minds; neither did I have the wherewithal to ceremonially commit suicide. Then I decided that the foundation of the national citadel must be fortified. I had a clear perception that if we must survive, the fingernails on our two primitive hands were just not sufficient for the battle for survival. In this age, machines must compete with machines. It is easy to die somehow or other, but not so to do apprenticeship[4] under *Vishwakarma*. It does not pay to be impatient; one would have to start from scratch: the path was long; the penance to be done was arduous.

I trained in mechanical engineering and managed to join Ford's automobile company in Detroit. Of course, I was gaining experience, but did not seem to be making much progress. One day I had the imprudence of telling Mr Ford that my object was not to seek my own prosperity, but to liberate my country; I had thought that as the high priest of freedom, America's conjuror of wealth would be pleased to hear it, and maybe even pave my way. With a snigger, Ford said, 'My name is Henry Ford, an archaic English name. Our maternal cousins in England are useless; I will make them useful: this is my vow.' I had thought that he might as well have felt interested in uplifting an Indian too. One thing was clear: the sympathy of the rich is meant for the rich alone. Another point I learned was that by turning with the wheel-making cycle, I would not possibly make much progress in acquiring expertise. In this context, my eyes were opened to another aspect: to learn mechanical engineering, one had to go into its fundamentals; knowledge of how to collect the machinery parts was necessary. For the powerful, the earth has her rich store of solids in her inaccessible womb, with which they have conquered the world, whereas for the poor, there is harvest on her surface; they are all skin and bone with a sunken belly. I started learning metallurgy. Ford had remarked that the fact that the English were useless had been proved in India: now they got down to indigo plantation, now to tea plantation. The bureaucrats sitting in their offices were busy enforcing 'law and order', while India's vast treasure of inner wealth, whether human or natural, remained unexplored. All they did was to extract the farmers' blood. I saluted JRD Tata from across the sea. I decided that throwing crackers was not for me; I must burgle into the stony walls of the underground vault. I would not keep mooing like the adult children tied to their mothers' apron strings. I would accept the poor of the country truly as the infirm, unfed, illiterate paupers that they were and not indulge in glorifying them with the appellation of 'Lord incarnate'[5]. Much did I play during my growing years, those games of 'moulding dolls of words'; sitting in front of the tinselled idol of the motherland made in the potter house of poets, I had shed profuse tears. Not any more. In this land of the intellectually awakened, I came to know what's what and learned how to be relentlessly enterprising without indulging in self-pity. Now going back home, this scientist from East Bengal would plunge into work with pickaxe and crowbar exploring the hidden treasure of his country. Maudlin admirers of the poet would not in any way recognise this work as the worship of the motherland.

After giving up the job in Ford's factory, I spent nine years studying mining and metallurgy. I travelled to various centres of learning in Europe, acquired practical knowledge and forged one or two mechanical devices myself as well. I received encouragement from professors, earned confidence in myself and castigated my former, enchanted, unfulfilled self.

All these big talks do not necessarily have any relevance to my short story: they might as well have been omitted, perhaps would have been better so. But while on this, one thing should have been said; let me say that. At the beginning of youth, when under the magnetism of women's spell, coloured bands of aurora keep moving across the polar sky of life, I had kept myself distracted, obstinately distracted. 'I am a *sannyasi*, a karmayogi[6]': with such homilies, I had kept my mind bolted. When fathers with maiden daughters were hovering around me, I had told them clearly that if the girl's horoscope predicted premature widowhood, only then should they contemplate me.

In the western continent, there is no barrier to keep off woman's company. There I was particularly vulnerable. In my native land, I had had no chance of hearing from the mouth of women in any language other than the silent language of their eyes that I was handsome. Naturally, this information was outside my consciousness. While in England, as I had discovered that I was more intelligent than ordinary people, so I had been aware that I was good-looking. Stories sufficiently intriguing to provoke my compatriot readers' jealousy had begun to form. But I declare on oath that I had not let my mind be beguiled by the delusion of fantasising over them. Perhaps I am of a strict temperament; unlike the delicate youths of West Bengal, I am not soaked with soppy sentimentalism over them. Making a stone chest of myself, I had locked my vow up there. To flirt with women and then leave them at an opportune moment is contrary to my nature. I was certain that if I slipped even once, I would be crushed under the debris of my vow with the obstinacy which now sustained me in my vow. For me, there was no evading this. Apart from that, I am a born rustic; I cannot quite overcome the traditional inhibition about women. So I have a disdain for those who make women's love an object of pride.

I had earned good foreign degrees. As they would be no good for any government work, I joined the administration of a king, by name, say, Chandabir Singh, of the Chandra dynasty in

Chhotanagpur[7]. Fortunately, his son Debikaprasad had studied for some time at Cambridge. I had chanced upon him in Zurich where he had heard of my fame. I explained my plan to him. He took great interest and employed me in the department of geological survey in their state. Such an assignment having been denied to an Englishman, the upper strata of the administration had been agitated. But Debikaprasad was a spirited man. Even though the old king vacillated in the matter, I just stayed on.

Before my coming over to this place, my mother had told me, 'Son, you've a good job. Now get married so my long-cherished wish is fulfilled.'

I said, 'You mean I spoil my work. Marriage won't accord with the nature of my work.'

I was firm in my resolve; all pleadings fell flat. Packing up my instruments, I arrived in the jungle.

Now on the horizon of my prospective countrywide fame, a speck of story that suddenly popped up had not only the illusion of a will-o'-the–wisp, but also the reality of the Evening Star.

I was then doing geological prospecting. The sky was absorbed in the riotous red of *palash*[8] flowers. *Shal* trees had sprouted flower-spikes; swarms of bees were buzzing around. Traders were busy collecting shellac, and from jujube leaves, harvesting silk cocoons for *tusser*. The santhals[9] were gathering ripe mahuas[10]. A lean river meandered across like a dancing girl with a flowing scarf. I had named it Tanuka. This was no factory shed or classroom; it was that realm of dusk absorbed in happy somnolence, where the enchanting nature works its colourful embroidery on the solitary mind as it does on the canvas of sunset.

My mind was engrossed in a trance-like infatuation. The tempo of work had become tardy; I was annoyed with myself, trying to find impetus from within. I was wondering if I had been entangled in the cobweb of the tropical weather. The fiendish tropics, ever since our birth in this country, had been transfusing through the hand-fan the instigation of defeat into our blood: its sweat-soaked spell must be overcome.

The day was melting into dusk. At some place, the river had bifurcated leaving a sandbank in between. On that sandy island a flock of herons sat brooding. Everyday at day's end, this scene indicated the time to turn the corner in my work. With samples of earth and rocks in my rucksack I was returning to my bungalow; there I would experiment in the laboratory. Intervening between afternoon and evening, the spare part of the day, which is like a fallow land, poses a veritable problem for a solitary man to spend; especially so in the loneliness of a forest. That is why I had allocated that time to doing experiments. Switching on a dynamo, lighting the lamps I used to sit down with my microscope, balance and chemicals. On some days, I worked late into the night. Today I had located signs of manganese ore at a certain spot. Therefore, I was walking fast with enthusiasm. Overhead, in the grey sky, crows were cawing their way to their nests.

Suddenly at that time, my returning to work was hindered. On a mound on my way through the forest, there was a circular array of five banyan trees. Anybody sitting inside that enclosure could be spotted only through one gap, or else escaped notice. That day, the clouds had displayed an amazing burst of luminosity. In that gap under the trees the crimson glow seemed to have spread fistfuls of gold. In the path of that light was sitting a girl leaning against the bole of a tree, her feet huddled up to her chest, writing something on a diary intently. In a moment, I felt a strange wonder, such as seldom occurs in one's life. Like the flow-tide of the full moon, waves of tidal bore kept lashing the shores of my heart.

I stood behind a tree trunk looking at her: an ineffable picture kept imprinting itself in the perpetually memorable archive of my mind. In my life of extensive experience, I had encountered many unexpected charms, but had gone past them, regardless. Today I seemed to have arrived at the edge of some unknown ultimate. To think like this or talk like this is not my wont. How did that blow strike me, a blow that can unlock a unique identity unbeknown to oneself? I had always known myself to be dry and solid like the hills. Fountains spurted out from within me.

I wanted to say something, anything whatever, but could not find out what the first word of the most important conversation with a human being could be. That might be the first words of genesis of the Christian mythology: Let there be light; let the hidden be manifest. I refrain from using the girl's real name, which I came to know later on. Let me name her Achira. What is the meaning? Achira is one who takes no time to be revealed, like lightning. Let that name continue. It seemed from her face that she had sensed someone was standing behind cover. I suppose presence has a silent sound! She had stopped writing, but seemed unable to rise, lest her escape should be conspicuous. I tentatively thought of saying, 'Excuse me.' What to excuse me for? What was my offence? What would I say? Going a little distance, I pretended to scoop the earth with my English trowel, picked up something into my sack; it was absolutely useless. Then looking down with a stoop, I went away scanning like a scientist. But I very well know that the one whom I had tried to deceive was not deceived. There is no doubt that she had had many more proofs of the weakness of the enchanted heart of males. I hoped that in this case she enjoyed it secretly. If I had advanced a bit further than this, then—well, what would have happened then I do not know. Would she have been or pretended to have been angry? With a very restless mind, I was walking down the way to my bungalow when I noticed an envelope torn in two. This was no geological sample, yet I picked it up and read. It was addressed to one Bhabatosh Majumdar, ICS, of Chhapra[11], written in a female hand. It had stamps affixed, but no postal seal: as if all this were the imprints of a maiden's hesitation. Mine was a scientist's acumen; it was clear to me that this torn envelope contained the scars of a tragedy. Our mission was to dig out from the ruptured strata of the earth the history of its revolution. That investigative hand of mine now resolved to reveal the mystery of this torn envelope.

Meanwhile I was wondering how profound the mystery of my own inner being was. I was astonished to discover for the first time now how under the impact of each particular circumstance its nature reveals itself crystallising into a new form. I had distinctly recognised the mind that had so far wandered from place to place assiduously in search of the aim of life. I had thought that that was my true nature; I could swear on the stability of its conduct. Now for the first time I found that in it lay hidden an ignorant being that was beyond the pale of intellect. A forest-dweller was revealed, one who was not amenable to reason, but yielded to infatuation. Forests cast a spell: the silent conspiracy of trees and woods, hymns of primordial life. The singeing midday reverberates with its distracting tune; the midnight with its deep sonorous voice keeps humming in its consciousness: it confounds the intellect with the secret instigation of primeval life.

Even as I was cultivating geology, this sylvan spell was working insidiously: I was searching for radium, trying to extract it from the rigid grip of stone; I happened to find Achira, bound in the shadow of a blooming shal grove. Before this, I had of course seen Bengali girls, but never had had the opportunity to see one so intimately, secluded from everything else. Here, to the tenderness of her darkish figure the leaves and creepers of the forest had added their own language. Of the foreign beauties, I had seen a good many and they were appealing enough, too. But a Bengali girl, it seemed as though I had seen for the first time now, just where she could be viewed in all her aspects. In the seclusion of this forest, she was not intermingled with the various familiar and unfamiliar realities: she did not look like the one who went to St. Diocesan's school swinging her plait or who was a degree-holder from Bethune College or at the tennis party at Ballygunge served tea amidst boisterous laughter. The songs of Haru Thakur or Ram Basu, which I had heard long ago in my childhood and thereafter forgotten and which were no longer played on the radio or resounded through the gramophone today seemed to envisage in their simple lyrics the beauty of that Bengali girl: 'The anguish of the heart, O dear, remained buried in the heart'. The pathos in the tune of this song today appeared in a vivid image before my eyes. Even this was possible. I had read in geology how a severe earthquake spews up the fiery substances buried underground. In myself, I saw that hot molten thing of the dark underground cellar suddenly thrown up into the light above. This upheaval in the unwavering inner core of the austere scientist Nanimadhab was entirely unexpected.

I could realise that every day as I had been going down this path back to my work, she had noticed me; absent-minded, I had not noticed her. Ever since my visit to England, I had grown proud of my figure. '*O how handsome!*' I had been accustomed to the whisper of this praise. But from some of my England-returned friends I have heard that Bengali girls have a different taste; soft womanly beauty is what they prefer in a male's looks. The popular saying is: 'Handsome like Kartik[12]'. A Bengali *Kartik*, whatever else he may be, is in no male like a commander-in-chief of the gods. From a female friend in Paris I heard that 'The white complexion of the British skin is in fact the absence of pigmentation. On the body of an oriental, the complexion tanned by the tropical sky is the true coloration, the colour of shadow, and that is the colour we like.' This observation is probably not applicable in the vicinity of the Bay of Bengal.

So far, none of these deliberations had occurred in my mind. It had engaged me for the last couple of days. Sun-tanned is my complexion, tall is my vibrant body, strong are my arms, nimble is my movement, and my eyesight, as they say, is sharp: with prominent nose, chin and forehead, well defined and imposing is my figure. Epstein had offered to do my portrait in stone; I could not afford the time. But an average Bengali in my view is his mama's child and their mothers too love to see the treasure of their lap as wax dolls. These feelings fermenting in my mind were infuriating me; I was quarrelling with Achira fictitiously in advance. I was telling her, 'What you call beautiful is a deity meant for immersion; it may get your worship, but does not last long. I spurned the garland of ovation that came my way in many of the advanced nations; you think you can ignore me?' This gratuitous quarrel was so puerile that I laughed out one day at my smouldering rage. On the other hand, my scientist's rationality was working inwardly. I told my self: it is also significant that she keeps sitting by the path I use mornings and afternoons. If seclusion were all she wanted, she would have changed her place. At the beginning, I used to glance at her obliquely as if I had not noticed her. Of late, our eyes met often enough. I believe, she did not consider it an ominous coincidence of four eyes.

Another test much stronger than this was done. Until now, I used to go along that path through the five-banyan-cluster only once when I returned home after my day's work with soil and rocks. Recently repetition of coming and going had begun. That this incident had no connection with geology Achira was mature enough to understand. I too became increasingly bolder when I noticed that even this clear indication could not displace the young girl. On some days suddenly turning back, I saw that Achira was looking on in the direction of my motion; the moment I turned, she cast her eyes down on the diary. I suspected that the flow of her writing had lost its previous rapidity. My scientist's mind began to analyse the mystery of her mind. I concluded that she had taken the vow of penance for a certain man. His name was Bhabatosh; he had been serving as assistant magistrate at Chhapra ever since he returned from England. Before that, while he had been here, the two were in deep love; on the eve of his appointment, a sudden upheaval had occurred. I must investigate the matter. It posed no problem, because my fellow student at Cambridge, Bankim, was in Patna University.

I sent a letter by post: 'In Bihar civil service, there is one

Bhabatosh Majumdar. In the guardians' circle, it is rumoured that as a bridegroom the man is quite enviable. One of my friends has requested me to help him trap the fellow for his daughter. I will be obliged if you let me know after collecting detailed information whether the road ahead is clear. I would also like to know about his plans and intentions.'

The reply came: 'Road closed. As for his intentions, if you still have any curiosity left, then listen.

'At college, one of my teachers was Dr Anilkumar Sarkar: quite a few letters of the alphabet are appended to his name. As extraordinary was his erudition, so childlike was his simplicity. If you saw his granddaughter, his only light in the world, you would think that being pleased at her perseverance *Saraswati* had not only appeared in her realm of intellect, but also descended with her beauty on her lap. That scoundrel Bhabatosh infiltrated into her heaven. Keen was his intellect; fluent were his words. First, it was the professor and then it was his granddaughter to be beguiled. Their intolerable intimacy made us seethe with rage. There was no way to prevent it; everything had been settled, except that she would have to wait until he returned as an ICS from England. His passage and all other expenses had been sponsored by the professor. The man had a constitution liable to catch cold. To the deaf Almighty we had prayed mornings and evenings that he might die of pneumonia before the wedding. But he did not die, and passed the exam too. Soon after passing, he went on to marry the daughter of a high-ranking officer of the government of India. Mortified with shame and grief, the professor resigned and disappeared with his granddaughter nobody knows where.'

Having read the letter, I firmly resolved that I must reclaim this girl from her shame, from her depression.

Meanwhile, I became restless somehow to pick up a conversation with Achira. If instead of being a scientist, I had been a lover of literature, or instead of being a native of East Bengal, I had been a smart fellow from West Bengal, certainly I would not have faltered in talking. But I feel inhibited about Bengali girls; they seem unfamiliar. I had a notion that a Hindu woman was unapproachable to any male other than her husband. If I gratuitously tried to talk to her, it would defile her blood; so blind is one's prejudice. Before I joined my work here, I had spent quite some time in Calcutta where in the circle of my friends and relations I had seen Bengali girls who frequented cinemas and theatres and who seemed born to be friendly; they were—well, let me spare them. But as for Achira, even though I knew nothing about her, she seemed to be of a different class: standing outside this age in pure self-dignity, she was a sensitive girl, wary of touch. I was only contemplating how to begin the conversation.

Around this time, one or two robberies had taken place in the area. I thought that on this pretext I would tell Achira, 'I'm thinking of requesting the king to arrange for your security.' Had she been an English woman, she might perhaps have considered this gratuitous favour an act of insolence, saying defiantly, 'That's my concern.' But how this Bengali girl might take my offer was not within my experience. Because of my long stay outside Bengal, my mental make-up had been mostly associated with British beliefs.

The day was almost over. It was time for Achira to return home or maybe her grandfather would take her along for a walk. Just then, an upcountry ruffian-like fellow swooped on the scene and snatched away Achira's handbag and diary. In a moment emerging from the woods, I told her, 'Don't be afraid.' And at once giving chase, as I pounced upon him, he dropped the loot and ran away. I brought back the stolen goods to her.

Achira said, 'Luckily you were –'

'Don't mention it. Luckily the rascal had come.'

'What does that mean?'

'It means that it was thanks to him that I had had my first word with you. So long I had been wondering what to say.'

'But he is a robber.'

'No, he is no robber. He is my footman.'

Lifting the deep-brown sari-end to her mouth, Achira burst into a giggle. How sweet it was! It sounded as though a fountain was gurgling through pebbles.

When she stopped laughing, she said, 'But had it been true, it would have been great fun.'

'Fun for whom?'

'For the one about whom the robbery is concerned. I've read a story like this.'

'What would have happened thereafter to the rescuer?'

'Inviting him home, I'd have treated him to tea.'

'And what do you propose to do about this fake rescuer?'

'Does he need anything else? All he had wanted was the first word of picking an acquaintance, isn't it? He got the second, third, fourth, and fifth words to boot.'

'I hope the numbers wouldn't come to an abrupt end?'

'Why should it end?'

'Well, had it been you, what is the first word you would have said?'

'I'd have said "What childishness is this you are picking clods here and there? Aren't you mature enough?"'

'Why did you not say so?'

'I was afraid.'

'Afraid? Of me?'

'Why not? You're a great man. I heard it from my grandfather. He had read your dissertation in a journal from England. Whatever he reads, he tries to explain to me.'

'This one too?'

'Yes. But the flourish of Latin names was forbidding. With joined palms I said, "Dadu, Put it away. Rather, let me fetch your book on quantum theory."'

'Is that something you can understand?'

'Not at all. But my grandfather has a fixed notion that everyone can understand everything. I don't wish to violate that conviction. He has another strange perception: the common sense of women is much keener than men's. That makes me apprehensive lest I have to listen to the explanation of the paired relation of 'time-space'. In fact, there's no end to his compassion for women. As long as my grandmother was alive, whenever he began to talk big things, she would stop him short. Naturally, how sharp women's intellect can be, he had not had any direct proof from my grandmother. I cannot disappoint him. I heard a lot, did not understand a thing; I will hear lots more and will not understand.'

Achira's eyes shone and brimmed over with curiosity and affection. I wished this pleasant talk in her refreshing voice would not end soon. Daylight faded; the first star of the evening twinkled over the shal grove. The *santhal* women having gathered firewood were on their way home as indicated by their song heard from afar.

At that point, a call came from outside, 'Didi, where are you? It's almost evening. Times are not good these days.'

'Of course not good, Dadu. That's why I've appointed a guard.'

As the professor came, I made him a *pronam* taking the dust of his feet. He felt ill at ease. I introduced myself: I am Nanimadhab Sengupta.

The old man's face lit up. 'Really? So you're the famous Dr Sengupta? You're almost a boy, I see.'

'Quite so. I'm not more than thirty-six.'

Once again, Achira laughed in her sweet warbling voice, as if jingling a sitar at double tempo in my mind. 'To Dadu,' she said, 'everyone in the world is a child and Dadu is every child's Agarwala.'

'Agarwala?' said the professor. 'You've coined a new word in Bengali. Where did you collect it from?'

'You remember that Marwari student of yours you loved so much? Kundanlal Agarwala? He used to bring me bottled mango pickle. I had asked him the meaning of the word "agarwala". "Pioneer", he had said.'

The professor said, 'Dr Sengupta, since we've been acquainted, you must come over to my place.'

'He need not be invited, Dadu. He's only too eager to come. He has heard from me that you will explain the space-time continuum riding on Einstein's shoulder.'

I said to myself, 'Good heavens! What a prank!'

The professor said with much enthusiasm, 'I suppose time-space is something you –'

I said hurriedly, 'I don't know anything about time-space. You'd be wasting your time trying to explain it to me.'

'Wasting time! Is there any lack of time here? Well, do one thing; rather come over for dinner tonight, what do you say?'

I would have jumped and said, 'Of course, right now.'

Achira forestalled me. 'Dadu, is it for nothing that I call you a child? By inviting people at any hour, you only throw me in trouble. Where in this wilderness am I to find a Firpo's shop? He belongs to the dinner-eating voracious tribe of England. Why must you earn your granddaughter a bad repute? At least bekti and mutton must of course be arranged.'

'All right, all right. Tell me when you can make it convenient, Dr Sengupta.'

'I can make it convenient tomorrow itself. But I don't wish to inconvenience Miss Achira. I have to go out prospecting in jungles and hills. For provisions, I keep beaten rice, bananas, tomatoes, green shoots of gram, and sometimes almond as well. I'll bring with me curd and other ingredients of refreshment. Miss Achira will mix them with her own hands and then serve. If you agree to this, there's no problem keeping your invitation.'

'Dadu, don't believe such people. You once wrote in a Bengali monthly on the role of vitamins in the Bengalis' food. He must have read it and so, merely to please you, gave a menu of banana, beaten rice and the rest.'

I thought she had put me in an awkward position. To read the vitamin theory written by a doctor in a Bengali journal was never possible for me. But how was I to admit it—especially when he asked me very eagerly, 'Did you read it?'

'Whether I did or did not read does not matter. In fact –'

'In fact, he knows that if we give him a dinner tomorrow, beast or bird, movable or immovable, nothing will be spared in his platter. That's why he so blithely chanted the praise of tomato. Just look at his figure: would anyone suspect that it has been nourished merely by leaves and roots? Dadu, you believe everybody too much, even me. That is the reason I do not dare to tell you anything in jest.'

Talking in this vein, we were walking slowly towards their house when suddenly Achira spoke forth, 'Now you go back to your apartment.'

'Why, I had thought I'd see you off at your door.'

'The rooms are in a terrible mess. You might remark Bengali women are all untidy. Tomorrow you'll find it so done up you'd be reminded of the memsahibs.'

The professor said, 'Please don't mind. Achi's talking too much, but that's not her nature. The place being lonely, she keeps my mind engaged with incessant chatter. And that has grown into her habit. When she keeps silent, it is then that my house seems eerie, my mind too with it. She knows it. I'm afraid lest anyone should misunderstand her.'

Hugging the old man, Achira said, 'Let them, Dadu. I do not wish to be absolutely blemishless. That'd be uninteresting.'

The professor interjected proudly, 'You know Sengupta, my Didi has a flair for talking, such as I have found in no one.'

'You say you've found no one like me, Dadu. I too have found no one like you.'

I said, 'Sir, you must give me a word before I leave.'

'Well, all right.'

'As often as you address me by *aapni*[13], I feel ashamed. If you make it *tumi*[13], I'll be truly honoured by your affection. To elevate me to the *tumi*-class, your granddaughter will also assist you.'

'O my God! I'm a mere granddaughter. I can't reach there all at once; you're so high. Better let there be a few days before I try. If I can forget your degree-holding image, everything will be possible. But Dadu's position is different; Dadu, you start calling *tumi* right away. Tell him, "Do come to dinner tomorrow. If Didi happens to add salt a pinch too many to the fish curry, bear with it like a good boy. Say, "Oh, how delicious! Can I have another helping?"'

The professor, affectionately placing a hand on my shoulder said, 'Bhai, if you had seen my Didi a few days earlier, you would know actually she is shy. That is why when she feels it necessary to be formal while making an acquaintance, she ends up talking too much.'

'Have you seen, Dr Sengupta, how sweetly my Dadu exercises control over me? As if with a sugarcane stick. He could easily have said, "You're so talkative; your frivolity is intolerable." But you must defend me, Dr Sengupta. How would you argue? Tell me, please.'

'Not in front of you.'

'Would it sound too harsh?'

'You know my mind.'

'Then you need not say. Now go home.'

'One more word. The feast you're hosting tomorrow is to celebrate my new name-giving. From tomorrow onward, Dr Sengupta shall be dropped from the name of Nanimadhab. Just as a comet on its journey to the sun sheds its tail, being left barely with its head.'

'Then call it name-shedding; why say name-giving?'

'All right, so be it.'

Thus ended my first D-day.

What a serene beauty, what placid image old age has! His eyes seemed to be casting a look of benediction. A polished walking stick was held in his hand; a folded chuddar hung from his neck; his dhoti was pleated carefully; he wore a tusser shirt; the hair on his head was sparse but neatly combed. All this bore clear imprint of his granddaughter's handiwork in his dress and daily life. It was only to please the girl that he suffered the torture of pampering.

My scientific data collection gave way to asking after them routinely. I will use the name Anilkumar Sarkar for the professor, one of the last generation PhDs from Cambridge University. Having resigned as the principal of a suburban college a few months back, he had rented an abandoned bungalow of this state and made it habitable with some renovation. This is the draft of the history; the rest can be compared with Bankim's letter.

Here ends the first canto of my story. There is no long interlude between the beginning and the end of a short story. I will not be tempted to narrate it in an exaggerated manner, for I do not wish to spoil its generic character.

Days of talking freely with Achira came soon enough. That day, a picnic was held on the bank of the river Tanika.

The professor, like a child, suddenly asked me, 'Nabin, are you married?'

The question was so clearly suggestive that anybody else would have held it back. I replied, 'No, not yet.'

No word escapes Achira's attention. She said, 'Dadu, that word 'yet' is meant for the consolation of doubtful parents of maidens. It has no proper meaning.'

'How did you conclude that it has no meaning whatever?'

'It is a problem of mathematics and that too not of higher mathematics. We already know that you are a mere child of thirty-six years. Simple calculation shows that by now at least five to seven times your mother must have told you, "'Son, I wish to bring a bride into my home." You said, "Before that I wish to bring money into the iron safe." Wiping her tears, your mother kept silent. Thereafter, you have had everything except being hanged. In the end, when you landed a job on a fat salary in this state government, your mother once again said, "Son, now you must get married. How many days are left to me?" You said, "My life and my science are one and the same. I will dedicate it to my country. I will never marry." Disappointed, she wiped her tears once again and has been waiting since. Tell me whether I have or have not committed a mistake in working out the arithmetic of your thirty-six years of experience. Be honest.'

It is dangerous to be off one's guard while talking with this girl. Only a few days back something had happened. Incidentally, Achira had told me, 'In our country you get women as domestic companions. To those who are unnecessary to the world even the women of this country are unnecessary. But in England, those who are ascetics of science are fortunate to find suitable partners as was Madame Curie to Professor Curie. Did you not find such a woman while staying abroad?'

The thought of Catherine came to my mind: we had worked together while staying in London. Even in one of my research papers, her name was associated with mine. I had to admit it.

'Then why did you not marry her? Was she not willing?'

Once again, I had to make an admission. 'Of course. It was from her side that the proposal had come.'

'Then?'

'My work concerned India, not merely science.'

'This means that the fruition of love is not an object of desire for devotees like you. The ultimate goal of women's life is subjective; yours is objective.'

I could not come up with the rejoinder to this. Seeing me silent, Achira said, 'Perhaps you do not read Bengali literature. There is a poem named *Kach and Debjani*[14]. It deals with the same theme: women's vow is to ensnare men, while that of men is to avert that snare and pave the way to the realm of immortals. Kach had extricated himself from the pleadings of Debjani, and you overcame your mother's imploring. It is all the same. In this perpetual conflict between males and females, you have emerged victorious. Let your masculinity be victorious. Let women shed tears, which you may accept as offerings of our worship. Offerings come to the deity, but the deity remains detached.'

The professor did not at all understand the burden of this discussion. He proudly said, 'How effortlessly my Didi keeps saying profound truths! People would think –'

He always feared outsiders would not quite understand his granddaughter.

Achira said, 'Outsiders can't tolerate precocity in women. Don't be worried about them. It's enough if you alone understand me.'

Achira used to say even serious things in a lighter vein, but today she was so grave. One thing occurred to me just tentatively: Bhabatosh had convinced her that the fact that he had collected his bride from the galaxy of the Indian government also had a very high and selfless aim. From the resources of the British government itself, he could collect the wherewithal to devote to national interest. It was not so easy to deceive Achira. That she had not been taken in had its proof in that torn envelope.

Achira once again said, 'Do you know, Nabin-babu, what curse Debjani had pronounced for Kach?'

'No.'

'She had said, "The treasure of your learning you can neither use for yourself nor gift to others." I find this rather strange. If someone were to utter this curse for Europe, he would have been saved. Treating what belongs to the world as their personal property, they have fallen prey to temptation. Tell me, Dadu, is it not true?'

'Absolutely. But what is surprising is how you pondered over all these things.'

'Not a bit in my own capacity. Just these things I have often heard from you. You have a great virtue: you are *Bholanath* forgetting everything you ever say. No one is afraid to tag one's own name to stolen goods.'

I said, 'Stealing is a great art. Whether it is in learning, or in statecraft, great emperors are great thieves. In fact, petty thieves are those who get caught even before sealing their names.'

Achira said, 'So many of Dadu's students just by taking down his lectures went on to publish books earning fame. He reads them to his amazement and is all praise. He does not even know that he is only praising himself. A share of this praise often falls to my lot also. Ask Nabin-babu: he will confess he has started writing about my originality in his notebook where he records the history of the Copper and Stone Ages. Do you remember, Dadu, once long ago when you were teaching in college, you read out the *Kach-Debjani* poem to me? Ever since then, I have acknowledged to myself the exalted glory of males, but never admitted it openly.'

'But Didi, I have never in my words made light of women's glory.'

'To imagine that you would! You are a blind devotee of women. I laugh to myself hearing women's praise on your lips. They swallow it all up unabashedly. To appropriate cheap praise has become a habit with them.'

All this conversation of that day was by no means any light talk. There was hint of a battle in it. Achira's nature had two aspects and she had two shelters: one, their own house, the other that five-banyan-grove. When my relation with her had been quite free, I decided that in the seclusion of that grove, on the pretext of laughter and fun, I would somehow raise the topic of the recent crisis of my life and steer the discussion to a resolution. But the road was closed there. Just as on the first day of our acquaintance the first word was not forthcoming, so also the Achira who was present here lacked the first word. I found no way to access the ultimate word of her heart to resolve the crisis. At the door of her house, her laughing garrulity stopped my advance of a single step and in her secluded sylvan shade she resisted my agitation with speechless silence. On some days, at the tea party at their place, there came a limited scope to open up my mind; Achira could sense that I was approaching the danger mark and it was then that the profusion of her words became unusually excessive; I got no opening. The atmosphere grew hostile as well. It seemed to me to be very much troubled. My work was being hampered to an extent that put me to shame. I had a proposal to get an additional grant for my research work sanctioned at the budget meeting at the headquarters. The supporting report had not been done more than half. Meanwhile, I had been hearing discussion on Croce's Aesthetics every day for some time. The subject was completely beyond my comprehension and interest, of which Achira was well aware. She encouraged her Dadu and enjoyed it thoroughly in her mind. Presently, he was explaining all possible counter-arguments about *behaviourism*. The miserable aspect of this expatiation was that half way through it Achira took leave to busy herself in gardening, saying, 'I have already heard all this discussion.' I kept sitting like a fool, at times looking at the door. The only redeeming feature was that the professor never asked whether I understood a particularly difficult point of the argument. He thought everything was as simple as that.

But this must not do any longer: the matter must be broached at any opportunity. On a picnic day, when sitting on the step of the deserted temple the professor was reading a recently imported book on modern chemistry, Achira suddenly told me, 'The blind vital power inherent in this eternal forest is gradually gripping me with fear.'

I said, 'Strange! An exactly similar feeling I noted in my diary the other day.'

Continued Achira: 'In any crevice of an old building, a peepul seed sprouts, unnoticed. Thereafter, spreading its roots, it brings about its destruction. The same is the case here. This is what I was discussing with Dadu. He said, "If you stay far away from human habitation for too long, your heart keeps growing weaker under the influence of nature and the influence of the primal life grows stronger." I asked, "What can be done in this circumstance?" He said, "We can bring along the human heart with us: we get it more intimately in solitude, rather than in a crowd. Look at the books I have brought." It was easy for him to say so; the same medicine does not work for all. What is your opinion?'

'All right,' I said, 'I'll tell you. Try to get at the point I am making. What I want to say is that in this condition, we must get both inwardly and outwardly the company of some person whose influence can fulfil our human nature. As long as we do not get it, we will continue to be defeated by the blind power. Had you been like ordinary women, ultimately I could not have spoken the truth clearly.'

'Speak out. Don't hesitate.'

'Being a scientist, what I'm going to say I'll say in an *impersonal* manner. Once you loved Bhabatosh very dearly. Do you love him equally so even today?'

'Well, suppose I do not.'

'It is I who drew your heart away.'

'Maybe, but not you alone, this formidable blind power inherent in the forest as well. That is the reason why I do not respect my withdrawal; I feel shy about it.'

'Why don't you respect it?'

'People build up their own ideals with the power of the heart over a long time, only to be shattered by the blind power of life. My love that flows towards you owes itself to that blind power.'

'In spite of being a woman, you are insulting love in this way!"

'Only because I am a woman. The ideal of love is an object of worship. That is what is called chastity. Chastity is an ideal. This virtue is not in the nature of the forest, but of a woman. In this solitude, I had been worshipping that ideal despite all adversities and deprivations. If I cannot maintain it, I cannot keep my purity.'

'Can you respect Bhabatosh?'

'No.'

'Can you go to him?'

'No. But he and that first love of my life are not the same. To me, that love is now *impersonal.* No receptacle is necessary.'

'I can't follow you properly.'

'It is not possible for you. Yours is the wealth of knowledge: on the highest peak, that knowledge is *impersonal.* Women's wealth is of the heart; if she loses everything—whatever is external, visible, tangible and enjoyable—still what is left is the ideal of that love, which is beyond understanding. In other words, *impersonal*.'

'Look, there is no more time for argument. You may have seen in the local newspaper that my work at this place has been finished. The assistant geologist has written to inform that prospecting has to begin farther away from this place. But –'

'Why did you not go?'

'From you –'

'From me you want to hear the final word; the first word has been obtained already.'

'Exactly so.'

'Let me tell you frankly then. Sitting in that banyan grove, I observed you unnoticed for some time. You worked hard all day defying the scorching sun. No one's company was needed. On some days you seemed to have been disappointed; you did not find what you had expected. But from the very next day, excavation was resumed in right earnest. It seemed as though with the strong body of the carrier, the powerful mind had been on its march to victory. I had never before seen such an austere devotee of science. I revered you from a distance.'

'And now perhaps –'

'No. Let me say. The more you advanced in your acquaintance with me, the weaker that devotion became. On many flimsy pretexts, your work got retarded. Then I became afraid of myself, this woman. Shame on me, what poison of defeat I have brought in me! So this is your side of the story. Now listen to my side. I too had a dedication; that too was a penance. I definitely knew that it would purify and brighten my life. But I observed that I was continually lagging behind. The restlessness that had possessed me had had its inspiration from within the breath of this shadowy forest; it was the inspiration of the primal power of life. At times induced by the night, an ogress, I thought that there was perhaps an ogre of desire who could snatch me away from my grandfather. It was spreading its tentacles around me. Immediately leaving my bed I had rushed to the fountain and jumped into it for ablution.'

Even as she said this, she called out, 'Dadu!'

'What is it, Didi?' The professor said with sweet affection, keeping aside his studies.

'Did you not say the other day that the truth of a man is manifested in his penance—that it is no biological manifestation?'

'Yes, that is what I believe. The savages of the world were at the level of beasts. Through penance, they developed into intelligent beings. More penances are ahead; more grossness has to be shed. Only then shall they attain godhood. The conception of gods has been introduced in the Puranas. But in the past, there were no gods; they are in the future, in the last chapter of man's history.'

'Dadu, let us now finish the talk between you and me. It has been raging in my mind for the last several days.'

I got up and said, 'Then I'll take your leave.'

'No,' said Achira, 'Please stay. Dadu, the principal's post you once held has fallen vacant again. The secretary has written very entreatingly to you to accept it. You had always been showing me your letters, except this one. That made me suspect your ulterior motive, and I read the letter secretly.'

'It was my fault.'

'Not at all. I have dragged you down from your throne. We are good only at dragging one down.'

'What are you saying, Didi!'

'I am saying only the truth. If the world ceases to exist, God's hands fall empty. Without students, you are in the same plight. Tell me whether I am right.'

'All through my life, I've been a schoolmaster, that's why –'

'You're a schoolmaster! You are a *born teacher*, a preceptor. Your devotion to learning is not for yourself, but for the sake of others. Did you not see him, Nabin-babu? When an idea comes to his head, I am at the receiving end of all the expatiation, three-fourths of which falls flat on me. Alternatively, he makes you his listener;

that's even more miserable. He has no idea at all where your mind is, thinks it is after pure knowledge. Dadu, pupils you must have, but take care to choose them properly.'

'It is the pupil who chooses the teacher; the necessity is his.'

'All right, we'll talk that over later. Of late, I have realised that of the one who is a teacher I am making a bookworm. Thus, I am breaking your penance in my own blind interest. You must accept that job; you must go back to your post immediately.'

The professor looked on at Achira's face confusedly. Achira said, 'Oh, I see, you must be worried about what will be my refuge. My refuge is you. Bholanath[15], if you do not like me[16], grandmother the Second has to be brought in and I'll make myself scarce. If you haven't grown too proud, you must admit that you can't do without me for a single day. If I am not around, the fifteenth of Ashwin passes for the fifteenth of October. The day you invite your colleague to dinner, you are cooped up in your library room working out a most difficult *equation*. Hiring a cab, the address you give has yet to have a house to be built there. Nabin-babu must be thinking I'm exaggerating.'

I said, 'Not at all. It's quite a few days I have been observing him; I'm convinced what you're saying is absolutely true.'

'Why are such inauspicious things coming out of your mouth today? You know, Nabin, she has of late been showing symptoms of talking such nonsense.'

'All those symptoms will abate, once you go back to your work. The pulse will return to normal; senseless muttering will cease.'

Turning to me the professor said, 'What is your advice, Nabin?'

Because he is a scholar, he has so much respect for the wisdom of a geologist. Remaining silent for a while, I said, 'No one can give you better advice than Miss Achira.'

Achira stood up and made me obeisance touching my feet. I retraced a few steps in embarrassment. Achira said, 'Don't be embarrassed. I am a nonentity compared to you. One day you'll know this. This is my final leave-taking. We won't meet again before our departure.'

Surprised, the professor said, 'What's this you say, Didi?'

'Dadu, you know many things, but about many other things my knowledge is far more than yours: this you should admit in all humility.'

I made a pronam to the professor. He held me in an embrace close to his heart and said, 'I know that the wide road to fame lies ahead of you.'

Here ends my short story. The epilogue to it is concerned with the geologist. Returning home, I sat down with the notes and records of my work. I had a sudden upsurge of joy in my mind. I realised that this was what is called freedom. In the evening, after finishing my day's work when I came to the veranda, I felt that the bird had come out of the cage, but a bit of the snapped chain stuck to its feet, which impeded its movement.

Phalgun 1346 (1939)

NOTES

1 Raga Basant: a springtime evening raga evoking the romantic mood.
2 Nabinmadhab: appellation of Krishna who was of darkish complexion.
3 Nabarun: rising sun.
4 Apprenticeship under Vishwakarma: to try to be a successful devotee of the architect of heaven.
5 The text has 'Daridra-Narayan: Daridra (the poor) idolised as Narayan (an aspect of Vishnu)'.
6 Karmayogi: one who practises yoga through work; yoga is the mystical union of the self with the Supreme Being in complete awareness and tranquillity through various mental and physical exercises, such as work, learning, etc.

7 A district in Bihar.

8 Palash: a beautiful red flower with no fragrance.

9 Santhal: an aboriginal tribe of India.

10 Mahua: a kind of butter-tree or its seed or flower; an intoxicating liquor is distilled from its honey.

11 A district in Bihar.

12 Handsome son of goddess Durga, and commander-in-chief of the gods.

13 The pronoun 'you' in English is universally used in direct conversation, irrespective of age, social status or relative position of the speaker and the person spoken to. Not so in Bengali (or Hindi, for that matter). Here three distinct forms corresponding to 'you' are admitted: tui, tumi, aapni. (see Glossary)

14 See Glossary.

15 An appellation of Lord Shiva for his forgetful nature.

16 Traditionally, grandparents in rural Bengal were, and still are, in crude or puerile joking terms with their grandchildren up to a certain state of maturity.

Glossary

Note: Words and phrases in the text retained as such in translation and not appearing here have been annotated in the ***Notes*** appended to each translated story.

Bengali calendar months

Baishakh/Jyaishtha/Asharh /Shravan/Bhadra/Ashwin/Kartik/Agrahayan/Paus/ Magh/Phalgun/Chaitra

Note: The Bengali New Year commences with Baishakh, correspondingly with the Gregorian calendar, on the 14th or 15th of April. The successive months in the above order begin around the middle of the corresponding Gregorian calendar month.

Subtract the number 593 (or 594 for a leap year) from the year in AD to arrive at the corresponding Bengali Year (*Bangabda*). Bengali Year 1416 commenced on 15 April 2009, for example.

Bengali seasons

Grishma: summer/***Varsha***: rains/***Sharat***: autumn/***Hemanta***: late autumn/***Sheeth***: winter/***Basanta***: spring

Note: Each season is supposed to last for two months. Often overlapping occurs with extended summer and rains.

Briefly appearing before winter, late autumn (hemanta) is generally not experienced as a separate season, often being overlapped by autumn and winter, although it finds an occasional mention in the stories.

kalbaishakhi: during the fortnight in late Chaitra and early Baishakh, a strong wind arises in the afternoon from the north-west, often playing havoc with trees and causing widespread destruction of mud houses.

Rivers

Ganges: the most sacred river to the Hindus with many places of pilgrimage along its banks, especially, Varanasi; length 2507 km; also known as Ganga.

Yamuna (Kalindi): a tributary of the Ganges, the confluence being at *Prayag* (in Allahabad)

Padma (now in Bangladesh) is particularly known for its destructive form.
Hooghly: a branch of the Ganges, flowing through the West Bengal districts of Howrah and Hooghly.
Narmada: the second most sacred Indian river; in central India.
Godavari: in central India, sacred to the Hindus.

Places

Lucknow: the capital of Uttar Pradesh, famous for its own style of thumri and ghazal singing.
Benares: a city on the Ganges, in UP, major place of pilgrimage for the Hindus, seat of the Hindu University, famous for its wedding saris named after it.
Ranchi: an industrial city in Bihar, also a health resort.
Puri: a district town in Orissa, on the Bay of Bengal, a tourist resort and holy place to the Hindus.
Kalighat: a place of Hindu pilgrimage in south Calcutta.

Trees, Plants and Flowers (and a bird)

peepul (ashvattha): a large tree, resembling the banyan; another name is *bodhitaru* or bo tree, tree of wisdom, from Sanskrit *bodhi*.
shal: a tropical tree that grows tall and straight, giving valuable timber for pillars and roof structure of huts.
jhau: an evergreen shrub with feathery clusters of blades of leaves.
kadamba: spherical-shaped mildly fragrant flower with bright yellow-orange hairy growth, a favourite with children; a flower of the rainy season.
bakul: a large ever-green tree of small, white, sweet-smelling spring flowers
bel: wood-apple tree; it bears sweet-smelling white flowers in summer; the leaves of the tree are an indispensable item of Hindu rituals; the sweet astringent pulp within the fruit's hard shell is a laxative and also makes cool sherbet.
champa: golden-yellow summer flower
kamini: sweet-smelling white flowers blooming by night and shedding at dawn, during the rains, unlike *shefali* or *shiuli, which* is a winter flower.
madhabi: a creeper with pink flowers, grown over a trellis, as part of a grove to give a decorative facade to premises.
gaab: a resinous tree bearing inedible fruits
neem: *margosa*, a large tree with crops of small serrated leaves and white flowers; its sweetish fruits are favourite bird feed; leaves have medicinal value; its huge leafy branches offer cool, healthy shade.
kaash: milk-white flowers sprouting on long, slender, wavy reed-like stalks that spread a white radiance across vast verdant fields at the advent of autumn, have an appeal to Bengalis as the harbinger of their great annual festival, the Durga Puja; finds frequent mention in the stories.
amlaki: generic name, *emblic myrobalan,* medicinal plant bearing small sour fruits, which taste sweet when chewed with water.
amra: hog-plum tree. Its sweetish-sour olive-green fruits make good chutney and pickles.
kalmegh: another medicinal plant of extremely bitter leaves.

kochu: plant cultivated in the tropics for its large, edible rootstock and tuber.
koel: a generic name for any of the several parasitic cuckoos; it is characterised by a shrill cry ending with a gentle cooing, the name 'koel' is preferred by poets.
Note: Words either naturalised into the English language or having their English equivalents have been mostly excluded.

Gods and goddesses of the Hindu pantheon

Hindu pantheon: believed to be 330 million in number
Durga: variously called *Parvati, Basanti, Mahamaya, Annapurna, Sati, Uma,* consort of Lord Shiva, conceived as the prime mover of the universe and the driving force behind human activity; worshipped as the principal goddess by the Hindus, especially the Bengalis, for five days during the bright lunar fortnight of the month of Ashwin (autumn) with fervour and festivity, which goes by the name of *Durga Puja* or the great autumn festival, often mentioned in the stories. It celebrates the slaying of the demon *Mahishasura* (erupting out of the womb of a buffalo), the symbol of all evil.
Kali (the *a* being pronounced as in *art*): a fierce-looking, with lolling tongue, unsightly manifestation of the consort of Lord Shiva, believed to annihilate evil, and worshipped for empowerment in any enterprise.
Lakshmi: goddess of wealth and prosperity; her idol carries a pitcher symbolising never-ending wealth; traditional Hindus associate this perception to their family coffers; thanks to her perceived benign nature, her name has come to be often referred to a docile boy or girl, or otherwise used as an affectionate term of persuasion; she is often alluded to by the epithet *chanchala* meaning fleeting or inconstant, for wealth does not last too long.
Saraswati: wife of Brahma; goddess of learning, speech and music; draped in white, which is perceived to symbolise the pure, transparent and serene; she is imagined to dwell in a lotus pool, carried around by a swan and playing on the *veena* (lyre).
Dashamahavidya: the ten manifestations of the primordial power, the goddess Durga. *Bharavi* is one.
Ganesh: eldest son of Shiva and Parvati, god of fulfilment, worshipped all over India by devout Hindus before launching an auspicious enterprise or proceeding to worship any other deity. Mythologically, Ganesh is elephant-headed; hence, he is also called Gajanan, *gaja* meaning elephant, and *anan*, face.
Kartik (kartikeya): commander-in-chief of the gods, handsome, youngest son of Shiva and Parvati, conceived for slaying the demon Taraka (dramatised by Kalidasa in Kumarsambhava); seldom worshipped as a god except for his good looks by a particular section of the Bengalis. To describe an extremely handsome male, he is traditionally likened to Kartik.
Madan: also known as Kamadeva, god of love, lust, desire (cf. Cupid, Eros);
Indra: held by the Vedas as the king of the gods, he lives in the palace *Vyjayanta* in the city of *Amaravati,* lounges in the garden *Nandan,* and rides a chariot drawn by two horses *Uchchaihshrava* and also rides the elephant *Airavata.* Yet, he is not commonly worshipped.

Varuna: god of the sea.
Yama: god of death; also called *Dharmaraj*, dispenser of justice after death for mortal acts according to divine decree of vice and virtue. *Yamapuri*, Yama's city, compares with Hades in Greek mythology.
Dharma: a word having wide connotation. From the simplest meaning 'essential property of matter, nature, or being', it extends to cover social, moral, and religious principles, codes, customs, and laws, and the conduct conforming to justice, piety and righteousness. Yama is held to be the custodian of the good, and hence sometimes referred to as Dharma.
Yaksha: a demigod supposed to protect treasure buried underground; a man, especially a child, left to die shut up in an underground cellar of treasure is believed to become its custodian; the term is sometimes referred to a niggardly hoarder of money.
Kubera: one of the four Lokpalas, guardian deity of the northern quarter of the universe, lord of wealth. He dwells in the jewelled city of Alaka, near Mt. Kailasa. He commands a host of gnomes (yakshas) who guard his treasure (cf. Pluto, Mammon); used to describe someone with immense wealth.
Krishna: an incarnation (avatar) of Vishnu, the most celebrated and beloved Hindu icon, whose life story is told in the *Bhagavata-Purana.* Associated with his pranks and feats in childhood in *Vraj* (Gokul in Mathura), his roaming exploits on the banks of the Yamuna, playing the flute and sporting with the *gopis* (milkmaids), his love for his consort Radha and her pique and placation, which is the staple of *Vaishnava* devotion. Celebrated as a perfect human being, and for the ideal he enunciated in the Bhagavad-Gita.
Shiva: a self-absorbed ascetic, the destroyer form of the three chief divinities of Hindu pantheon, the other two being Brahma the progenitor and Vishnu the protector, of the universe; used as an epithet of someone notoriously self-forgetful (*Bholanath)* or something fiercely destructive (*Rudra)*, and to symbolise the good, austere and auspicious. *Bhutnath* is another name for Lord Shiva who, after drinking, roams the burning *ghat*s with his retinue in a state of narcotised abstraction; *bhut* means 'ghouls and charnel house spirits', and *nath* means 'lord'. Nandi and Bhringi are his chief retainers and accomplices in this. *Bhairav* is one of the eight destructive images of Shiva.
Brahma: the creator who, with Vishnu and Shiva, constitutes the triad known as the Trimurti (See above); also called *Prajapati* (butterfly) Brahma who is believed to predetermine the fate of every individual on earth since birth through marriage until death as a fait accompli called *Prajapatir Nirbandha* or *Bidhir Bidhan* (the decree of fate). The phrase occurs in many stories, particularly, in 'The Elder Sister'. Also, the ultimate and divine reality, from which all being originates and to which it returns.
Kali (the *a* being pronounced as the o in 'so'): the presiding deity of the fourth and last age of creation called *Kali Yug,* which will end in total annihilation according to the Hindu scripture; used to mean an approaching doomsday or times vitiated by evil instincts and strife, marked by degenerate tastes. The other three *Yuga*s are *Satya, Treta, Dwapar,* the four making up a *kalpa* equal to one day of Brahma.

Historical, religious and scriptural sites, events and personages

Manwantar (the Great Famine): the term has a mythological allusion: the tenure of each of the fourteen imaginary sons, *Manu,* of Brahma is called a *manwantar* or transfer of power from one *Manu* to another; this is believed to be associated with great upheaval and apocalyptic devastation. Hence, a famine causing large-scale death and destruction has been given this name. The two great famines that ravaged Bengal are that of the Bengali eras 1176 (1769 AD) and 1350 (1943 AD) brought about by governmental negligence, hoarding, black-marketing, and profiteering.

Sepoy Mutiny: the great Indian mutiny of 1857 was triggered by the army being required to bite off the cartridges smeared with animal fat, allegedly of the cow, taboo for the Hindus, or of the pig, taboo for the Muslims.

Aryavarta: northern part of India where the Aryans settled, as compared to the Deccan separated by the Vindhyas (see *Agastya).*

Partition of Bengal: Lord Curzon in 1905, ostensibly to meet administrative requirements, announced partition of Bengal into East Bengal, a Muslim-majority province, and West Bengal, a Hindu-majority province. It sparked off a great agitation, which spun into a national movement; as a result, the partition was revoked in 1911.

Chanakya (Vishnu Gupta): a scholar of keen intellect and cunning in the court of Chandragupta Maurya, whose ascension to the throne was facilitated by his machinations against the Nanda dynasty. He is credited with *Arthashashtra* (treatise on economics), and what is popularly called *Chanakya-sloka*, Sanskrit couplets on time-tested lessons of practical wisdom and social morality.

Subhadra: sister of Krishna and Balaram.

Tantia Topi: a leader of the Sepoy Mutiny, joined the troops of Nana Saheb and later Rani Lakshmi Bai of Jhansi and carried on a desperate fight in Central India. He was hounded from place to place, was given up to the British, early in April 1859, by Man Singh, a feudatory of Sindhia, and was hanged on charges of rebellion and murder.

Kach and Debjani: Kach was the son of Brihashpati, pre-eminent in the knowledge of the Vedas and the teacher of the gods. Debjani was the daughter of Shukracharya, teacher of the demons. Though Debjani loved Kach passionately, he refused to marry her, raising intricate points of morality evolving out of the circumstances of her rescue and his resurrection by her father.

Religious texts, rites, and places

Shashtra: deriving from the Sanskrit root *shas,* which means 'to rule', it signifies the law, code, decree or writ meant to regulate man's behaviour on earth, enunciated by the ancient sages as perceived by or revealed to them through meditation. In a broader sense, any treatise on religious teachings is a shashtra.

Puranas: oldest Sanskrit texts recounting the births and deeds of the Hindu gods, the creation, destruction and recreation of the universe; they number eighteen .

Vedas: the most ancient scripture of Hinduism, four in number, written in Sanskrit around four thousand years ago. The Rig (nature of God), Yajur (rituals for use by priests), Sama (hymns to gods), and Atharva (spells and incantations) are the source of all mantras and sacrificial rites of the Hindus.

Vedanta: one of the six main philosophical schools of Hinduism; the last part of the Vedas, written by Vyasdev, expounding the monism regarded as implicit in the Vedas according to the doctrines of the Upanishads. It teaches that Brahman is the only reality, the whole phenomenal world being the outcome of illusion (maya).
Vedanta-Bhasya: eighth-century AD Hindu theologian and philosopher Shankara was the leading exponent of the Vedantic (Advaita) school of philosophy; his commentaries on the Vedanta and the Bhagavad-Gita are esteemed.
Patanjal-darshan: the philosophy of sage Patanjali who lived in the third century; it consists of four parts: yoga, meditation, divine glory, and the uniqueness of the soul. He wrote a commentary on Panini's Grammar.
Yoga: a Hindu system of philosophy which aims at the mystical union of the self with the Supreme Being in a state of complete awareness and tranquillity through certain physical and mental exercises. Patanjali expounded the essentials. A yogi is a mystic, a master of yoga; a female mystic is a *yogini* (different from the sixty-four companion goddesses of *Durga).*
Agastya: a sage of Vedic and Puranic antiquity, said to have subdued the Vindhya Mountains (which divide India centrally into Aryavarta and the Deccan) when they threatened to cut off the sun's rays reaching the Deccan plateau; a phenomenon held to symbolise colonisation of southern India by the Aryans. He is believed to have crossed the mountains (on the first day of *Bhadra*), never to return, thus stunting its growth in height forever. Traditionally, someone setting out on a mission and never returning is said to have gone on an *Agastya jatra* or 'Agastya's journey'.
Manu: any one of the fourteen sons of Brahma. *Vaivasvat* (son of the sun) Manu is held as the primordial progenitor of mankind and lawgiver; the Hindu code of jurisprudence is attributed to him.
Devanagari: Goddess Saraswati is credited with the invention of the Sanskrit language and its Devanagari script, the script of the devas.
Mahabharata: one of the two ancient epics of India, the other being the Ramayana. Written in Sanskrit by Vyasdev, it deals chiefly with the struggle between two families of the same clan and contains many episodes the most notable of which is the Bhagavad-Gita.
Ramayana: written in Sanskrit by Valmiki, this epic recounts the feats of Ramachandra (one of the three human manifestations of Vishnu), held as the model of goodness and valour. His wife Sita is the model of Hindu womanhood.
Bhagavad-Gita: the most revered and sung Hindu scripture; written in Sanskrit verses, it epitomises the teachings of the Upanishad and is incorporated into the Mahabharata as yoga counsels of Lord Krishna to Arjuna before the battle of Kurukshetra. Krishna, as Arjuna's charioteer, advises him on his duty in times of war, the nature of being and of God. Young Bengali revolutionaries held it as a sacred text.
Bhagabat: Puranas narrating the life and exploits of Krishna.
Puja: prayer or worship, whether austere (as with just an offer of flowers to one's deity) or ceremonial (as with elaborate ritual and offering on a particular day to a particular god or goddess); in Bengal, it is almost exclusively the goddesses who

are worshipped except for the family deity *Narayana*. Unless specifically mentioned, *puja* in Bengal refers to Durgapuja with wide connotation beyond worship; for instance, puja spirit, puja holidays, puja market.

pujari: worshipper or priest, more often a Brahman who officiates for a devotee.

ishtadevata: a guardian deity of a Hindu family who is worshipped as part of a routine often in a separate quarter or shrine allotted to it in the household.

sannyasi (sannyasin): originally, a Brahman who having attained the fourth and last stage of life as a beggar will not be reborn; a Hindu male bound by vows of celibacy, poverty, chastity and obedience, living on alms and the barest of clothes. Credulous people often fall victim to the deceptive garb of a fake sannyasi. The corresponding Muslim term is *fakir*.

sadhu: a Hindu wandering holy man.

chariot festival: the festival of Jagannatha going on a chariot for his sea-bath annually; Jagannatha is an idol of Krishna worshipped throughout Orissa and Bengal; at an annual festival in the month of *Asharh* the idol is wheeled through Puri town in Orissa on a gigantic chariot; centring this event fairs are held with great enthusiasm and merriment.

mantras: Vedic metrical psalms; religious incantation during worship; political counsel; instigation.

namabali: a chuddar or scarf, usually saffron-coloured, printed with the names of gods, especially, Hari (Krishna) and Rama: *Hare Krishna, Hare Rama,* over and over again, worn by the Vaishnavas and other pious Hindus.

ekadashi: Hindu widows observe the eleventh day of each lunar fortnight by keeping fasts.

Vrindavan: the grove beside the Yamuna, a rendezvous of flirtation for Krishna with his principal consort Radha and other herdswomen (*gopis*), regarded as a holy place by the Vaishnavas.

Vaishnava or Baishnav: a member of a sect devoted to the cult of Vishnu, strongly anti-Brahmanic and anti-priestly in religious persuasion, and stressing devotion through ecstatic songs and simple rituals. Lyrical poems on Vaishnavism (the cult of *bhakti* or devotion) called *padabali* form an important component of Bengali literature.

sakhi: applied to females, a friend or an alter ego, to whom private matters are confided, itself a form of address also. A male friend would be a *sakha*.

ashram: a religious retreat or community where a Hindu holy man lives; a cloistered educational community for the hermitage life of learners in ancient India.

Kalighat: a spot of pilgrimage in Calcutta, famous for its shrine of the goddess Kali, which devotees visit to: (i) redeem a pledge after supposedly receiving the boon they prayed for, and (ii) perform ritual worship to ward off the evil effects of conjunction of stars. The place has a notorious association with animal sacrifice.

chandimandap: a permanent site, public or private, generally with a thatched structure where the goddess Chandi (one of the manifestations of goddess Durga) is worshipped, and hymns in her praise (from the Markandeya Purana) are sung. When not in use as such, it is a favourite spot for village elders to gather and gossip.

ghat: stairs or a passage way, usually paved, leading down to a river or any water-body (also means: a mountain pass; mud path; a fault); a jetty or landing place where boats moor, and people gather for taking bath, drawing water or performing pujas and funerals; a meeting ground of women especially in villages to discuss local politics and scandals.

Writers, literary works and forms

Kalidasa: the greatest poet and dramatist in Sanskrit literature, associated with the court of King Vikramaditya (fifth century?). His works include *Meghaduta, Kumarsambhava,* and *Shakuntala.*

Jaydev: fifteenth-century Bengali poet, court pundit of King Lakshman Sen, wrote *Gitagovinda,* a dramatic poem about Krishna and Radha.

Kasidas (Kasiram Das): c. seventh-century poet celebrated for his Bengali translation of the Mahabharata by Vedavyas.

Krittibas Ojha: c. fifteenth-century poet celebrated for his Bengali translation of the Ramayana by Valmiki.

Ishwarchandra Vidyasagar: a nineteenth-century Sanskrit scholar, so celebrated a name that the honorific title of erudition, *Vidyasagar,* has virtually replaced his surname Banerjee. He was a pioneering force of social and educational reform in Bengal. There is hardly a Bengali who has never read his *Barnaparichay* and *Kathamala* as primers. He was a great philanthropist as well. Kathamala, his book of animal fables, is the Bengali equivalent of Aesop's Fables.

Madanmohan Tarkalankar: a Bengali poet with a Sanskrit title for erudition in logic and rhetoric, contemporary of Vidyasagar, with some widely-read primers to his credit.

Bankim Chandra Chatterjee: Bengal's first and arguably greatest novelist anticipating Tagore by about a quarter of a century, he wrote fourteen novels, mostly with a historical background. His *Vande Mataram* slogan, from the eponymous song composed in praise of the motherland and appearing in his first novel *Anandamath,* was accepted as the national song and became the rallying cry for nationalist revolutionaries. Besides, he was a redoubtable writer of essays and commentaries, especially satires on social degeneration of Bengali youths, Hindu rites and even the British Raj, creating a fictitious opium-addict and unsparing character Kamalakanta as his medium for the latter purpose.

jatra: an extended dramatic work performed in the open air by itinerant troupes enacting historical, mythological or epic themes.

panchali: a type of traditional ballad celebrating the glory of a deity, often set to music with a recurrent refrain. The writer most acclaimed for his *panchali*s is Dashu Ray.

kabigan: a type of song-contest where poets sing extempore verses usually on mythological themes.

kirtan: a type of traditional religious song, devoted to the love of Krishna and Radha.

kathakata: the vocation of a reciter and expositor of Puranas and mythological stories.

agamani: a class of folk songs celebrating the homecoming of Parvati from Kailas to her mother Menaka, sung in Bengal heralding her at the advent of Durga Puja.

baul: < *batul* (Sanskrit) or madcap. A sect of mendicant singers without religious creed who seek communion with God by making the mind levitate in the omnipresent air in intoxicated abstraction (the euphoric effect nearly always achieved with *ganjika* or *ganja,* that is, marijuana).
Mangalkavya: a genre of narrative poems glorifying besides goddess *Chandi* (see above), other lesser deities such as *Manasa* (snake-goddess), *Dharma* (a non-Aryan tribal god conceived from *Yama* and the Sun god of the *Purana*) and *Shitala* (goddess of the scourge of pox). These, Bengal's very own, local deities being finicky have to be kept in good humour with propitiatory offering (by women, each on a particular day in a particular month of the year). *Chandimangal* written by Mukundaram Chakraborti is the most celebrated of the *mangalkavyas*. 'Kabikankan' is an appellation for his distinguished poetic achievement. *Manasamangal* was written by Vijaygupta, and *Dharmamangal* by Ghanaram Chakraborti.
Vidyasundara: a narrative poem by Bengali poet Bharatchandra Ray *Gunakara,* a title meaning 'a literary virtuoso'. Vidya is the heroine.
Meghnadbadh-kavya: an epic by Michael Madhusudan Datta on the slaying of Meghnad (or Indrajit, Ravana's son); based on the Valmiki Ramayana, composed in blank verse, inspired with the humanism of the nineteenth-century Bengali renaissance, it seeks to alter the original by relegating its divine status to the background, in an ornate, rather convoluted, language, which found little favour with the Bengalis traditionally inspired by the Krittibas version. His genius was dissipated trying vainly to make a name in English literature.
Nabagopal Babu: Nabagopal Mitra was the editor of a newspaper started by Tagore's father. Tagore mentions him in *My Reminiscences* while recalling the day his elder brother asked him to his great embarrassment to read a poem to Mitra.
Kabikankanchandi: a ballad in praise of the goddess Chandi by the sixteenth-century poet Mukundaram Chakraborti. See 'Mangalkavya' above.

Social customs, rites, and festivals

Brahmin (or Brahman): a member of the highest or priestly caste in the Hindu caste system. By virtue of their supposed superiority, they were the most privileged class of the society; offering them land, food, and money was held to count as a virtuous act in the next world. Bengali *dwija* means 'twice-born'; it refers to a Brahmin who is believed to be regenerated or reformed by wearing the sacred thread; it can also mean 'a bird' because it hatches from an egg.
kulin: the highest sub-caste of the Brahmans; a pernicious and degrading system of polygamy was introduced by King Ballal Sen of Bengal, which permitted a kulin Brahman to marry as many girls as he liked—sometimes even girls his granddaughter's age—to extort dowry and satisfy lust. The system died a natural death under the changing social conditions.
polygamy: beyond the kulin system, polygamy was socially permissible for the purpose of preserving the continuity of one's family line, as for example, if the first wife proved barren.
Kayastha: a member of the traditional writer and other white-collar professional class, such as, lawyers and teachers; second in rank to a Brahman in social hierarchy.

Shudra: lowest of the four hereditary classes into which Hindu society is divided; traditionally, the working class. The other two castes are the Kshatriya (warrior class) and Vaishya (trader class), in that order.
outcastes ('untouchables'): those pursuing the so-called 'unclean' trades, such as, oilmen, cobblers, scavengers, relegated to a separate cluster. The lowliest of them is the *dom*, whose duty is to remove corpses and carcasses and burn corpses at the crematorium.
Santhal: an aboriginal tribe of India, chiefly inhabiting parts of Bihar and West Bengal.
kabiraj: physician practising in the traditional Indian system of medicine, *Ayurveda,* a treatise on the art of healing and prolonging life, sometimes regarded as the fifth Veda.
pundit (pandit): an expert; a learned person; formerly a Brahman learned in Sanskrit language and literature, especially in Hindu religion, philosophy and law (as Pandit Ishwarchandra Vidyasagar), later extended to any scholar as an honorific title, acquired or assumed; sometimes a sarcastic appellation for false pedantry. In British India, teachers at schools, besides those at *tol*s, were known as pandits, irrespective of the subjects they taught.
tol: a Sanskrit grammar school, but its adjectival form *tulo* was used only to demean someone who had not graduated beyond the primary levels. Often, wrongly, confused with *Chatushpathi*, where the four Vedas would be taught, besides grammar.
Raja: king; formerly, also a ruler or landlord, locally within his territory; sometimes used as a form of address or title preceding a name (as Raja Rammohan Ray).
Ray Bahadur: an honorific title conferred by the government on aristocratic Hindus as a recompense for their abject loyalty to the British Raj. *Khan Bahadur* is the Muslim equivalent.
Young Bengal: a collective term for the young men of nineteenth-century Calcutta, who were progressive-minded, thanks to the advent of English education and culture mostly followers of the progressive Anglo-Indian, Derozio.
orthodox marriage: conventional marriage decreed by scriptures, according to which girls had to be given away in marriage, within the same caste, within a certain age, normally twelve years (but sometimes it was even before puberty). Failure meant possible social ostracism.
sacred thread: male members of the Brahman caste wear it as an insignia of superiority, in a cluster of several rounds of cotton string, transversely across the left shoulder down to the right knee; also means the ceremony celebrating the auspicious assumption.
Ramnaam (Rama's name): held most sacred by the Hindus to: (i) scare off ghosts by uttering 'Ram' or 'Rama' in a rapid burst, (ii) express their mortification at seeing or hearing something ugly or shameful, by uttering it twice in exclamation, the first being somewhat long-drawn, (iii) express relief from some crisis, (iv) chant in funeral processions, (v) swathe themselves with Rama's name printed in a repeated design on scarves, (vi) as a form of greeting, and (vii) as prayer ('Hey Ram!').

pranam (or ***pronam***): an expression of respect for elders or superiors, either uttered with a gesture of joined palms and bent head, or performed by touching the feet, or more piously, wiping the dust from the feet and placing it on one's own head.
namaskar: said with joined palms as a usual form of greeting between two persons less familiar with each other; Muslim equivalent of *salaam.*
salaam: a Muslim form of greeting consisting of a deep bow with the right palm on the forehead.
shradh: a Hindu ritual of offering libation to the departed soul; solemnised on a prescribed day (usually, eleventh or thirteenth) after death, rightfully by the eldest son, or wife by default.
shanti-swastyayan: the first part means appeasement, the second part, bringing prosperity; the ritual for this purpose.
zamindar (jamidar): originally, contract agent holding land, collecting revenue, paying 9/10th to the Viceroy and retaining the rest; he inherited his zamindari and was responsible for policing his jurisdiction. Under the Permanent Settlement Act of Lord Cornwallis in 1793, zamindars were elevated to landowners with (i) the government's land-revenue demand permanently fixed, (ii) recovery provision through sale of proportionate land, and (iii) withdrawal of the magisterial power. The system was abolished after 1947. The Tagores were zamindars in East Bengal (now Bangladesh).
dewan: formerly, a chief minister or finance minister of a state ruled by an Indian prince. Extended to similar positions under a zamindar.
taluk: part of a zamindar's landed estate, usually named after the place.
Brahmatra: rent-free land given to a Brahman.
tehshil: firstly, the revenue receipts; secondly, the office where the revenue is paid.
tehshildar: the revenue collector of the government.
gomasta: the rent collector or steward of a zamindar; the bill collector of a businessman or a mercantile firm.
korfa: a cultivator who has no right in the land, but holds it as a tenant-at-will, and is not recognised by the zamindar; a *ryot* under a *ryot.* In *Shashti* (Punishment), Ramlochan is the original tenant; Dukhiram and Chhidam are korfa tenants.
kachhari: a court or office where any public business is transacted; thus, there was a government *kachhari* as well as a *zamindari kachhari.*
nayeb: the highest official in a kachhari; secretary, steward to a zamindar.
piyada (or peyada): a footman, messenger or agent of a landowner collecting revenue, often using third degree methods; bailiff of a law court.
paik: same as piyada except that he often joins a barkandaz as a lathiyal (see below).
barkandaz: a sepoy carrying firearms, an armed bodyguard of a zamindar; a member of his private army.
moktar (mukhtar): a legal representative appointed by a defendant or plaintiff with the power of attorney.
munsiff: a judge of the lowest civil court.
chaprasi: a liveried servant; an orderly or bearer or peon in an office.

lathi: a five to six-feet long wooden stick, seasoned by oiling and sunning, used as a weapon.
lathiyal (or lethel): expert in wielding lathis; professional fighter or guard on the payroll of a zamindar.
lagi: a ten- to twelve-feet-long bamboo pole used for punting a country boat.
gadabanduk: a flintlock gun, in which the charge is ignited by a spark produced by a flint in the hammer.
kuthi: office, business house, mansion, or bungalow.
nilkuthi: factory producing indigo dye from plantations, and the associated office.
aatchala: a house with a roof of thatch in the shape of an octagon, walled up with coarse mats made of palm-leaves or date leaves or bamboo slips and plastered with mud; sometimes left without walls, when meant for public use, for example, for pujas as a chandimandap.
durbar: formerly the court of a native ruler or a governor; a formal meeting at such places.
zenana: from Hindi *zanana,* a woman; a Muslim's wives and concubines collectively. Part of a house reserved for the women and girls of a household; a seraglio or *harem* in a Muslim palace. In Bengal, a rough equivalent is *antahpur* or *andarmahal,* where strangers, especially males, are forbidden.
mohar: or sovereign is an ancient gold coin of India and Persia; seal or stamp.
mudra: coin, legal tender; in the context of the stories, gold and silver coins; also means signs made with fingers during prayer; pose or gesture of dancing; mannerism.
paisa: in the context of the stories, one sixty-fourth of a rupee or one sixteenth of an anna; since 1956, one hundredth of a rupee; then made of copper, now of nickel.
rathjatra (chariot festival): Lord Jagannath going by chariot; on the second bright lunar day of Asharh, the idol is taken out in a procession.
brothers' day: in Bengali, *bhai-phonta* or *bhratri-dwitiya,* a festival where sisters put sandalwood paste marks (tilak) on their brothers' foreheads, wishing them a long and prosperous life, with exchange of gifts and sweetmeats. It is held on the second day of the bright lunar fortnight following Kali-puja.
kabaddi, or kapati (ha-du-du): a simple originally rural game of India, still played, needing strength and stamina. Two teams stand across a line; anyone then starts the game by crossing the line, while holding his breath, uttering 'du-du-du...' or 'chuuu...', at the same time trying to touch any rival player and returning, before running out of breath. If he can do it, the player touched is 'dead'; if he is caught while trying to make good his return, he is 'dead'.

Wedding:

dowry: the Hindu custom of a bridegroom's father extorting money and goods from the bride's father in consideration for and commensurate with his son's worth.
engagement and blessing ceremony: in Bengali *pakadekha,* formal approval of the pair by both sides; legally validated according to the Hindu code of marriage by signing up a detailed document and solemnised with gifts of gold rings or some such valuable items attended with a feast.

turmeric ceremony: in Bengali, *gayehalud,* a ritual in which turmeric paste is touched on the brow of the bridegroom in the small hours of the wedding day, and this turmeric is carried ceremonially along with fish and betel leaves to the bride to dab on her brow before she takes her ritual bath.
bridal party: customarily, the bridegroom sets out in a procession of friends and relations for the bride's house where the wedding takes place.
auspicious sighting: in Bengali, *shubhodrishti,* a ritual where the bride and the groom formally see each other, and especially in the period of the stories, for the first time. This is an occasion for merriment and exchange of repartees among the couple's friends and cousins.
seven-turn ritual: in Bengali, *saatpaak ghora,* the bride sitting on a wooden plank is taken seven times round the groom who keeps standing still. This is held to bind them forever invisibly in sacred ties.
ritual gifts: in Bengali, *tattva,* information, message, enquiry, etc., is extended to mean various goods and sweets traditionally exchanged as part of the ritual between the bride's and the bridegroom's families during the wedding ceremony, and thereafter, in its original meaning (exchanging information) on seasonal occasions as a form of courtesy.
vermilion: bright red cinnabar powder used in the parting of their hair by Hindu married women not widowed. This also marks the solemnisation of marriage when it is first worn.
shwashur-bari: father-in-law's house; for a bride, her husband's father's house where she goes to live; for a groom, his wife's father's house where he goes occasionally on a visit; used in village parlance occasionally as an imprecation to mean prison.

Dress

Benarasi sari: a rich silk fabric woven with raised design, often in gold or silver threads, once specialised in at Varanasi (Benares), the traditional dress for Bengali brides.
tusser: fabric of coarse silk yarn; when ochre-coloured, used during prayer or worship.
garad: fabric of the finer quality silk yarn; worn as sari; makes the Bengali bridegroom's wedding attire.
chapkan: long, loose upper garment for males, normally worn with *pyjamas,* chiefly as part of official dress.
choga: waist coat; a toga-like open-breasted vest worn over chapkan ('choga-chapkan') by the affluent gentry.
jobba: a knee-length, open-breasted vest, denoting office, authority or rank.
chadar (chuddar): a length of cloth, decorative or plain, wrapped around the upper part in winter. At other times, neatly folded and put on the shoulder, completes the respectable attire of the average Bengali gentleman going out on social occasions.
jamiyar: a richly embroidered shawl, indicating high social position.
gamchha: a kind of serviette; a rectangular two-yard length of coarse coloured cloth, used as a towel, sometimes worn as a *lungi* or loincloth, or slung over the shoulder by labourers or domestic servants.

dhoti: six-and-a-half yards length of white cloth for men worn in various styles to cover the body from the waist down.
pyjamas: full, flared, ankle-length trousers of fine fabrics, used by either sex, especially, for leisure wear.
kurta: a long, flowing shirt with full sleeves and without collar, worn with dhoti or pyjamas.
khaddar: or *khadi,* is hand-woven coarse cotton cloth made of hand-spun threads, introduced and popularised by Gandhi. Dhotis and caps made of khaddar were once a proud apparel for the *Swadeshi*s.
puggree: a man's headdress, worn ethnically by the Sikhs, and occasionally in the past by respectable Hindus, made by swathing a length of linen or silk.
shamla: a chiffon-embroidered turban worn by clerks and lawyers.
ghagra: an ankle-length skirt worn mainly by north Indian women
attar: an oil from flowers, especially the damask rose or jasmine petals, used pure or as a base for perfume; applied to the face or hair, or sometimes dabbed on the earlobes.

Food

rice (bhaat): the staple food grain of India, especially of the Bengalis, who eat it twice, or even oftener a day, thereby earning the dubious distinction of *bheto* (given to eating rice) due to the lethargy induced by it.
roti: or 'ruti' in Bengali, called *chapatti* by North Indians, a type of hand-made unleavened bread made by kneading a mix of coarse flour of wheat and water, rolling out into a disc and baking first on a frying pan and then direct on the flame when it balloons up; forms a staple food of most Indians.
luchi: Please see the Notes to The Royal Mark. Paratha and puri are variations on luchi.
paan: betel leaf wrapped with a mixture of areca chips, catechu powder, lime paste, and optionally, some addictive and aromatic preparations; the juice aids digestion.
sandesh: a Bengali speciality sweet, made of curdled milk (milk coagulated by acid) and sugar or jaggery in various shapes, consistencies, and garnishes; traditionally offered in pujas, and as a treat to guests.
mohanbhog: a sweetened dessert made of *suji* (coarse-ground flour of wheat) usually cooked in milk and ghee sprinkled with raisin and cardamom.
payes: a milk preparation of sunned rice, sugar or jaggery and raisin, cashew nut, etc.
doi: a thick custard-like food, resembling yoghurt, prepared from milk that has been curdled by bacteria, often sweetened.

Music:

shehnai: a classical wooden wind instrument, consisting of a conical tube fitted with a mouthpiece having a double reed. It has a penetrating nasal but sweet tone, played during pujas, and especially, at weddings. A recurring instrument in Tagore's stories. The other wind instrument most played is the bansuri or flute, which is Krishna's instrument in his dalliance with Radha and other herdswomen.

veena: a seven-string instrument in various shapes and sizes is of the oldest origin, and held as the symbol of music in *Saraswati's* hand. Other frequently played string instruments are *sitar, sarod* (both played with a plectrum), and *sarangi* with a bow. The main strings in the sitar and sarod overlie others, the tuning depending on the raga being played, rendering the music continuous (*meend*) and melodious.
taanpura: a stringed musical instrument, usually of four strings, sometimes of six, played by stroking with the fingers, helps the vocalist maintain a perfect tune.
tabla: a percussion instrument for any kind of classical or light music, consisting of a pair of drums played by the fingers and palms of both hands.
khol (or shrikhol): a single-piece variation on the tabla, both ends of which are played simultaneously, to accompany *kirtan* and *baul* songs.
alap: similar to talking about a theme, as we do through language, when developing an idea, logically and meaningfully. Thus, it means exposition of the idea of a raga, in a slow tempo without rhythmic accompaniment (*tala*), in vocal or instrumental music.
raga: a melodic framework, a basic note-pattern formed by selecting notes from the thirteen tonal intervals conventionally established in the octave space, usually associated with a particular mood, *rasa* (sentiment), time, season, and even region, on which a vocalist or instrumentalist can improvise creating new tonal patterns. The musicological tradition recognises six *raga*s and thirty *ragini*s, mirroring, at the metaphysical level, *Shiva-Shakti* or *Purusha-Prakriti* pairs, and represents the masculine-feminine principles in music.
bhairavi: a morning ragini exciting a sober, meditative mood with a tinge of sadness.
desh: a light, meditative evening raga.
malhar: a monsoon group of *ragas,* it forms rich combinations with other *ragas*: *Deshmalhar, Meghmalhar, Mianmalhar,* all late-night ragas.
basant: a springtime evening raga evoking a romantic mood.
sahana: a late evening exhilarating raga most often used in the stories in wedding references.
thumri: with *Ghazal, Bhajan, Tappa,* etc. forms a category known as classical vocal light music. Thumri (from *thumakna,* which means 'to walk with dancing steps so as to make the ankle-bells tinkle') is a form connected with dance, dramatic gestures, mild eroticism, evocative love-poetry, and folk songs of Uttar Pradesh, with regional variations. While the dignified Benaras *gharana* exhibits an approach similar to khayal, the Lucknow *gharana* shows an affinity with ghazal. Originally sung by courtesans and court musicians, it thrived in Lucknow, once the leading centre of Hindustani classical music.
ghazal: originally meant 'love-song in Persian'. Later, Urdu literary tradition extended the thematic range. From the beginning, the love of God was interwoven as a strand of the thematic fabric by *sufi* saints.
bhajan: a genre of light classical music; derived from the root Sanskrit word *bhaj* which means 'to serve', the name is applied to a class of songs which had been composed as well as sung by saint-poets in the wake of the devotional movement that swept the country from the eighth century onwards. The common ragas used

were desh, sarang, bhairav, kalingda, mand, and malhar with rhythms of eight or sixteen beats. Notably, this is different from the kind known as *Kirtan,* which has nothing to do with the ragas or the complexities of classical music.

Terms of address

baba: father; also, a respectful term for any father figure; reciprocally used as a term of endearment for son and occasionally extended socially to other boys or men.
ma: mother; reciprocally used as a term of endearment for daughter and extended socially to other girls or women; applied by a servant to the wife of the master. *Chhoto ma* and *baro ma* are the terms for the youngest and the eldest wife in an extended family; also, uttered in a sigh of desperation (*Ma!*), as Baidyanath in 'The Golden Deer' did when he drew a blank in his search for hidden treasure.
ma-thakrun: an address for the mistress of a house used by her servants or others. *Note:* The Bengalis traditionally regard a woman, especially a married one, as a mother figure. Hence, using *ma* as a suffix, they call their father's sister *pishima,* mother's sister *mashima,* uncle's wife *kakima* or *jethima*, and maternal uncle's wife *mamima*, also with their corresponding shorter forms without the suffix.
kaka (kaku) ***or*** khuro: younger brother of one's father, also extended socially.
jyatha: father's elder brother.
dada: elder brother with respect to younger brothers and sisters, whether siblings or cousins; extended by social courtesy to people of similar age; also, a form of address for grandfather, especially, maternal grandfather, *Thakurda* being the address for paternal grandfather. *Dada* or *dada-babu* is also applied by servants to the son of the master.
didi: elder sister with respect to younger brothers and sisters, whether siblings or cousins; extended by social courtesy to people of similar age; also, a form of address for grandmother, and for the wife of one's husband's elder brother.
Note: The last two forms of address above are reciprocal between grandparents and grandchildren.
bhai: literally, brother, an affectionate term of address for the grandson and extended by social custom to other boys and men. Also, a friendly form of address in general, or when making a request, among men as well as women
bou-didi: elder brother's or elder cousin's wife; also used socially for women of similar rank; an alternative form is *bou-thakrun.*
thakurpo: husband's younger brother or cousin.
babu (babuji): used by people of lower class, as for instance, by a servant speaking or referring to the master; likewise, Ma (Maji), *ji* being a respectful suffix, for the master's wife. Also used at the end of first names, sometimes surnames as well, but never with both, as a formal address between social acquaintances, e.g., Kailash-babu ; *other meanings:* a term of respectful address like *Mr* or *Sir,* nearly equivalent to *Esquire;* scribe, clerk; the word once meant an indigenous equivalent of a British title like Ray Bahadur and referred to wealthy, fashionable, ostentatious gentry (see the story Grandfather); now used ironically for one given to prodigality, foppishness and triviality.

thakur: used to address a Brahman, priest, deity or a saintly person; used after dada (dadathakur) to refer respectfully to a Brahman.
mashai (or mashay): added to babu to mean the master, added to dada to mean grandfather, and to thakur or jyatha to mean the priest and one's father's elder brother suggesting some degree of intimacy mixed with respect; also, used between any two persons of either sex who are on joking terms with each other; used after the surname as an address between two respectable male acquaintances, such as, Chakraborti Mashai and Kundu Mashai; used after *master* as a respectful address for a teacher.
khoka: address of endearment for one's son, often the youngest, or any other small boy (see *baba)*; similarly, *khuki* or *khuku* for a girl.
bouma: address for the wife of one's son or one's younger brother, and by extension, wife of others of similar age (see *ma*).
bou: sometimes the address for a daughter-in-law in an extended family or by social superiors. *Chhotobou* and *barobou* respectively refer to the younger and the elder ones in a joint family.
sahib (or saheb): a white man, a form of address or title placed after a man's name or designation, used as a mark of respect. It is also usually the Muslim equivalent of 'babu'. *Bibisaheb* is the corresponding address for a Muslim married woman. *Memsaheb* is the term for the wives of sahebs.
shala: one's wife's brother. See below.
shyalika (shyali): wife's sisters or her female cousins; the younger ones are traditionally permitted to be on bantering terms with the husband, but flirting is taboo. Similarly, her husband's younger brother or his male cousin, *debar,* stands in the same relation to her. Contrarily, her husband's sister, *nanad* is not traditionally on amicable terms with her while the wife's younger brothers bear an affectionate relation, *shala,* to her husband. Strangely, *shala* is a term of abuse also, used as such or muttered under one's breath.
Note: The pronoun 'you' in English is universally used in direct conversation, irrespective of age, social status or relative position of the speaker and the person spoken to. Not so in Bengali (or in Hindi, for that matter), where three distinct forms corresponding to 'you' are admitted: *tui, tumi, aapni. Tui* is the affectionate address for children in the same family, and friends, and the pejorative address for so-called low-caste people. *Tumi* is the reciprocal address of endearment among the members of a family irrespective of age, between lovers, and by elderly people to their unrelated juniors. *Aapni* is reserved for teachers and other social or chronological seniors or superiors.